PROMISED SPLENDOR

Cecile opened her eyes and watched Iaian walk to the bedside.

"My lord," she whispered sleepily.

Iaian felt a tightening in his loins as he gazed down at her by the light of the candle he carried. He had, he assured himself, come merely to see that she was well cared for. But he had not counted upon the feelings that would wash over him at the sight of white sheets slipping from bare shoulders, revealing the delicate lines of bone beneath creamy flesh.

Quite naturally, Cecile flung the covers aside to welcome him, feeling languorous and safe in the lingering sleepiness that gripped her.

With an oath, Iaian extinguished the candle and placed it on the washstand. He shed his clothes hastily, deriving some comfort by telling himself that this was his wife, after all. It was his duty to bed her.

"Emotionally charged and powerful, *Exiled Heart* is a passionate portrayal of the times in the strong and compelling style that typifies Ms. Tanner's writing. She always makes us hungry for more!"

—Libby Sydes
Author of *The Lion's Angel*

Other *Leisure Books* by Susan Tanner:
CAPTIVE TO A DREAM
HIGHLAND CAPTIVE

LEISURE BOOKS  NEW YORK CITY

For Aunt Nita and Papa Pelham

A LEISURE BOOK®

August 1993

Published by

Dorchester Publishing Co., Inc.
276 Fifth Avenue
New York, NY 10001

Printed in the United States of America.

EXILED
HEART

Prologue

Anne Gillecrist looked at the man she had loved for nearly twenty years—the man their world thought of as her husband. Tears filled her lovely dark eyes and spilled slowly down her cheeks. "How can I tell him, Geoffrey? How can I face him with this." *This* was a crumpled missive, twisted and retwisted by nervous fingers as she foresaw the end of her preciously happy existence.

Sir Geoffrey Lindael took the paper from her fingers gently. "We've always known this day would come, my love. We will face it together."

As she allowed him to pull her into the comfort of his embrace, Anne admitted the truth to herself. She had prayed that this day would never be. She would have lived a lie until the moment of her death and allowed her son to live that lie as well. Damn Alasdair Gillecrist. Damn him!

Even in death, he would wound her. For a brief moment, she considered continuing the deceit, sending to Scotland the news of her son's "death" in childhood. Swear that the only children left to her were those born to her English lover, Sir Geoffrey.

But, until today, she had stolen her happiness only at the expense of a man who had never loved her, had abused her. If she lied in the face of his death, she would keep her son from his birthright, from the wealth and the title that belonged to him. Lord Alasdair Gillecrist had died a very wealthy man, with several properties scattered the length of the Scottish border marches. And he had died without remarrying, without any other legal issue. His only heir was her beloved son, Iaian.

Geoffrey touched her hair tenderly. "I have never regretted the moment I took you from Scotland, my love, but I regret having brought you to this grief."

"Hush." She pressed her finger to his lips. "Never say you have done so. You have gifted me with a lifetime of happiness. My life with Alasdair would have been an eternal torment."

His embrace tightened at the thought of never having known this woman. Though it had begun almost as a lark, a border raid of the kind that rarely took place in these enlightened times, it had been the turning point of his life. The young Englishmen, made reckless with liquor, had stolen horses and cattle and the young wife of Alasdair

Gillecrist, a man twice her age. And it was true, Geoffrey Lindael had never regretted the moment he had come upon her riding alone just at dark, sweeping her from her horse to his. Returning home, he had fended off his friends when they would have dishonored her, and he had never let her go.

There had been only one time, after Geoffrey had fallen in love with his captive, that he had offered to return her to Scotland, to her husband. She would not leave him. But they had made a mistake, the two of them. They had pretended the son she had carried in her womb was his, had told all of England, and Iaian as well, that Geoffrey Lindael was his father. Only one person had known the truth.

Anne, knowing her only brother loved her, had not wanted him to live with the grief of thinking her slain, but she regretted having written, as well, of the birth of Alasdair's son. Because he had known how bitterly unhappy Anne had been with Alasdair, Ros Donnchadh had acceded to his sister's wishes and kept silent concerning the birth of the boy. Though Lord Gillecrist might turn his back on his errant wife, he would have moved heaven and earth to regain a son. Now Ros had stepped forward at Gillecrist's demise to claim the Gillecrist properties for his nephew, the rightful heir.

He had then written to Anne with the news of her husband's death, and of her son's inheritance. Ros would never let her relinquish Iaian's birthright. She would have to lie to him now, and continue the lie to her son. Or she could send Iaian to Scotland to claim that which was his and know she had forever lost his trust and his respect.

"I cannot do this," she said in a choked voice, and then broke into sobs against Geoffrey's broad chest, soaking the fine linen with her tears.

Geoffrey stroked her hair, thinking how soft and lovely it was even after all these years. And, even after so long, his body responded to the closeness of hers, and he knew he would desire her until his dying day. Pressing his lips to the dark curls, he knew his own heart would break, too, when Iaian looked on him and did not call him Father. Another man had sired the son of his heart, but even the children who came after Iaian, sons and daughters of his own loins, had not held the place Anne's firstborn had with him.

He said nothing of his own fears and regrets to the woman he loved. Even he, in his love for his son, could not keep Iaian from that which was rightfully his.

Chapter One

Scotland, March 1548

A soft morning wind rippled the meadow grasses and the new growth of leaves on the small trees. With that same wind caressing her face, Cecile Lotharing lifted her chin and breathed deeply of the cool air of spring. The River Clyde, scarcely a river at all this far below the small burgh of Lanark, swirled gently at her bare toes. She was out later than she had intended to be, and those bare toes were going to earn her a scolding. Her lips curved slightly in a smile. She was well used to scoldings from her brothers' wives.

At the thought, her smile faded. One was wife no more. Memory brought a bittersweet image of a laughing brother, tall and blond and blue-eyed, as were all her brothers. Odwulf had died the past September at Pinkie Cleugh, fighting the

English, just as Waren, the second oldest of her father's sons, had died at Solway Moss, five years earlier.

Dashing away the tears that came to her eyes, Cecile turned from the river toward Ciaran. It rose from the meadowlands, the proud walls and graceful towers embodying all that she loved, all she had ever known. She was sixteen years of age, and Nearra, her eldest brother's wife, warned her frequently that the day was coming when she must leave. Not that Nearra considered it a warning. She teased Cecile with hints of a husband and a home of her own. But that was not foremost in Cecile's mind. Her mother, Giorsal, said she would feel differently were she at court, surrounded by other young girls her age, all of them sent to make fine matches so that their minds were ever on the subject. But Cecile had pleaded not to be sent, and Saelec, her father, would not hear of her being made unhappy, as she was sure she would be.

Even now, when her father had begun to speak more often of the need to arrange a fine match for her, she gave little thought to marriage, other than to tease her parents with mention of anyone they would be certain to consider unsuitable.

A rabbit rustled through the broom and knapweed, stirring her from her thoughts. She would surely have been missed by now, and though no one would be alarmed to find she had slipped from her room before daybreak, it was time to return. With a gurgle of laughter for the rabbit, who froze when he spied her, then turned in a scramble, she strode through the meadow grasses toward Ciaran. She paid no heed to the heavy stalks that tugged at her woolen skirt, dyed yellow as bracken.

The sun overhead, more pale than the moon had been earlier, was just breaking through the morning mist. She had missed Mass yet again, and Father Aindreas, who could not seem to like her, would frown yet again. She set her jaw at the thought. She, who usually liked everyone, could not like him either. He had not been long at Ciaran, just since their beloved Father Lucien had died, and she did not think her father would tolerate his overbearing manner many more weeks.

Ciaran's gates stood open as they had done from the moment she left the bailey. And she knew the sharp gaze of more than one of her father's guards had followed her every instant she was beyond the safety of Ciaran's solid walls.

Amalric was waiting for her in the bailey, and he chuckled at the sight of her bare feet. Amalric was nineteen, the brother closest in age and temperament to her. "Our Rilla is going to love the sight of you with your skirt hem muddied and snagged with weeds."

Cecile smiled in turn. "I suppose 'tis too much to hope that she is yet in her chamber or the nursery." Odwulf had left two small sons to comfort his young wife and to bring sunshine to Ciaran when the first pain of his loss had dimmed.

"It is," Amalric warned, his smile fading. "And, Ceci, 'tis not safe for you to leave Ciaran without a guard. The English are still shedding Scots blood south of Edinburgh." He sighed at the flash of his sister's blue eyes as she prepared to launch into an argument and lifted a hand to forestall her. "You've no need to rail at me. You're going to hear the same from Father."

As he watched, her shoulders drooped and the fire slowly died. She might tease their father as unmercifully as she did her brothers, but none of them defied Saelec. Amalric smiled encouragingly, sorry he had made his sister unhappy. She was the shining jewel of the Lotharings, with her hair as pale as the first rising sun and her eyes as darkly blue as purest sapphire. Though all of them were fair-haired and blue-eyed, the colors were most brilliant on their Ceci. And she was tiny like their mother, while Amalric and his brothers matched their father's massive size.

"Do not fret," Amalric said gently. "I'll go out with you any morning you wish. You'll be safe enough with me."

Cecile pictured his body broken by the English the way Waren's and Odwulf's had been and hid her quick shudder. Amalric would be insulted to think she feared for him, as if he were some green lad who could not defend himself and her. "Thank you, Amalric. But," she squared her shoulders with a sigh, "I'd best go in now before I need your protection from Rilla or Nearra."

"Too late for that, I think," Amalric warned at the sight of Nearra and Father Aindreas leaving the keep.

The pair paused on the bottom step, staring at the disheveled appearance the daughter of Ciaran presented. Nearra recovered first, stepping forward even as she shook her neatly coifed head. As always, she was the picture of modest womanhood, her gown of soft blue silk fitting her trim figure neatly. She managed to smile when she reached Cecile.

"You've been about early again, Ceci." Her voice was as calm as her golden brown eyes.

Surrounded as she was by blue-eyed kin, Cecile was always fascinated by Nearra's brown coloring, made more evident by the cream of her smooth skin. Cecile relaxed under Nearra's smile and returned it ruefully. "Aye, and I know I shouldn't have been so long, and Amalric tells me I shouldn't have gone at all. Not alone."

Nearra laughed lightly. "Then I'll spare you another scolding."

Cecile lifted her shoulders in a resigned shrug. "Well, if you will," she said wryly, "*he* will not."

Nearra turned to glance at the priest who followed in her wake. Father Aindreas was a favorite with none. He was tall and lean, so that he always had a hungry look to him, even in the sharp, pale green eyes that missed nothing. Where Father Lucien had been the embodiment of all that was good and loving in the church, Father Aindreas practiced only those extreme elements of harsh and unloving discipline.

He nodded curtly at Cecile. "You were not at Mass, Mistress Cecile." He could not help but feel that Father Lucien, who had been here before him, was responsible for the laxness allowed in this household.

"I'm sorry," Cecile answered, feeling guilty for the mistruth.

Father Aindreas accepted her words. "Well enough, then, but I'll hear your confession now."

Cecile looked pleadingly at Nearra, who pretended not to see. "Yes, Father Aindreas," she returned dutifully, wishing she could stick out her tongue and flee. She might well have done so a few years ago, though it earned her the back of her father's hand. For a moment she wished she were not quite so grown.

The priest frowned at her lack of enthusiasm. The entire family, though sincere in their faith, lacked the devout adherence to its tenets that he wished for them. He feared the girl could easily be led astray if a strong hand were not taken with her. "There are those whose souls yearn for the opportunities you scorn, though their minds turn them from the truth."

Cecile grimaced. She already knew the fiery response the mere thought of reformers brought to Father Aindreas. And though she truly tried to bite her tongue on a reply, she failed. "Perhaps 'tis their hearts that lead them, rather than their minds." Her tone was polite, but she knew her words would be as glowing coals.

"The fires of hell burn hot for such!" he thundered, aghast that she would doubt the evil in those lost souls.

"The fires of man burn hotter!" Daringly, she referred to the many who had gone to the stake for their defiance of the Holy Roman Church. Scotland still reeked of the burning flesh of George Wishart, two springs past. Cecile had been fourteen and would never forget her horror on hearing of it. Even now, she felt slightly nauseated at the memory.

Father Aindreas could not ignore the angry tone of her words and responded in kind. "Do you mistake the retribution of God for that of mere mortals?"

"If God had meant for heretics to burn," Cecile retorted, "he would have given them wooden feet!"

His face livid, Father Aindreas drew back his arm and slapped Cecile sharply across the cheek. Nearra gasped in shock, but before she could move, Amalric had the priest pinned in a furious grasp.

"Get you from here," Amalric said through clenched teeth. "If you are very quick, you will be gone from Ciaran before my father seeks you out and ends your miserable existence."

Flinging the priest from him, Amalric gathered his sister in his arms, feeling her trembling. He glared at the priest, who returned his glance defiantly. "You'll rue this day," the man warned as he straightened his cassock.

"I rue the day Ciaran first saw you." Amalric released Cecile to Nearra's arms and stood with clenched fists until the priest turned away, cassock flapping against his angular body as he strode toward the chapel. More thoughtfully, Amalric watched Cecile pull away from Nearra and walk with shoulders held proudly into the keep. And he wondered if ever a day would come that Cecile Lotharing could keep herself from stirring trouble about her.

Nearra took Cecile straight to her mother, entering the morning room with no indication of the diffidence she still felt after four years of marriage into this family. They were all so exuberant, so confident—even the tiny woman who was her husband's mother.

Giorsal Lotharing put aside the delicate altar cloth she was embroidering to smile at her daughter and her eldest son's wife. Sunlight filtered through a narrow window and highlighted her daughter-in-law's pretty features, but Nearra's usually golden brown eyes were dark with dismay. Giorsal turned her gaze to her daughter, and the bright spot of color on Cecile's cheek told a partial story of the reason for that emotion.

Giorsal rose to her feet, her mouth thin with anger as she studied the dark imprint of fingers against her daughter's fair skin. "Saelec will stripe whichever of your brothers dared lift a hand to you." It was inconceivable to her that anyone else would do so. Cecile was forever tussling with her brothers, and her quick tongue had enraged each of them at one time or another. But to strike her! Nay, they would not.

"Mother," Nearra said softly, "'twas not any of your sons."

"Who dared?" Giorsal's voice was as sharp and cold as the crack of breaking ice.

Nearra, who loved her mother by marriage and knew her well, was respectful of the fierce protectiveness she displayed for her young. Though she was more tiny than any woman imaginable, her age showing in the silvering of her fair hair and tired lines about her mouth and eyes, she was formidable. Nearra would rather face a wild animal than Giorsal Lotharing when she defended any of her children.

Cecile patted Nearra's hand reassuringly and answered her mother. "'Twas Father Aindreas who struck me. I provoked him," she added simply.

"I shall kill the man," Giorsal breathed, blue fire sparking from her eyes. "'Twill be more merciful than what your father will do to him should he reach him first."

"I would imagine he is long gone from Ciaran by now," Cecile told her calmly. "Amalric witnessed the scene."

At her daughter's obvious lack of distress, Giorsal relaxed a bit. "Just what did you do to provoke the man, Ceci?"

"I but spoke the truth!"

Nearra sighed at the simplicity of Cecile's view. "In his eyes, she blasphemed," Nearra explained, repeating Cecile's words to the priest.

With difficulty, Giorsal kept her lips from twitching in a smile. How could she condemn her daughter for stating something she herself believed? She knew, however, that Nearra would never have dreamed of voicing so defiant a belief, though she, too, agreed. "Ceci does not mean to be irreverent, Nearra."

Nearra was not deceived by her mother-in-law's soothing response. She knew nothing would be done to curb young Cecile's tongue, and nothing, she feared, *could* be done to curb the girl's thoughts! "Tell Father Aindreas!" she said ruefully. "We will be fortunate if we do not incur the archbishop's wrath in this. He may even question our faithfulness to the church." She shuddered visibly at the possibility.

"Father Aindreas has dealt with far worse than my daughter's tongue, I assure you. Surely he should be able to control his temper under more difficult circumstances than a child's honesty."

She smiled at Cecile's look of affront at being termed a child. And, truly, Ceci was a child no more. At sixteen, she was blossoming into a woman with a tiny waist, gently curving hips, and breasts no longer flat beneath the bodice of her gown. "And there is no harm in speaking our minds here at Ciaran."

Giorsal thanked God for that. Saelec had made the border keep a haven for them all, and though he had prospered in the years of their marriage, gaining other properties south of Edinburgh and Glasgow, they had remained at Ciaran.

"Well," Nearra said, reluctant to give up the battle, even though her arm tightened lovingly around her young sister-in-law's shoulders, "not everything that is true must be spoken. Silence is often wiser than speech."

Giorsal inclined her head in agreement. "I'll not argue that, Nearra, and I know you hold your tongue frequently when your thoughts would give argument to those around you. But sometimes, just sometimes, I wish you would not! That boar-headed husband of yours would do well to have a taste of your intelligence on occasion—though I wonder if he would have the wits to recognize it."

"Mother Giorsal!" Though shocked, Nearra was pleased as well. There were times when she thought Giorsal was truly the only one who recognized that she had more in her head than the jangle of the heavy keys that swung at her waist, her badge as Ciaran's chatelaine. Her husband, Berinhard, surely did not.

Smiling, Giorsal touched her daughter's cheek lightly as she walked past them both. "Nearra, I've some soothing oil in my chest for Ceci's face. I fear I must seek Saelec 'ere he harms a man of God."

Giorsal's giant of a husband was striding around the courtyard looking furiously helpless. He was enraged at the thought of anyone laying a hand upon his daughter, but he could not very well ride down a man of God and slay him!

His youngest son hid a smile at his father's agitation. Saelec Lotharing was a legend in battle, his weapons as bloodthirsty as any, his prowess greater than most. In things of home and family, however, he yielded always to his wife, and he eyed her approach now with obvious relief.

"Ceci?"

"Is fine," Giorsal said reassuringly, casting her gaze upon her youngest son, standing at his father's side. Straight and tall, he never failed to fill her with pride, for he was as good as he was handsome. "What of Father Aindreas?"

Amalric blushed at her faint tone of censure. "He is gone from here, but I did not harm him."

"I would have dealt with the man first." At Amalric's crestfallen expression, she relented. "But I've no doubt you did well enough, my son. I'd not have a man of God injured here, but I'll not tolerate harsh treatment of my family!"

Now that the priest was gone from reach, the man had ceased to interest Saelec, and he turned his mind to another concern. "Do you know what she said to the man?" he asked indignantly.

"Aye. And I've no quarrel with the sentiment, though perhaps she could have worded it more politic." Giorsal's eyes twinkled at Saelec's dumbfounded look. "Now, Saelec, 'tis no more than you've thought and said."

"Not to a priest! God's blood, have I taught my children naught?"

"You've taught them much of courage and honesty," Giorsal said soothingly, but she knew as well as her husband that there was often danger in the truth.

"'Tis time she was wed," Saelec growled. "A husband would tame her."

"Perhaps." Though, as her mother, Giorsal doubted that greatly.

"With Alasdair Gillecrist gone, we'll have new blood at our boundaries. Perhaps his heir will be of marriageable age and yet unwed."

Giorsal did not argue the possibility. She would not find it amiss to have her daughter wed and settled at the very edges of Ciaran's properties. It was time for Cecile to be safely contracted, and no eligible young man had yet caught her eye. And an alliance with the new lord of Daileass would strengthen Ciaran's stand against the English. Though Gillecrist had died unexpectedly only a few weeks earlier, there had yet been no word of his successor.

Amalric frowned. "I've heard it rumored that his by-blow might well expect to gain at least a portion of Gillecrist's lands. With no legal heir, he stayed much in Gillecrist's pocket, hoping for just that."

"I'd not think it," Saelec returned, shaking his head. "Arran and the Council of Lords will be looking for a show of strength for Gillecrist's border holdings. Someone who would wield a strong arm against the English. I've not seen much strength of character in Tavis."

"Well," said Giorsal more practically, "'tis early days to speak of our own plans for the new Lord Gillecrist." She looped her arm through Saelec's, tugging him toward the keep. "You've not broken your fast, my heart."

But they'd taken only a few steps when the gate sentry shouted warning of approaching riders. Saelec and Amalric turned as one to wait.

"'Tis Berinhard," the sentry called reassuringly, when Saelec's own banner became apparent above the group of horsemen.

"Thank God for his safe journey," Giorsal said, relieved that her firstborn son had met no mishap while he was from the safety of his home.

Saelec looked at her in disgust. "Sweet Jesus, woman, he's not been gone two weeks seeing his brother board ship."

Lifting her chin, Giorsal sniffed. She had lost too many of her sons, one in infancy and two to the English, not to worry when one was away from her sight. And now, Raimund, her sixthborn, sailed to Germany to wed the betrothed he had never seen and would remain to assume control of Saelec's inherited properties there. She feared she would not live years enough to look upon his dear face again, but at least she could think of him well and prospering.

The clatter of heavy hooves on Ciaran's flagstones prevented Saelec's saying more on her fearfulness where her sons were concerned. Not that he had anything new to add. He could but remind her, as he was wont to do, that all they had was of God, and could be safely left to His will.

Berinhard dismounted, removing his helmet and embracing his mother before he grinned at Saelec. Of all Saelec's sons, his eldest was his favorite; most like him in nature, least like him in looks. His hair, though streaked with gold, was almost brown. His eyes held as much green as blue. And he was slender and wiry, where his brothers carried the solid mass bequeathed to them by their father.

"You traveled well?" Saelec asked in a growl, refusing to show that he, too, was relieved to see his son safely surrounded by the walls of Ciaran once more. These were difficult times in the south of Scotland, with the English at their very doors.

"Easily and safely." Berinhard was not fooled into thinking his parents did not need reassurance, even now that he was within hand's length. "And I've news of Gillecrist's heir." He paused. "He's English."

"What?" Saelec's booming question drowned the sound of Giorsal's whispered denial. "How can this be?"

"Well, he was raised as English," Berinhard amended. "'Tis Alasdair Gillecrist's own son by Anne Donnchadh."

Giorsal's brow furrowed. "But she was slain by the English the year you were born, Berin. Twenty years ago."

"She was not slain," Berinhard said, trying to remember every detail of the rumors that had been flooding Edinburgh on his arrival. "She was held by the Englishman who took her and has been living with him since then."

"Willingly?" Giorsal did not hide her shock.

"Aye. And passed Gillecrist's son off as the Englishman's."

"Christ's wounds," Saelec swore feelingly. "That was a low thing to do to a man."

Though she could not argue that point, Giorsal reminded him of Gillecrist's treatment of his young bride, adding, "I cannot blame her overmuch for taking any means of escape. Still, to take a man's heir ..." Her voice trailed away, for she could not say with any certainty that she would not have done the same under similar circumstances.

"Does this young man come to Daileass?" Saelec asked.

"He goes first to Coire, and 'tis said Coire will stand against him."

Saelec scowled. "Though I mislike his English upbringing, I do not envy him the claiming of his inheritance. Does Tavis stand against him?"

"Gillecrist's bastard? I've not heard it said. Some believe he will, some say not, but no one has heard from his own lips."

"Well, his uncle will stand with him and I doubt any, even Tavis, would stand long against Donnchadh," Saelec said thoughtfully. "Donnchadh makes a formidable ally."

At the speculative tone of his voice, Giorsal looked at Saelec in dismay. Surely he would not still consider linking their daughter with Gillecrist's heir—even for the ties it would bring with Donnchadh! Not now. For all his Scots blood, Anne's son could only be English in his thoughts and his loyalties. Nay, surely Saelec would not think to marry their Ceci to this man now!

Chapter Two

Iaian Gillecrist stared at the massive gray stone of Daileass Castle and felt—nothing. No sense of homecoming. No edge of anticipation. Not even the pull of ancient ties. He could not honestly say he had expected to feel anything, though. And that was almost a relief, because it meant that even the anguish of the past months was gone for the moment. The anguish of hearing from his mother's own lips that the man he had called Father for nearly twenty years was not, in fact, his father. Nor was the man her husband.

Anne Lindael's—nay, Anne Gillecrist's—husband lay in a newly covered grave in the border marches of Scotland. The Englishman at her side was no more than her lover, her one-time abductor.

Iaian's horse shifted beneath him, returning him to the present, to another of Lord Gillecrist's many properties. The first Iaian had tried to claim, a small keep just miles from the border of England, now lay in ruins, an example to his remaining properties. And a monument to the day his mother had been stolen from within the boundaries of its lands—her unborn son with her.

No more examples had been needed for the castellan of Daileass, the next of Lord Gillecrist's holdings. When Iaian's advance had reached its gates, they had been flung open, his orders implicitly obeyed. Iaian had been almost sorry at the news, for his blood-lust had not been assuaged by his destruction of Castle Coire.

"Lord Gillecrist?"

Iaian started at the title, still unused to anything more than Sir Iaian, a status duly earned. He glanced at the captain, who was waiting anxiously.

Freyne swallowed. By the Virgin, this man was not like any other he'd ever served, for he spoke scarcely at all and smiled never. Now that he'd foolishly interrupted the lord's thoughts, the captain was not at all eager to continue. But Lord Gillecrist was waiting—less than patiently, judging by the look in his eyes.

"Do we approach?" Freyne knew there was to be no battle. Fully half of the men in Daileass Castle were in the pay of Lord Gillecrist. The other half had been cowed by the tale of his ruthlessness at Castle Coire.

Iaian lifted his reins. "Indeed. I've no wish to spend another night in these godforsaken hills." Forsaken by God. As was he.

As they approached, Iaian studied the lines of the castle. Positioned in a smooth valley created by knolls that could barely be called hills, it was well built, with square walls and an L-shaped tower. From without it looked solid, but Iaian had quickly learned two things about the stranger who had been his father: Alasdair Gillecrist had been very wealthy and very frugal. Coire, though it had been on the edge of the England, had been shamefully undermanned and underarmed, with walls near crumbling even before the first attack.

Not that it would have made a difference in the end. The castellan had yielded with the first cannonball, but Iaian had been filled with the cold fury that had been with him since the day his mother had learned of his father's death. And destroyed all her son's dreams. After allowing the inhabitants to leave, Iaian had painstakingly destroyed every wall of the castle, leaving scarcely two stones intact.

Before him, the clean lines of Daileass Castle blurred with an image of the English stronghold of his youth. That was hardest of all to bear. He could have forgiven his mother for having given her heart and life to a man not her husband. He could have forgiven her the lie that he had lived. But she had stolen from him his very identity. He who had been English to the core; he was now

Scots. The land he had secretly disdained was his homeland. The blood he had secretly scorned flowed through his veins. Secretly, because his fa—Sir Geoffrey had never let his household or his children deride Scotland or its people. Now Iaian knew why.

"My lord."

Lost in his thoughts, Iaian was again pulled to the present by the warning in his captain's voice. He glanced up to see a small party leaving the castle gates, riding toward him. He cursed that he had been so lax as to be caught unaware, then realized that if he had been, his men were not. They were in position around him, prepared for battle. He stayed them with a gesture and drew rein on his mount.

After a moment, he relaxed. There was nothing warlike about the small group of men riding to meet him. Indeed, they might well have stepped out of a drawing room, so richly dressed were they. Brilliant colors rivaled the gold in the morning sun and the blue of the sky. Jewels winked on velvet doublets and lightweight cloaks. Iaian recalled his slur on entering the ruins of Coire Castle—that there did not appear to be much in Scotland worth plundering. That was not true of this group.

One man stood out from the rest, riding at the center and just in front. Iaian's stomach muscles tightened as he studied the once dark hair, now graying, the straight nose, and the dark, piercing eyes. This, he saw from the resemblance, was his mother's brother. The man who had put in motion all that had torn the very fabric of his life in twain.

Iaian reached up to sweep off his helmet so that his own likeness to this man could be seen. Not, he knew, that there was any need. Ros Donnchadh would have been waiting, watching, his men ready to carry word of any of Iaian's movements. As he waited for Donnchadh's approach, he relished the cool breeze lifting his hair.

Donnchadh reached him and stopped his horse. "Nephew." His gaze assessed Iaian thoughtfully, the weary lines etching the handsome face. The young man's dark eyes were intelligent and guarded; his strong jaw set firmly. Aye, Iaian would enhance the Gillecrist lineage as much as that of his Donnchadh legacy.

With ill grace, Iaian inclined his head. "Donnchadh." He did not yet think of this man as his uncle.

The older man's lips twitched in a brief smile as he studied Iaian's armor. "You are prepared for war?"

"I've not had a warm reception thus far," Iaian acknowledged dryly.

"Did Coire's reception of you warrant the destruction of one of Scotland's defenses?" Donnchadh allowed a moment of anger to became apparent.

Rage seared through Iaian's veins and was gone as abruptly as it came. "Do you expect me to care for Scotland's defense? Against England?"

Donnchadh flushed slightly as he realized the incongruity. He sighed. "Perhaps not yet. But, nephew, you'd do well to remember this is your home now. If you are not willing to defend what is yours—even from England—you will lose all."

"I will defend what is mine," Iaian said grimly. "Do not doubt it."

Sadly, Donnchadh acknowledged his nephew's right to bitterness. "How much will you destroy in the process?" he asked searchingly.

"No more unless I'm given cause. I did not arrive unprepared. Coire was destroyed because it was the poorest of Lord Gillecrist's holdings and the first to defy me. I considered carefully before I acted. Every outbuilding, every league of ground of every keep, is as familiar to me as reports can make it."

Donnchadh nodded. If this were true, his nephew would do well enough once he was used to the thought of being Scots. The lad was clever, though perhaps a bit cold-blooded. At his gesture, his men fell into line with Iaian's, and his nephew followed his lead as he turned toward the gates of Daileass. "Will you stay here long?"

"As long as I must to ensure that my commands are obeyed, whether I am here or leagues distant."

"I should think your show of arms at Coire did that."

"Nay," Iaian said emphatically, his eyes taking in every aspect of the bailey as he and Donnchadh rode through the castle gates. "There are far too many ways for retainers to disobey the wishes of their lord, ways that have nothing to do with weaponry."

Ros Donnchadh looked at his nephew with new respect. He would do very well, indeed.

Iaian was not displeased as he entered the wide-flung doors of the hall. The castellan, who hovered in the background anxiously, was obviously worth his hire, for even after his lord's death he had not allowed any signs of neglect in the ancient fortress. The weapons on the long walls gleamed dully in the scant sunlight that found entrance through narrow slits of windows high on both sides of the huge room. There were some tapestries, exquisitely stitched, but each was of a battle scene, grim and all too real.

While Iaian studied the room, Donnchadh studied him. He regretted not having had the rearing of the lad, but he acknowledged ruefully that even had Iaian not been removed from Scotland, his uncle would have had little influence. Alasdair would have seen to that. Donnchadh hoped there was none of his father in the young man. Cruelty became no man.

"Well, nephew, what do you think?"

Iaian smiled faintly. "I'm glad 'twas not this keep that defied me. It would not have been easily leveled, I think."

"Nay," Donnchadh agreed, "it would not, and your return to Scotland would have been far less comfortable."

The smile on Iaian's face faded. "There is no comfort for me in any of this. I would to God I'd never heard of this place, or you."

Donnchadh did not take offense. There was no anger in the younger man's voice, only deep despair. He placed his hand on his nephew's shoulder. "Scotland is your birthright, Iaian. I know 'tis difficult for you and will be more difficult in weeks ahead. But you've a heritage of which you can be proud. Alasdair Gillecrist was not an easy man, but the courage and the wit of the Gillecrist line is not to be disdained." He grinned slightly. "Nor is that of my forebears. Donnchadhs have ever made Scotland proud."

Iaian met his gaze without flinching. "'Tis no easy thing to trade one life for another. I'll succeed, Uncle, but I do not have hopes that I'll ever thank the day I was forced to it."

Pleased that his nephew had finally acknowledged their relationship, Donnchadh nodded. "You'll not find yourself faced with it alone. You are my heir, my only family. Donnchadhs take care of their own."

Turning to take the heavy goblets crusted with jewels from a servant, Donnchadh handed one to Iaian. He lifted his own in a toast and waited for Iaian to do the same, smiling at his nephew's reluctance. "Welcome home, lad." His smile broadened as Iaian lifted his wine and drank.

Iaian, sprawled in a deep leather chair, stretched his legs before him, wearier than he'd ever been in his life. And lonelier. His uncle, asleep now in another of the many upper rooms, was affable as well as astute, but a stranger. Still, Iaian found he could no longer harbor any animosity toward the man for the actions that had wrested him from a comfortable life in England. Donnchadh had done what he believed to be in Iaian's best interest, and in the best interest of their family line.

Iaian still had difficulty in remembering that Ros Donnchadh was his family, perhaps his only family, except for his mother. Iaian recalled his uncle's rather blunt statement that Iaian was his heir. Though curious, Iaian had not yet reached the point that he could ask him about other kin. Nor had he given his mother any opportunity to impart such information once he realized the enormity of what she was telling him that day in England. He'd not wanted to hear more about a family whose existence he'd never known until that moment.

Stifling an urge to hurl his goblet into the cold hearth, Iaian glanced restlessly around the room. It was elegant by any standards. Every wall was covered with costly hangings in exquisite colors. Gold plate lined a massive shelf of chiseled stone above the hearth. He was a rich man now. With an oath, he left the chair and paced to a window with shutters flung open to the night air. The chill of early spring seeped into the room.

Iaian gazed out at the dark sky sprinkled with stars and thought of England, of home. He recalled his mother as he'd seen her last, weeping, and his heart ached at the memory. But even as he considered sending word to her that he was well, he felt the ripping pain of having lost all that was dear to him. Not yet. He could not say the words she would need to hear from him yet. Not when the pain of losing England, and Edra, was with him still. Lady Edra Byreham, of the soft, honey-colored hair and the mesmerizing brown eyes. His betrothed, who had not wanted the taint of scandal that now accompanied the man she had promised to wed.

By his own choice, he had been the one to tell her. She had been so beautiful that day, though he could not now recall the color of her gown. He could remember only the look in her eyes as she heard his words—and her response. "Lord Lindael is not your father. Your mother . . ." Repugnance had dawned in the tawny depths of her eyes. "Your mother is his mistress, the wife of a Scot?"

"I've spoken with your father, Edra. 'Twill be no hindrance to our contract."

At his words she had taken a step backward. "No hindrance? How can you say so? I'll not bear your mother's shame! And do you expect me to journey with you to Scotland? 'Tis a barbaric nation." She shuddered delicately. "I'll not have Scots blood running through the veins of my children."

She had fastidiously tucked her skirts about her and stepped away from him, forcing him to realize the depth of his loss. He was twenty years old and suddenly without family, country, or future. He, who had been heir to the Lindael estates, was little better than a bastard. England was no part of his blood nor his heritage. And he was no longer contracted to wed the most beautiful of England's daughters.

No. He could not send word to his mother until he could give his forgiveness. And his anger and pain burned too deep, still, for that.

Giving in to exhaustion, he flung himself atop the softness of the massive bed and slept, awakening to a confusion of noise in the early hours of dawn. He dressed quickly in tunic and woolen hose, leaving his room with his sword in hand. The great hall below was deserted; not even a servant moved about in the gray light of dawn streaming through the high leaded windows.

As he pushed open the heavy door of the hall, the rumblings that had awakened him increased to a roar. Every person of his household, it appeared, was in the bailey, with his uncle and his uncle's men.

A small troop of men, still mounted, were the center of the disorder. Iaian's steps slowed as he descended the stairs of the keep. One man caught his eye, tall and broad-shouldered, with hair and eyes as dark as Iaian's own.

The man met his gaze, then dropped his glance to the sword Iaian held loosely in one hand. A slow smile curled his lips before he slid from his horse and swept Iaian a mocking bow. "My Lord Gillecrist, is it not?" His jaw was square, his brow high and intelligent. And his eyes were sharp, seeing much but revealing nothing.

Iaian stopped before him and nodded. "I am Iaian Gillecrist."

"Welcome to Scotland . . . brother."

Iaian stiffened, glancing at Donnchadh, who met his look evenly as he responded to the question in Iaian's eyes. "This, nephew, is your half-brother, Tavis."

"Your *bastard* half-brother," Tavis drawled, amused at Iaian's expression. "You did not know, then?" He threw back his head and laughed bitterly. "Pity, but no matter. The joke is on me, of course. I did not know of you, either. Until after our blessed father's death."

Thoughts raced through Iaian's mind as he tried to discern this Tavis's true reaction to the arrival of a rightful heir. Had Alasdair Gillecrist led his illegitimate son to believe he would inherit all? He would have been right to do so. After all, he did not even know of Iaian's existence.

"Welcome to Daileass," Iaian said at last, scarcely knowing what else he could say until he knew better how things stood.

Tavis laughed again, still without mirth. "My thanks . . . brother. 'Tis pleasant to know I stand welcome, once more, in the home of my youth."

Despite his sympathy for the other man's position, Iaian began to mislike his tone. The unholy disorder of Gillecrist affairs was no fault of his. He'd wished more than once, and wished still, that he'd never heard the name Gillecrist, much less that he bore it for all time! "You are welcome," he said at last, "until you make yourself unwelcome."

Donnchadh looked at him sharply but without censure, while Tavis's face tightened.

"Do not mistake me, my lord," Tavis said in a harsh voice. "I'll do nothing to usurp your place."

Iaian did not apologize, though he nodded gravely. "Then let us see if there is food to break our fast." He glanced at the small troop who remained astride. "Your men are welcome also."

Without regard for treachery, he turned his back on the group in the courtyard. Though there was much he did not yet know, he was sure he would do well to show no fear to this man. His brother. The thought was daunting. Iaian wondered what else he did not know.

Somewhat to his surprise, Donnchadh and Tavis conversed easily over a repast of bread and cheese and ale. Clearly, they knew each other well. For the first little while, Iaian did no more than listen, for they spoke of a Scotland he did not know. Familiar though he was with political intrigues—Geoffrey Lindael ensured his children were well versed in the affairs of their homeland and its volatile neighbor—this was a side to Scotland he'd not heard.

Tavis brought news to Donnchadh. "Our little Mary has been moved to Dumbarton. 'Tis thought Stirling is no longer safe."

Donnchadh nodded. "That whoreson Somerset left hordes of his bloody bastards south of Edinburgh. And Arran hasn't manhood enough to lead an army of Philistines against them—much less men who are sick at heart of being led into battle and then abandoned to slaughter."

Iaian was surprised to hear his uncle speak so scathingly of Scotland's regent. Apparently Arran was no more liked by his nobles than was Somerset, who had been named Lord Protector of England upon the death of Henry VIII in January of the previous year.

Silently, Iaian thought that neither country was in good stead at the moment. England had as king a frail ten-year-old, and Scotland's queen had been born just days before her father's death five years earlier. Somerset was a sour man, unpopular with the baronage and commoners alike. And it appeared that Arran was more noted in Scotland for his cowardice than for his leadership.

"What do we hear of France?" Donnchadh asked when Tavis did not remark on his scathing comment on Arran.

Tavis's gaze slid to Iaian, and Iaian caught the flash of mistrust in their depths. It was common knowledge that Marie de Guise, Scotland's dowager queen, sought desperately to contract her daughter to Francis, the Dauphin of France. This would ensure the strong hand of France in Scotland's protection, as well as the troops Marie needed to quell the rising of the reformers against her beloved church.

All this Iaian knew. And he knew, also, that Somerset would pay dearly for knowledge of whether or not a marriage contract had yet been signed between the royal families of France and Scotland. It was this that Tavis feared to reveal.

Iaian smiled bitterly at his half-brother, lifting his goblet in a mocking toast. It would be just as well that Tavis guarded his tongue. As yet, Iaian was of divided loyalties. Though his wealth and heritage belonged to Scotland, he was not yet Scotland's man.

Donnchadh merely snorted at Tavis's reluctance. "Though you like it not, my boy, Scotland is home to the Gillecrists, and any man of them will die in its defense."

And, though the words were directed at his half-brother, Iaian knew their message was for him. He could not help but wonder how his uncle could be so sure of him when he was not at all sure of himself. But Donnchadh's eyes were on him, steady and assured, and Iaian bit his tongue on the doubts that clamored in his mind.

Chapter Three

"Mother Giorsal, you must do something about Cecile!" Nearra entered the room, wishing she did not have to complain about her young sister-in-law yet again. 'Twas barely a fortnight since the debacle of Father Aindreas's departure.

Giorsal Lotharing looked up from the skein of silk she was untangling. She liked Nearra, truly she did, but sometimes the younger woman could be very tiring. "And what has my young imp done this time?"

"Despite Amalric's warning, she has slipped out again. She is not in her room, nor in the bailey. The guard tells me she is at the river again. He has been watching her, but . . ." Nearra stopped helplessly.

Unalarmed, knowing Ciaran's guards would die to protect the daughter of the household, Giorsal patted the low couch beside her. "Come, Nearra," she said invitingly. "Rest for a few minutes."

Her eldest son's wife was weary, she knew, from preparing Ciaran for visitors. The powerful Earl of Arran, Scotland's regent, would grace them with his presence within the week. Not that Ciaran needed much readying. Nearra was a far better chatelaine than ever Giorsal had been. In the four years since Giorsal had relinquished her duties with a sigh of relief, there had not once been a hitch in the smooth running of the household. A very opposite state of affairs from the haphazard manner in which Giorsal had ruled after her mother's death fifteen years before.

Giorsal smiled at Nearra's bemused expression. Her mother, Kyrene, would have loved Nearra's gentleness, though she would have abhorred her diffidence around men. Giorsal was more inclined to accept both as being a part of this lovely girl. And Nearra accomplished more with Berinhard than many a lass would have. Giorsal was well aware there were times when she could have gained much in her own arguments with Saelec had she not been as stubborn and vocal as he. She and her husband were as alike in temperament and coloring as they were opposite in size. With hair as golden and eyes as blue, Giorsal reached only to her husband's upper ribs, but that did not make her less formidable in a disagreement. Nearra rarely disagreed with anyone, yet more frequently had her way than the other females of this household—except for Ceci.

With a sigh, Nearra accepted her invitation. "I do not mean to vex you with Cecile's behavior, Mother. Forgive me."

"Nonsense." Giorsal chuckled before admitting, "Cecile has been vexing us all since the moment of her birth!"

"Perhaps if I had children of my own, I would be more understanding of her." Nearra's eyes held a hint of old pain and longing.

"You will have." Giorsal touched her hand in commiseration.

"I think not. Not if I've had none in four years of marriage. 'Tis a sadness to Berin and to me."

"On the day of Berinhard's birth, my mother told me he would be the father of as many sons as his own father. You are but late in beginning." A smile teased her lips. "And once they begin you will wish it had been later still!" After bearing eight sons, six of whom had survived the womb and infancy, Giorsal could speak on the subject with authority. She felt a sharp pang at the memory of two sons lost to England's determination to rule Scotland, but did not let her smile falter.

The sadness did not lift from Nearra's eyes. "If that is true, I fear it will be with some other wife."

"Nay," Giorsal answered gently, "for she told me also a thing that I did not understand until I met you." She paused until Nearra looked into her eyes. "She told me that my son would marry the one nearest to him and that she would be the mother of many and the helpmate of my old age. From his fourteenth year, I watched every young girl who entered this household. When he wed very young, I was disappointed in his choice and wondered if my mother had been wrong for the first time in my knowledge. I confess I could not like the young flirt and could not weep at her death. Not after the many tears her behavior cost my son! And then, when I had given up hope that he would wed again, he brought you into my home and into my heart. I believe 'twas your name she saw. Nearra—nearest one. Aye, sweetheart, you will bear sons. I promise you this."

Before Nearra could reply, Cecile made her usual precipitous entrance into the room, the bright green silk of her gown swirling about her gracefully as she moved. Her face was lit with the joy of the morning. All Cecile's days were joyous, it seemed to her mother, who prayed they would remain so.

Cecile stopped abruptly at seeing Nearra with her mother, their faces so sombre. But then Giorsal smiled at her and bade her enter. Cecile did so with more reluctance. No doubt, Nearra was complaining about her behavior yet again. She *liked* Berin's wife, but she could not *be* like her. She would not want to!

"I'm going with Father," she began in a rush, "and Amalric and Berin."

"And where are Father and Amalric and Berinhard going?" Giorsal was noncommittal concerning Cecile's accompanying her father and brothers. Saelec was fond of taking the girl where she would be far better not going!

"To Daileass—to greet the new lord there."

Cecile's eyes were bright with the thought of being away from the keep, of being on horseback for almost an entire day. And they were pleading. Giorsal felt herself weakening and knew Nearra would frown, but the journey would be safe enough. "We've had word then? He's arrived?"

"Aye, just three days ago. 'Tis said he brought nearly an army of men with him!"

For weeks, Ciaran had been flowing with rumors of the rearming of Daileass to suit its new lord—and with that lord's destruction of Castle Coire. Giorsal was less comfortable than Saelec with the tales surrounding the man. Of course, Saelec would find nothing amiss in the warlike legends that surrounded Lord Gillecrist, nor in the fact that he was more English than Scots. Though German-born, Saelec considered himself as much a Scot as any other. He would deem it likely that the new Lord Gillecrist would make the same transition.

"Please, Mother?"

Giorsal wondered if any of them would ever be able to refuse this child anything. She was the heart of the family, and so beautiful she brought sunshine to the darkest day. Her hair was more pale than Giorsal's had been before time had robbed the strands of their silk and their gold. And though Cecile was careless with it, rarely taking the time to do more than comb the tangles from its length, it was lovely; satin-textured white-gold that fell in heavy waves to her waist.

Giorsal looked into her daughter's blue eyes and smiled. "Aye, then, you can go . . . *if* your father plans to return this same day."

"He does, but he says it will be late."

Nearra rose gracefully. "Well, if you will go, Ceci, I'll do your hair. You'll not leave here like a young hoyden with no sense of style!"

Cecile felt a wave of pure affection for her eldest brother's wife. "Thank you, Nearra. And I'm sorry I left the keep unattended. Sim told me you were anxious." Cecile glanced cautiously at her mother, who did not look pleased, but did not seem inclined to scold. This time.

Nearra's lips curved slightly at Cecile's sincere tone of apology. Cecile was always sorry when she transgressed, but the fact never seemed to sway her not to do so on the next occasion. "Well, there's no harm done, I suppose. Just please take a groom with you in the future."

Though Giorsal smiled at the older girl's response—truly, Nearra was a blessing to the household—she fixed her daughter with a sharp glance. "'Tis more than a request, Cecile. Do not leave this keep alone again. Not until the English are routed from Scotland's boundaries."

As the two girls left the room, she rose to her feet, feeling the ache of old age. She would speak with Saelec before he left the keep. Though she wished to see her youngest child, her only daughter, safely wed before her death, she did not agree with Saelec's most recent thoughts. And she would not allow this visit to be the beginning of any plans he might have. Lord Gillecrist might be most wealthy, and his Daileass might be their nearest and strongest neighboring keep, but he was far too violent to take her Ceci as wife. And he was English.

Nay, she thought, as she descended the stairs in search of her husband, Cecile needed someone as kind-hearted as she. She was spirited but had no meanness in her with which to protect herself from hardness in others. Giorsal wanted someone for her who was, perhaps, more like her brothers. Like her father. Gentle giants, capable of fighting, perhaps even loving it, but not warlike for the sake of violence itself. That Lord Gillecrist had left Castle Coire in ruins had alarmed her and made her give pause to Saelec's belief that they might look to Daileass for their daughter's husband.

Giorsal did not argue that her daughter should be wed, for she had suffered the first frightening shortness of breath but a few weeks earlier and several times since. Aye, it was time for Cecile to be safely contracted before her mother was not alive to see it, and no eligible young man had yet caught her eye. Cecile would have no argument to a marriage her father arranged—at least Giorsal hoped she would not.

She found Saelec in the outer bailey, and he swung her into his arms before she had a chance to open her mouth. When she did, it was not to scold. She loved her Saelec more with each passing year. The thought of leaving him, even for the peaceful arms of death, frightened her. She closed her eyes briefly and pressed her cheek to his, savoring the rough texture of the beard he had but lately adopted. When his hand slipped to her hip, she opened her eyes abruptly.

He was laughing into them. "Can you not bear to be away from me for one day even, wife?"

She laughed but said in warning, "Beware lest you lose that hand, husband."

For answer, he slipped his broad palm lower, caressing her buttock, caring nothing for who might watch. This was his woman. After nearly thirty years, the hunger was still there.

"Saelec!" At her tone, he dropped his hand obediently, but she blushed at the look in his eye.

"So then, if this was not what you wanted, why did you hurry down upon learning I was to be gone?" He paused. "I assume our young rapscallion gained your permission for her to go?"

"You should not call your daughter such," Giorsal scolded, spoiling the effect by adding, "though she is. And, yes, she has my permission to go, but I do not want you even hinting at an alliance between her and Lord Gillecrist, not to him nor to Donnchadh."

Saelec feigned an innocent look. "And would I, when you have so steadfastly said you will not have it?"

Before Giorsal could scoff at the false protest, as Saelec knew she would, he groaned at hearing the sound of Cecile's voice behind him.

"Nor will I have it. I will wed Reynard."

"You will not," Saelec roared.

Giorsal winced, as much from Saelec's certain rage as from the thought of her daughter married to Rilla's brother. Rilla was the widow of their third eldest son, Odwulf. Odwulf had married Rilla in Germany four years earlier, coming home to Scotland only the previous year. Reynard had journeyed with them, returning to Germany after enchanting Cecile with his poetry and musical ability. Poor Reynard was *too* gentle. Never would he be able to keep Cecile in line, much less protect her and their home. The lad needed a keeper of his own!

"Now, Cecile, do not tease your father."

Cecile's bright blue eyes twinkled merrily. "Disbelieve it, if you will. But Reynard is my choice, and I will wed no other."

Giorsal pushed at Saelec's arms until he lowered her feet to the flagstone, so that she could stand face to face with her daughter. "And would you leave Scotland to be with him?"

"If I must."

Giorsal stared at her daughter's complacent expression. Was she not jesting, after all? "We will speak of this later, Cecile." When Saelec was not about!

"We will speak of it whenever you wish, Mother. But if I do not wed Reynard, I'll not marry at all." Cecile's tone was polite and sweet, but determined.

In truth, she had not a great deal of desire for marriage, having seen its effect on her brothers' wives. They yielded to every silly thing that was spoken to them, whether it made sense or not. Nay, she did not want that for herself. But if she must wed, then Reynard would be the one for her. He worshipped her. She could not believe that even marriage would cause him to scoff at her thoughts and order her about! Besides, she did want children and rather suspected she would find herself at death's door if she decided to gain them without marriage—though she knew of more than one fine lady who had borne children, even an heir, during a husband's lengthy absence.

"I'll bare your backside to my hand if I so much as hear that pup's name on your lips again!" Saelec glared down at his daughter in helpless fury. Truly, he would beat her before he let her marry such a weakling.

"Saelec." Giorsal placed a pleading hand on his arm. "Later, my love." She caught her breath at the sudden sensation of weight against her breastbone. This time, there was pain with the pressure.

"Mother!"

Giorsal heard the panic in Cecile's voice and knew she felt the fear that pulsed through her mother with the rippling of pain. Cecile had inherited her grandmother Kyrene's gift for feeling the strongest emotions in those closest to her—and even in strangers she chanced to touch. Giorsal felt it was more a curse than a gift, and had been relieved when Cecile had never shown any indication that she possessed knowledge of the future, which ability Kyrene had also had. She willed herself to take a deep breath, fighting both the pain and the fear. "'Tis nothing, Ceci. Look, there." She nodded toward a groom. "Your mare is ready for you."

"I'll not leave you." Cecile's delicately square chin was set in stubborn lines.

"Indeed you will. And when you are gone, I'll spend the day doing naught but resting while Nearra waits upon me hand and foot." Her eyes pleaded with her daughter to obey.

"What's this? Are you ill." Saelec's voice held fear.

"Nay, merely tired of listening to the two of you quarrel," Giorsal lied, holding Cecile's gaze with her own.

Slowly, Cecile nodded, brushing Giorsal's cheek with her lips. "I love you, Mother."

"And I you. Now, *behave* for your father. Please."

With the abating of her mother's strong sense of fear, Cecile drew a steadying breath. "I will. I promise."

"Are you two coming?" Amalric shouted. He and Berinhard were already mounted and waiting.

Nearra stood near the steps of the keep, watching longingly. Swinging up into her saddle, Cecile gave her a pitying look. Nearra would adore coming with them, but she did not sit a horse well, and Berinhard did not often take her on lengthy rides. Another example of the reasons not to wed!

With a last look at her mother to reassure herself, Cecile turned her gaze and her thoughts to the countryside just beyond Ciaran's walls. The River Clyde flowed in the distance, begging her to follow. Far northward lay burghs she dreamed of seeing, Glasgow and Edinburgh and Linlithgow. She had been no farther than Lanark, while two of her brothers, Waren and Odwulf, had journeyed to Germany, their father's birth nation, to find wives.

Waren's wife had died soon after her journey to Scotland, before his own death at Solway Moss, where King James had been defeated by the English. They had left no children. Odwulf had returned the previous year only to die fighting the English at Pinkie Cleugh. His Rilla remained at Ciaran with her two sons. Konraet made his home in the Highlands with his bride, who would soon bear his parents' third grandchild, while Raimund, older only than Cecile and Amalric, was betrothed to a German girl named Alarice, whom he had never even seen. Even now he was on his way to Germany to wed. Cecile had longed to go with him.

With all but one of her brothers safely married, the family line would be assured. And even the one unmarried, Amalric, was betrothed to a Scots heiress, though she was only yet a child of twelve.

Cecile was certain she would be allowed to marry to please herself. And it would please her to marry Reynard! Although, she admitted only to herself, she did not care for him to touch her, which would make it very difficult to bear children by him. Not that he had tried often to touch her. Reynard would do nothing she did not like, and she had found his one attempt at a kiss unpleasant. It had not been overbearing, but rather light and dry, without feeling.

Cecile glanced at her father. She would not mind so much being treated as he treated her mother. He yelled at Giorsal and argued with her, but he respected her. When Giorsal spoke her mind he listened as if she were a man. But, she sighed, her brothers had not followed his lead. That gave her little hope that any other man would treat a wife in the same way her father did.

Cecile bit her lip thoughtfully. Did her father know of the pains her mother had of late? Of her fear that the pain boded ill? She wondered if she should tell him, but knew she dared not. It would distress her mother, and that was something she did not want to do. Both for her mother's sake—and for her own when Giorsal learned of it!

Amalric's question broke into her thoughts. "Father, why do you suppose Lord Arran journeys to Ciaran?"

Cecile listened intently, always curious about that which occurred in her world.

"Well," Saelec began slowly, "with the English still swarming the countryside below Edinburgh,

I'd warrant any governor would be looking to his defenses. We're too near the border for him to chance our loyalty."

Berinhard growled deep in his throat. "And do you think he doubts that loyalty?"

Saelec chuckled grimly. "I do not. He but woos us to be sure that we remain loyal to Scotland—and to him. His place is precarious, at best, now that there will be no marriage betwixt the little Mary and his own son."

Berinhard nodded. All of Scotland knew that Arran was to receive a French duchy in exchange for assisting with the marriage contract between the son of Henri II of France and Scotland's five-year-old queen. Mary, the only surviving child of James V, had been the subject of many proposed marriage contracts since the hour of her birth, just weeks after her father's grim defeat at Solway Moss.

"Where is Queen Mary now?" The idea of a woman ruling all of Scotland—though she was just a baby now—fascinated Cecile.

"At Dumbarton, since February. Awaiting the French fleet of ships to remove her to the care of France."

"And she'll be safe there?" Cecile persisted.

"Safer than that fool Arran can keep her, though there are few enough Scots who will like to see her under Henri's thumb."

Cecile did not need to question why her father thought Arran a fool. 'Twas his inept leadership that had lost the day at Pinkie Cleugh, losing their

Odwulf's life in the process. None of them would forget that bitter September for many a year to come.

Abruptly, Cecile's attention was claimed by the massive walls of Daileass Castle rising before them. A thrill of excitement swept through her. Though she would never consider marrying a man more loyal to England than to Scotland—and surely he must be after his upbringing within its boundaries—she could not help but wonder what he was like. Was he a barbarian, as she pictured all Englishmen? Bloodthirsty and cruel? She shivered and glanced at her father, wondering if the guards surrounding them would be enough if this new neighbor proved as treacherous as his English countrymen.

Chapter Four

"Lotharing seeks a son-in-law, I'd warrant, as much as he seeks an ally at his elbow," Donnchadh commented without looking at Iaian. "Ciaran is your closest neighbor, and the match of Daileass in strength and wealth, though Saelec Lotharing is only a baronet."

He stood between Iaian and Tavis as the three watched the approaching riders from the battlements of Daileass. Late-morning sun glinted from the trappings of the horses splashing across the shallow burn that watered the meadows surrounding the castle.

"I've no wish for a wife, but a loyal neighbor would not be amiss." Iaian hid a sharp pang of regret. Had the news of his Scots patrimony come but six months later, he would have brought a wife with him—albeit an unwilling one.

Tavis grunted at Iaian's words. "There's many a man has offered for the maid already. Lotharing is overparticular."

Something in the twist of his lips as he spoke made Iaian wonder if Tavis had been one of those to offer. He'd not blame a man, even a commoner with no more than a title of honor, for refusing a bastard his daughter's hand.

"Lotharing can afford to be particular," Donnchadh murmured thoughtfully. "He has riches enough to buy more of a title than that he gained in reward for his faithfulness to Scotland. And it was little enough reward. More than men and arms and his own blood, he's given two sons thus far."

"Then," Iaian remarked, "he can buy a son-in-law as well. Elsewhere." His eyes upon the visitors who neared the gate, he wondered aloud at the large number of guards.

Donnchadh gave a harsh bark of laughter. "The borders have not been safe since September last. A man had best be well armed if he would survive the shortest of journeys."

"You forget, Uncle," Tavis said, breaking his silence with a bite to his words, "Gillecrist properties need no longer fear the English."

Without thinking, Iaian dropped his hand to his weapon at the tone of insult, only to find Donnchadh's heavy fist upon his arm. "Nay, nephew. 'Tis not from your brother that you will have to defend your lands—and your right to hold them. Save your sword arm, and know this.

If you gain his trust, Tavis will be loyal unto death to you." Donnchadh's gaze moved from Iaian to Tavis, who walked away from them.

Iaian noted the stiff set of his half-brother's shoulders as he descended the stone steps to the bailey. Meeting his uncle's eyes, he voiced what he could not help but think. "Do you deny he would take what I hold if it were possible?"

"I tell you that 'tis not lands or wealth that Tavis Gillecrist would have, half as much as he would have a family. Think you on that, lad." And Donnchadh turned to follow Tavis down to greet Daileass' guests, leaving Iaian to follow as he would.

Saelec eyed the inner bailey of Daileass with a critical gaze. There was nothing to indicate a change in ownership, which was good in this instance. Though Saelec had heard that Gillecrist's other properties suffered from neglect, that had never been true here. From a quick study of the inner defenses, he turned his attention to the new lord and the men beside him.

Donnchadh was at his nephew's elbow and greeted Saelec first. "You are gladly met here, Lotharing. Is all well with your lady wife and your sons?" His smile included the two sons Saelec had with him and the daughter who shifted her horse forward a bit, the better to see. Donnchadh's smile broadened at her open curiosity. He'd always favored the lass, for she was a pretty thing, and spirited.

"Well enough, Donnchadh. 'Tis good to see you here and not much of a surprise, truth be known." Moving his glance to the new Lord Gillecrist, he dismounted to proffer his hand in greeting. "My lord, I'm glad to welcome you to Scotland." From the young man's wry smile, he wondered if others had made him less welcome. Alasdair's bastard, perhaps. And then thought, nay, more like he did not wish to be welcomed to Scotland by anyone. Rather he would be welcomed home to England if it were his choosing.

Iaian took Saelec's hand willingly, liking his neighbor at first glance for his open look of honesty, although he reserved his trust until he could know the man better. "Daileass is privileged to give you hospitality. Will you sup with us?"

"We cannot. I promised the lass's mother I'd return her 'ere dark. And, in truth, we'd not impose on you, though a light repast after our ride would not come amiss."

The castellan, who had watched attentively from a distance, nodded respectfully when Iaian glanced in his direction, then hurried within to have food prepared for the visitors.

Iaian turned his gaze to the young men who had dismounted behind Saelec. There was no mistaking them for the man's sons. He greeted them, judging their age close to his. Their straightforward gaze denoted an honesty equal to that he perceived in their father. Without turning his attention from them, he was aware of Tavis moving forward to aid the girl in dismounting.

His half-brother was looking at her besottedly, and Iaian knew he had guessed rightly. Tavis was one of the number who had been refused her hand. Iaian wondered if it had been her decision as well, though she looked glad enough to see his half-brother, now.

Iaian's first thought of Cecile Lotharing was that 'twas a shame such a lovely countenance should grace so tiny a maid, one clearly unsuited to bearing sons. His second thought was that he'd pity any man who dishonored her, for her father would tear him asunder. Iaian was not small, but Sweet Mary, Saelec of Ciaran was mammoth-sized.

As the man gestured his daughter forward to greet him, Iaian recalled Donnchadh's words as they'd watched the approach of the visitors from the battlements. The man sought a noble son-in-law, but upon seeing her, Iaian was of no different mind than he had been. The girl was comely, even beautiful, but she was far from the elegant stature of the woman he had sought in marriage. Her beauty was piquant, with sharp little features that came alive when she smiled at him. Hers was a warm beauty, lacking the cool sophistication of Edra Byreham. Another man might find her fascinating in her very difference. He did not.

He smiled faintly in return, greeting her politely before returning his attention to her father and her brothers. His interest was in the men who would be his neighbors, who would stand at his back in the face of threat. Though he could not imagine that threat coming from Englishmen. By God, *he* was English, though his blood told it not!

Cecile was fascinated. Not that she would ever consider marrying the man, no matter how her father pressed for it. Nor did she fear being forced. Her mother would not allow it—at least, Cecile did not think she would. But never had she seen a man so well favored. He was as dark as her own family was fair, with eyes the same dark shade as the thick curls that clung to his neck. Every line of him exuded strength, from the strong cut of his jaw to the sinewy muscles outlined beneath his woolen hose.

And if his coloring was opposite that of her male kin, his size was not. He was nearly as tall as her father, with a breadth of shoulder to match. She found herself staring at the muscles that rippled beneath his shirt as he led the way into his keep. And she found herself, also, fighting a tiny bit of chagrin that he had dismissed her so easily once she had been presented to him.

There was only the smallest consolation in Tavis's wholehearted attention and in the fact that she did not truly want the man to notice more of her. At least, not enough for him to wish to fall in line with Saelec's half-conceived plans for the alliance her mother had expressly forbidden.

Saelec paid scant heed to the inner hall as they followed their hosts into the keep and were served ale at the massive plank table. The hall was very like Ciaran's, as fine and comfortable as such a large room could manage to be in the face of constant drafts and cold stone. But the stone was warmed by hangings, though no fire burned in the enormous hearth, as it did at Ciaran. Likely if the man had womenfolk here, it would. It seemed women were forever cold even after spring showed its face.

That thought reminded him of his earlier hope for a union between the two houses. Not that he had entirely given it up, but he was dismayed at the anger he sensed barely banked in the young man who had inherited Daileass. The anger seemed not directed at anything, was almost unapparent, as Gillecrist talked comfortably and easily with his guests of his plans for crops and defenses at Daileass. Another man might not have even realized its existence, but Saelec knew. He had not lived with his wife's mother for near fifteen years without learning to read people with something of her insight. His Giorsal had developed her natural abilities in the same fashion as he had his, but in Cecile, Kyrene's unnatural ability had manifested itself. He looked to her sharply and found her studying Iaian Gillecrist with something of a perplexed look.

Abruptly, Saelec spoke. "Do you think you will be given wide berth by marauding English because of your upbringing?"

Anger flared in Iaian at the question, then subsided. It was a reasonable enough question from a neighbor, and if he could not ignore the fact of his past, how could he expect anyone else to do so? But he could not keep the bitterness from his faint smile as he responded. "I would guess that would depend upon the Englishman. There may be those who would feel a certain loyalty to one who was so recently an heir to Geoffrey Lindael. My . . . stepfather is well loved in the northlands of England. And then there are certainly those who harbor a jealousy for what the Lindaels possess." What he would have possessed, had not fate and his mother betrayed him.

"Will you find it difficult to stand against them should they attack?"

Iaian knew he did not speak of courage or of ability. "Difficult," he acknowledged, "but not impossible. Not if they stand at my gate with weapons drawn. I will defend what is mine against all comers." He did not glance at Tavis, but his thoughts were there, too. Despite what his uncle claimed, he had seen the look of naked wanting in his half-brother's eyes. Perhaps Tavis would do nothing to slake that wanting. Perhaps, someday, he would try to claim that which he had once thought to be his. If that day came, he would not find Iaian unprepared.

Abruptly, Saelec changed the subject, looking at Donnchadh. "Arran travels south. Ciaran expects him one week hence." His glance moved to Iaian. "You will no doubt receive a visit as well."

Iaian had been watching his uncle and knew he was not surprised by the news.

Donnchadh saw his look and flushed slightly. "Aye. I've had word that he comes."

"And that he comes here?" Iaian asked evenly, his tone no match to the irritation he felt. His uncle would soon learn that he was his own master. He hoped they did not come to blows over the lesson.

"Aye," Donnchadh admitted uncomfortably.

"What was it you did not trust, Uncle? My reaction to the news . . . or was it more?"

Donnchadh's expression darkened at this. "I would not suspect you of treachery, nor of lacking wits to handle yourself. I but waited until I knew better how to broach the subject with you."

Saelec shifted uncomfortably. He had no wish to witness an altercation between the two men.

Iaian felt an unexpected smile tug at his lips. "Am I so prickly then, Uncle?"

Relaxing, Donnchadh shrugged without apology. "Rather, you are an unknown to me yet. And truth be known, even I am not always sure which side I am on in this struggle between Arran and Marie de Guise."

"Struggle?"

"James's queen would have the regency, if she could. And Arran fears daily that 'twill be wrested from him."

"Should it be?" Iaian recalled what he knew of the cowardice of Arran in the face of battle, and what he had learned of the contempt in which Scotland's nobles held their governing force.

Donnchadh shook his head. "I know not. Would to God I did."

"A man is fit to rule or he is not," Tavis commented.

Iaian looked up in surprise. Tavis had been so quiet, he'd thought his brother not attending the conversation. For a brief moment, his gaze traveled farther, to the little maid of Ciaran. She was watching him with disconcertingly wise eyes. As if she could read his soul. He gave her a deliberately bland, polite smile and returned his gaze to Tavis, but not his attention. For some reason, it stayed with the girl.

"'Tis not so easy," Saelec said in response to Tavis's statement. "I am of like mind with you, Donnchadh. 'Tis no easy thing to judge the best move for Scotland in this. Arran is a fool and a coward, true enough." He spoke openly, for if Donnchadh trusted his English-bred nephew in this, he would also. "But should Marie de Guise take the regency, we face more bloodshed in the name of religion."

Iaian looked at him in surprise. "Are you reformers?"

"Nay. My household is faithful to Rome, but I've no liking for the smell of burning flesh. And it would take no more than a resurgence of French influence and power to fan the flames against those who would break with the church."

"But it is in the power of France that our little Mary's surest safety lies," Berinhard added, joining the conversation for the first time. "And it is in Mary that Scotland's future must be protected."

"Aye," Donnchadh agreed heavily, "and that is the crux of the matter. Mary must be safeguarded. France has the power, but once that power is upon us, God help those named heretic."

"And will that divide Scotland?"

"Divide it?" Donnchadh met Amalric's questioning gaze. "Nay, but 'twill wound it, of a surety."

The conversation lagged when servants carried in platters of cold meat, freshly baked bread, and candied fruits. Talk resumed with a question from Donnchadh concerning Raimund's departure for Germany.

Iaian was surprised to learn that Saelec's sons went so far afield as Germany to find brides. "Are there no Scotswomen suitable?"

"There are," Saelec admitted, "but there are many who consider *us* not suitable. Though their mother is Scots, my sons have not the blood of Scots nobles running through their veins, and though I've wealth, I've no title to overcome what is there."

Saelec felt a moment's chagrin as he realized he'd just given his new neighbor sufficient reason not to consider a match with his daughter. But, as viscount, the man had title enough of his own. He could afford to overlook the lack in his wife's father. If it came to that, considering Giorsal's adamant opposition. Of course, if Cecile persisted in this matter of Reynard, she would only help his case with her mother.

"How many sons have you?"

"Four living. The eldest is Berinhard." He nodded at his son. "Waren, the second eldest, died at Solway Moss, and after him was Odwulf, who died at Pinkie Cleugh. Konraet is next, then Raimund. Amalric is my youngest son. And Cecile," he added with a smile, "is our lass, and the youngest and most biddable of all my children."

That drew Iaian's eyes back to the girl, and he was surprised to see a flash of impudence in the smile she gave her father. When he realized her father jested in the matter of her meekness a reluctant smile dawned for the look of pure impishness on her face. 'Twas just as well he was not looking to her for a wife. He needed nothing else to make his life uncomfortable.

As they finished eating, their conversation stayed on lighter matters of court rumors. Donnchadh had many to relate, though he was discreet in what he brought up. There was a lass among them, after all.

It was only as their guests were escorted to their horses that the subject of Arran again arose, this time from Saelec. "You might do well, my lord, to meet Arran for the first time amongst a friendly crowd."

Iaian looked at him sharply. "And why would that be?"

"Arran will surely try to sway your thinking to his favor in the matter of the regency. You've had no chance 'ere now to study the man. If you come first to Ciaran and meet him there, you will have longer to know your own mind."

Relaxing, Iaian nodded. "I would not quarrel with the opportunity, though if my uncle cannot know his mind after all the time that he has known him, I do not know that I will be any the quicker to choose. And must we make a choice, after all?" They had reached the bailey, and Iaian stopped to face his guest squarely. "Is it likely that the matter will come to an opposition of forces?"

"Nay, but where your favor is seen to lie can influence many things over the course of the years, depending upon who is regent and where your loyalties are considered to be. There are many of us who still walk a narrow line, preferring not to tumble to either side."

Cecile was only half-aware of their conversation as Tavis asked her a question of his own. "What think you of my brother?"

She glanced at Iaian Gillecrist, knowing Tavis did not want to hear her breathless response to his physical magnificence. In fact, she suspected Tavis did not want to hear her utter any praise for the new Lord Gillecrist. She was aware he had asked her father for her hand and been refused. 'Twas not that he was a bastard. The man Saelec admired most, the man he had followed from Germany those many years ago, was a bastard. But Gavin MacAmlaid had made his own way in the world, earning his fortune and titles enough for several men. Tavis had done naught but hang on his father's coat sleeve, hoping to be given that which he did not seek to earn.

Still, for all his lack of drive, Cecile liked him and did not seek to wound him, so she answered with care. "I'd say 'tis early days to judge the man. I've not liked what I've heard of the destruction of Coire."

"Nay, that was necessary." Tavis surprised her in his defense of the man who had taken away his hope of inheriting. "Else Iaian would have had to fight for every keep he sought to claim, regardless that they were his by rights."

"Then," Cecile said reasonably, "I've little enough to judge him with. I know not what to think of the man, Tavis, save the fact that there is a sadness in his eyes." And an anger, though she did not speak of that, not knowing its source or direction. Could she but speak with him, she did not doubt that knowledge would come to her. But, like her grandmother, she did not seek to know that which was not her concern. There were times enough that she could not protect her heart and mind from knowledge she did not wish to have.

"Think you he remains faithful to England?" Tavis knew of her gift, though he had never discussed it with her. There were few of their circle who had not heard of the ability the woman Kyrene had passed to her granddaughter.

"I do not know this, Tavis," Cecile answered simply, her eyes meeting Iaian's unexpectedly as he glanced her way. She blushed, hoping he did not know they had been discussing him. But as his piercing gaze traveled to the man at her side, she sensed that he did. Well, they had said nothing amiss, and it could not surprise him that he would be the subject of curiosity, now and for a long time to come.

Her embarrassment was well covered amid the flurry of farewells as they mounted, but when she glanced back from beneath the archway of the gates, she found Iaian Gillecrist watched her still. And the pain and anger and bewilderment she had sensed in him was clearly visible in his eyes.

Iaian was rocked by the quick look of sympathy that was upon the girl's face. Rocked and quickly infuriated. How dare any slip of a Scots female pity him! He'd not much use for any woman after Edra Byreham, and he certainly had no use for this one. He hoped his uncle was wrong in thinking that Saelec Lotharing would seek a betrothal between them, but in the event he was not wrong, Iaian would do what he could to avert the subject. He would prefer not to openly refuse the man if he could help it. But if he could not help it, then he would do so.

Chapter Five

"You must have an heir," Donnchadh said reasonably. "Therefore, sooner or later, you must wed." He waited out the silence in the small anteroom where he and Iaian had been arguing the issue for the better part of an hour.

"But not Lotharing's lass."

Donnchadh was startled by the emphasis Iaian placed on the words. He had seen nothing amiss in any exchange between the two of them, and the lass was sightly enough for any man. "Do you have a preference for another?" God help them if his nephew wished to place an English lady at his side.

"Nay," Iaian said bluntly. "I've no wish to marry anyone. Why can Tavis not be my heir? My father all but promised him my place, did he not?"

"It would not do. Tavis would lose all within a

year of inheriting. I said as much to Gillecrist." Not that Anne's husband had paid much heed to the council of her brother.

"He does not seem lacking in courage," Iaian grumbled. Foolhardy courage at that. Iaian already tired of his half-brother's baiting. It almost appeared that Tavis wished to stir him to a quarrel.

"Courage? No. 'Tis wisdom he lacks." Donnchadh raked his fingers through his hair distractedly. He did not want to give Iaian a dislike of his half-brother, but there was a warning he knew he must make. "Tavis becomes embroiled in every court intrigue he stumbles across. And there are far too many for him not to find ample opportunity for trouble. Even now, he dabbles in Marie de Guise's desire for the regency."

"Are you against her?" Iaian asked in surprise, despite what his uncle had said that morning against choosing sides. He would have thought Arran's well-known cowardice would cause his uncle to hold the man in aversion.

"Not against her, but 'tis early days for too open a move. Tavis has no caution. He acts upon his heart, not his mind."

"Tavis's indiscretion is not reason enough for me to wed." Iaian brought the conversation around to its origin, wanting to lay the matter to rest so he did not hear of it again. At least not from his uncle.

"But Tavis's mistrust of you is reason for you to think on the advantages. His thoughts are but a reflection of what you will encounter in others. Your claim to all of your father's properties is tenuous, at best. You will be forced to hold your lands against those who will seek to take them, openly or through subterfuge."

"I do not need the aid of Lotharing to hold what is mine."

"Not if open force is used, but you will not likely be so lucky. More damage could be done if someone were to question your loyalty to Scotland and feed the doubt into royal ears." Donnchadh held him with a piercing gaze. "Marriage to a Scots lass, into a family well known for loyalty would undermine any such attempt." Seeing the stubborn set to his nephew's jaw, Donnchadh sighed. "Think on it, lad. Marriage is not such a bad thing and could do you great good."

"I'll think on it," Iaian said grudgingly and knew he would, though the need to do so grated on him.

"There's nothing to dislike in the lad," Saelec insisted.

"He's English." Giorsal snuggled closer to Saelec's broad shoulder, feeling the same security and peace their marriage bed always brought to her. And wishing her beloved husband would cease his argument for a marriage between Cecile and Gillecrist so that she could sleep.

"He's Scots. And, if it comes to that, I'm German."

"Germany is not our enemy."

Saelec chuckled at that. "Germany is too busy with feuding amongst its own people to fight with anyone else. And Gillecrist is our neighbor, not our enemy."

"Does he wish for this marriage?" Giorsal asked at last in exasperation.

"I've not broached it to him. How could I when you are so set against it."

Giorsal groaned at the extreme reasonableness of his tone, when she knew very well he would do as he thought best. "You seem not to care for that!"

Hearing the exasperation in her voice, Saelec drew her closer. "You know that is not true. I'd do nothing you mislike."

"'Tis the first time I've wished for my mother's gift," Giorsal admitted, relaxing at this sincere reassurance. As long as Saelec did not act against her wishes, she could deal with his persistence in arguing the matter. "This once I would know that which is hidden to me."

"Whether such a match would be good for Cecile?"

"Aye. I would have my daughter happy. And safe."

"No parent can make such a guarantee." Saelec lay in silence a long moment. "Though Cecile cannot tell what will happen, she has an intuition of people that I trust. I think I would trust her in this."

Surprised, Giorsal drew back so that she could see the outline of his face in the dim light. "Has she said she wants the man?" She had said nothing to her mother, neither yea nor nay.

Saelec shook his head. "I've not asked," he admitted. "I fear to hear Reynard's name upon her lips again."

Giorsal chuckled. "'Twould be only to bait you, I warrant. Her love is that for a dear cousin. He does not stir her excitement."

Saelec had no more argument—for now. He lay in the dark thinking of the young lord he'd met that day and wondering if he would be right to push for a marriage between the man and Cecile. Beside him, Giorsal's breathing evened, and he pulled her closer. Thinking she slept, he was surprised when she spoke to him once more, her voice drowsy. "If Ceci should want to marry this new Lord Gillecrist, I'll not object longer."

Cecile woke to an aching feeling of regret, bringing with her to wakefulness an image of Iaian Gillecrist, dark and handsome and wounded deep within. Staring into the darkness above her, Cecile struggled to recapture the dream, but it had faded as she woke. She could recall only that it centered on the lord of Daileass and a pain he carried within him. When she slept again he was with her still.

Her second awakening that day was to the bustle of her maid on the far side of her chamber.

Iseabal smiled at her as she stretched. "You've gotten lazy since Father Aindreas left, but no more. The new priest has arrived and would bless this household with Mass this very morning."

"But 'tis scarcely light yet," Cecile protested. "Doesn't the poor man need to rest? He must have traveled all night to be here at this hour."

"Indeed, he did. He told your father that Father Aindreas made him quite concerned for the 'spiritual' safety of this household."

Iseabal's grin was cheeky, and Cecile groaned. "Not another like Father Aindreas? I was truly hoping otherwise. I miss Father Lucien."

But despite her protests, she allowed Iseabal to assist her in donning a heavy silk gown of moss green embroidered with black thread at the tight cuffs of the sleeves and the scoop of the neckline. She insisted her hair be left unbraided beneath a modest cap of black velvet.

"These colors are not right for you," Iseabal grumbled, thinking all the while that they deepened her loveliness but also brought a maturity to Cecile's features that Iseabal was not ready to see.

"Well, they shall have to do," Cecile replied, not at all concerned with Iseabal's lack of a compliment for her looks this morning. She liked the soft feel of the gown, and textures affected her more than visuals. She knew the fact never failed to cause Iseabal anxiety in the choosing of materials for her gowns.

It was with great reluctance that Cecile joined her family in Ciaran's small chapel, but she, along with the rest of the household, were soon happily surprised in their new priest. He was not round and comfortable-looking the way Father Lucien had been, but rather tall and angular like Father Aindreas. There, however, all resemblance ended. Instead of a burning light in his hazel eyes, there was a warm glow of love. Father Micheil's blessing on his new home was just that, and not a veiled condemnation and warning of doom to come.

Cecile was still savoring her relief when the family emerged from the chapel to the excitement of a messenger on a lathered horse.

Saelec recognized Arran's badge immediately. "He comes then?"

"Aye, my lord, they leave Melrose at first light." The man was breathing more heavily than his horse.

"Then they'll be here by eventide," Nearra murmured, already thinking ahead to the preparations that had been made and those that must yet be attended.

Cecile's thoughts jumped with her father's, and she was not surprised to hear him summon a messenger of his own.

"Berinhard, have word carried to Lord Gillecrist of Arran's arrival. If he wishes to be here, we will welcome him this night. And his uncle and Tavis as well."

Nor was Cecile surprised to see the sharp look her mother had for her father, and she knew Giorsal was thinking that Saelec wished to use any opportunity to pursue a marriage between herself and Iaian Gillecrist. This morning Cecile's own thoughts were mixed on the subject. Though there had been nothing in their new neighbor's manner to attract her, she had her remembrance of the disturbing dream that had moved him to a firm place in her thoughts.

"Come, Cecile." Rilla, though still clothed in somber mourning, shone as quietly beautiful as when Odwulf had first brought her home to Ciaran. She touched her young sister-in-law on the arm. "Let us help Nearra so that your mother does not need to do so."

Rilla's concern for her mother brought back Cecile's sharp fear from the previous day. "She is truly ill, is she not?" Cecile asked quietly.

"I fear so," Rilla agreed, warm sympathy in her eyes of pale green. All her husband's family adored their mother, and Rilla knew too well the pain of loss. "But she does not wish to speak of it, so we must not."

"She's always so strong. It frightens me that she might weaken," Cecile admitted.

Rilla slipped an arm around her shoulder as they walked toward the keep. "We will take care of her, and all will be well."

As they entered the hall, Nearra looked up in relief. "There you are! Rilla, could you please see to the placing of fresh linens in each bedchamber? And, Ceci, if you would go over this menu with Cook once more?"

Rilla and Cecile exchanged smiles at Nearra's distracted tones. Ciaran was always well and smoothly run. The servants loved Nearra dearly and would never let her be disappointed in them. There was no need for hovering, but if Nearra wished them to hover, they would do so.

When Cecile assured herself that all was well in the kitchens, Nearra had another task for her, and another after that, so that it was late in the day before either she or Rilla had time to attend their toilet. Not that Rilla cared for that, but Cecile did. She found she did not wish for Iaian Gillecrist to see her with her skirts smudged and her hair lying limply against her face. Hurrying up the stairs to her chambers, she chuckled at the realization that she cared not a whit for what the regent might think of her. She could polish the silver in his presence with her hair in a kerchief and wearing her oldest gown and be quite comfortable.

Iseabal began to grumble the moment Cecile sailed into her chamber. "Well, I thought you'd not even bother to change your gown. And your bath water is quite cold!"

"No matter," Cecile said carelessly. "'Tis not overly cool in here."

Nevertheless, she made short work of her bath in the tepid water and shivered as Iseabal poured water over her to rinse her hair.

"You'll catch your death of a chill." The age lines deepened around Iseabal's mouth at the thought.

"'Tis not likely," Cecile retorted, rising from her bath to let Iseabal towel her briskly. "I'm disgusting healthy, and you know it." Cecile was aware that the fashion was to be not quite so obviously strong of constitution.

Iseabal took comfort as she always did in the undeniable bloom of health on the girl's cheeks. 'Twas her size that gave them all misgivings, but her mother was tiny and had always been strong. At least until just of late. "And beautiful as well," Iseabal conceded, her eyes softening as she used the square of linen to absorb the dampness from Cecile's silky hair.

"And a trial to you all, if you would but admit it!" Cecile was used to Iseabal's silliness where she was concerned. Though the older woman was fond of scolding her, Cecile knew she loved her young mistress unconditionally. "Now, what shall I wear? Green or blue? 'Tis too warm for velvet, I think."

"Aye," Iseabal nodded, "though I've seen it worn in full summer by some thin of blood. What of the plum damask?"

"'Tis not my best color," Cecile said uncertainly, thinking more of the stiffness of the gown.

"Indeed it is," Iseabal said, affronted that anyone beside herself should dare to say such a thing.

Aware of the passage of time by the shadows deepening in the room, Cecile yielded to the choice and allowed Iseabal to slip the gown over her head and shoulders and settle it about her tiny waist. She hid a grimace when Iseabal pulled it snugly against her ribs. True to her memory, the gown was very stiff. Moments later, however, when a chamber maid entered to light the tapers, Cecile caught the glimmer of the gold thread shot through the cloth and was consoled that she would be pleasing to the eye if not completely comfortable.

She was curiously aware of the rapid beating of her heart by the time Iseabal was satisfied enough with her appearance to let Cecile leave the room. As she walked slowly down the stone steps leading into the hall, her velvet-shod feet made little whispers of sound that blended into the soft rustle of her skirts swinging with each step. Each of her senses was vibrantly alive so that even the shadows between the blazing torches seemed a tangible thing.

Every corner of the hall was brilliantly lit. Cecile's gaze swept the room, and she realized she was the last of the family to descend. She felt a quick disappointment upon seeing that none of their guests had yet arrived.

Rilla and Nearra were standing near the hearth, though there was no fire there to draw them. They smiled in relief at her approach, though Cecile suspected different reasons for each. Nearra was no doubt pleased that she was gowned befitting her station, while Rilla would have wondered until this instant if she would appear in their company at all. She had been known to disappear from sight when august guests were entertained at Ciaran.

"Ceci, you look lovely," Nearra murmured sincerely.

Cecile smiled, but her response was never uttered as the wide doors of the hall were opened to emit their first guests. She tried not to stare at the trio of men who joined her parents.

Her reaction to Iaian Gillecrist was disconcerting. He was truly handsome with his dark hair and eyes and features that were classically arranged. Yet those same features were harsh in a way that saved them from any hint of softness. But it was not his handsomeness that drew her. It was the bleakness that she knew was in his eyes, though his back was to her as he conversed with Saelec. Even so, the feminine side of her noted that his shoulders were broad and muscled beneath a gray satin doublet, just as his legs were sleekly muscled under black woolen hose.

Next to the emerald of his uncle's garb and the sky blue of Tavis's, Iaian might have been expected to look almost drab clothed in gray. His presence did not allow that. He was, rather, the more elegant and impressive for the restraint of his clothing. Where Tavis's sleeves were slashed to show an undercutting of gold cloth, Iaian's sleeves were embroidered with heavy black thread. And while Donnchadh was draped in gleaming chains and cut stones, Iaian wore only one heavy chain of beaten gold around his neck.

And from the moment he had entered the room, he had not once glanced her way, a fact Cecile found more disappointing than it should have been.

Iaian was very aware of Cecile, a fact *he* found galling as he shifted slightly so that she was within his line of vision. He did not find her perfectly shaped features any more attractive to him than previously. Nor did her well-proportioned though small-dimensioned body stir his lust. But his senses were acutely alive to her existence, the rippling sheen of her pale hair above the brilliance of her gown drawing his gaze again and again. Each time he could not keep his eyes from straying to her, he felt a renewed sense of angry frustration. 'Twas Donnchadh's words that kept her in his thoughts, surely. The thought that he might be coerced into marriage to secure his inheritance was infuriating.

It was a relief when Arran arrived in a flurry of excitement, drawing all their attention, though Iaian was not looking forward to the audience. He was surprised to realize that Arran was less sumptuously clothed than most of the half-dozen nobles attending him. But, perhaps 'twas not so surprising, when Iaian considered that he held reformer tendencies. He recalled Donnchadh's comments on Arran as they had traveled to Ciaran that afternoon. "For full five years he supported that faction, but his wish to retain his regency made such beliefs unwise. He was confirmed as regent in January of 1542, and in September that same year he did penance for his apostasy and received the sacrament in the church of the Franciscans at Stirling."

"He had a change of faith?"

"Nay. Of fortune. It was clear early on that if he did not cast his lot with the church, he would never hold his position. He may lose it yet, but 'twill be because of ineptitude, not his choice of faiths."

This conversation was in Iaian's mind as he was presented to Arran. He found him an unprepossessing man, entirely lacking in that charm that drew men to a natural leader. He could not decide, however, if he would have felt the same had he not known how easily the man could turn his back on his beliefs in his grasping for power. Such a man could as easily turn his back on those who supported him if it were safest to do so. And so fickle a man was not to be trusted.

Arran smiled at him genially, but there was an assessing quality to his gaze as he greeted the new Lord Gillecrist. "And how do you find Scotland, my lord?"

Beside him, Lotharing shifted abruptly, and Iaian smiled to himself. The man feared he would make a hasty and unwise reply. Was he already allying himself with Iaian? And was it as neighbor? or as son-in-law? "Unfamiliar," he answered cautiously, catching his uncle's look of relief and wondering if they all thought him an imbecile.

Arran nodded, as if he had said something very astute. "When do you travel toward Edinburgh? You've properties there and at Dunblane, do you not?"

"I have, but there is much to be done at Daileass, yet. Perhaps by mid-summer I will be in Edinburgh."

"I trust the walls of your remaining properties will be left standing?" It was a dry reference to Coire.

"I trust I will not be refused entrance to mine own keeps," Iaian replied with a hint of sharpness.

Saelec exchanged a glance with Donnchadh. Perhaps he did not wish to join Ceci to this brash young man after all.

Iaian was aware of the exchange, but gave no sign of it. Even if Cecile Lotharing was the very goal of his existence, he would not answer otherwise.

Rather than irritation, Arran's expression held amusement as he answered, "I trust not, my lord. I trust not. And if they do, I pray they do not petition the crown for intervention."

"Would it not be given?" Iaian asked bluntly.

This time Saelec actually groaned. Nay, 'twould not be a good match. The lad was as blunt of speech as his Ceci. They would be at daggers drawn at the first quarrel—if Iaian survived his own tongue that long!

Still Arran showed no offense. "Nay, my young lord, it would not."

Saelec's attention was taken from the conversation by Donnchadh's muffled oath and sudden grip on his forearm.

"Sweet Mary, Lotharing, who is that beauty?"

Saelec was answering even as he turned to look. "I am not familiar with all of these noble ladies, my . . ." His voice trailed away as he followed Donnchadh's stare. Why 'twas their Rilla! He turned back to look at the bemused expression on Donnchadh's face. "'Tis my daughter, my son's wife." Even as Saelec realized his mistaken wording, Donnchadh's face fell. "My son's widow," Saelec corrected himself. There were times he still could not believe Odwulf was dead.

Donnchadh nodded gravely, hiding his relief. "She is still in mourning." That much was apparent by the unrelieved dark of her clothing, but nothing could dim the radiance of her lovely complexion and soft green eyes. Nor could any sack have hidden the graceful curves of her breasts and hips.

"'Tis six months, now, since Pinkie Cleugh. Would you speak with her, my lord?" Saelec was not averse to the thought. Sooner or later he would wish for Rilla to remarry. He was fond of the girl and would like to see her smiling again.

"Speak with her?" Donnchadh felt bemused. "Aye. I would speak with the lass."

Hiding a smile, Saelec led the way after they had excused themselves from Arran. As was proper, he introduced Nearra, as Berinhard's wife, first, then Rilla, before nodding toward Cecile. "And you know our Ceci." Not wishing to alarm the object of his true attention, Donnchadh gave each of them equal greeting, though his gaze returned to Rilla after each. "Perhaps we shall be able to talk more later," he told her at the last.

Rilla felt disconcerted, her glance going quickly to her father-in-law. "Perhaps, my lord." But then she lowered her eyes, unused to male attention since her husband's death.

When he walked away with Saelec, however,

she followed him with her gaze, scarcely hearing Cecile's teasing comment about his interest in her. The two men reached Arran, still conversing with Iaian, and she met Giorsal's curious look and blushed at thoughts that seemed traitorous to Odwulf. But though she had well and truly loved her husband, she could not but admire the fine figure that Ros Donnchadh presented.

A short while later, Donnchadh found himself seated next to Rilla Lotharing. Meeting Giorsal's twinkling glance, he knew he had cause to be grateful and took full advantage of his captive audience to be all that was pleasing to a woman.

Iaian, however, was less fortunate in his dinner companion and found himself parrying verbal thrusts with one of Arran's nobles, who seemed determined to force him into defense of the English.

"Somerset is brave now, but his forces will soon be routed from Scotland." Dunmar spoke to Iaian, but his glance strayed frequently to Cecile, who was seated across from him.

Iaian, noting the interest with which the other man eyed Cecile Lotharing, did not comment on the fact that six months of Scots fury had not yet accomplished that boast. He smiled faintly and answered, "I'm sure all of Scotland hopes that you are correct in your belief."

"And what do you hope?" The man's sharp eyes and strong jaw were as challenging as his tone.

Iaian's lips thinned at the open invitation. "I've

given little thought to matters past the claiming of my inheritance and the hope that I will not be forced to slay any man who challenges my right to it." He noticed almost dispassionately that Cecile Lotharing was staring at him now.

"No doubt there are many who would dispute your right to Scots lands," Dunmar sneered.

"No doubt," Iaian agreed quite evenly. "But I'd hope none would be so foolish as to voice it."

Cecile heard the banked rage in his voice, felt it in the very air around him, and prayed the handsome Lord Dunmar would be silent on the subject. He did not realize that he faced a man goaded by his situation almost to the point of murder. Even as she completed the thought, she saw Dunmar open his mouth and knew whatever he said would not be wise. Knowing she was equally unwise to do so, she spoke before Dunmar could. "Even if they are, my lord, surely no one would defy the crown that recognizes your birthright."

Iaian could not believe the girl had joined the conversation. Could not believe she had dared feel the need to defend him. Good God, did the chit think he could not defend himself? His jaw twitched as he let his gaze touch on her face then move away, as if she were not worthy of an answer. He looked instead at Dunmar, meeting his contentious stare without hesitation. But Dunmar said no more, whether he realized he'd attracted the notice of others or because he recognized Iaian's fury.

The fury was not all for Dunmar's goading, nor even for Cecile's interference, but was also for one fact that was borne home: there might well be truth in his uncle's words. If there were many such as this one to dispute his rights to his father's property, he might well need the alliance of someone known loyal to keep that which was his. He knew already that Arran was a man easily swayed. He might well be swayed to the viewpoint that Iaian Gillecrist would never be Scots at heart.

And, Iaian acknowledged silently, there could be truth in that, but it was a truth not of his making, and he would be damned if he would allow it to keep him from that which was his. Scotland was his future, whether he desired it or not. There was nothing in England left for him. He could but build upon that which his father had left behind.

He let himself look at Cecile again even though he knew he would look elsewhere for a bride if he were forced to that path. The girl was not to his liking. And he was further infuriated by the sympathetic understanding he read in her gaze. It was almost as if she sensed something of his rage and his pain.

Stifling an oath, he looked away. Nay, he would not marry Cecile Lotharing.

Chapter Six

While minstrels entertained the remainder of his guests, Saelec answered Arran's request for a private audience by taking him to a small anteroom. Saelec loosed the heavy arras so that it dropped to cover the doorway, noting with a cynical smile the two guards that positioned themselves on either side. Arran might do well to keep his back well protected when he was at court, but there was no such need here at Ciaran.

Arran glanced sharply around the tiny, plainly furnished room. Satisfied they were alone, he sat in one of the straight-backed chairs drawn up to a small table and gestured for Saelec to do the same. Then he came to the true purpose of his visit. "We await the arrival of the French fleet."

Saelec did not need to hide his surprise; he felt none. "Has the Council of Lords agreed to the marriage, then?"

"Individually—though not as a body. But they will."

"Queen Mary will be removed to France? To safety?"

Arran's lips thinned at the reminder that he could not be trusted to keep his ward safe. "Aye. Her mother insists." His contempt for Marie de Guise was ripe in his voice.

Saelec said nothing. No words of his would ease Arran's dyspepsia over the situation, for he was of the same belief as the dowager queen. Little Mary would be far safer in France with King Henri than in Scotland with the wavering Arran.

"But," Arran stirred restlessly, "I intend to personally select most of those who will travel with her, and I would have one of your sons."

Saelec almost growled at his choice of words. Scotland had already claimed two of his sons. He was not of a mind to give another. Especially if Arran thought to embroil that one in a dangerous intrigue. "To what purpose?"

Though Arran bristled at the tone of suspicion, he knew he could not afford to alienate any more of his nobles than he had already. "For no more purpose than to surround Mary with those who would keep her safe."

"And if I cannot oblige?" Carefully, Saelec kept his tone neutral.

"I will look elsewhere—though with great disappointment. Scotland has many brave families, many sons willing to die in defense of their queen. But few with the intelligence to watch for other than the obvious enemy."

Arran met his gaze evenly as he spoke, and Saelec knew he was not flattering the Lotharings. Arran was perhaps seeing phantoms, but he obviously feared deceit on the part of the French. Saelec stifled an oath. He did not want his family drawn into this, but Arran was waiting, clearly ready to force the issue. Saelec would have to answer, and there was but one answer he could give. "I'll not send my heir, Arran, and I've few enough sons left to me. I'll send my youngest, Amalric, but God help you if harm comes to him through fault of yours."

"It shall not," Arran said forcefully, hoping he never had to face this man again if he proved wrong. "But it will earn him a place of his own in Scotland. Valor and loyalty do not go unrewarded."

They talked very little more before returning to the crowded hall. Saelec's glance swept the room, falling with displeasure upon the sight of Dunmar leaning attentively over Cecile. The man was rumored to be readily attracted to innocence, which it then pleased him to destroy. Before he could move in that direction, however, his eyes widened at the sight of Iaian Gillecrist striding toward the pair, a scowl upon his face. After a moment's hesitation, Saelec stayed on his side of the room, though he kept the trio within his sight.

Iaian was furious. With Dunmar, for the wolfish way his eyes lingered on the creamy flesh above the bodice of the Lotharing girl's gown; with the girl herself, for being too naive to realize the source of the man's attraction to her, and with himself—mostly with himself—for feeling the need to intervene, to protect. By all that was holy, where was the girl's father that he could not see to her chastity?

He'd never seen Dunmar before this eve, but he'd seen his kind many times. And he'd seen the tragic results left in their wake. His sister had been almost such a victim, but Geoffrey Lindael had taken care that the man thought better of his attraction.

"Mistress Cecile, your brothers tell me you enjoy the hunt." Iaian smiled rather grimly. Her brothers had told him no such thing.

Cecile was wondering which of them had gone daft. Berinhard and Amalric both knew she cringed from the sight of an animal in the throes of death. She had not been taken since she was perhaps twelve, and had wept for days after the scene.

Dunmar, seeing the cold way with which Gillecrist was eyeing him and noting Cecile's confusion, was not deceived. "Perhaps 'tis not the outdoor sport to which they referred, Gillecrist."

"Careful, my lord, 'tis not some court lady whose name you tarnish." Iaian's harsh tone gave warning of protective instincts he had no wish to harbor but found he could not ignore. He was very aware of Cecile watching him with widened eyes, but he kept his own fixed upon Dunmar.

A short burst of laughter gave lie to the irritation Dunmar felt at this intrusion from one he considered less than acceptable company. "Soothe yourself, my lord. I but jest, and the lady in question has a father and brothers to see to her reputation."

"Shall we test their reaction to your jest?" Iaian's voice was smooth as silk. To his pleasure, Dunmar's face darkened with anger. And all the while, Iaian felt Cecile's gaze touching him, probing his feelings. He could feel the very intensity of her curiosity, as if he were some foreign animal she would understand. 'Twas because he was English, he knew, and her reaction served to fuel his ever-present anger.

He wanted Dunmar to challenge him, wanted to feel his bare fists grow raw and bloody against the man's face, to hear the crack of the other man's bones against his knuckles. He wanted to place his hand's on the girl's shoulders and shake her until tears fell from the depths of her eyes and she ceased to stare at him.

But Dunmar was merely smiling at him in a condescending manner, as if no better behavior could be expected of someone reared in England. And then he turned his back on Iaian and bent low over Cecile Lotharing's hand. "I fear, my lady, that my simple words have been taken amiss. If I have offended you, I am deeply sorry."

Iaian could barely hear her reply over his own throaty growl of frustration. Then Dunmar was gone, and there was no one between him and the girl.

"Why did you do that?" she asked quietly.

Iaian did not pretend to misunderstand her. "You are no match for him." She tilted her head, so that the light caught in her hair. The shimmer, as if from a thousand candles, caught and held his gaze.

"As he said," she commented reasonably, "I have a father and brothers to see to my protection." Cecile was far from angered by his interference and knew she should back away from the dark feelings that engulfed the man before her. But she could not.

Iaian cast a swift glance around the room, at the crowds of people Arran had brought with him mixed with servants and Lotharings. Those whose attention was not on their food and drink had it fixed upon the minstrel singing for their entertainment. Or upon some flirtation they hoped to pursue to a satisfying end. With a practiced movement, Iaian slid an arm about Cecile and swept her into the small passageway behind them.

Feeling breathless, Cecile was not sure if it were emotion that had unbalanced her or the quickness with which she had been removed from the presence of a crowd to find herself alone with a very angry young man. That alone reassured her.

Had it been Dunmar, she would have been chilled at having to deal with his blatant sexuality. While Iaian was much more the masculine, she was quite comfortable handling anger. And that was what faced her now. *Why* he was angry eluded her, but she was confident nevertheless.

"And now?" she asked softly, very conscious of the tense grip of his fingers on her shoulders as he held her facing him. His touch was not painful, but she felt the force of his emotions through his very fingertips. The swirl of anger, frustration, and dark brooding caught at her far more effectively than had Dunmar's overt desire.

"I'll not be forced to marry," Iaian said between clenched teeth, more in answer to his own thoughts than to her words.

Cecile blinked in surprise, then her lips twitched. "I'm relieved to hear that, my lord. May I return to the hall 'ere we are missed?"

Iaian met her steady gaze and found himself drawn into the depths of her dark blue eyes. The compassion he saw there infuriated him. He wanted to rage at the unfairness of the position life had handed him, to punish as he felt punished, and in answer to that urge, he lowered his lips to hers.

Taken by surprise, Cecile gasped, unwittingly parting her lips to the touch of his. Even before the pressure increased to a punishing force she knew this was not a kiss such as Reynard had given. Nor, she suspected, was it a kiss of desire such as Dunmar might have given had he found an opportunity. This kiss was meant to wound as Iaian Gillecrist had been wounded. And it was devastating.

The pain, his pain, as she had felt it through the tips of his fingers against her shoulders was nothing to what she experienced now. His fingertips were still there, though lightly, yet they burned her flesh through the heavy damask of her gown. Heartache, impotent rage, and despair washed over her in drowning waves so that they, even more than the pressure of his lips to hers, left her weak and gasping.

Instead of the reaction she knew she should give, despite the danger of being discovered clasped in a man's arms, Cecile responded to those emotions by moving up on her tiptoes, placing her hands lightly against his chest to steady herself. With a knowledge born of a desire to comfort, she moved her lips caressingly against his.

Iaian shuddered at her movement, feeling physical desire replace the need to hurt. Sudden realization backed him away from the soft, comforting touch of her lips. For that was what he suddenly realized she sought to give. Comfort. Damn her!

He drew slightly away, intending a scathing comment on her morals—and was stopped cold by the sight of the tears filling her eyes. "Nay," he said hoarsely, "do not."

This was the physical reaction he had wanted from her. Tears. Pain. Even though he had known the desire to hurt her was not rational. But the tears and the pain were not for herself. They were for him.

"Do not," he repeated, pulling farther away from her so that she almost lost her balance, and he was forced to steady her to keep her from falling. The hand he held to her elbow burned at the touch, though the silken fabric of her gown was cool against his flesh. What manner of girl was she to have such a reaction, to cause such a one in him?

Still she said nothing, simply stood looking at him with a pain in her wide, tear-filled eyes that was his pain. Stifling an oath, he gestured toward the doorway. "Return to the hall. 'Twas a mistake to bring you here." That was as close to an apology as he could give.

When she did not move he gave her a light shove. "Go."

Reluctantly, she stepped away from him, scarcely noticing the trembling in her knees. She blinked at the glittering, raucous crowd in the great hall, people who knew nothing of what had just occurred, cared nothing, though she knew that a single kiss had changed the course of her life forever.

Nearra saw her first after she reentered the room and gasped at the sight of her flushed cheeks against an otherwise pale face and the brilliance of tears in her eyes. "Cecile?"

"I . . ." Cecile's voice failed her momentarily. She found it difficult to speak past the ache in her throat. "I need to speak with Mother."

Panic caused Nearra to grip Cecile's arm almost roughly. "What's amiss, Ceci? Are you hurt? Should I call Berinhard?"

"Nay, Nearra. I am well, but I need Mother."

Nearra glanced around the hall helplessly. Certain that something was terribly wrong, she feared leaving Giorsal to deal with it.

Cecile placed a hand on her arm comfortingly. "I am well," she repeated. "Please, Nearra."

Reassured by the return of normal color to Cecile's face and by the calm in her voice, Nearra nodded. "Go up to Iseabal, then. I will send Giorsal to you as soon as she can leave our guests without comment."

Barely aware of her surroundings, Cecile made her way across the room to the stairs, smiling at the people she passed, greeting one or two she knew. Feeling an intense stare, she glanced up to see Dunmar just ahead of her. His piercing glare seemed to reach into her very soul, but it was followed immediately by a mocking smile. She smiled in turn, as if there was nothing amiss in the way he looked at her.

Only Donnchadh caused her steps to falter. He was at the base of the stairs that lead to the upper corridor, and when she met his gaze she knew he had seen his nephew pull her from the room. His smile was kindly, and her eyes filled with tears.

She stumbled as she started up the steps, and she blinked the tears from her eyes. What had Iaian Gillecrist done to her? She was used to dealing with the emotions of others, to hiding her tender feelings from their sorrows and their rages. But she had found herself actually drawing Iaian's pain from him as if to share it and somehow make it less. That realization shook her as much as anything. She had ignored the ways her mother had taught her to protect herself, had deliberately opened herself up to the turmoil of another human.

Reaching the haven of her room, she closed the door behind her and stood with her back pressed against it. The room was peaceful. A very small fire burned in the hearth, mostly for Iseabal, who felt the chill of Ciaran's stone walls more than Cecile. The maid dozed in a comfortable chair close to the flickering warmth. Cecile moved from the door and called to her softly.

By the time Giorsal entered the room, the stiff damask gown had been removed, and Cecile luxuriated in the soft linen of her nightshift.

Giorsal studied her daughter's serene face and wondered at Nearra's anxiety. "Leave us, Iseabal. Ceci and I must talk. I'll call you afterward." She smiled at the maid as Iseabal swept her a deep curtsy and left the room.

Cecile scooted to the center of her bed and patted the space beside her. Giorsal obliged by stepping up to sit beside her. "You alarmed Nearra."

"I did not mean to do so."

"Are you ill?"

"Nay, Mother." Cecile was not at all sure how to proceed. Though she knew what must be, she knew she could never explain it. And she knew her mother was going to ask questions she could not answer. Finally, when Giorsal did not speak but merely sat watching her face, she sighed. "I would marry Iaian Gillecrist."

Giorsal's brows lifted in her face and her lips tightened. "To please your father?"

"To please myself." That wasn't entirely true, but it was as close as she knew how to come. It would please her far more never to have heard the name Gillecrist, but she could not now ignore what had passed between them. There was a bond and a link there that she could not deny. And she could never wed another when she knew that link existed.

"Why?"

That was the question she had known would come but knew she could not answer. She plucked at the bedcovers with nervous fingers, finally meeting her mother's steady gaze. "Because I must. I do not know why I must, but it is true."

"Oh, Ceci," Giorsal breathed. There was about her daughter a calm acceptance that Giorsal could not deny. This knowledge of who her mate was to be held an old familiarity. Too many years ago, that same knowledge had been in Giorsal herself as her eyes had met those of Saelec for the first time—a heartbeat after she had thrust a knife between the links of his maile. She had wed without demur and never been sorry, for that sense of completeness had never left her. Saelec had been her life's mate, and she could not refuse to acknowledge that Cecile could experience the same.

Cecile wondered at the emotions that flitted across her mother's face, even as she wondered that no more questions were forthcoming—nor any protests. "Mother?"

"Very well," Giorsal said quietly. "I will speak with your father, and it will be so."

"If he will have me." Cecile admitted the truth that he might not wish to marry her. Would probably not. The passion she had felt in him had not been the passion of a man for a woman.

"He will have you." If the bond was there, Giorsal knew it could not be otherwise. She only hoped the two of them would find the shared strength in their bond that she and Saelec had found. She could not help wishing, however, that it had been anyone other than the angry young Gillecrist. And, if she had not felt so weak of late, she would surely delay any plans to see her only daughter wed and gone from the safety of her mother's home.

Giorsal kissed her daughter on her forehead and quietly bade her good night. She returned to the hall to find her guests much as she had left them, with few even aware of her brief absence.

Iaian was among those who had watched her leave the room soon after her daughter—and had watched for her return. His gaze followed her as she moved among her guests, greeting those she knew, smiling at those she did not. He noted the taut lines of her body, and as she reached her husband's side every muscle in him tensed for action. He relaxed only when she made no effort to immediately claim her husband's attention from his conversation with another. Perhaps there would be no need to fight his way from Ciaran after all.

"Do you seek to have the girl first then, English?" The coldly mocking voice behind him drew his attention, and with it, his anger.

Iaian turned to look at Dunmar, who was regarding him with an icy expression. Without doubt, the Scotsman had seen him pull Cecile into the shadowy passageway and was furious at his presumption. Iaian had no desire to fight him for the girl, like two dogs with a single bone, but he felt a strong antipathy for the man and responded accordingly. "It matters not if I have her first, last, or never. You'll not have her at all."

Dunmar's smile of derision tightened into a near snarl of bared teeth and thinned lips. "Do you place yourself as her protector, English? I will bed the girl, and be damned to you."

"Touch her," Iaian said softly, ignoring his question, "and it will be your death." The girl was no longer the issue. Dunmar stood for the country Iaian still felt so at odds with, an example of the hostility he could expect to find wherever he traveled. A reminder of what was now and what should have been. He knew a strong urge to bury his fist—or his sword—in the other's flesh.

Dunmar stepped very close, so that there was no chance another could hear, and spoke in a quiet intense sneer. "I will bed the Lotharing lass if only to prove you wrong. And should you try to interfere, I will kill you as surely as your other countrymen will be killed for having dared to step foot on Scots soil."

"They live yet." Iaian's mocking tone reminded him of the English who were still within Scotland's borders.

"Bastard," Dunmar spat, lifting clenched fists.

But Iaian merely stared at him in disdain, knowing the other would not dare to start a brawl in the presence of his regent. When Dunmar turned away Iaian knew he'd made a sure enemy, and probably one for the girl as well.

He stood alone, listening to the swirl of conversation around him but thinking on his uncle's words. Dunmar was an example of his uncle's warning. He would not be accepted as Scots, not by his efforts alone. And he could not kill every Scotsman who looked upon him as English. Nor did he trust his half-brother not to take advantage of any opportunity to regain what he had once considered his rightful inheritance.

Squaring his shoulders, Iaian strode to where his uncle stood talking attentively to a pretty young woman who had been introduced as one of Lotharing's daughters-in-law.

Donnchadh looked up at his approach, and Iaian wasted no time on words or amenities as he pulled him aside. "I am for Daileass. Offer for Lotharing's girl on my behalf." He turned on his heel, scarcely aware of his uncle's astonishment.

Donnchadh watched him take leave of his host and shook his head. Whatever had changed his nephew's mind on the matter of marriage did not sit well with him. He hoped it would not bode ill for any contract he could arrange with Lotharing for his daughter's hand.

Chapter Seven

Long after most of Ciaran was abed, Saelec considered the words of the man sitting across from him. They were in the same small anteroom where Arran had requested one of his sons attend the little queen on her trip to France. Now Donnchadh was requesting another of his offspring—his daughter. "Why does Gillecrist offer for her?"

It was what Saelec had wished, but now he was not so sure. He wanted his daughter to marry well, and Gillecrist was as high in rank as he could hope for her. And he would like to strengthen Ciaran's position. But foremost he would have his daughter happy, and there was something about young Gillecrist that made him uneasy.

'Why does any man wish to wed?" Donnchadh answered, feeling less than honest, for it was a question he had asked himself as well. Iaian had made his aversion to the subject of marriage with Lotharing's lass clear enough earlier. What had changed his mind?

"For heirs or wealth or influence or any of a hundred other reasons." Saelec studied Donnchadh with a piercing gaze. "But why my Cecile? She should bring him heirs if she does half as well as her mother, but so would many another. And though her dowry will not be meager, you've asked little enough there, and I've no influence at court—far less than you. Why my Cecile?" he repeated.

Donnchadh decided on the truth, in as much as he knew it. "I can tell you only that he was against the marriage when I first mentioned it, but that was before he had opportunity to know her. She is an enchanting child, Saelec, no one could deny that. And they had a moment or two of private conversation earlier." At least he hoped it was no more than conversation. He recalled Cecile's flushed face and overbright eyes. "Who could spend time with her and not lose his heart?"

Saelec snorted. "Anyone who had to deal with her for more than a 'moment or two'! Enchanting she may be, Donnchadh, but she is not a quiet miss. How will he deal with her when she is determined to have her way? When she looks him in the eye and tells him she cannot do as he bids? I'll not have my Cecile beaten as are some." Saelec ignored for the moment how frequently he had threatened to beat her himself. What he did and what he allowed in another were not necessarily one and the same. And he could not forget the treatment Iaian's father had dealt his mother. What if the lad were of the same temperament?

"I admit I do not know my nephew well, Lotharing, but I'd swear he'd not be one to mistreat anyone weaker than he. And I'd stand as her protector should she ever need one."

"I don't know," Saelec said, worried about Giorsal's reaction to this. She'd made her feelings very clear. "Besides, Dunmar offered for her this evening as well."

"Dunmar!" Donnchadh was incredulous. "Surely you'd not give him serious consideration?"

"Nay," Saelec admitted, "I would not. But 'tis an indication Cecile may pick and choose from amongst Scotland's nobles if such as Dunmar would offer for her. He has as much power as any."

"Aye—but there are no others whose lands border yours, Lotharing."

"True." Saelec rubbed his jaw. This needed discussing with Giorsal. She would know what best to do. "Let me think on it, Donnchadh. I'll have your answer by tomorrow at last light."

Donnchadh finished his wine and nodded. "I'm for bed then. I'd swear 'tis been more than a single day since this dawn."

They climbed the stairs together and parted at the door to the chamber Donnchadh would share with one of Arran's nobles. Saelec turned his thoughts to Giorsal. He had yet to tell her of Amalric's imminent journey to France and did not like to think what her reaction to that would be. Nor was he eager to tell her of Gillecrist's offer. His Giorsal could be quite stubborn when she wished to be.

She waited for him in bed, her tiny frame nearly lost within the plush coverlets. A smile crossed her face as she saw his expression. It was the one he always wore when he was about to tell her something he wished to do or to have done and feared her reaction. She pieced that with Cecile's earlier comments and sighed. "He's offered for her, then."

Closing the door behind him, Saelec shook his head in amazement. "I vow you've your mother's sight."

"Only where you are concerned, my love."

"You are not shrieking." Saelec's words were muffled as he pulled his shirt over his head without bothering with the lacings.

"Cecile wishes for the marriage."

"Did he speak of it to her first?" Saelec's voice was thunderous. "I'll thrash the pup if he dared!"

"I think not. She feared he would not accept *your* offer."

"Well, then, and why would he not? Our Cecile's a lovely young girl."

Giorsal grinned broadly at his swift change of tone. Rage that Iaian might have spoken of his intentions to Cecile before he spoke to her father became indignation at the thought that anyone would refuse the offer of her hand in marriage.

Saelec eased his woolen hose from his legs and tossed them atop his shirt and doublet. A frown drew his brows together as he slid into bed with her, not bothering to extinguish the candle on the bed stand. "What do you think passed between them? Donnchadh tells me Gillecrist would not consider marriage but a short while ago, and Cecile would speak of none but Reynard.

"I do not know," Giorsal admitted, "but if they both wish for it and you still think it a wise match, I'll not speak against it."

"Dunmar offered for her as well."

"Nay," Giorsal gasped. "I'd not have that!" Not even if Cecile and Saelec and God himself wished it!

"Nor I, but the fact both reassures and alarms me. I am relieved to know that my blood in Cecile does not stand in the way of a good match for her, and I am fearful that she should draw the interest of one such as Dunmar."

All the more reason to see her safely wed to Donnchadh's nephew, Giorsal determined silently. She loved Saelec dearly, but she did not trust his wisdom with people. He was too honest to always perceive dishonesty in others. And though she had doubts yet about Iaian Gillecrist, she trusted Ros Donnchadh implicitly.

"I will speak with Cecile in the morning," Giorsal said as Saelec drew her against his broad chest. "If she has not changed her mind, then you will arrange the match."

As Saelec felt her snuggle her face to the mat of fur at the base of his throat, he thought of Amalric and of Arran's request. He knew he should tell her now, but the movement of her hands along his ribs made it seem more prudent to broach the subject on the morrow. This was a mood he would not spoil.

Cecile had not changed her mind. She could not have explained it to anyone, but it was as if every muscle and nerve of her strained toward Iaian Gillecrist. Her dreams had once again been of him, and once again she could not recall any details. All she knew was that they had saddened her beyond belief. It was almost incomprehensible that one human could carry as much pain and anger as she felt to be in him.

Weighted by remembrance of the dream, she opened her eyes to bright sunlight and her mother's face.

Giorsal smiled at her sweetly, her expression at once loving and troubled. "Gillecrist has offered for you."

Cecile hid her trembling reaction to the words. "Father accepted?"

"He will—if you still wish it."

"I do."

"Gillecrist may not remain at Daileass." Near Ciaran. Near the safety of family.

"It matters not." In truth, Cecile was at once loathe and eager to leave the safety of her childhood home. She loved her family but felt the pull of the world beyond Ciaran's walls. Her mother, she knew, understood her feelings, though she did not share them. Her father, who had seen too much of that world, had never understood.

"Very well, then," Giorsal said with a smile that was tinged with sadness. "We must begin to think of your wedding clothes."

Cecile felt a shaft of fear at the poignance in Giorsal's tone. Would the pain of her leaving increase her mother's illness? She realized her terrors were revèaled in her expression when her mother pulled her close.

"Every mother faces this moment, Ceci, and dreads it. But every mother knows it will come with the birth of each child. So will you learn, also. If 'tis a girl, there will be the moment she leaves for the home of her husband. If 'tis a boy, there is the day he is fostered and, God forbid, the day he rides to war." Her heart ached at the memories of Waren and Odwulf. She drew a steadying breath and pulled away so that Cecile could see her smile. "But we will be joyous as you wed, for you have chosen this man and not been forced to it as so many are."

"Nor were you." Cecile loved to hear the tale of her parents' marriage. Her father had ridden with the legendary Berinhard to claim Ciaran from her grandfather, who had sold his loyalty to the English. Her mother had stabbed Saelec in defense of her home, but Saelec vowed he'd known at once that Giorsal was fated to be his life's mate. They'd wed immediately upon his recovery, though her mother had not quite reached her fourteenth birthday.

"Nay." Giorsal chuckled, knowing Cecile was once again reveling in those tales of old. "I was not. But many are, and you and I both have cause to be grateful. Now I shall call Iseabal to help you dress while I speak with your father. He and Donnchadh entertain themselves with sports."

"What of Arran? Is he not with them, also?"

"He and several others left at first light with your brothers to hunt." Her lips thinned. Saelec had told her this morning of Amalric's journey to France. It would be soon, she knew. Too soon. She was losing all of her children so quickly.

"Mother?"

She forced herself to relax. It was too easy to forget Cecile's gift of empathy. "Nay, child, 'tis just that I'll be glad when Ciaran returns to normal. So much company unsettles me."

Cecile looked at her uncertainly, but held her tongue. It did little good to argue with Giorsal when she denied her feelings, and there were so many other things to think about now.

Giorsal called Iseabal to attend Cecile, then left them alone as she went below to tell Saelec of Cecile's determination to wed Iaian Gillecrist. She found him with Donnchadh, watching some of the younger lads fostered to Ciaran train at arms in the bright morning sun. For several moments she stood watching as they wielded small timbers carved in the likeness of heavy swords. Their tunics were darkened with sweat, more of which streaked foreheads and cheeks, as they strained against the realistic weight of their "weapons." These youngsters were at the very beginning of their training as knights and warriors, but even now each small face was grave with the importance of the task ahead.

Becoming aware of his wife's presence, Saelec slipped an arm about her shoulders, though his attention remained on the young lads before him. They were a mixed lot; two were French, one German, and two of them Scots. When the warrior who worked with them gave a signal, they relaxed their stances, weariness in every young line of their bodies. But when he gave a second signal, dismissing them for a few hours, the weariness dissipated as if by a miracle and, giving whoops of pleasure, they raced off as a group.

The warrior turned toward Saelec, who shook his head with a smile. "If leaders of state could behave as those lads, there would be no need to train for war."

To Giorsal's amusement, the warrior's own smile was pained. He was a simple man who clearly treasured his life's calling. No war would mean no opportunity to use those skills upon which he prided himself.

He cleared his throat before answering. "There are no English among them." Clearly he thought that would make a difference.

"There could easily be," Saelec replied. "And I think you would find an English youth treated the same as any of the others. These lads have not yet learned to hate and distrust."

"But they will," Donnchadh said with a tinge of regret. "They will."

The warrior took his leave awkwardly, not sure how to converse with Ciaran's lord when he spoke so strangely.

Saelec turned his full attention to Giorsal. "Have you spoken with her, then?"

"Aye." She glanced from him to Donnchadh. "She will have him." She would not say more in front of Donnchadh. Cecile's feelings were her own. She would share them with whom she would.

Donnchadh looked satisfied. "Theirs will be a good match. Aye, one for Scotland's good."

"I'm more concerned for their own good," Giorsal said sharply, causing Saelec to look at her in surprise.

"Have you misgivings?" His brows drew together in a frown as he studied her eyes.

She sighed. "No more than any mother would for her daughter's future. Nay, this is as Cecile wishes. I am content."

Donnchadh relaxed visibly and clapped Saelec upon the shoulder. "When shall we ride to Daileass?"

"Tomorrow morn Arran leaves for Stirling. Send word to young Gillecrist to expect us then. And now that that has been settled, I'd break my fast. What of you?"

Nodding, Donnchadh fell into step with his host and hostess, his mind racing as he wondered if it was too soon to broach a subject dearer to his heart than even his nephew's future. He hesitated to speak, then gave a mental shrug. It could do no great damage. They would consider his suit or they would not. "The girl, Rilla," he began gruffly, as a servant attentively opened the door of the hall to permit them entrance, "do you think to allow her to wed again?"

Saelec and Giorsal exchanged glances, their eyes twinkling, but their faces solemn. It was Saelec who answered. "It would be considered under the right circumstances."

"Which would be?" Donnchadh's mind went to the two Lotharing grandsons. Few mothers would willingly relinquish their sons, and few men would willingly give their heirs to another's keeping. The lads could well be the stumbling block to his hopes.

"If 'twas what she desired," Giorsal retorted. "If you'd have her, you'd best begin to woo her, for she'll not leave here until she comes to me as did Ceci and says it is her wish."

Donnchadh felt a quick relief, though he suspected he should not have been so greatly surprised. These Lotharings were more enlightened than many. Saelec seemed to consider his wife's views as important as his own, and Giorsal clearly considered those of her family equally so.

Giorsal was still smiling when she took her leave, calling a servant to her lord and their guest as she did so.

Cecile waited for her anxiously. She sat before her mirror watching Iseabal's careful plaiting of her hair. Iseabal's eyes were suspiciously red, but Giorsal pretended not to notice as she stepped into the room and shut the door.

With difficulty, Cecile waited until her mother had seated herself in a padded leather chair before asking, "How soon shall I wed?" There was an equal amount of anxiety mixed with the anticipation in her question. It was still difficult for her to sort out her feelings on her own decision.

"That is something I do not yet know. Gillecrist's offer came through Ros Donnchadh, and no date was set. Your father had to content himself with my agreement—and yours—before he would speak further on it."

"Father has not met with Lord Gillecrist?"

"Nay, Lord Gillecrist left Ciaran last evening. Saelec will likely go to him when Arran has left us. Now," she added briskly, lest she think too long on the changes ahead of her, "what cloth shall we have for your bride's gown?"

"Something soft."

The answer was so typically Cecile that Giorsal closed her eyes against a wave of fierce, protective love. This child that so loved things soft and lovely must never know the harshness of life that Giorsal had endured before Saelec. God would keep her safe. He had to.

Arran was jovial as he took his leave of Ciaran. The previous day's hunt had not been fruitful, but he was more than content with the results of his visit. He'd spoken at length with Amalric

Lotharing and was satisfied that the lad was sufficiently wise and cool-headed for the task that lay ahead with his journey to France.

And he'd met the new lord of Daileass, though he was less sure of his thoughts there. 'Twas plain Gillecrist was a man of strength and honesty, one who would hold to his loyalties. But where did they lie? Arran knew he would bear watching until that much was clear.

But, aye, he was happy with his visit, and he smiled broadly at Lotharing when he took his leave of the man and his lady. "We would be pleased to see you at court." To his knowledge, no one ever had. At least not the lady.

"Perhaps when the borders are quiet again, and we've no English to threaten our peace." Saelec did not think he would ever again walk through a royal residence, but he was not dismayed at the loss. He'd not cared for his surroundings when he was there so many years before.

Arran nodded gravely. "'Tis fortunate, Scotland is, to have so many loyal border lords."

Overhearing, Dunmar's lips tightened as he thought of Iaian Gillecrist. That one could never be loyal to Scotland, not with his upbringing. And somehow Dunmar would make that evident. His anger made his hands rough on his reins as he mounted, and his horse wheeled in protest. Aye, somehow he would make it clear to all that Iaian Gillecrist would never be other than English.

Chapter Eight

Evening was a soft whisper of bird calls and insect noises as Iaian stood on the battlements and watched his uncle and Cecile's father ride up the steady incline to Daileass. That they came together was answer in itself. Ros Donnchadh could have carried any refusal alone. Even now Iaian was not sure how he felt about the offer he had made. Wise or foolish, it was done. He would not allow himself to feel regret nor try to guess if he had acted in a haste that he would soon repent.

With firm steps he descended the stairs cut into the gray stone of the castle walls, arriving in the bailey at almost the same moment his guests rode through the portcullis raised at their approach. Tavis stepped from the hall to watch Donnchadh and Saelec dismount. Iaian wondered almost idly if he were unwise to allow his half-brother to remain. But, then, there had been no reason so send him away as yet. In fact, Tavis had proven remarkably good company on long evenings, and had even helped Iaian plan the taking of the next keep should force prove necessary.

Iaian put Tavis from his mind and concentrated on greeting his guests, though his uncle was scarcely that after his lengthy stay at Daileass. "Your royal visitors have gone?" There was no mockery in Iaian's words, though he had seen little enough in Arran to respect.

"This morn," Saelec replied. "He bade you good luck on claiming the remainder of your inheritance."

"'Twill not take luck," Tavis said unexpectedly, a gleam in his eye. "Iaian needs only the Gillecrist wits, and he has that, I ken."

Saelec was pleased that Alasdair's bastard did not seem inclined to quarrel over Iaian's rights. 'Twould be one less worry he'd have for his Ceci. He did not want her embroiled in a family dispute over inheritance. "Well said." His smile included Iaian, and it was then he noted the strong resemblance between the two. And it was then he recalled that Tavis Gillecrist had also wanted to marry his daughter. His smile faded with his recall of the young man's anger at his refusal. Tavis had been sure it was because he was baseborn and had refused to heed Saelec's assurances that it was, instead, that Ceci had shown no partiality for the lad.

Iaian stiffened upon noting Saelec's suddenly grim expression. Was he going to refuse Iaian's suit after all? He could not help the slight curtness to his voice in bidding them enter the hall, where they could be served food and drink after their journey.

Donnchadh frowned at his nephew's cool tone and wondered if he had regretted his impulsive offer for Cecile Lotharing's hand. He sighed and followed the others into the hall. There were times when he wondered if he should not have left Iaian Gillecrist in ignorance of his heritage.

No mention was made of the offer while serving wenches placed strong ale and cold meat before them. Tavis, however, set nerves jangling when he commented on the plain sustenance and Daileass's obvious need for a woman's touch.

He smiled inwardly as he noted the angry set to Iaian's jaw and the embarrassed look in Lotharing's eyes at his words. They took him for a fool, but he was not. Though he had left Ciaran shortly after Iaian, he had seen enough to know what was in the wind. Inwardly he shrugged; he was not in love with the lass, after all, and he had found warm comfort in the arms of another after his rejection. Still, he could not help but feel chafed at how easily all fell to this stranger who was his brother. His home, and his hope of wealth, and now the girl he had wished for his wife. Nay, he would not make it comfortable for Iaian. Why should he?

Donnchadh changed the mood quickly with mention of the improvements he had noted in Daileass over the course of recent weeks.

"And I've equal plans for the properties at Edinburgh and Dunblane, if they've need of them."

"The house at Edinburgh is as fine as any of its neighbors," Tavis commented. "You'll need to do little enough there." He shrugged. "Waytefeld at Dunblane is another matter. Neither Father nor I spent much time there."

Iaian's gut tightened, though he kept his face expressionless. How easily Tavis spoke of their father and his years at his side. That was a loss Iaian could never regain. Yet, for all his resentment, he knew if he'd been raised to watch his father mistreat his mother, he would have grown to hate the man. As it was, he disdained his acts while yet wishing he could have known Alasdair Gillecrist for himself. But Tavis was watching him, and he responded easily, "Is Waytefeld as neglected as I found Coire to be?"

Saelec saw the quick flare of resentment in Tavis's eyes and groaned inwardly. Nay, all was not as peaceable between these two as he might have hoped. He'd have to warn Donnchadh that he'd not stand for his Ceci to be caught in the middle of whatever war the two brothers thought to fight.

With a sigh, Donnchadh once again changed the topic of discussion, hoping he did not exhaust his supply of thoughts for conversation before Alasdair's sons came to blows over one of them. It was a relief to him when Lotharing finally pushed his goblet away and requested a private audience with Iaian.

Iaian led the way to a small chamber, closing the door carefully behind them and gesturing to a pair of chairs placed comfortably near a cold hearth. "Would you care for wine?" Anticipating the need, Iaian had requested wine and fresh goblets brought to the room earlier.

"Nay." Saelec cleared his throat. "I would talk of your petition for my daughter's hand."

Iaian relaxed suddenly, taking a seat in the chair beside Lotharing. He nodded for the other man to continue.

"Your mother was a fine woman," Saelec said unexpectedly, looking uncomfortable. "Your father's treatment of her was a disgrace to him—and for those of us who did not intervene in some manner."

Iaian said nothing.

"'Tis no easy thing to interfere in another man's marriage, and likely would have done little good—Alasdair was a hard man—but I should at least have spoken to him on the matter." He got to his point abruptly. "I'll have no daughter of mine treated so shamefully. Ceci is not used to harsh treatment."

"Nor was I raised with such an example before me." Iaian kept a tight rein on his temper. He was not his father, but this man would learn that for himself. "My stepfather treated my mother with gentle respect."

Saelec looked relieved. "I'll not say what she did was right, Gillecrist, but I am glad she's been happy all these years."

"But we are not here to speak of my parents, are we?" Iaian had no intention of discussing them further. "You accept my offer?"

"Aye. Because Ceci does." Saelec wanted that much clear. "If she did not, I would not."

"That is an uncommon way to arrange a match, is it not?"

"Perhaps. Even for Germans," Saelec added deliberately. "Does my background bother you?"

Iaian gave a shout of laughter at that. "Less than mine does you."

A smile tugged at Saelec's lips. He liked this young man more and more, though he could not help but worry for his daughter's future with him. "You've been generous in your settlement on her, and you've asked little by way of dowry."

"I've no need of more wealth. I've yet to learn all there is to managing that which I have."

"You'll learn that quickly enough. 'Tis managing a wife that will likely cause you the most trouble," Saelec retorted, thinking of his Giorsal.

Iaian pictured Cecile Lotharing as he'd seen her last, her face tear-stained by his actions. Ruefully, he acknowledged the truth of Saelec's words. He'd made a bad enough beginning and wondered if he would not regret having created the need to continue. He could have walked away from Cecile

Lotharing without a backward glance and been free of the peculiar fascination she held for him. Or could he?

Cecile sat quietly beside her betrothed, who seemed no more inclined to converse than she. At least not with her. He spoke more to the serving girls, with their full platters of food, than he did to her. But she could hardly expect more. They had not seen each other since the disastrous night of Arran's visit two weeks earlier. No doubt his memories of that evening were as clear as hers—and as uncomfortable.

She sighed softly, trying to forget the stiff discomfort of her gown. Nearra and Rilla, both, had insisted upon a brilliant green brocade with scratchy lace at the collar and cuffs. And they had insisted, too, upon dressing her soft hair in piles of curls that cascaded from the crown of her head. The style made a mockery of the discreet cap of black velvet embroidered with emerald thread to match the gown.

She felt a prick of dismay when Iaian's eyes fell upon her, and she knew she had stirred restlessly once too often.

"Are you tired, mistress?" Though his query was polite, his gaze held no warmth.

"I'm well," she returned, equally polite, striving to keep her smile from trembling upon her lips. Had she not still felt that incredible pull upon her senses for this man, she would be convinced she had made a dreadful mistake in thinking she wished to marry him. And she did wonder if she had dreamed the earlier feelings that flowed from him, for now there was only a cold calm surrounding him. In reaction to her own doubts, she lifted her chin higher. She had made her choice—she would not question what she had decided mere days earlier.

That was another source of dismay: the speed with which all had been arranged. Dismaying not only Cecile, who had expected a betrothal of months in which to become acquainted with the man who would be her husband, but her parents as well. Especially her father. Her mother seemed more accepting and far less distressed. It was Giorsal who had explained the need for haste to Cecile. "Lord Gillecrist has several properties at least as rich as Daileass that he must claim. He would be wed before he leaves to that end. Your betrothal will be announced in two weeks, formally. And you will be wed in late May."

Cecile had stared at her aghast. "'Tis only two months from now."

Giorsal's lips had twisted in a wry smile. "He argued for one month. Your father would not agree."

"Where . . . where will we live?" She prayed it would be at Daileass, near her family.

Here Giorsal had faltered. "He is rebuilding Coire."

"So near England?" Resolutely, Cecile had squared her shoulders and lifted her chin at her mother's hesitant nod. "Well, 'tis not so very far away." But inside she was thinking only how difficult it would be to learn to live with the stranger that would be her new husband without the strength of her mother beside her. And wondering how strong his ties to England must still be to make him wish to live at its very edge.

And her thoughts were no less tumultuous when she rose to stand at her betrothed's side and listen to her father proclaim them formally contracted. Her hand was cold in Iaian's as Saelec presented them to guests and family, and she wondered what thoughts ran through Iaian's mind. Was he any more sure than she?

A sideways glance revealed nothing save that he was as handsome as any man she had ever seen. His lean face was not that of a courtier, for it held a certain harshness of expression. But each time he smiled she caught a glimpse of the man he could, perhaps, be. If she could help him to banish the devils that both grieved and angered him.

Iaian was aware of her surreptitious gaze and knew he was doing nothing to reassure her. But God help him, he could not. 'Twas discomfort enough that he found it expedient to wed. He'd have no lovestruck lass on his hands, and the sooner she knew that the better. He would wed her and bed her as was his duty, but he'd not have her hanging on his coat sleeve. Nay, she would stay safely at Daileass until his business was complete in the middle marches of Scotland. Then he would see to the rebuilding of Coire. There would be time enough after that for them to establish a comfortable relationship. He did not, after all, intend to neglect her.

And, with a sidelong glance, he admitted that it would not be too difficult to bed her. The rounded tops of her breasts pushed against the lace of her gown, her flesh gleaming in the light of a hundred torches. Her gown curved sharply at the waist, and somehow he was sure that beneath that rich fabric the touch of her would be soft flesh and not stiff binding that forced an unnatural narrowing of her body. His eyes lifted to hers, and he realized she was watching him warily. Almost in spite of himself, he smiled reassuringly. She returned the smile faintly, but that wary look did not ease.

Cecile was relieved when the last toast had been lifted to their good health and to his virility and her fertility, so that they were free at last to seat themselves once more. Had she allowed herself to listen to the toasts, which grew more ribald with each healthy drink their guests took, she would have been mortified. Instead she concentrated on wondering how it would be to be mistress of her own home. That proved entertaining enough until she caught Iaian watching her.

His stare in itself did not bother her, for she had been guilty of the same in turn. She was, however, bothered at the subtle shift in his emotions. Where there had been antagonism and frustration at the evening's beginning, there was now something else. Something she could not easily define. A hunger blended with resentment. Somehow she feared their life together would not begin as smoothly as a bride could wish. And when he spoke to her but moments later under cover of the conversation around them, she wondered if *he* were not reading her thoughts.

"Why did you agree to this marriage when I seem to make you so uncomfortable?" He was leaning toward her, offering the heavy goblet they would share throughout the meal.

She took it, lifting the rim to her lips and using it as a shield for her emotions. "Why did you offer when you clearly have no interest in me as a woman?" she countered.

His eyes widened. For some reason he persisted in thinking of her as meek and modest when she had proven herself to be something out of the ordinary. Not brazen, but bold in a way that had nothing to do with sensuality. She was innocent, he would swear to that. "Why do you think I do not?"

She chuckled. "The strongest thing you have felt for me thus far has been a great urge to strangle me."

He burst into laughter, drawing the eyes of those around him. Then he sobered enough to admit, "And to protect you."

"From Dunmar?" she guessed. "Perhaps that was only because he brought out a base instinct in you. If we were not so civilized, you could simply have struck him dead, and you would not, perhaps, have felt compelled to offer for me."

For a brief moment, Iaian wondered if she were seeking lavish compliments from him. If so, she was doomed to disappointment. Then, seeing the steady look in her brilliant blue eyes, he knew she was not—and perversely felt a disappointment of his own. Was she not, then, attracted to him at all? "There were other reasons for my offer as well," he said, not caring for the churlish sound of his own voice.

"Will marriage to me safeguard your properties?"

His eyes narrowed. She was either more astute than he would wish in a wife or she listened well to those around her, proving he had been the subject of at least one conversation. Not that that surprised him in any way. "'Twill help," he admitted. "But I also wish an heir." And no man, he thought fiercely, his mind on his own father, would wrest that heir from the security of his home. The thought brought a sharp pain at the reminder of the man who had taken him from Scotland before his birth. Even now he loved Geoffrey Lindael as his father. Damn him.

Cecile watched the play of emotions in his eyes, the only place any were revealed. His face remained passive, and she wondered at the self-control he possessed. It made him seem cold and unapproachable. That was something she was not used to in the men of her family. "The thought of making an heir with me does not seem pleasing to you."

Iaian choked on the wine he was sipping and glanced around to see if she had been overheard. Mother of Jesus, did the girl have no sense of what was proper? If she had spent any time at court with her open ways and frank comments, she would have been raped by now. He would have to teach her to hold her tongue, and there was no reason not to begin now. Deliberately, he let his gaze rake her from the tiny cap nestled against her hair to the curve of her hip, which was as far as he could see. "'Twould not be too unpleasant, though I doubt you know much in the way of pleasing a man."

"I've no doubt I can learn," she retorted, stung by his comment. "If I've the desire to do so and the right man to teach me." She saw the rage leap into his eyes and wished fervently that she had held her tongue. If he struck her, her father would kill him where he sat before she could even admit she deserved it. "I'm . . . I'm sorry," she gasped miserably. "I should not have said that." But then she added with a faint touch of defiance, "And I would not have if you hadn't provoked me quite deliberately."

Unexpectedly, Iaian felt his rage die. Aye, she was innocent and far too trusting, but she was wise. "And I am sorry for that," he responded, surprising himself as much as her. He smiled at the widening of her eyes. "Have you not heard a man apologize when he was wrong?"

"I've never before heard a man *admit* he was wrong," she countered. "Father simply blusters and pretends he was misunderstood."

"And your brothers?" Iaian had grown curious about the family that had produced such a strange girl.

She smiled openly. "Berinhard blusters like Father. The rest all raise their voices until they cover the words of anyone who could prove them wrong. You must come from a rare family—" Immediately she wished she could retract her thoughtless words, but it was too late, she knew, for his expression closed over his feelings once more.

"A rare family, indeed," he said as he reached for the wine goblet, turning from her.

Cecile fell as silent as he. Their brief beginning was at an end. But there would be another and another until they knew one another and were comfortable and trusting. And next time she would be much more careful.

She was less confident by the evening's end. Never had she known a person who could close himself off so effectively. He spoke and was polite, but he was as distant from her as the farthest isles to the north. And as lacking in warmth, she was sure. By the time they parted, she was quite ready for a sympathetic ear and was glad when Rilla followed her to her room. She could not have confided easily in her mother, who had burdens enough with her weakening health.

Rilla smiled at Iseabal, who had waited up for her mistress. "I'll help Ceci tonight." She was silent until the maid left the room, then turned to her sister-in-law, who stood smiling at her. "Yes, I know I'm nosy," Rilla admitted to that knowing look, "but I saw him laughing with you once, and I'd begun to think the man did not know how!"

"I think laughter might once have come easily to him, but he is so sad now. And angry." Cecile turned her back and lifted her hair that Rilla might reach the fastenings of her gown. She was more than ready to be out of it.

Rilla's hands were as busy with the tiny hooks as her mind was with Cecile's words. "I've tried to imagine how I would feel if I had suddenly found that my father was a man I never knew and my country was one I had always considered an enemy."

Cecile faced her, allowing her gown to slide to the floor. She shivered with the brush of cool air against her warm skin and undergarments. "How did it feel to marry a stranger and come with him to a strange land to live with people you'd never met?" She remembered when Rilla had first come to Ciaran, how lost and alone she had seemed.

A smile touched Rilla's lips as she lifted a warm nightshift over Cecile's head. "I was homesick," she admitted, "but I'd had nearly three years to learn to love Odwulf by the time he brought me to Scotland. And I had our son. Valdemar was so tiny, but I could hold him and remember my mother holding him. It brought me peace to think of it. And by then I was pregnant with Theudoric." A faraway look came into her eye. "I thank God he was born before Odwulf was killed."

"I did not mean to make you sad thinking of

him," Cecile said softly. She sat before her mirror, her eyes meeting Rilla's as the other girl began loosening the coils of her hair.

"My thoughts of Odwulf bring me comfort. Those and my sons are all I have left of him. I would never wish to forget."

"Do you ever wish to return to Germany now that he is gone?" It was something Cecile had often wondered in the weeks after her brother's death. But no mention had ever been made of Rilla leaving their family as those weeks turned to months.

"My sons belong here," Rilla said quietly, "and I feel as if I, too, belong with this family."

Cecile turned to hug her impulsively. "And so you do. I will miss you even more than my own brothers when I wed."

"Which will be soon," Rilla said remindingly.

"And I will be so very far away," Cecile said mournfully.

Rilla's light colored brows lifted in surprise. "Daileass is but a morning's ride, is it not?"

"We will not live there. He is rebuilding Coire."

"But that will take months. You will be more adjusted to your marriage by then and will not miss us so very much." Rilla smiled at Cecile's look of open disbelief. She knew how frightening marriage could be, but did not doubt that Ceci could tame the fierce Iaian Gillecrist. The day would soon come when she no longer thought of Ciaran as her home, though Rilla knew she would not believe that now.

"Perhaps. But I will not be at Daileass long enough to adjust. We must go to claim Iaian's other properties." Though Cecile forced herself to speak his name aloud, still it sounded strange on her tongue.

Rilla looked shocked. "Surely he will not take you to do so! There could be danger."

"I would not have him go without me! A wife's place is at her husband's side." Even when she did not feel like much of a wife.

"Not in wartime," Rilla retorted, "and if he were so careless as to take you, your father would put a stop to it, I am sure."

Cecile stood to face Rilla, taking the brush from her hand to lay it aside. Then she clasped both Rilla's hands in hers. "Lord Gillecrist . . . Iaian does not go to war. He merely takes possession of that which is his. And if there is danger, then I *should* be with him. Rilla, I am marrying him because he needs me. I could not fail him in this."

Rilla's mouth grew pinched in a worried frown. "Needs you? How can a man like Lord Gillecrist *need* a sixteen-year-old girl?" Unless it was in a physical sense, which she knew was not what Cecile meant.

"I cannot explain, but I know that he does. And I will not fail him."

"Of course you will not," Rilla said soothingly, even as she wondered what her precious sister-in-law's peculiar nature had convinced her of this time.

Cecile smiled at Rilla, knowing the other girl would never understand her, but knowing that she loved her just the same. "I am truly going to miss you, Rilla." As she would miss each of her family, but her life was now with Iaian. He would hold her loyalty, and, God willing, her love.

Father Micheil smiled benevolently on the couple kneeling before him. He had officiated at many weddings, but never had he seen a bride so lovely. Of course, it did occur to him that he thought the same at each wedding, but he was convinced he would never see the match of Cecile Lotharing. Her silvery hair caught and held every bit of the sunlight streaming through the windows and reflected it back against her ivory skin. Even the cascades of very old, fine lace could not dim the glow. Only her eyes shone brighter than her hair, a rival for the brilliant springtime sky.

As he intoned the final blessing solemnly, it occurred to him that nature had blessed this union as well. After weeks of stormy spring rains, the day had dawned as fair as any bride could wish. At his gesture, the groom assisted his bride to her feet. Father Micheil sighed at Lord Gillecrist's stern face. That was the only thing he had found to mar the day. Neither of the newly joined pair seemed to find the pleasure he wished on every married couple.

Ah well, he sighed to himself, as he stepped back for the family to surround the young couple, God was good and would teach them all they needed to know of love for one another. He was even more convinced of that when the dear girl cast him a shy smile over her shoulder. Her sweet temper would surely ease the harsh set of her new husband's face soon enough.

Chapter Nine

Though Rilla did not begrudge her young sister-in-law her happiness, she could not help thinking of her own wedding day. She had been equally young and confident that she had all of the future ahead of her to mold to her hopes and dreams. Odwulf had been no less handsome than Iaian Gillecrist, and, though she would never claim Ceci's beauty, she knew she had never looked prettier than the day she exchanged vows with Odwulf Lotharing. Now, such a little time later, Odwulf lay cold in his grave, and she faced her life alone.

Pensively, she crumbled a bit of sugared cake between her fingers. It had taken only three short years for all her dreams to crumble as easily as the little cake.

"'Tis not easy to suffer a loss."

Rilla looked up in alarm at the low spoken words. Donnchadh stood before her, wonderfully handsome in sand-colored doublet and breeks. She felt the heat rise to her cheeks that she had been so easily read and glanced in alarm at the newly wedded couple, but they stood greeting guests and seemed unaware that she could not completely enjoy their moment. Though, in truth, *they* did not seem to be enjoying it overmuch, either.

"Nay," Donnchadh assured her, "no one else has noticed the sadness in your eyes. And that is perhaps because I, too, can remember the trust with which I faced my own future on my wedding day."

"And was that future as brief and bittersweet as mine proved to be?" Rilla lifted her eyes to his, glad for a chance to be unburdened of some of her thoughts.

"Not so brief, but bittersweet . . . Aye, it was that. I'd thought to found a family of Donnchadhs, as did my father before me. But my wife was barren, and 'twas a sadness we never quite put behind us."

The sorrow was there in the man's dark eyes, but Rilla did not think it remained because he'd had no babies. "But your marriage was long?" And happy, she guessed, but could not ask.

"Long enough for me to feel as if I'd been cut in twain when she died." He studied her, his gaze a gentle touch on her face. "You were not married long."

"Three years. But I thank God I bore Odwulf two fine sons before his death. They are the single joy of my life now."

Donnchadh admired the soft green of her eyes and the way her short, heavy lashes framed them. "But sons mature and leave home. What then will bring you joy?"

A sad quirk of her lips acknowledged the truth of his remark. "Grandbabes?"

"Do you think never to marry again?"

She shrugged, and he thought the movement more graceful than that of a swan.

"'Tis not something to which I've given any thought at all," she answered.

"I suppose 'tis much too soon, at that." After all, Odwulf had been killed but eight months earlier at Pinkie Cleugh. He, too, had suffered loss in that battle, when his two remaining brothers had not returned—along with so many others of Scotland's finest.

He saw the faint quiver of her lips as her thoughts followed his. Fool, he scolded himself, you were to make her smile, not make her heart heavier. But only one thing had made her look less sad. "How old are your sons?"

"Valdemar is two, now, and Theudoric is one."

Donnchadh hid his surprise that Odwulf had bestowed German names on his sons. "And do they favor you or the Lotharings?"

"In looks they are both their father's sons. In temperament . . ." She shrugged. "Valdemar is much like me, I suppose. Theu is more demanding.

If he has not yet the words to make himself known, he simply stamps his foot and points. Unfortunately, both his brother and his nurse jump to obey."

"And you?"

Her eyes twinkled. "I did not jump for Odwulf, though I loved him, and I will not jump for his son, though I love him equally well."

"Perhaps one day I could visit the nursery," he said easily.

Rilla felt a quick surprise. "You would be quite welcome, I'm sure." She could not imagine why anyone of Ros Donnchadh's station would wish to visit two grubby lads.

"I'm quite fond of children," Donnchadh told her in response to her questioning look.

"And do *you* think never to marry again?" she repeated his question back to him and felt bold for the asking. "You could yet have sons of your own."

"Unless it was I and not my Catriona who was barren." He laughed at the shock in her eyes. All knew a man's pride was at stake in the issue. "Did you never think to hear a man admit to that possibility?" It had never been a point of virility with him, only a cause for regret. He sobered. "Or have I offended you?"

"Of course not," she said hastily. "But I am surprised, for you are right. Lack of children in a marriage is not something many men would even think to take the blame for."

"Only God can know why a marriage is not fruitful."

Rilla realized she had not spoken so easily with any but a Lotharing man since Odwulf's death. The realization made her suddenly shy. "'Tis almost time for Cecile to retire to her chamber. I must be with her."

She blushed to recall her own bedding. It had been the most embarrassing moment of her life, made bearable only because Odwulf had been so considerate. For dear Ceci's sake, she hoped Iaian Gillecrist would prove as much a gentleman.

Though she took her leave of Donnchadh and made her way to Cecile's side, thoughts of the man went with her. He was much older than she, yet he possessed an air of vitality that far surpassed most men. Her own thoughts made her blush as she hurried across the room.

Iaian stood by Cecile's side, but stepped away at Rilla's approach. With a trembling smile of gratitude for her presence, Cecile grasped Rilla's hand almost desperately. Rilla gasped as the other girl's fingers closed around hers. They were like ice.

As if on a silent signal, Nearra appeared at Cecile's opposite side and took her other hand. She glanced at the top of the stairs, hesitating until Giorsal had ascended to the highest step. Around them, goblets were raised in yet another toast to the couple, and Nearra mouthed a silent "Now" to Rilla.

Cecile's feet felt like lead as her sisters-in-law urged her to a run. But she ran. Halfway up the stairs, she was gasping for breath, both from the exertion and fear of what lay ahead. Not that she did not know the specifics of what to expect. She did—Giorsal had seen to that. But Iaian Gillecrist was the unknown.

Her mother was smiling down at her reassuringly. Then they reached the top of the stairs, and Giorsal, too, turned to run. Iseabal waited at the opened door to her chamber, slamming and bolting it shut behind them. Cecile stood panting, listening as the first raucous guests reached the barred door.

Rilla chuckled. "We'd best make haste if we do not want the door battered down."

For answer, Nearra removed the lace headdress from Cecile's soft curls. Iseabal began unhooking the tiny fastenings at the back of her gown while Rilla's hands worked at the tiny hooks along the fitted sleeves.

With each layer of her wedding garments lifted from her slender form, Cecile's dread grew greater. She knew her mother realized her growing fear when Giorsal pressed a goblet of wine into her hand.

"Drink, sweetheart. 'Twill warm you."

Cecile sipped it gratefully. Then Rilla removed it from her cold fingers for Nearra to lift a nightshift over her head. It was not *her* nightshift, of comfortably soft white linen, but one made for this night. Still of virginal cut with high neckline and long sleeves, the sheer, ice blue silk molded her body so that every curve was outlined.

Too soon, Giorsal moved to open the door, lifting the bar with one last reassuring glance for her daughter.

Cecile froze as her brothers thrust Iaian Gillecrist into the room. They did not follow him in but backed away to prevent any other guests from slipping in with Saelec and Donnchadh.

Iaian felt as if the breath had been knocked from his body at his first sight of his bride. Tiny though she was, she had no lack of curves to prove she was a woman. Her hair cascaded down her back, rippling where the clasps had held her hair in unnatural twists. Her face, though pale, looked composed, save for the tiny giveaway sign of the edge of her lip caught between small, even teeth.

Saelec smiled reassuringly at his daughter, recalling her mother's nervousness on their wedding night. And Cecile looked so like her mother in this moment. Shy and waiting. He cleared his throat uncomfortably and looked at Iaian. "Donnchadh says you take her as unblemished?"

"I do." Iaian had no desire to have his wife unclothed before witnesses to prove she was not disfigured. He thought it a barbaric custom.

Saelec nodded his relief. "We leave you then." He glanced uncertainly at Cecile, then back at Iaian. "I give her to your safekeeping."

Iaian's lips quirked, for it was clear Saelec had no real wish to do so. He could only hope Saelec's misgivings were the natural ones of any father and not a true regret for having allowed his daughter to wed an English-reared groom. But Iaian voiced none of that. He simply nodded and waited for the host of people surrounding his bride to retreat.

The reluctance with which they did so was almost comic. Giorsal left first, kissing Cecile gently on the cheek and patting her new son-in-law on the shoulder. The two younger women followed reluctantly. Iaian noted with interest that his uncle still seemed to find one of particular fascination. Cecile's maid lingered until Cecile was forced to quietly assure her that she should go.

Saelec and Donnchadh were last to leave, and it seemed to Iaian that his uncle's parting glance held something of a warning. Iaian wondered if he expected his nephew to beat his wife on their wedding night. His irritation rose at the thought.

"He means well." The words came softly.

Iaian jerked his head around to stare at her. He did not feel soothed at the realization that she had seen the look as well. Rather, he felt even more vexed.

She stared back ruefully. "And now I've made it worse."

Without answering, Iaian moved to pour himself some wine. What manner of girl was she? She read him too well and too easily. He liked it not.

Cecile waited quietly, not knowing what to do. Not knowing what was expected of her at this point. She was ready to slip into bed, but found it preferable to stand and watch the back of Iaian's head. He had a nicely shaped head, at that. As a matter of fact, there was no part of him that was not perfectly formed. His hair curled crisply against his strong neck, and she wondered how it would feel to the touch. She blushed to realize she would soon know. She could not recall anything from their one encounter save the force of his emotions washing over her. She wondered if it would be like that again.

He turned unexpectedly and caught her staring, and she blushed more deeply. And just as openly, he studied her, lifting the goblet of wine to his lips while his eyes traveled from the top of her head, very slowly, to the bare toes that peeped from beneath her night shift. Cecile wanted desperately to speak to break the tension of the moment, but her tongue felt thick in her mouth and no words came to her. For once, she actually desired to know what another person was feeling. This time, however, it was clear he was in control of his emotions. If she touched him, she would know, but she was not ready to touch him. Not yet.

"Well, Lady Gillecrist, we are where we wished to be, are we not?" His glance was mocking.

Actually, Cecile was not at all sure this was where she had wished to be. She truly had not thought this far into her decision to take Iaian Gillecrist for her husband. It occurred to her, she had not done much thinking at all. And it was too late now to wish otherwise. She lifted her chin. "Aye."

Iaian smiled more kindly. Her uncertainty made her less irritating. If he could keep her thus, they might deal better than he had feared. The thought amused him. He was amused, too, that he felt not much more sure of himself than she appeared to be. He had bedded his share of women, but never a wife. And never one so young. His inclination had been for women grown jaded with their marriage bed. Then he need not worry about any attachment one might form for him.

He took a step toward her and was pleased that she did not shrink from him. Rather, she continued looking up at him with a mixture of trust and curiosity. The realization was a soothing balm. For all she kept him off guard and for all she had proven her ability to sting him to anger, he was now her lord and master. And the fact did not seem to cause her distress.

Still staring into her eyes, he slipped a hand behind her neck and pulled her closer. Only then did he feel her hesitate as her eyes widened in a flash of confused surprise.

The force of him had caught Cecile off-guard. She had known what to expect but not the strength of it. Whatever doubts she might have had vanished. Surely there could not be another human in existence whose feelings would flow so openly to her at just a touch, flesh against flesh.

What he was feeling also surprised her. She had anticipated lust, and perhaps anger, for it had been so strong in him before. But there was no anger now. And if this was lust, it was not the ugly thing that it was in one like Dunmar.

She stepped forward experimentally so that mere inches separated them, and she could feel his breath against her cheek. She could tell by his quick glance that this time he was caught off-guard. The thought pleased her.

Iaian felt himself smiling. So, she was curious about this business of being bedded. Well, then, he would satisfy that curiosity, and she would long remember the experience. He would have to be careful, though, or all she would recall would be pain. He did not love her and did not plan ever to love her, but she was his wife. As much as it was possible, he would be protective of her.

Cecile was sifting through the emotions she felt from him, when all coherent thought fled at his touch against her breast. Even through the thin material of her gown, she felt the heat of it, so that she was suddenly warmed. Blood that had rushed icily through her cold hands and feet now flowed like fire through her veins. Instinctively, she lifted her lips toward his.

Iaian had not thought to feel exultant at this moment, but he did. This was not, after all, Edra Byreham in his arms, as it should have been. It was not the fullness of her breast against his hand. He would not have had to lift Edra to her tiptoes to meet his lips as he did Cecile. But where he would have thought to care about all those things, he did not. His senses were completely filled by the girl he had wed. Her nipple was hard against his palm, and she was moaning faintly against his lips. Lust made him grow hard and full, and he knew he would have to be very careful if he were not to tear her apart in the act.

He set her away from him slightly and untied the ribbon at the neck of her gown. The opening fell away on either side, baring her breasts to his gaze. They were full for one so slender. He placed his hands under the weight of each, bending to kiss the pale curve of one, then the other. When he straightened to look into her face, he found her watching him through heavy-lidded eyes, her breath coming in little gasps between parted lips.

Almost in pain from wanting to thrust into her, he eased her gown over her head, then caught his breath at the sight. She was perfect. Every sculpted hollow and curve blended to form high, full breasts, a narrow waist, hips that tapered to slender thighs. Her lashes lowered at his heated stare, and color tinted her pale cheeks.

He picked her up easily and carried her to the bed, leaving her alone only long enough to shed his own garments. He noted that she held her breath as he eased onto the bed beside her, but she let it out again slowly when all he did was caress her cheek. When he felt her relax a bit he let his fingers trail slowly down her neck to her collarbone, then lightly to the tip of her breast.

Moving gently, he replaced his fingertip with his tongue, caressing and sucking at her breast while his hand searched lower, finding the soft curls between her legs. Though she shrank from his touch at the start, he persisted until she thrust toward his hand instead.

At her movement, he found it more difficult to remain in control of his body and hers. He rolled his weight over her, careful to balance on his arms so that he did not crush her. He felt her grow still as she realized what moment was at hand.

He entered her carefully, with agonizing slowness. Agonizing to her, he realized, as much as to him. He was too big. The realization made him pause and draw back slightly. When he looked down at her she was watching him steadily.

"I could stop." But he was not sure he could. Not now.

"Then it would only be to do over," Cecile said reasonably.

Iaian was not sure he liked her answer. He had hoped that the desire he'd created in her would carry her through this moment, but clearly it would not. She was far from caught up in the throes of passion. But his body would not delay long enough for him to try to recreate in her the earlier physical need he had brought her to. And it would have been of little avail, after all. The pain would only return her to this point when he began again.

"I'm sorry," Cecile heard him say as he thrust into her abruptly. She stifled a cry so that it was no more than a gasp of pain. Dear God, the man was a giant. Surely this was not the normal way of things. Her mother had said 'twould be a slight discomfort, not a feeling of being torn in half! She bit her lip until she tasted blood, but slowly the worst of the pain subsided.

And then she was caught up in the desires raging through Iaian. She did not need to look into his face to see that he had moved beyond himself into a pleasure that was almost a pain. She slipped her hands up so that her palms lay against his chest, and she could feel his heart pounding against them. What was this he felt, then? 'Twas like nothing she had known or known in others. It was devastating, yet it was beautiful.

In spite of herself she strained closer, trying to absorb the feelings that gripped him. They swirled around her, teasing and tantalizing, promising exquisite pleasure. She drew her knees up, moving her hands to his shoulders to pull him down to her, to pull him closer so that she, too, could experience the overwhelming passion that gripped her husband of so few hours. Still, all she felt was a rawness, the discomfort her mother had told her was what she could expect from this first coupling.

But her actions were more than Iaian could take. With a groan, he spilled his seed into her.

For just a moment, Cecile lay staring up into his face, then her palms clenched into fists and she brought them hard against the muscles of his chest. "I want to feel that," she said in frustration. "I want to feel what you felt!"

His thoughts still dulled by the physical release, Iaian looked in bemused surprise at the girl whose virginity he had just taken and knew beyond a shadow of a doubt that his life would never be the same.

Chapter Ten

Cecile's earliest awareness her first morning as wife was that she was faintly sore—and alone. She lay quietly, sifting these two things in her mind. As to the soreness, it took but a moment before realization flooded over her, causing her to be glad, just briefly, that Iaian was not there to see her blush. His absence took a bit more pondering.

Somehow she knew that he had not been pleased by her reaction to her initiation into the marriage bed. A wife, perhaps, should not be demanding. True, after a first start of surprise, he had laughed at her words, but he had promised nothing. And she had been too dismayed by his laughter to try for any other conversation. It was afterward, as they both lay in the shadows with their thoughts, that she had felt the change. A darkness had settled over him, so much so that she could feel the weight of it. She had the uncanny feeling that another woman had come to his mind, and that she was being unfavorably compared to that other woman.

The fact bothered her on two levels. She had never been able to read thoughts and did not want to start now, in even the slightest degree. And, if she were right, Iaian was being terribly unfair. He had offered for her—not any other. She did not want a man at her side who was not content with his choice.

But then, he was *not* at her side. The thought brought her sitting upright. At almost the same moment, her mother entered the room, carrying the morning tray that Iseabal usually brought to her.

Giorsal smiled at her daughter and was saddened to see that Cecile's answering smile had a faintly pensive tilt to it.

"Where is Iaian?" Cecile asked quietly.

Giorsal stared at her. "He did not tell you?" She would not have believed the young man so cowardly. He must surely have known what a wife's reaction would be to being left alone without word on the morning after her wedding night.

"Nay, he did not tell me." Cecile watched her quietly as she arranged the tray across Cecile's knees. "And I am not hungry."

"Well, you will eat," Giorsal said firmly, "while I tell you where your husband is."

Husband. Cecile considered the word. It had a strange sound to it when applied to her. Obediently, she picked up a spiced oat cake while her mother climbed up to perch on the edge of the bed.

"Iaian spoke at length with your father yesterday. They decided between them that you would be safer and happier here while Iaian secures the remainder of his inheritance. He does not know, yet, if he will encounter resistance." She sighed to see the familiar stubborn tilt of her daughter's chin. "He wishes only for your safety."

"He wishes only for his convenience." As he had wished only for his pleasure on their wedding night. Well, he would soon find he could not have his way in all things.

Giorsal knew a moment's exasperation, but yielded to the hint of pain in her daughter's eyes. She did so want Cecile to be happy in her marriage. And she had hoped that good would come of this union, though it would not have been the one she chose for her Ceci. Perhaps she had been wrong to let Cecile have the choosing of it. "Aye," she said softly, at last, "men do like their convenience. And a good, obedient wife."

That brought a smile to Cecile's lips. "Then why is Father so happy with you?"

Ruefully, Giorsal smiled back. "Your father is of a different cut than most men."

"Iaian is different." And, God help her, she did not know yet how to deal with him.

Giorsal nodded soberly. "He is that, but he is your husband. To be obeyed." Cecile's knowing stare drew a sigh. "Aye, I know I'm not the best to speak of obedience, but I do obey your father when he is right."

A gurgle of laughter preceded Cecile's answer. "And when he is wrong?"

"Then I needs must cause him to think he has changed his mind."

Cecile smiled, but the smile did not quite reach the depths of her eyes. "Husbands are also to be protected . . . as you protect Father from the pains in your chest."

Giorsal's smile was sad. "That knowledge would make him unhappy, Cecile, and do no good. My happiness depends upon his. I am being selfish not to tell him."

Cecile's fingers picked restlessly at the embroidery along the edge of the bed cover. "I am afraid, Mother. I do not want you to be ill or to . . ."

Giorsal placed a finger against her lips. "I will stay with my family as long as I can, dear heart. And I will love you forever." She patted her daughter's face and said more briskly, "But now you are wed and have a life of your own to lead."

Accepting the change in subject and mood, Cecile made a face. "Aye, if my husband will not choose to lead it for me!"

"I do not fear that you will allow that."

"I will not," Cecile said adamantly. "And I begin today in making that clear. My home is at Daileass until my husband returns and chooses where we will live. May Amalric escort me there this morning?"

Her mother looked at her in dismay. "Your father will not allow it."

"Aye," Cecile responded with a twinkle in her eyes. "He will allow it. Before I am done, he will beg for it."

That proved not quite true, but Giorsal felt no great surprise when her daughter gained her way. The argument began the moment Cecile sailed downstairs dressed for riding, smiling sweetly at her father and brothers, who broke their fast after their morning ride. Each day they traveled the boundaries of Ciaran.

Cecile fixed her eyes on her youngest brother, who smiled at her knowingly. Amalric always read her well. "I would go home this morning, Amalric, will you ride with me?"

"He'll not," Saelec answered before her brother could, "because *you'll* not." He glared up at his daughter. Somehow he'd known her husband's plans for her would not fall smoothly into place.

"I will," Cecile returned serenely, descending the last few steps. Her light woolen skirt swung gracefully against her legs. "And if you'll not allow Amalric to go, I'll ride alone."

"Beat her," Berinhard inserted calmly, watching his sister as he lifted his mug of ale to his lips. He'd not want Nearra getting ideas from his sister's defiance of her husband's wishes. Had Gillecrist wanted Cecile at Daileass, he would have taken her there when he rode that way but a few hours earlier.

Cecile wrinkled her nose in his direction but did not honor him with a response. She kept her eyes upon her father, pleased that he had looked uncertainly past her to her mother, who had followed her down the stairs.

"Gillecrist wished her to stay here," he addressed his wife.

"But she wishes to go home."

"This is her home," Saelec growled. He ignored his dainty daughter, standing patiently just at his shoulder. Berinhard had the right of it. But he should have beaten her when she was younger. He feared it was much too late now.

Giorsal paid no heed to his ill temper as she replied, "Not as of the moment Iaian Gillecrist became her husband. His home became hers."

"He left her here."

"Had he known her better he would not have." By now Giorsal stood at her husband's side. She lifted a hand to the graying hair at his temple. Her next words were spoken softly for him alone. "I would not have allowed anyone to keep me from my husband's home."

Saelec brought his glance back to his daughter. The look was filled with exasperation. "Why can you never do as you are told?"

Cecile did not bother to try for an answer to that. She would be wrong no matter what she said. "Father, Iaian should never have left me here in my father's home, as if I would be too frightened to take my place in his. I wish to begin as mistress of his home, and 'twill be easier done sooner than later."

Meeting his daughter's steady gaze, Saelec saw the strength in her that was in her mother. How could two such tiny females stand so strong? "And what will you do when faced with his anger at your disobedience?"

"I will have long to think about it, will I not," Cecile said bravely. "'Twill be months before his return to Daileass."

"Aye. When he is gone. He does not plan to leave until tomorrow morn. If you go there today, you face his wrath."

"Then I will face it." She lifted her chin. "He is my husband, and I will not fear him." But she saw the spark of concern in her father's eyes and knew he recalled Iaian's parents. "He will not harm me, Father, no matter how great his rage," she added softly.

In truth, it suited her plans greatly that Iaian had not yet left. She had never intended to remain obediently at Daileass, but to ride after him. Now she could leave soon enough after to be right on his heels when he left Daileass. The thought of a journey excited her and stiffened her resolve to escape her father's protective care. Much as she loved her home and family, she was ready to begin her life in a role that looked to hold much freedom.

"What of your belongings?" Saelec felt himself weaken.

"I'd never thought to be left here." The fact that she had been rankled. Iaian Gillecrist would pay dearly for that. "Iseabal and I began packing weeks ago. I will take a few things with me this morn, and Iseabal can bring the rest in a day or two."

"Iseabal does not travel with you now?" Saelec lifted his brow in surprise. Iseabal had been with Cecile every day for more than half of her life.

"There will be servants at Daileass enough to spare one for my use for one evening," Cecile answered. She did *not* want Iseabal with her now, for Iseabal would never let her follow Iaian Gillecrist north to Waytefeld. "Now . . . will you allow Amalric to ride with me?"

Saelec cast one last pleading look at Giorsal, then nodded reluctantly. "I will—but I do not think you are wise to do this. And if Gillecrist beats you for it, I'll not interfere." But the very thought tore at his gut, and he looked sternly at Amalric. "You'll stay with her until you are assured all is well."

Amalric grinned at his inconsistency and nodded.

Cecile kissed her father's forehead. "I love you, Father. I'll be fine." She felt a lingering sadness at the touch of his leathery skin beneath her lips. Her father had protected and loved her all her life. Though Saelec patted her cheek affectionately, he said nothing. Cecile wondered if it were because speaking would have been too difficult.

Her parting from her mother was even more

poignant. They strolled the bailey while horses were saddled and Amalric readied himself. Fear clutched Cecile's heart when she realized she might not see her mother again. "Have a care for yourself, Mother. Let Nearra take care of you."

Giorsal smiled reassuringly. "I will cradle your first child, my love. Do not fear otherwise."

Their glances met, and Cecile stopped abruptly. "Oh, Mother, I shall miss you." Her mother opened her arms in embrace, and for just a moment, Cecile was a child again, securely held against the warmth of her mother's breast.

But Cecile was child no longer, and at the sound of Amalric's voice calling to her, she straightened reluctantly.

"Go," Giorsal whispered, knowing how very much she would miss this child of her heart. "Your husband awaits you." Life awaited her, and Giorsal wondered what her daughter would make of it.

Moments later, Cecile lifted her chin to the world beyond Ciaran as she and Amalric rode through the gates. Through the guards that surrounded them, her parting glimpse of her parents was a familiar one. Saelec's arms were about Giorsal's shoulders, and her head rested against his broad chest.

Cecile smiled when she turned to face Amalric, but tears glittered in her eyes.

"We'll all be leaving soon, I suppose," Amalric commented pensively. He would miss this little sister of his.

"All?" Cecile questioned in surprise.

"Well, I leave for Dumbarton and then for France with the wee queen. And I think it will not be long before Rilla and her sons are gone from Ciaran as well."

"Rilla! But where would she go?" It would break her mother's heart to lose Odwulf's sons.

Amalric snorted. "Have you not noticed the way Ros Donnchadh looks at her?"

Cecile thought of Odwulf and sighed. "Aye . . . but I'd not noticed her looking back overmuch."

"It would be good for Ciaran," Amalric said practically, "and Donnchadh would be a fine catch for any woman, much less a widow with a small dowry." Not that Saelec Lotharing would be stingy. But though they were prosperous, the Lotharings did not have the wealth Donnchadh could boast.

"I'd be more concerned for her happiness."

Amalric cut her a look of pure exasperation. "She'd not be pushed to it. No one wants her to leave with Theu and Valdemar. But there's no denying it would be an advantageous match. And he *is* taken with her."

Cecile thought on that. She couldn't think that a woman who had been a wife would be forever content to stay in the home of her dead husband's family—no matter how much she was loved and welcomed. And Donnchadh was a handsome man, though not a young one. But, then, perhaps he would not look as old to a woman of twenty as he did to a girl of sixteen. Especially when that woman was a mother who must look to the security of her sons. Cecile nodded almost to herself. Perhaps it would not be a bad match. And it would place Rilla, whom she loved, in her family on two counts: through Odwulf's sons and through Iaian's uncle.

They fell silent through the remainder of the ride, and then Daileass towered before them. Though set in peaceful hills, it was not a pretty castle. Not like Ciaran. The lines were strong and bulky, with none of the intricacies of architecture such as she was used to seeing in her home. But, then, this would not be her home for long. They were to live just on the border of England. The thought was vaguely disquieting. Not that she was frightened by the thought of the English at such proximity, but rather it was a reminder that her husband thought of himself as English. What were his ties there? How strong?

Amalric caught her anxious look and reined in his horse. Their guard stopped about them.

Cecile looked at her brother in questioning surprise.

He cleared his throat uncertainly. "I'd have you happy, Ceci. There's more than one lass who changed her mind after her wedding night."

Touched, Cecile refrained from smiling. She rather suspected Iaian Gillecrist would tear her brother apart if Amalric tried to keep her from him. Not, she admitted freely, that it would be because he cared for her. He simply had too much pride to brook any interference. "I've not changed my mind, Amalric. 'Tis just that it is a bit frightening, beginning a new life."

He looked at the imposing edifice of Daileass, then back at her. "Say the word and I'll take you back to Ciaran."

She shook her head, smiling gently. "Nay, Amalric. I'm a wife truly wed, and I do not fear to be with my husband."

Her brave words came back to her several hours later when she faced her husband's wrath. He had been icily contained while he played host to her brother, and she had been uncomfortably aware that she had yet to reap the results of her actions. But she was careful to smile and keep her growing reluctance to be alone with Iaian from Amalric, who left with the expression of one reassured that all would be well.

When she finally stood alone in the bailey with only Iaian beside her and only his men within calling distance, her spirits flagged, though she took care to keep her shoulders straight and her chin high. As he glared down at her, she was forcibly reminded that there were some distinct advantages to height that she had not yet considered. She felt like a very small child called to task.

"Had I wished you to reside at Daileass, I would have brought you when I left Ciaran this morning."

"You did not even bid me safekeeping until your return." Her words were not so much a delay as a bid for attack. In all things, she was better there than in defense of her actions. She had learned that at a very young age. There had certainly been enough of her actions that needed defending.

Iaian softened slightly. She sounded like an aggrieved child. "Perhaps I was wrong in that." Actually, he had not thought she would care one way or the other. It was rather pleasing to him that she had.

Cecile blinked. She had not expected so easy a capitulation. She needed more of his resistance to bolster hers, for when she followed him north he was going to be furious indeed. "And wrong, too, to give me no choice as to whether or not I wished to remain at Ciaran. I did not marry to live like a child in my father's home."

"Why did you marry?" he asked, feeling very reasonable that he had not yet given way to his rising irritation.

There he had her. She had not the answer to that any more than he. She could not lie and say it was for love. And she did not yet trust Iaian Gillecrist with her feelings that she could tell him of the bond she had felt between them from the first. Nor could she admit that her decision was tinged with a desire to protect him—to ease the pain she knew dwelt within him.

She lifted her chin. Obviously, it would be better to attack yet again. "I married to gain a husband. But why did you? You surely did not wish a wife, else you would not have left me at Ciaran." She watched his jaw twitch from the force of holding his teeth clenched together. Perhaps she would have been wise not to push him quite this far.

Iaian lifted his eyes heavenward for one moment and took a deep breath. When he looked at Cecile again he saw her flinch, then tense, and knew she feared him if only a little. Why, *indeed,* had she married him? "Perhaps I was wrong there, too," he said in reaction to the feeling that hit him as he looked at her. She was not tall and elegant nor cool and poised, as was Edra. But she was his wife. She would be the mother of his children, and he did not want her to fear him.

Now Cecile was truly disconcerted. Never would her father or Berinhard have admitted to being wrong even once. And not even Amalric would have admitted to the second.

"Your father and I discussed what faced me in seeing to my inheritance at Waytefeld," Iaian continued. "There could be battle and bloodshed. I . . . we felt it best if you were to remain with your family until all was secure. Your father—and I—did not care to think of you waiting here, alone."

Cecile gritted her teeth. She had no intention of remaining here, alone or otherwise.

Neither of them had noticed Tavis's approach, and Cecile jumped at the sound of his voice behind her. "Alone? You need not fear, brother." He drawled the term so that there was no doubt it was not an endearment. "I'll remain at Daileass to see to her safety and well-being."

He smiled pleasantly, pretending not to notice Cecile's look of aggrievement and Iaian's look of annoyance. He touched his hand to his chin, glad that he had bothered to scrape the beard from his face. If he had known to expect Cecile at Daileass, he would have exchanged his leather jerkin for a doublet of some finer cloth. He did not think to steal her from his brother—she was not worth his life. And there was Elspeth to keep him content now. But he would not mind if Cecile noticed that he would not have been such a poor choice for a husband, after all.

Iaian's face darkened as he glared at his half-brother. "You will come with me. I will have need of any able hands." He'd never be so foolish as to leave his new bride with the man who had desired her. And perhaps did still. Angered, he glanced back at Cecile. It was no wonder Tavis looked at her like a besotted fool. The sun's rays lit her hair like finest gold and drew lights of pure sapphire from her eyes. "And, in future, you will obey me in all things."

Embarrassed that he should speak to her so in front of another, Cecile gave in to her quick tongue. "Aye," she replied with apparent calm, "I will be an obedient wife or I will flee an unhappy marriage—as did your mother before me."

Rage leapt to Iaian's eyes, and for a moment she thought he would strike her. His rage wrapped around her, dark and burning. But as she watched, he visibly regained control. It was almost frightening that he *could* control such fury.

"Never," he said in a low and furious voice, "never make mention of my mother to me again."

As he turned away from her, Cecile knew she had made a terrible mistake. It shamed her that she would wound him so deliberately. She had married him to ease his pain, not increase it. She stood watching as he walked toward the guard-house, her underlip caught between her teeth. She did not think it would be easy for her to overcome her own actions. Not this time. Not with this man.

Chapter Eleven

Father Aindreas strode through the narrow wynds of Edinburgh with a definite feeling of satisfaction. This was where he should have been all along. This was where God's servants were most needed. Not, as he had been, in some provincial little keep where the denizens played at religion. He shuddered to think he could have remained there for years, out of the true battle for God's lost souls.

But here the sure hand of Marie de Guise was felt throughout the royal city. True, those who called themselves reformers were not entirely subdued, but they were learning their place at the risk of life and limb. Even the heretic English were slowly withdrawing from Scotland since the death of their king, early in the previous year. And though his successor was Protestant, Edward was a weak child, which meant that a Catholic might yet gain the throne of England.

Aye, it was good to be a part of the crusade for papal supremacy. The Lotharing lass had done him an unwitting favor, though never would he forgive her for causing him humiliation at the hands of her ill-bred brother. If he could make her pay for that, he would. After all, it was not his dignity she hurt, but God's, for what was he but an emissary of the Father?

Glancing around him at the gathering dark, he rapped sharply on the door of his destination. It was a large house, a fine one, hinting of old wealth and power. He had been summoned to an audience with one of Marie de Guise's most trusted minions—at least, the man was trusted as much as she trusted anyone. She was always too conscious of the insecurity of her position to be lax in her watchfulness of others. But this noble was always assured of having her ear. Some rumored that he watched Arran for her, always at his side, and then was seen frequently in her antechamber in whispered conversation.

A servant ushered Father Aindreas into a small paneled room where he waited with ill-concealed patience.

For just a moment, Dunmar stood in the doorway, watching the priest who had not yet seen him. This was the type of churchman Dunmar despised, devout to the point of madness, never realizing that the true basis of Christianity was gentleness. But then, Dunmar had no need for a gentle man.

Nor did he have much use for Christianity except as it aided his plans.

The room was ill-lit at his orders, but even in the dim light he could see the brilliant glitter of the priest's eyes as he studied the costly appointments. No doubt, the man was seeing gold that could better be applied to God's great cause. But Dunmar had other uses for his gold. He had his own great cause: his climb to power. And the downfall of Iaian Gillecrist. There was, also, the small matter of the Lotharing girl, who had dared to snub him in favor of that English-reared barbarian.

He stepped from the doorway, drawing the priest's eyes to him. "Father Aindreas." It was more of an acknowledgment than a greeting.

"Lord Dunmar." The priest spoke in a voice equally smooth and unrevealing.

"Would you care for wine?"

As if on silent cue, a servant entered the room with a carafe and two goblets on a silver tray. She placed the tray on a small table, and Dunmar dismissed her with a sharp gesture. He poured the wine himself, handing a heavy goblet to the priest.

Father Aindreas met his eye boldly as he took the wine. "You have need of me?"

"Our goals are very similar. Perhaps we have need of each other." Dunmar sat, careful to take a seat that did not allow the room's single light to illuminate his expressions.

Father Aindreas sat also, not waiting to be invited. "Goals?" He did not care that he sounded dubious and slightly arrogant. What were this noble's needs when compared to his own holy calling? "My single goal is the destruction of God's enemies."

"Which will happen all the more quickly once Marie de Guise has the regency." That one act would be a stepping-stone to Dunmar's goals as well. But the priest had no need to know that Marie de Guise's success was but a means to his own ends.

The priest inclined his head at Dunmar's words. That was true. The dowager queen's devout faith and her ties with France would do much to end the dangerous proliferation of dissidents in Scotland. God's holy representative on the French throne would provide men and arms to crush the religious revolt.

"What can *we* do to ensure de Guise's ascent to power?"

"We can help by ensuring the downfall of any who appear in favor with Arran." Dunmar paused. "You were recently in the service of Saelec Lotharing, were you not?"

"I have never been in the service of other than God Almighty," Father Aindreas thundered. His sense of humiliation had not faded.

"But you were at Ciaran," Dunmar persisted.

"Aye," the priest almost whispered, enmity choking his voice.

"The Lotharings are in Arran's favor."

"I know nothing of their politics."

"Perhaps you know more than you realize. Perhaps I could help you to understand the meanings behind things you heard and saw and thought innocent."

A light of comprehension dawned in Father Aindreas's eyes. "It is possible," he said at last.

"And were you ever at Daileass?" Dunmar asked too casually.

"Never. Does it also house vipers?"

"Arran courts Gillecrist's heir—and Lotharing's daughter has married him."

"The heir. He was English-reared, was he not?" Father Aindreas studied Dunmar's expression through the dim light as he asked the question. There was much here he was not being told.

"Aye," Dunmar said softly. "For twenty years he believed himself to be English."

"How could such a man be loyal to Scotland?" the priest questioned.

"How, indeed?" Dunmar agreed with a cool smile that held no mirth. How, indeed?

Chapter Twelve

The morning after her unwelcome arrival at Daileass, Cecile found herself rudely shaken awake. She struggled against being dragged from the depths of sleep and from her dreams. Again her dreams were of Iaian, but they held a strange sense of urgency that she had not felt in earlier ones. But again, she could recall nothing of the dream save for the poignant feelings that remained upon awakening. She opened her eyes to face her husband's sternly set face.

"Get dressed," he said brusquely. "You will travel to Waytefeld with me."

Cecile needed no urging, and she blessed the nature that allowed her to wake clear-headed. That clear head went to work so that she hastily grabbed her nightrobe from the stand. No delay of hers would cause him to change his mind.

Iaian did not leave the room, but crossed to fling open the shutters and stare down into the bailey below. Early-morning sun poured around him into the room, stroking Cecile's arms through the thin material of her gown. Though she watched and waited for a moment, he did not turn, and she shrugged. He was her husband. He had every right to be in her chamber, though he had chosen not to be there the previous night. A small amount of resentment slipped out with the thought.

Keeping a wary eye on his back, she discarded her shift and bathed quickly in the basin of cool water on the washtable. Iaian did not stir, even as she dressed hastily in the riding skirt and over-blouse she had placed on top of a small chest. Though she argued with herself, curiosity won, and when she had completed dressing, she braced herself for his reaction and asked, "Why?"

At last Iaian turned to face her, his eyes taking in the simple braid of her hair and the practical garb she had chosen. With his eyes upon her, he felt a renewed warring of emotions. Why, indeed? He had lain awake an entire night, to his own disgust, considering what to do with the bride he had never really wanted but now had to deal with. It had not helped his disposition that his body remembered and longed to claim her again. Nor was his body the reason. He had wanted many women, and claimed many. He would never be slave to his own desires. But the truth was—and he could not admit it to her—he was unsure of his ability to control her from a distance. And he read her better than she knew.

Just when Cecile thought he would not answer, a mocking smile crossed his lips. "Because if I do not take you with me, you will follow, will you not?"

Cecile's mouth dropped open, and she considered not answering. She *could* not lie. Nor did she particularly want to give him the truth.

"I will not believe you if you deny it." His tone was almost good-natured, though he knew full well he should beat her for her disobedience. Even for thinking disobedient thoughts. If he did not, she would ever lead him a merry chase.

After silent debate, Cecile settled on a *politic* answer. "A wife's place is with her husband."

"A wife's place is where her husband wills it to be," Iaian corrected, though without much hope of convincing her.

"But you will take me?"

Iaian studied her upturned face. Eager anticipation sparkled in her eyes, a longing for adventure and excitement that he'd never seen in a female. He did not delude himself that she was driven by any great desire to be with him. Nor did he want her to be. She was a convenience, a necessity in this strange new life through which he was learning to negotiate with all the care needed in a game of skill.

"Aye. I will take you, but I do not think you will find it comfortable."

Cecile lifted her chin, feeling challenged. "You will not hear me complain."

Iaian stifled a smile. No, he did not think he would. She was tiny and delicate and as lovely as any woman he'd ever known, but she was as determined of will as any man he'd ever known. If he broke her with the journey, he did not believe he could ever make her complain.

He offered her his arm and saw the quick, questioning look that entered her eyes. But she merely placed her hand on his forearm, as if it were a natural beginning to her day, and walked with him to the stairs.

Donnchadh waited for them in the hall below. He was seated at the well-polished plank table already spread with the morning meal of fresh oat bread, cheese, cold meat, and ale.

Assessing him, Iaian lifted a brow in query. "You do not look dressed for travel."

Taking her place at the table, Cecile silently agreed. He looked, as a matter of fact, quite handsome in a soft-hued doublet and stockings. His garb was a sharp contrast to Iaian's leather jerkin and breeks.

"I will catch up with you," Donnchadh said smoothly. "I have an obligation this morning."

"Something that cannot wait, no doubt." Iaian flashed him a knowing look tinged with exasperation.

"Something I do not wish to wait."

Donnchadh did not appear the least ruffled as he replied, and Cecile wished she knew the two of them well enough to enter the conversation. She sighed and held her tongue as she reached for her mug of ale. Perhaps one day.

She held her tongue, too, when she realized that Tavis had not joined them to break his fast. Somehow, she suspected her husband would not appreciate her interest. Not that he had cause for concern. If she had wished to marry Tavis, she could have. There was no conceit in the thought; her father had told her so. And she had told him that Tavis could never be more than friend to her. Just now, however, the thought of having a friend for a husband was more attractive than it had seemed at the time.

Not until they were mounting their horses in the outer bailey did Cecile learn of Tavis's whereabouts. And then it was only because Donnchadh asked the question, looking about him in surprise.

"I sent him to Edinburgh." Iaian did not look at Cecile, but then, he had scarcely done so since they had left her bedchamber. "He is to ensure that any servants unwilling to be in my employ are replaced by those with less delicate sensibilities."

"And what do sensibilities have to do with it?" Donnchadh asked gruffly, knowing full well what his nephew meant.

"Well," Iaian drawled, "my background is hardly respectable."

Cecile heard the note of pain, or perhaps felt it, for Donnchadh seemed to notice nothing amiss. If he did, he did nothing to ease it.

"Few servants care for more than the gold that pays them and a roof over their heads. There's some, I suppose, who care as much for the station of their employer, but they are no more loyal than any other."

Perhaps that was the way to handle Iaian, Cecile thought, as he nodded and swung into his saddle. Carelessly, giving no credence to how the world must view him. His eyes went briefly to her to ensure that she was mounted. Very briefly, then, his look turned back to his uncle.

"When shall I expect you?"

Donnchadh flashed him a smile. "Somewhere before you pass through Dunblane."

Cecile's mind seethed with questions. When had Iaian sent Tavis to Edinburgh? And why? Iaian had been less than pleased at Tavis's suggestion that he remain at Daileass with Cecile. Had he also not cared for the thought of them being in close proximity on the way to Waytefeld, even with Iaian present? Cecile pondered the possibility that Iaian was jealous, then discarded it. He would never be that, nor did she want him to be. She fixed her gaze on his back. Of course she did not.

Rilla stared in frustration at the cook's assistant. "Certainly the remainder of the wedding food is to be given to the poor!"

"Cook said not the sweets." The young man's voice trembled slightly, but he stood his ground. This was not, after all, the real mistress of the household, although he did think Lady Giorsal would say the same.

Rilla felt fury rise within her. He would not argue with Nearra, she was sure, no more than he would have Giorsal. But as the widow of a younger son, he did not hold her in respect. Yet!

She walked past the assistant into the kitchen, her skirt lifted delicately in one hand, her back stiff and proud. The hapless young man stared after her and wished he'd not been the first one she encountered in her task of seeing to the disposition of the remains of the wedding feast.

The cook looked up from the hot liquid he tested gingerly. "Ah, Mistress Rilla, would you care to taste this broth I am preparing for Lady Giorsal? I am sure it is strengthening. I wish for it also to be tempting."

With a smile, Rilla did so, nodding her approval. "I am sure Mother will enjoy this. You are very thoughtful of her." A compliment or two could not hurt at this point.

"We are all careful of our lady."

"Wonderful. Then you will not wish to have her disturbed over something so trivial as the wedding sweets. They are to be handed out at the door with other foodstuffs when the poor come begging." There were always the poor to feed.

"But, my lady, the poor need meats for strength."

Though his protest seemed sincere, Rilla thought she saw greed in his eyes. He could sell the sweets to the villagers and have a tidy profit.

"I quite agree." Rilla held on to her smile. "After they are given meat, the sweets will be a nice gift they don't often receive. And since neither of us wish to distress Lady Giorsal, if you have further questions, I will inquire of Sir Saelec's wants in the matter."

Gritting his teeth, the cook nodded. "There is no need. I am sure you are quite correct."

Rilla turned away, satisfied. It occurred to her that perhaps she could, someday, be mistress of her own home. She had rarely had to deal with the higher servants and, so, frequently found herself intimidated by their lofty manners. With Mother Giorsal weaker almost by the day, she had taken on a few of the multitude of duties normally handled by Nearra, for it was Nearra who tended Mother. Of course, she knew full well Nearra could easily take care of all, but there was no need. And Rilla found she rather enjoyed the experience.

All in all, she felt quite pleased with herself by the time she sailed into the great hall—and Ros Donnchadh.

Having been told that Rilla could be found in the kitchen by an openly surprised Nearra, Donnchadh had started that way. Stepping into the narrow passage that led out to the cook's domain, he barely had time to stop as the object of his attention walked straight into his chest. It was no great hardship to steady her by placing his hands gently upon her shoulders. The fragile lines of her bones sent a surge of feeling through him. She was a woman to protect, to cherish.

Rilla felt the color flood her face as her eyes met his. "My lord Donnchadh, I am sorry. I was not paying attention."

"No harm done, if you are not hurt."

"Of course not," she stumbled over the words. "Are you seeking Sir Saelec? I think he is with the captain of the guard."

Reluctantly, Donnchadh removed his hands. "I've spoken with Lotharing. I have his permission to visit you, mistress." Of a sudden, he felt uncertain. Damn, but he had not meant to be so blunt with it. What if she did not *want* his attentions?

Stricken, Rilla smoothed her hands over her skirt. She had dressed for household duties, not for guests. And not this guest! The contrast between them only made her feel worse, though she could not help admiring the way the soft cloth of his fine French doublet lay against the muscles cording his shoulders. She had seen many men who had to add padding to attain such a physique.

She realized he still waited for a response to his words, and she moistened her lips with the tip of her tongue. "I . . . I would be pleased to greet you at any time, my lord. Though I would not find it amiss to have some warning," she added with a touch of asperity.

Donnchadh smiled in relief, for he had seen the flash of sheer joy in her eyes as she considered the fact that he had indeed come only for the pleasure of her company. Even her mild scolding could not dismay him now. "I will give you ample warning, mistress, if you will call me Ros. Do you need warning, also, that I wish to visit with your sons each time as well?"

Rilla's smile was slow and sweet and warmed him to the heart as she answered softly, "I will anticipate it, my . . . Ros."

Once she had done so, speaking his name seemed as natural as anything she had ever done. If he had been young and dashing, she knew she would be stricken with grief and guilt for Odwulf's memory. Because Ros Donnchadh was so much older than Odwulf had been, so steadying and secure, a feeling of safety outweighed any other. And somehow the fact that he was also very attractive was of less importance. She had known Odwulf well, and his had been a loving and generous nature. He would wish her to be happy and he would wish his sons well provided for. She suspected Ros Donnchadh could accomplish both.

And then she recalled how she was dressed. "If you would give me but a moment, I would change into something suitable for visitors."

"You look lovely," he protested.

Her nose crinkled in response. "Five minutes," she promised, gliding past him as her father-in-law entered the hall. She smiled at Saelec without pause.

Saelec sighed to see Donnchadh's happy expression. "We will be sorry to lose the girl. And Odwulf's sons."

"I will not take her far. And Odwulf's sons will always be Lotharings. I will take good care of them. I promise you."

"You'd better," Saelec said gruffly. He did not doubt it would come to that, and soon. He had seen the happiness in Rilla's smile and the impatience in Donnchadh's.

After a full day's travel by horseback, Cecile was aware of two things: She was as sore as she was happy. It hardly even mattered that her husband had said scarcely two words to her. The others of their group were not loathe to converse with her. One older soldier, in particular, had named each of the keeps whose lands they had crossed, telling her tales of the lords who occupied them. She doubted all of them were true, but they were entertaining. And if she looked wistfully from time to time at Iaian's broad back, she said nothing to attract his attention to her.

Iaian made no concessions to the fact that his bride of one day traveled with them, but fortunately Cecile was young and strong and bothered not one wit by the long hours on horseback. Nor was she dismayed when she found their resting place for the night was in a small dip of land, scarcely deep enough to be called a valley, with low hills all around. To her fascination, camp fires soon dotted the small encampment, and the pair of hunters Captain Freyne had dispatched early in the afternoon returned with their booty.

Before long, her mouth watered at the smell of crisply roasting fowl. Their brief luncheon of cold meat and tepid ale had done no more than sustain her strength. When twilight turned to full darkness the warmth of the day turned to chill. Even as Cecile shivered and wondered if she dared ask Iaian to have someone unpack her cloak, he was standing before her, holding it.

She wrapped it around her shoulders while he spread a blanket upon the ground and gestured to her. Cecile sank to her knees, suddenly realizing she was indeed exhausted. Excitement had carried her through the day, but her energy was waning. It occurred to her to be glad they were surrounded by others, for she did not think she had strength enough for Iaian to bed her. Not that he seemed to need her for the act—he had seemed quite content for her merely to be present on their wedding night.

A soldier brought them mugs of ale. Iaian handed one to Cecile, then joined her in sitting on the blanket.

She had thought, perhaps, they would rest in tents, but when she realized her mistake, she could only be glad she had not mentioned expecting more shelter than a blanket to wrap around her. Iaian would be sure to think she complained. In truth, she rather liked the notion of having only stars above her, though she did study the heavens for clouds with a tiny bit of apprehension. She would not enjoy a drenching as she slept.

"It will not rain."

Cecile turned with a start to find Iaian staring at her. "No," she agreed quietly, "the sky is clear."

"There will be clouds by morning, but it will not rain."

"How do you know the clouds will come?" She heard the fascination in her voice, and felt very young and ignorant.

"By the feel of the wind and the smell of it." Iaian found himself studying the moonlight's effect on her hair. It shimmered with her every movement, as if jewels were embedded in the rippling curls. He stifled an urge to touch it. There was no place here for the result that one touch might have on him.

"I do not feel or smell a dampness," she protested.

Iaian was surprised that she was not bored by the subject at this point. "That is why it will not rain. But the wind usually dies at sunset. When it does not it brings clouds."

"You've spent a great deal of time in the open, have you not?"

"Some," he said cautiously. He did not care to discuss his early years with this girl, the hours spent at Sir Geoffrey's side while he was trained in manners and warfare. He'd not been fostered out, as other youths, as his own brothers had been. At the time, he'd assumed it was because he was the oldest, his father's heir. He knew better now.

"Were you ever at the English court?" Cecile knew she was being very daring. She felt his reticence, an apprehension of where her questions would lead him. But the emotions flowing about him were not hostile, rather wary, and there was much she would know about this husband of hers.

"I was there," he said at last, not offering more than an answer to her question.

"Was it grand? Have you been to Scotland's court?"

He realized then that she was not probing in an effort to discover secrets, his or any others. She was merely very young and curious. He knew, after all, that she had never traveled more than a few hours from her home in any direction.

He relaxed a little and smiled. "I was there several years ago when Henry yet lived. And the court of Henry VIII was very grand indeed. I was green enough to be very impressed with the riches and the proud ceremonies."

"And would you be now?" she asked softly.

"Now I find I am impressed with very little." He knew he sounded cynical, but could he not be, when he considered how very little Henry's splendor had gained him—unfaithful wives and a puny son.

"You were not impressed with Arran."

It was an astute observation, and Iaian looked at her sharply. Although he had not toadied to Arran—and never would to any man—he had thought himself politic in his interview with Scotland's regent. What had the girl heard?

"'Twas not anything anyone has said to me," Cecile assured him.

Iaian choked on his ale. "You knew my thoughts!" He heard the harsh accusation in his tone.

"Nay, I merely felt your suspicion. I only guessed it was because you disliked others talking about you. You have cause, after all. I am sure you're the subject of much gossip, here and in England."

"You're very brave," he said dryly, deciding not to be angered at her daring.

"My father says, rather, that I am very foolish. I never seem to know when to hold my tongue." She thought of Father Aindreas and sighed. She was not sorry for that incident, though she'd had cause for regret many times when her quick tongue had wounded those she loved.

"'Tis not a trait to be admired in a woman." He was half-teasing, but kept his voice stern. It would not do to let her know he did not mind some boldness in a wife.

Cecile looked at him in pleased surprise. She would like to be comfortable enough with her husband to jest with him. "Well," she returned, "you can list it with the many other traits you find unadmirable in me."

He heard the laughter in her voice. "How did you know I was not serious?" he asked curiously. "*Can* you read minds, after all?" He'd never known anyone who could, but he'd heard claims enough from those who swore they'd encountered the ability in others.

"Truly, I cannot. But," she hesitated, suddenly uncomfortable, "I can sometimes feel what others feel. Not all the time and not in everyone." She met his gaze honestly. "Usually 'tis just with those who are very close to me. Very rarely, in strangers who touch me." As he had touched her that night at Ciaran. She recalled the flood of emotions that had overwhelmed her, convincing her that there was a bond between them not to be denied.

Iaian was thinking of another time. Of their wedding night, and the moment she had drummed her fists against his hard muscles, begging to feel what he had felt. He had a disquieting feeling that he had cheated her of something rightfully hers.

Cecile felt his sudden embarrassment and wished she *could* read his thoughts.

Looking into her suddenly perplexed face, Iaian was glad she could not.

They fell silent, for one of the men approached just then with the roasted fowl that smelled so heavenly to Cecile.

Iaian watched to ensure that she had adequate to eat and drink. And when a steaming mug of hot cider was brought to her with his sharp whiskey, he noticed she cupped her hands around the warmth and shivered. He felt a twinge of conscience at the thought of the thin blanket he'd expected to suffice for her through the night.

He told himself it was merely to ensure that she did not take a chill and sicken that he spread his blanket next to hers after they had eaten. And when he returned from assuring himself that their camp was well guarded and lay down to draw her close to his warmth, he told himself that it was merely the damp night air that made her turn in his embrace and press her cheek against his broad chest.

Two mornings later they passed near Dunblane, and that night they lay beneath the towering walls of Waytefeld Castle—Iaian's third inheritance.

Chapter Thirteen

Tavis reached Edinburgh in the midst of a foggy afternoon. He passed unchallenged through the gates of the city and rode confidently to the richer section of town, passing thatched houses and taverns with scarcely more than a glance. Since he was a lad, he had made his home here for a part of each year. Every filthy cobblestone was dear to him, particularly now that he could lay no real claim to the house that had been his father's. Though he did not blame Iaian for that, it did not endear his half-brother to him. It was a damnable quirk of fate that he, the bastard, had been raised to believe all would be his, while the real heir had been raised to believe he was heir to another's wealth.

Tavis tugged his collar higher against the drizzle as he dismounted at the rear of the house in front of the stables. A lad rushed out to grab his reins, while the head groom grinned at him from the doorway of the stables. "Master Tavis, 'tis good to have you about again. Will you be staying long?"

"You know me, Murray. I'm too restless for being long in one place. We'll see. Do you suppose I'll find aught to eat inside?" He had considered stopping at a tavern, because he was not expected. None of the heavy-timbered entrances with their layers of the city's grime had appealed to him, however.

"Mistress Elspeth will always cook for you." Aye, but she'd let the rest of them starve, himself included! Haughty bitch.

Tavis just smiled and turned toward the house. The thought of Elspeth gladdened his heart. She always had a ready welcome for him, whether his needs were in the kitchen or the upper chamber.

The door opened easily to his touch, and for just a moment he stood in the back entrance, absorbing the rich odors of the house. Through the faint smell of disuse came the scent of the beeswax that had been used to bring a sheen to the heavy wood furniture through decades of cleaning. No cheap tallow lit these rooms, nor stinking rushlights; just candles of the finest wax with a light scent of dried flowers blended into them at their making.

A young woman descended the stairs, stopping on the last step when she caught sight of him, squealing her excitement. With a laugh, Tavis opened his arms to her, lifting her in a crushing embrace. "Elspeth, lass." He whirled her around, laughing down into her cinnamon-brown eyes with their fringe of light gold lashes the same shade as the sprinkling of freckles across her cheeks and nose.

"Ah, Tavis, I've missed you. It's been forever since you were here."

"'Tis just been four months, sweetheart. I'd not stay gone from you longer than that." If there was ever a woman he'd come close to loving, it was this one. He'd wanted Cecile Lotharing, and his body had been stirred to passion at the thought of bedding her, but he'd never felt the tenderness for her that he did for Elspeth Leathann.

"Four months can bring many changes," Elspeth told him with a faint hint of sadness in her eyes.

"But never in the way you feel for me," Tavis said almost fiercely, letting her slide to her feet. Surely she did not mean that. Her affection was the one solid thing he could count upon, though it perhaps meant more to her than it did to him.

"Nay," she assured him softly, stepping back so that he could see the length of her clearly, "never that." But with the words, she folded her hands over her apron, smoothing it against her rounded stomach.

For an instant Tavis felt gut-kicked. There was no mistaking what she was revealing to him. Had he been in Iaian's shoes at this moment, heir to all that Alasdair Gillecrist had owned, he would be shouting with joy. But what was there to celebrate in the bringing of another bastard into the world with nothing to his name?

Elspeth saw the sick look in his eyes, and the sadness deepened in hers. She knew the demons that drove Tavis Gillecrist, poor lad. "I'll love him all the same," she said with a smile, though tears filled her eyes.

"We'll love him," Tavis said almost harshly, then tried to smile. "And it could be a girl." It did not occur to him that had he inherited all he would scarcely have been willing to bind himself to a housekeeper, even one with impoverished noble bloodliness such as Elspeth's. Nay, more likely he would have settled a small sum on her and sent her on her way, perhaps taking the babe from her when it was weaned.

Elspeth's tears fell in relief. He would not abandon her, as she had feared. She had known he cared for her, but she knew also how desperately he despised his station in life and the disdain he'd endured in being a nobleman's bastard.

"Why do you cry?" Tavis said roughly, feeling like weeping himself. "A bairn is no cause for weeping. I'll not have your tears marking my son."

His son. And what did he have to bequeath him? A bastard's standing and the handouts of Iaian Gillecrist.

It was barely dusk when Tavis eased from the bed. "Where are you going?" a drowsy Elspeth asked softly. She had fed him and loved him, reveling in the thought that she could sleep in his arms at last. Perhaps soon as his wife, though he had not said so.

"I've acquaintances to renew." Tavis looked at her pretty face in the fading light. "I inherit nothing from Alasdair Gillecrist. I've got to make my own fortune for our bairn."

"You do nothing dangerous?" She sat up in alarm.

"I'll not leave you a widow before I've made you my wife," he said lightly. Aye, there might be danger in what he did, but what recourse had he now? He'd always been interested in linking his fate to Marie de Guise. If he were among those who helped her attain her goal of regent, he would reap the rewards along with the others. Enough money made even a bastard respectable. But, he wondered uncomfortably, could even money do as much for a servant?

He dressed in his finest—at least Alasdair had not been stingy with him—and kissed her hard on the mouth. "On to sleep with you, love. My son needs his rest."

She smiled and snuggled closer into the covers. Aye, she'd be Tavis Gillecrist's wife, and it mattered little to her that he came by his name from the wrong side of the blanket. *Their* child would not!

Tavis patted her gently on the hip, then strode from the room and down the stairs. The butler let him out of the house, greeting him as if there were nothing odd in his going straight to bed with the housekeeper right after the evening meal. Tavis grinned to himself. Iaian had gained some impeccable servants. The grin faded. For the first time Tavis wished he could challenge Iaian for his inheritance.

It did not take Tavis long to reach his destination, even on foot, accompanied only by a single armed servant. Not that Tavis felt need of a guard, but he visited wealth tonight, and nobility. Though not of that class, he would dress and travel as such. Alasdair had taught him long ago to lift his chin and dare any to tell him he had not the right.

Indeed, at his destination Tavis found himself welcomed as if he were as blue-blooded as his host, and though he did not stay long, he left with a gilded invitation. It had engraved upon it a day, time, and address, but it made no mention of any social gathering. Aye, there was danger in what he did, and Elspeth had reason to worry, but what else was there to do but make his fortune where he could?

Two nights later, Tavis presented his invitation at the appointed hour and place. The home he entered proved even more elegant than the one he had visited on his first night in Edinburgh, its owner more highly placed in titled society. Tavis recognized several of the richly garbed guests, among them Lord Dunmar, whose eyes flickered slightly when they were introduced. Neither acknowledged that they recognized the other, nor mentioned to their host that they had encountered each other before this night.

Tavis nodded faintly and moved away to greet another. Softly spoken words echoed of near treason from every corner of the room. Treason, because, by law, Arran ruled. But these men—some here by virtue of their faith, some by their determination to have the power of Scotland in their debt, and a few because of the thrill of danger—were determined that Marie de Guise should rule Scotland. She had been James's queen, after all. Mary was her daughter. But, foremost, as a daughter of France, she had the force of that country behind her.

After a few moments, however, Tavis became aware of a vague disquiet. Nowhere did he hear mention of solid plans to attain this common goal among them. There was much talk of what would be and how grand life would prove when it was accomplished. There was talk, too, of sure rewards for those loyal to de Guise. But that was all any of it seemed to be. Talk.

"You frown," a smooth voice said close to Tavis's ear. "Do you hear aught that is displeasing to you?"

Tavis turned to face Dunmar, quickly shielding his expression from that one, though he could not have said exactly why. "Nay," he replied just as smoothly, "nothing displeasing, but I hear little to please anyone who has real hope of placing Marie de Guise at the head of Scotland."

To his surprise, Dunmar burst into laughter, drawing several pairs of eyes. Tavis bristled, and

Dunmar lifted a conciliatory hand. "Nay, do not lambast me. 'Tis merely that I had been having the same thoughts in my head. There are a great many 'if only's' and then 'all shall see's,' but little is being said that could bring it about."

Tavis looked at him with more interest and less animosity, admitting, "I am little better than those I disdain, for I, too, have voiced no great plan for success."

"Ah, but you look like a man suited to action—and one not afraid of it." There was a challenge in Dunmar's eyes.

"A well-thought plan would find me a willing participant," Tavis said recklessly. Almost any plan would find him in its midst, well thought or otherwise.

"Arran's very weakness would be his own downfall if we were patient enough to wait." He laughed again at the flash of disappointment in Tavis's eyes. "But I am not a patient man." He lowered his voice. "And I *do* have a plan."

Tavis glanced around at the milling nobles. Like so many sheep they were, content to follow. "Do you share it?"

"Here? Nay. I'll pick and choose those I wish to have a hand in it. Would you be one of those, Tavis Gillecrist?"

Tavis met his gaze fully. "I would."

Dunmar studied him for a long moment. "Within the week I shall send someone to you. He will tell you of my plan and then you will decide how truly you are committed to Marie de Guise."

Moments later, Tavis left. He had met the only man who appeared ready to take action. These others could be left to their weighty discussions.

As he exited the room, Dunmar stared after him, a slow smile lighting his face. Elation sang through his veins. This, then, was the unwitting aid he needed to defeat Iaian Gillecrist: Gillecrist's own flesh and blood.

Chapter Fourteen

At daybreak, Iaian roused Cecile from the warm cocoon she had made of her blanket and his. "I would send you to a safer point from which to watch the battle."

Cecile's eyes opened wide as she sat, feeling the chill of the morning air when the blankets fell away from her. There appeared no trace in Iaian of the loneliness that had radiated from him the previous night. As on the two nights before that, he had slept beside her, holding her but not touching her other than in an impersonal embrace to keep her warm. At least, it had felt impersonal to her. His thoughts were not on her, she knew. They were on things far away, things that would never be his again. But by morning's light, Iaian was self-assured, coolly in control once more.

"You fight today?" Cecile asked in dismay. "So soon?" They had arrived at the fortress of Waytefeld just the previous afternoon. Cecile was not sure what she had expected, but she had not thought the attack would be immediate.

Iaian's lips thinned. "My messenger was turned away by a shower of arrows—as the previous ones have been. There is no need to delay. We are prepared for battle, and I'd not have my men grow weary with waiting." He smiled down at her rather bleakly. "I'd not have my wife in the midst of bloodshed, either. After you break your fast, you'll be taken to the farthest edge of the clearing and well protected."

"What of you?" Cecile knew it was a stupid question, but she could not help it any more than she could help the sudden clutch of fear she felt for his safety. He was her husband, after all.

Iaian looked at her in surprise. "What *of* me?"

"You'll . . . will you have a care for your safety?"

A small stab of pleasure lightened Iaian's mood, undeniably dark at having to fight to claim that which was rightfully his. "Aye, madam, I will have a care. I've no wish for death."

The sun glinted off his mail as he turned away from her, blinding her momentarily. Or, more honestly, she was blinded by the tears that could not entirely be blamed upon the shards of sunlight. For a brief moment, she wished that he left her with a parting caress, even no more than a touch of his hand. She wondered if twenty years hence they would be as distant.

Less than an hour later, from the farthest copse of trees, she watched in fascination as Iaian and Donnchadh, who had finally joined them the previous day, commanded their troops. Men spread out around the sprawling fortress of Waytefeld in a formidable display of strength. Cecile thought herself surrounded by almost as many, for Iaian had assigned what seemed a full company to her protection.

Most of Cecile's fascination lay not with what was occurring around her, but with Iaian himself. She knew his voice would be low and controlled as he gave the orders that would breach the walls of Waytefeld should the castellan continue to defy him. No cannon had traveled with them, but there were cannon there now, ready. Cecile touched the arm of the soldier nearest her. He turned his head, his expression a mixture of irritation that he would not be in the midst of the battle and pride that he had been among those chosen to guard what Lord Iaian clearly considered his most treasured possession. Cecile smiled at him. "When did the cannon arrive? In the night?"

"Nay, my lady. They were sent ahead—as were most of the troops." He turned his attention back to the scene before them.

Cecile sighed. The man was polite, but not inclined to chat. "Why did they not travel with us?" she persisted.

"Lord Gillecrist plans well." The soldier gave into his desire to brag of the man he admired more with each passing day. "He did not want his men fighting on unfamiliar territory, and it is always useful to have a show of force visible. The waiting wears on the nerves of anyone in the keep and builds fear where quick action sometimes builds courage."

"That is very clever," Cecile said with a touch of pride. Iaian's moves might well have averted a battle altogether, if the inhabitants of the keep had been sufficiently intimidated. She looked with new insight at the men surrounding them with such fanfare.

"Look, my lady!"

Cecile's gaze followed the soldier's upraised hand, though it was difficult to see what he indicated for the many helmeted heads about her. But when she lifted her eyes to the battlements of the castle, she saw what he saw. An elderly man garbed in scarlet lifted his fist heavenward in a gesture of defiance. At almost the same moment, the gates of the castle opened and men poured from beyond the fortress walls.

"Bloody whoreson," the soldier breathed, forgetting his lady's presence. "He dares to fight."

Of a sudden, Cecile's heart ached with fear as her gaze desperately sought Iaian. There would be no opportunity to use cannon, now. 'Twould be man against man, and she feared Iaian would not keep to the background of the fray.

"Why does the man resist?" Cecile asked, her voice sharp with her fright. "It can avail him nothing. Alasdair Gillecrist is dead, and my husband is his lord."

"This man is of noble birth. If he could defeat your husband in battle—perhaps even kill him—he could petition the crown for Waytefeld. He has held it all these many years."

Cecile gasped in outrage. "What king would reward such villainy?"

The soldier's lips twisted ruefully as he reminded her. "King, my lady? We have Arran."

Cecile looked at him in dismay and fell silent. They did, indeed, have Arran.

The battle was short; mercifully so. It was the first time Cecile had been surrounded by dying and wounded men. She did not think she could survive a second. Their fear and suffering emanated from the battlefield in waves of agony that washed over her, drowning her with pain. With the first death cry she flinched as if struck, and with each thereafter, until the pain of the fallen men was her pain. Their shrieks echoed in her ears. Long before it was over, she was gasping for breath, clinging weakly to her saddle and praying that she would not disgrace her husband. She prayed, too, that she would be recovered from her humiliating weakness before he sent for her.

He did not send for her. When the last of the castle's troops had dispatched their arms in the face of defeat, he came for her.

Iaian took one look at Cecile's pale face as she swayed atop her mount and turned his fury on the man nearest her. "Bloody hell! Why is she still astride when she can barely sit her horse?" Even before he completed the question, Iaian swung her from her palfrey to his destrier.

The soldier, his eyes having been on the battle, turned in amazement at Iaian's attack. What could be amiss with the lady? No one had come near. He blanched when he realized her condition. Though he stammered an apology, he feared for his very future. He could not hope to remain in Lord Gillecrist's pay, but he prayed he would live.

As Cecile's hands clutched at his mail, Iaian cursed himself for a fool as he recalled her words. *I sometimes feel what others feel.* If she suffered half of the agonies of the wounded littering the battlefield, it was a wonder she remained conscious. He swore again, feelingly. He should have placed her much farther from the fighting.

The soldier flinched again. Aye, he would be lucky to escape with his life.

Deliberately, Iaian skirted the places where the dead and dying lay thickest. He pressed Cecile's face to his chest and rode toward the castle gates. They stood open now, waiting. Before he reached the gates, Freyne had Iaian and his lady surrounded by a full guard. Freyne rode at their head. "I will enter first, my lord."

Iaian glanced down at Cecile's silky head. There could be treachery yet, and he dared not give her over to another's safekeeping. "Aye," he agreed finally, allowing Freyne and several of his men to move in front of them.

There was no treachery. The courtyard was deserted, though Iaian felt a hundred eyes watching his every move. There was no sign of the scarlet-robed figure who had defied Iaian to the bitter end.

With a sharp gesture, Iaian sent Freyne up the stairs to the battlements, where he had last been seen. Within moments, Freyne returned, his face grim. "He is dead, my lord. By his own hand."

Iaian nodded. He could not be sorry. Had the man lived, Iaian would likely have had to see to his death himself.

In all this time, Cecile had not stirred, but she did so now. Lifting her head, she gazed blankly about her, then turned her face to Iaian. He caught his breath at the wounded look in her eyes. Their brilliant blue was awash with tears that did not fall, but clung trembling to her silky lashes. For a moment there was no recognition of him in those eyes, and he wondered fearfully if her mind had fled a pain it could not endure. "Ceci?"

It was the first time he had called her by the intimate name her family used, and for a moment the sound of it brought back a feeling of being cherished. Hearing the touch of fear in his voice, she tried to smile at him reassuringly, but her lips trembled with the effort. "I am better, my lord. I could walk."

Iaian ignored that, keeping her in his arms as he dismounted as effortlessly as if he were not weighted with mail and his bride. "Freyne! A guard for my lady." He did not look back as he stepped into the great hall of Waytefeld and stopped thunderstruck. Here were all the riches he had not seen displayed at Coire and that had only been hinted at in Daileass. Gold plate studded with jewels, rich tapestries, ancient weapons polished to a gleam of precious metal. Below him, his booted feet trod carpets of the east. 'Twas no wonder the castellan did not want to give it to the keeping of another.

His anger deepened as he wondered if the castellan had milked his father of more than the property's share of its rents. He recalled Tavis's comment that they had rarely visited the keep. Tightening his jaw, he placed Cecile in a stuffed chair placed where it could be drawn near the hearth in cold weather. No doubt the ancient bones of the dead castellan had ached in the winter. Those bones would moulder in a cold grave now. He glanced at the young man Freyne had sent to him, assessing him sharply. "Guard her as you value your life."

Satisfied with what he saw in the soldier's eyes, he turned away. Cecile felt oddly bereft when he did so. For a few brief moments she had felt cherished. A wry smile touched her lips. 'Twas likely as much in the way of tenderness as she would ever have from him.

With his wife safe, Iaian turned his mind to more pressing matters with Freyne. "Have the captain of their guard brought to me. Or if he is dead, the highest in command that still lives."

The captain lived, but he clutched a grievously wounded arm. His face blanched gray as he stood before the rightful owner of Waytefeld keep, the man whom he had tried his best to defeat, if not kill. "My lord." He kept his chin lifted, though it was an effort. Underlying the pain of his wound and the weariness of battle was his shame that he had followed orders he knew to be dishonorable. Yet, what choice had he?

"Your name?" Iaian's eyes and voice revealed nothing.

"Leodlow, my lord."

"Your men fought well." He assessed Waytefeld's captain and did not find him lacking. He was a large man, perhaps in his fifties, with the muscular build of a true warrior. His gaze met Iaian's steadily, and a spark of pride lit his eyes at Iaian's compliment.

"They are well trained, my lord. And brave." Sadness replaced the pride. And so many were now dead.

"You followed your lord's commands and led them into battle."

Leodlow knew a moment's uneasiness. He could not follow this line of conversation. The new lord of Waytefeld spoke almost casually, as though he had not had to battle for what should have been given to him willingly. Leodlow had expected to be questioned sharply, then dragged from here to his death. "Aye, my lord," he acknowledged. "'Twas my place to do so." He was not excusing himself, just making a statement of fact.

"Where lies your loyalty?"

Leodlow knew true confusion now. "With the holder of this keep, my lord. Always."

"He is dead." Iaian watched the man's face clear with his words.

"Sir Amhuinn is dead," Leodlow agreed, "but I served two others before him."

"And now?"

"As you command, my lord." Leodlow began to feel that he might yet have hope of keeping his head attached to his shoulders. He discerned no anger in the young lord facing him. Nor did he appear vengeful that a man would do that which he was paid to do.

Iaian nodded abruptly. "See to your arm. We will talk again later."

Relief flooded Leodlow as he exited hastily.

A small band of Iaian's men clattered down the stairs, and he looked at them expectantly. Their captain, who was called Galen, stepped forward at his questioning look. "There's naught but womenfolk above. He left none to defend the keep or his women."

Iaian was not surprised. If Iaian had been slain on the battlefield, his troops defeated, there would have been little use for further defense of the keep. Sir Amhuinn would have known that. "Had he a lady?"

"A leman, only, from all we can see." Galen shifted uncomfortably, recalling still that one's curses. She would have made an old campaigner proud.

"Then take my lady abovestairs and make her safe and comfortable. Her life is in your hands." He did not expect treachery, but a man could never know.

Iaian had started toward the door to the bailey when he chanced a glance back to where Cecile faced Galen. She was clearly arguing, but even as she did so she swayed in her tracks, and he realized she was weak yet. He watched while the young captain caught at her arm clumsily. With a stifled curse, Iaian strode back to her, catching the last thing she said to the man.

"I've work to do. The wounded must be tended."

Exasperated, Iaian swooped her up in his arms once more. "You are much troubie, my lady," he told her softly, taking the steps easily. She was featherlight in his arms.

"But the men," she protested weakly.

"I assure you I know how to take care of my men. And my wife." He looked down at her, noting the dark smudges of exhaustion beneath her eyes. "Which is fortunate, for I fear you would collapse atop them were you to try to do anything at all."

As if to prove his words, Cecile's lashes lowered over the brilliance of her blue eyes, despite her efforts to remain alert. She was incredibly weary, for it seemed her own body had fought the effects of every pain inflicted upon the battlefield. Somewhere within the depths of her she knew she should be strong and brave, as her mother would surely have been. And she could be if she were not so unbelievably exhausted.

Even before Iaian reached the room his man suggested to him, he knew Cecile slept. Through his concern for her, he felt a surge of triumph. For this moment, at least, Cecile was completely dependent upon him, for once neither arguing nor defying. And her trust in him was absolute. It was a heady realization—and a rather frightening one. Having the lives of fighting men dependent upon him, men who knew they lived but day to day, was one thing. Being solely responsible for the safekeeping of his wife—and the children who would come of their union—was something else entirely.

Iaian's arms tightened about Cecile. Though he could not love her, he would do all within his power to keep her safe.

Cecile awoke gasping for breath. Heavy coverlets clung to her, dragging at her limbs when she fought to emerge from their depths. Pulse pounding, she freed herself and sat up. Her breath came in gasps, and she struggled to calm her racing heart. A terrible sense of urgency clung to her. And once more she knew her dreams were of Iaian, though no vestige of memory remained to tell her of what she had dreamed.

Slowly she quietened enough to gaze around the darkened room. The shutters were closed to a midday sun, and she felt the dampness of perspiration. 'Twas only that she had grown overwarm, she consoled herself. She frequently had nightmares when she became too warm in the night.

Too, she was unused to sleeping during daylight hours. And after the morning's battle, it was surely no wonder that her dreams had not been pleasant. 'Twas only remembered fear for Iaian's safety during that battle that clung to her now.

She rose and crossed the room to fling open the shutters. She could see distant crags beyond the castle walls, but she could not see into the meadows just beyond the gate. A mental image of the dew-sparkled grass littered with dead made her shudder. Feeling a renewed weight of sorrow, she made the sign of the cross. God protect their souls.

A quick glance about the room proved no servants had tended her needs while she slept. The ewer held no water for washing. And no wine or ale had been brought to nourish her upon awakening. Her lips thinned. Iaian would have enough to concern him without having to deal with servants. Though she had not had to do much along those lines in times past, she was sure she could manage. Nearra had taught her well.

Flinging open the door, she startled the soldier placed to guard her. "M-my lady?"

She smiled at him reassuringly. "Fetch the chatelaine of this keep to me."

The soldier stared at her in consternation. That one had been Sir Amhuinn's whore, and not likely to be biddable to his lady's wishes. But he did not know how to explain that to her delicately. He cleared his throat. "She . . . she grieves yet for her master."

Cecile did not miss his dark flush and realization dawned, for she had heard the answer to Iaian's query concerning Sir Amhuinn's lady. She blushed in turn. "Very well. Send any maid servant to me."

"Aye, my lady."

She closed the door once more and paced the room, waiting. She had not long to wait before a very fearful woman was thrust into the room. The woman looked perhaps ten years her senior, but well aware of her station in life. Her hands twisted nervously within the folds of her apron.

"What are you called?" Cecile asked quietly.

"Sorcha, my lady. I am Sorcha." At Cecile's calm manner, she quieted the tense movements of her hands.

"What is your position here?"

Sorcha's shoulders lifted more proudly. "Second only to Mistress Mairi."

"For the time being, Sorcha, you will be second only to me in matters of household." She watched in satisfaction as Sorcha's expression reflected the honor she felt at the statement.

"Aye, my lady." She hesitated, still feeling unsure. "And what be your wishes?"

"Is food being prepared for my lord and his men?"

Sorcha frowned thoughtfully. "I think so."

"Then my first wish is that you make *sure* it is so. Then I wish fresh water for bathing. And request that my belongings are brought to me. Do not disturb my husband's soldiers. Have a lad carry the request to the master of baggage."

The woman curtsyed. "Aye, my lady. Aught else?"

"Not at the moment." Cecile smiled kindly. "I will be most grateful to bathe." She had traveled several days with the most cursory of washings. Iaian seemed not to believe in tents, but if she traveled many miles more with him, she would have to change his mind. And if he traveled, so then would she.

Less than an hour later, Sorcha preceded one young man carrying the single chest Iaian had allowed Cecile to bring and another carrying a steaming kettle of water. And less than an hour after that, Cecile descended the stairs, still followed by her protecting soldier and feeling much refreshed.

The first person to greet her was Ros Donnchadh, who smiled at her warmly and inquired of her health. She lifted a brow at the heavy bandage over his shoulder. "Better than yours, I should think, my lord." She liked Donnchadh, but still felt slightly unsettled around him. She could not forget the moment just after her first tumultuous encounter with Iaian when Donnchadh's eyes had seemed to read into her very soul.

"Could you not be comfortable calling me Uncle?" he asked with a smile. "'Tis little enough, and I've finally convinced your husband to do so."

"Very well . . . Uncle. Does your shoulder pain you greatly? I'm not so skilled in medicines as

Rilla, but I could perhaps make you more comfortable."

Donnchadh felt unaccountably gladdened just at the mention of Rilla's name, and the painful burning beneath his collarbone faded somewhat. "Nay. I'm doing well enough, but I thank you, my dear. I suppose you're relieved that that young whelp you married was not injured."

A deep voice just behind Cecile made her glad she'd not had the opportunity for a quick retort. Her jest that Iaian was surely too dour for any sword to pierce might not have been taken as jest by her husband. She did not yet know him well enough to judge.

"Have a care what questions you ask of Ceci," Iaian drawled. "She will dare any answer honestly, whether it is in her best interest or not."

"Would you think me not careful of your good health, my lord?" She smiled when she turned to look at him, relieved to see the harsh look of battle-readiness gone from his face. Nor did he seem as cold and distant as in days just past. That iron control had given way to relief that Waytefeld was secure with no more losses than had been sustained.

"Careful? Perhaps, though I think you've wished me to the devil himself once or twice."

There was a teasing light in his forest-dark eyes, and Cecile knew a blaze of joy. She would make him glad of their marriage yet. She let a smile touch her lips. "No, my lord husband, 'tis merely that I thought *you* were the devil."

Donnchadh gave a shout of laughter at her reply, and Cecile knew a quick relief when Captain Freyne approached seeking further orders. Iaian would have no time for a fitting reply.

"The wounded are tended as much as may be," Freyne told him. "And the dead are buried."

"Both sides equally so?"

"Aye, my lord."

"How stand the defenses of this keep?" Iaian asked, only out of politeness for Freyne's position. He had already made a judgment of his own.

"Well enough, my lord. Though I'd arm it with cannon. The walls are secure and in good repair."

Iaian nodded. "Send Leodlow to me now."

Cecile kept very quiet through Iaian's audience with Waytefeld's captain. She was interested in every aspect of her husband's business and did not wish to be sent away to things of interest to females only. She liked Captain Leodlow at first glance, liked and trusted him, but knew she dared not say as much to Iaian. Her opinion did not yet count for anything with him, she knew. But one day it would. She vowed that it would be so.

Leodlow stood with shoulders as straight as his wounded arm would permit, awaiting his final judgment by Waytefeld's new master. "My lord," he said proudly.

Iaian saw no need for polite speech. "Will you be as loyal to your new castellan as to the old?"

Joy blazed in Leodlow. He was not to be turned

out of his post. "Aye, my lord. I vow to serve you well and obey whomever you appoint as castellan in all things." He hesitated. "Waytefeld will not be your home?" It was an indication of his judgment of the young man that he dared even to ask a question at this point.

"Nay. But I've a half-brother that I think may do well here." Iaian did not miss his uncle's quick look of pleasure nor his wife's quickly veiled surprise. He hoped he was not being foolish to place Tavis in a position of such power. And he hoped, too, that his judgment was not tempered by his very real desire to keep Cecile from being constantly near the man who had wished to wed her. And he dared not question *why* he wished to keep them apart.

At the end of a long evening, Cecile huddled in her bed and wondered if her husband would come to her. He had slept with her while they traveled, but she suspected it was for other reasons than a burning desire to be with her. He had certainly not touched her in an intimate way. In fact, she had not noted any desire in him for her at all since the morning she had awakened after their wedding to find him gone. She suspected it was as much because she had been demanding of him on their wedding night as because her actions had forced her presence upon him on the journey to Waytefeld. Her husband, she was learning, liked neither demands nor force.

Just when she had decided he would not come to her and had forlornly allowed herself to drift into sleep, the sound of the chamber door opening aroused her. She opened her eyes and watched Iaian walk to the bedside.

"My lord," she whispered sleepily.

Iaian felt a tightening in his loins as he gazed down at her by the light of the candle he carried. He had, he assured himself, come merely to see that she was well cared for. But he had not counted upon the feelings that would wash over him at the sight of white sheets slipping from bare shoulders, revealing the delicate line of bone beneath creamy flesh. Though he could not see their color, her eyes sparkled at him in the flickering light.

Quite naturally, Cecile flung the covers aside to welcome him, feeling languorous and safe in the lingering sleepiness that gripped her.

With an oath, Iaian extinguished the candle and placed it on the washstand. He shed his clothes hastily, deriving some comfort by telling himself that this was his wife, after all. It was his duty to bed her, and a necessity if he would have heirs.

The first touch of her cool flesh against his heated skin gave the lie to his self-assurances. He craved the touch of this small sprite. For surely she was such, a tiny elfin creature with magical powers. It must truly be magic that she could feel what others felt, could draw the very emotions from him through her fingertips. He could only pray that it was not evil magic.

When she slid her arms about his neck all such thought fled. There was room in his mind only for the feel of her. Full nipples that tautened at his caress. Silky ribs that rippled with goose flesh when he trailed his fingers downward to her hips, pulling her against the pulsing, aching part of him that demanded to be satiated. He caressed her slowly and at length, touching each gentle curve, nipping at her ear lobe and the delicate line of her jaw.

Cecile gave herself up to his touch, feeling an increasing warmth that grew until she was aware of nothing save Iaian's movements against too tender flesh. She gasped at the sensations flooding her, exquisite, blinding feeling that made her arch against his questing fingers, forgetting any thought of modesty. She moaned as his hand parted her legs, seeking, probing, moving against her with increasing intensity. "Please," she begged, terrified that he would cease. This time the feeling was hers, not gleaned from some maelstrom gripping Iaian. She did not even know what he felt. She knew nothing beyond the almost painful sweetness with which he tortured her. And she would surely die if he took it from her now.

Iaian was almost bursting with his own need but could not cheat Cecile a second time. He held his control, encouraging her with soft words, but almost lost that control when a gasp caught in her throat. With a soft growl of triumph, he plunged one finger deep inside her, feeling her spasms against his calloused flesh.

Groaning, he withdrew his finger and replaced it with the hard, aching center of his own burning need. He felt Cecile's teeth graze his collarbone, and felt his seed spurt deep within her.

Chapter Fifteen

Iaian could never be sure, later, what had awakened him, but he knew he would never forget the moments that followed. In his first brief consciousness, he was aware only of the soft breathing of the girl beside him, the fragile feel of her body cradled against his. A fierce protectiveness flooded him, a protectiveness and a tenderness that was foreign to him.

His second awareness was triggered by something equally subtle. A whisper of movement. A glint of steel in moonlight. An instant before his senses registered what that quick flash portended, the blade began its descent—toward Cecile's peacefully sleeping form.

Iaian's movements were no more than instinct. He sought to shield Cecile and strike out at the shadow looming above her. With a powerful lunge, he rolled over her and thrust himself at the midsection of her would-be murderer. Cecile's startled cry mingled with his curse as the blade glanced off his ribs, slicing flesh along its way. The assailant recovered quickly, but no more so than Iaian. Relentlessly, the blade was lifted high once more, this time aimed at Iaian's chest. Iaian launched himself upward, scarcely hearing Cecile's shouts for Donnchadh, anyone, to assist him.

The blade never descended, for the force of his body flung the attacker backward. Not waiting for a chance of recovery, Iaian reached for the throat before he had even caught his breath from the fall. Rage flooded him that Cecile had very nearly died at the hands of this assassin. Almost immediately he heard the snap of bones and just as quickly realized the snap of flesh between his hands was too fragile for that of any man. He loosened his grip and started to rise, but the flow of blood from his wound, increased by his exertions, left him oddly weak.

"God's mercy, what is this!"

Through the drumming of blood in his ears, Iaian heard his uncle's stunned voice as if from a great distance. He was aware of the flickering of candlelight about him and of Cecile's soft touch on his side. The sickening knowledge that he had just murdered a woman or a child made him not so eager to remain alert. As Cecile called for bandages, he slipped into unconsciousness.

* * *

"She's dead." Donnchadh straightened from his examination of the woman.

"'Twas her own doing," Cecile said hotly, pressing a sheet tightly against Iaian's ribs in an attempt to staunch the flow of blood until a servant arrived with fresh bandages. "She tried to kill Iaian—he but defended himself!"

Donnchadh looked at her in surprise. "I was not faulting him, lass."

Cecile looked up and sighed. "I'm sorry, Uncle." She bit her lip. "Iaian has lost a great deal of blood. I'm frightened that he does not awaken."

"'Tis best he does not yet, lass. We'd only have to drug him into insensibility for you to sew the wound." Donnchadh stepped away from the fallen woman to look down at Iaian's ashen face.

"I?" Cecile paled. She could not even stitch a piece of embroidery without ruining it.

"There are others who could do it, if you wish."

Cecile fancied there was disappointment in his expression. She touched Iaian's brow gently. "Nay." Resolve strengthened her voice. "Nay, 'tis my place. I shall do it."

Within moments, the room seemed filled with people. Vaguely, Cecile heard Freyne's whispered conversation with Donnchadh while the dead woman was carried from the room. Amhuinn's whore, Freyne called her, never realizing Cecile could hear. There was a servant with a basin of hot water, and another with fresh bandages and sewing implements.

Cecile felt oddly calm as she washed the blood

from Iaian's side, then threaded a needle carefully. She prayed she would not disgrace Iaian—nor injure him more greatly than he already had been. Taking a deep breath, she placed the first stitch. Her hand remained steady, though she had to swallow hard. Donnchadh placed a reassuring hand on her shoulder, and she continued.

When she was through she heaved a sigh of relief, feeling a warmth at Donnchadh's whisper of, "Well done, lass."

She glanced around, surprised to find the room empty once more. Only Donnchadh, herself, and Sorcha, who held the light just above her, remained with Iaian. And then Donnchadh ordered even Sorcha away, bidding her to light several candles before she departed.

"'Tis several hours until daylight, Ceci. Take yourself to another chamber to rest. I'll stay with the lad."

Cecile looked at him in quick surprise. "Nay, Uncle. I'd not leave him. When Iaian awakens 'twill be to find me at his side. Always."

Donnchadh smiled broadly. He'd begun to wonder if their marriage had not been a mistake, after all. They seemed so cool with each other until this moment. Still smiling, he pulled a chair close to the bed. "Then sit comfortably. He'll not awaken for hours yet, if I'm any judge."

He placed a second chair nearby and eased into it with a sigh of weariness. Cecile knew he would not leave even if she suggested it. Somehow Donnchadh sensed as readily as she that

Iaian needed a great deal more from them than he ever let show. They were all the family he had now. Cecile made a silent vow that she would fill the void created by the loss of his mother and stepfather.

"Is Iaian like his mother?" she asked softly, curious about so much concerning this husband of hers.

"More like her than the bastard that sired him. I rue the day she was ever given to the man."

"By your father?"

The taste of regret was bitter. "Nay. Our parents were dead by that time. Anne was in my keeping, and 'twas by my hand she was given to Alasdair Gillecrist."

Cecile touched his hand in commiseration. "You could not have known."

"Nay," he returned heavily, "I did not. But that does not make it any easier to bear. I loved Anne dearly, and by my own misjudgment, I lost her. And missed watching Iaian grow to manhood." Iaian might well have made up for all the childless years with Catriona.

"She must surely have been happy these last many years with her Englishman."

"Aye, but now she's lost her son. This, too, by my hand."

"I think that time will see all wounds healed." Cecile ached at the sadness that streamed from him. "And I think you've wounds of your own that will soon be mended." She hesitated, wondering that she dared, for he was, after all, little more than a stranger. But he was her uncle by marriage, and she would do much to ease his unhappiness. "Rilla is a wonderful person."

As she expected, he brightened at her words. "Aye." His smiled turned almost boyish. "And she seems not affronted that I would woo her."

"Of course she would not be!" Cecile forgot her own misgivings at the age of the man. In strength and health, he seemed no older than Iaian. And he was as handsome as any young woman could wish.

"And she has fine sons who bear a fine name." It had been a relief when they took to him so readily.

Cecile felt a pang at the reminder of Odwulf. "Aye," she said softly, "they will make you proud."

Iaian stirred and moaned, quieting at once when Cecile lay her hand against his cheek. "He is cool, yet." Her tone relayed her fear of fever.

"'Tis too early yet to know if he will take ill of this," Donnchadh cautioned. "But the wound was clean and you were careful of it." He was proud of her steadiness in the sewing of it, for he sensed how difficult the task had been for her.

"I would it had not happened." But she shuddered to think Iaian might not have awakened. They both could have felt that length of steel slide into their hearts. Yet she could bear no hatred for the dead woman maddened by her grief. Already, Cecile did not know if she could bear Iaian's death, and she did not even love him. "Please, Uncle," she said softly, "have masses said for the soul of that woman."

Donnchadh looked at her in surprise. He could not be so forgiving, but he would do as she asked.

"I think mayhap 'twould have been better for me if you'd taken that steel through the heart." Cecile glared at Iaian. He'd been an ideal patient only until the moment he had regained consciousness. From that moment on, he'd railed at his weakness, lashing out in irritation at anyone who came near. And since he insisted upon Cecile tending him, she was the person most often near enough to bear his temper.

"'Twas not my heart that knife was held over when I took this wound," Iaian reminded her irritably.

"Well then, I suppose you wish you'd let it follow its course!"

Iaian could not help it. He laughed at her look of outrage and affront. "Nay, but what I wish is that you'd consider I lie here wounded by my defense of you and not try to bleed me to death nor to scrape the very hide from my face."

"I told you, I'd never shaved a man before," Cecile said defensively. "And I'd no desire to do it now!" Nor did she consider it too poor a job for a first attempt. True, his skin was raw in a place or two, and she'd had to dab at a nick where blood had welled in response to her unskilled ministrations. Still, the whiskers were gone, and Iaian was still alive.

"But you do my bidding because you are an obedient wife."

This time it was Cecile's turn to laugh. "You know I am not, nor like to be, try though I might. I'm sure you were warned before you wed me."

"Indeed not," Iaian lied. "I was assured that you were meek and biddable in all things and that I'd never hear cross words from your lips." It pleased him to see her eyes sparkling with laughter. For these three days she had jumped to his every word, those lovely eyes showing the strain of her fear and her care for him. Both he and Donnchadh had tried to tell her that he was not likely to die of such a wound, but only time had reassured her.

"Oh, Iaian, the truth is not in you." She sobered somewhat, though the smile lingered on her lips. "And I am glad that we are learning to deal with one another. 'Tis good that we can be friends though there is no love between us."

Iaian hid a scowl. Though he did not want a clinging wife, he found he did not like to hear from her that she did not love him. "I've had enough of this bed," he growled. "Bring my clothes."

"I don't think you should rise yet," Cecile said calmly, putting away the blade she'd used to scrape his whiskers. She knew by his expression it would do no good to argue, but she felt compelled to voice her caution.

"And I care not what you think!" Iaian flung the covers away, gritting his teeth against the sharp pain his incautious action brought to the tender flesh over his ribs.

"I know that very well," Cecile said in exasperation. She'd been around ill-tempered men enough not to take offense at his words. With a small sigh, she brought a plain woolen shirt and hose and doublet.

Abashed by his own display of ingratitude for all her efforts, Iaian took the clothes with a rueful smile. "I'm amazed that you do not flee this very room, shrieking that you have married a madman." He knew he'd been so difficult that another woman would have left him to the care of a servant at the very least.

Cecile fought an urge to smooth the hair back from his forehead, knowing instinctively that he would not appreciate any wifely display from her. She shook her head in answer. "I am more like to bring a washbasin down over your head."

Iaian hid his smile as he bent over the fastenings of his shirt. He suspected Cecile was capable of doing just that if he angered her greatly enough with the bite of his tongue. Lady Edra would have retreated behind cool affront or tearful, wounded feelings. The comparison had come unbidden, and Iaian's smile gave way to a scowl. He did not care to think of Lady Edra or any other part of his past.

Cecile saw the scowl as he stood to fasten the thick hose at his waist and sighed. For every small victory she made in chipping at the defensive wall surrounding her husband's feelings, she encountered resounding defeat. She hid her chagrin and was glad she did so when he offered his arm as they left the room.

They were seated comfortably at the table, well tended by a beaming Sorcha, when the door to the courtyard was flung open and Donnchadh strode into the hall.

He smiled broadly to see them there. "I had begun to think you would lie abed forever. Of course, if I had someone to tend me as lovely as our Ceci, I might be tempted to do likewise."

"Our Ceci tried to cut my throat," Iaian grumbled, aware that she was having to stifle her chuckles beside him. For some reason he did not examine too closely, his uncle's praise of his wife irritated him.

"And if you've been as touchy as I suspect these past few days, I might have been tempted to *that,* also." He took a seat and helped himself to a slab of warm bread.

"It appears there are none who are not against me," Iaian commented as he smeared honey on his own slice of crust.

"Actually, lad, I think your luck has finally changed. I've good news."

"I could use a bit of good news—and good luck."

Beside him, Cecile could not help but wonder what kind of luck he considered their marriage to be.

"You had a messenger late in the night. It appears the castellan at Hagaleah has had word of your exploits in claiming that which is yours. He requests to know your wishes concerning the keep, so that all may be as you would like."

Cecile frowned even as Iaian broke into a smile. "What is Hagaleah?"

"The fourth and last of Alasdair Gillecrist's legacy to Iaian," Donnchadh answered.

"I've not heard mention of it 'ere now. Is it nearby?"

"Within a day's ride," Iaian replied. "'Tis a small holding with but a modest revenue. No doubt 'tis where I'll send you should you ever become displeasing to me." But even as he spoke, he moved his hand to grasp hers.

Cecile felt a warm thrill that he chose thus to share his feelings with her. There was hope yet for a marriage as strong as that her parents had built even if it could not be filled with the same kind of romance. She knew a deep contentment when Iaian's fingers gripped hers. If this was all she could have, she'd take it and gladly.

Chapter Sixteen

Elspeth shivered faintly beneath the pale green eyes that regarded her narrowly. It was almost as if the priest could see into her very womb to the child conceived in sin.

"I wish to see Tavis Gillecrist," Father Aindreas repeated impatiently. Of a mercy, was the young woman dim-witted? Surely he'd not been given directions to the wrong abode.

Hastily, Elspeth stepped back from the door, permitting him entrance. She gestured toward a carved bench in the entryway. "If you will wait here, Father, I'll bring Tavis—Master Gillecrist to you."

Father Aindreas did not miss her slip and frowned. Such familiarity from a likely looking servant toward her master told much of the way of this household. He prayed God would forgive him for dealing with such men as these, but God had ever used sinners in his battle with evil. Perhaps there was holy irony there—defeat the devil with his own minions. The thought comforted him.

"Father?" Tavis stood at the end of the hall.

Slowly, the cassocked figure rose and faced him "I am Father Aindreas." He glanced about to be sure they were quite alone. "I come from Dunmar. May we speak?"

Tavis's heart raced faster, though he wondered at Dunmar's choice of conspirators. A priest? Then he shrugged mentally. He'd had stranger bedfellows in the past. And who was more likely to keep confidence than a man of God?

Tavis gestured for the priest to follow him into a small drawing room. He tugged at a bellpull before seating himself at a small table. Father Aindreas followed suit. Neither man's expression revealed anything of their internal wonderings.

Master Gillecrist was younger than Father Aindreas had anticipated. He had the look of a green lad about him, the smooth face of untried youth. But then, what did he, a priest, know of the way of conspiracy? Perhaps older men were too wise to involve themselves. Yet, though Dunmar was young, he was of a much harder make than this Tavis Gillecrist appeared to be.

Tavis had begun to think it a great jest that his co-conspirator was a priest. Faith, if he lost his head at least he could be certain his soul was secure.

Elspeth came on soft feet to the doorway in answer to the summons of the bellpull. "Aye, sir," she inquired, as any good servant would, as if she had not just this morn slipped from the man's bed.

"Bring us wine, please, Elspeth. And perhaps a light repast?" The second was asked with lifted brows of the good father, who shook his head. Tavis turned back to the woman. "Just the wine, then." There was only a hint of the warmth they shared in the smile he gave her.

The two men chatted of inconsequentials until Elspeth returned and the wine was served. As she left the room, Tavis called to her softly. "The door, Elspeth." She closed it obediently in her wake.

Tavis looked expectantly at Father Aindreas, offering nothing in the way of an opening.

"Dunmar feels the way to reach a man is through those loyal to him," Father Aindreas began obliquely. "And Arran, for all his folly, still has many who look to him."

"I've little enough gold to convince any man to change his loyalty." Tavis's smile held a touch of bitterness.

"Ah," Father Aindreas said slowly, "but it serves us best if the loyalties themselves do not change. We would seek to change the fortunes of such men. Those brought low cannot lift another up."

"And many carry Arran on their shoulders, though he does not deserve it." Tavis felt daring in openly denouncing Arran to one he had known but a few moments of time. But trust had to be given somewhere if they were to succeed. As Dunmar had sent this priest, so then would Tavis trust him.

"But few whose future we could sway by our knowledge of them. If Arran becomes convinced of the treachery of those he should most trust, then there will be the fewer in his confidence, the fewer to support him." Father Aindreas studied his reaction, but could discern nothing yet. That pleased him. Perhaps Master Gillecrist was not so green as he feared.

"That seems a slow way to gain the regency." Tavis had expected quick, decisive action, though of what nature he could not have said.

"But the best way to keep our heads upon our shoulders." Though, in truth, Father Aindreas would gladly have sacrificed his neck for the good of the one true church.

"And you have those names?" Tavis asked finally.

"I have those you are to know."

Tavis's grip tightened slightly on his goblet before he forced himself to relax it. "Dunmar doubts me?"

Father Aindreas smiled in an attempt to be reassuring, but his face was unused to smiles—he felt its clumsiness. "Dunmar is cautious that no man involved know enough to endanger the lives of any of the others. 'Tis as much for your protection as for those working alongside you that you and your part remain unknown to them as they do to you."

"How many others?"

The priest shrugged. "Even I do not know for certain. Enough to ensure success. Each man of you will have the names of those whose fortunes you will work to alter."

Tavis took a deep breath, then expelled it slowly before asking, "And those Dunmar would have me seek to bring low?"

Father Aindreas watched him closely as he answered in a quiet voice, "Saelec Lotharing . . . and Iaian Gillecrist."

Feeling the bitter sting of disappointment, Tavis answered quietly, evenly, "Nay."

The priest frowned. Dunmar had assured him that of all people in Christendom, this one man had the most cause to wish Iaian Gillecrist out of his way. "Nay?" he repeated questioningly, as if he could not have heard aright.

"Tell Dunmar any other names can be given to me, and I'll act in whatever way I can. But not Lotharing—and not Iaian."

Dunmar did more than frown at the news. He cursed until Father Aindreas knew several new phrases. "The young fool," Dunmar said finally, bitterly. "Will he betray us?" His own lack of judgment was hard to accept. He seldom misread a man so thoroughly.

Father Aindreas shrugged. "He says he will not, but that he will take no part in the downfall of those two men. I assured him we'd do no real harm—at least none to life and limb."

Dunmar smiled grimly. A man's fortune was his life in many circumstances. He'd known men to end their existence after a devastating loss at the gaming table.

"Shall I approach him with other names?" Father Aindreas asked into the silence that had followed his last comment.

"Nay." Dunmar paused, thinking hard. Tavis Gillecrist's social circle was small, though his father had tried hard to have him accepted more widely. "He could have no influence on the others. And he cannot be used as a common footpad. I've no more use for him. 'Tis a pity."

Father Aindreas cleared his throat. "Would it not be wise to involve him in some small way so as to bind his tongue?"

Dunmar stroked his jaw thoughtfully. "Mayhap you are right, but I must give some thought on how best to do so. I trust him less now that I know of his misguided family feeling."

The priest left some few moments later, and Dunmar prepared himself carefully for his audience with Arran. Arran considered him one of his more trusted advisers, for Dunmar carefully relayed every detail of Marie de Guise's comings and goings to him. Details that he and de Guise spent long moments concocting for Arran's ears, with just enough of importance sprinkled amongst the trivial so that Arran thought himself well served by Dunmar's activities.

As usual Dunmar dressed himself richly but not ostentatiously. He had never considered it wise to outshine the peacock, and in Arran's case the peacock cut a quiet figure. Dunmar chose a doublet that was of French cut and very fine, but a quiet, deep midnight blue. Smooth hose fit the muscles of his legs like a second skin. A slouch hat, also of so deep a blue as to be almost black, topped his dark hair.

Once dressed, he strode confidently to the crowded outer chamber, where he gave his name to Arran's chief steward. Within moments, he was ushered into the Presence Chamber, where he took his place with those privileged few awaiting Arran's pleasure. His passage was followed by the envious eyes of men who had been cooling their heels many hours while they begged audience with their regent.

All the while he had been dressing and all the while he waited, Dunmar's mind sped. He'd trust no one else with Iaian Gillecrist's downfall now that the fool half-brother had failed him. The scheme was already well in place that would secretly recall Iaian to England. All Dunmar had to do was ensure that his haste in leaving Scotland would appear cause for suspicion. By the time he was bowing before Arran, he had the beginnings of a plan. By the time he was given leave to rise, he was smiling at its simplicity.

"Your Grace," he greeted smoothly. As always he noted that Arran, though garbed in all the trappings of his princely position, did not cut an imposing figure. And his surroundings, despite frescoed and friezed walls, did not contain the sumptuous luxuries that monarchs and the regents of monarchs generally gathered to themselves. Dunmar often wondered if this were not due to Arran's reformer tendencies, renounced but perhaps not suppressed.

"Dunmar, you are welcome here." Arran's smile was warm, though his eyes remained cool as always. Arran trusted this man, yet he had never cared for him. Perhaps, he told himself, 'twas because the man lied so easily to the former queen whose trust in him appeared implicit. There was ever a touch of idealism in Arran that he had never tried to stifle. He would do what must be for the good of Scotland, but he did not necessarily respect those men who helped him in his aims.

Arran took a cushioned chair and bade Dunmar be seated as well. They spoke at length, and when Dunmar had told him all of the inconsequential things purported to be de Guise's latest secrets, Arran sighed. "You tell me nothing I do not already know . . . and nothing to lighten my mood."

Dunmar stilled. He was easy on the first score. He'd deliberately said nothing of importance. But if Arran had heard aught that darkened his mood, that could only be good news for Marie de Guise. He waited, knowing Arran would confide in him without his having to question.

"I've word d'Esse landed this morning," Arran said at last.

The French fleet landed at last! Carefully, Dunmar schooled his features so that no trace of elation showed. He knew that Marie de Guise would have heard the same news in almost the same instant as Arran. And he knew that in her chambers there would be much rejoicing and merrymaking at the occasion. "Has the Council of Lords given consent for the marriage?"

"'Tis but a formality, I think. They will contract Mary to Francis when they've assurance that Scotland's independence will be respected."

Dunmar felt ill-served by Arran's mournful tone. He knew well enough that Arran was to gain a French duchy for giving up any hope of a match between his son and the wee queen. Of course, even a French duchy could not make up for the loss of a kingdom. "Could any such assurance be trusted?"

Arran lifted his chin, and for the first time Dunmar perceived true nobility in his demeanor. "Scotland will never become a French pawn. Not while one drop of Scots blood goes unshed."

"Aye," Dunmar agreed, seeing his chance, "but we must be cautious indeed not to be caught in the many snares laid by our enemies in France—and in England."

Suspicion brightened Arran's eyes at mention of England. "Have you word of evil afoot?"

"None I've yet been able to bring into the open. But there have been whispers, silenced as I approach."

"But you've heard something?" Arran prodded.

"Little enough. I've heard it said that the fortunes of Geoffrey Lindael have ever been linked with that of Somerset."

"Lindael?" Even as he questioned the man's identity, Arran hid his bitter reaction to mention of England's Lord Protector. Memory of his ignominious defeat at Somerset's hands was still an open wound.

"Sir Geoffrey Lindael . . . the English lover of Anne Donnchadh. And the man Iaian Gillecrist called father for the first twenty years of his life," Dunmar finished smoothly.

"You think Gillecrist plots with Somerset?" Arran tried to recall details of the young man who had wed the Lotharing girl. "I would think him too well snared in claiming his inheritance."

"Which actions give him just cause to travel the length of Scotland. A man can discern much in the way of a country's strengths and weaknesses by simple observation."

Arran stirred restlessly in his chair. Had he trusted too quickly? Gillecrist had been reared as English, after all. "I can have him questioned," he said finally.

"You would learn nothing. 'Twould be far better to have him carefully watched. Give him ample opportunity to prove his colors. Somerset would pay richly for the simple news that the French fleet sits on Scotland's shore."

"Gillecrist's path does not lie along the sea coast," Arran protested.

"It could," Dunmar suggested, "if he were called to join the young Lotharing, who is to travel to France with our Mary."

"And what if he does simply that?"

"With no messenger leaving his side in haste for England?" Dunmar shrugged. "Then the whisperers will be proven wrong, and you will know that Gillecrist can be trusted. Is it not better, after all, to be sure?"

"Aye." Arran frowned thoughtfully. "Aye, far better to be sure."

Dunmar kept his face suitably grave. How simple this was all proving to be.

Tavis twisted in his bed, his movements bringing a sleepy protest from Elspeth, who slumbered at his side. What was he now to do? If he kept silent and Dunmar succeeded, Iaian would be brought to his knees, perhaps sent back to England in disgrace. Would all not then be as it should? Every holding that should have come to Tavis when his father last drew breath would finally be his.

Yet did Iaian deserve disgrace? Whose fault was it that he had been called to claim that which Tavis had once considered his? Not Iaian's. Nor yet Tavis's. Nay, the blame lay with people and events of long ago over which neither of them had any control. Now or then.

But, a tiny voice whispered, does not your own son deserve better than the handouts of others, or what could be gleaned from the fortunes and misfortunes of royalty? Tavis thought again of the fact that his child's mother was at present no more than a servant. Aye, perhaps, 'twas all the bairn did deserve, after all, no more nor no less than his father before him.

But despite everything, Tavis could not regret spending his seed on Elspeth Leathann. 'Twas only she, after all, who had brought him any tenderness in years past. With his questions still unanswered, he drew her into his arms, cradling her gently as he once more courted the sleep that would not come.

Chapter Seventeen

Donnchadh returned to Daileass with an easy mind and a heart filled with thoughts of Rilla Lotharing. He knew 'twas long past time he should be looking to the care of his own holdings, and now that he could feel reasonably certain that his nephew's affairs were secure, only his longing for Rilla held him to these border marches.

He and his small guard rode into the cobbled bailey at Daileass with darkness falling swiftly about them and were met by an anxious steward. Donnchadh's heart sank at the expression on the man's face as he proffered a sealed scroll with a stammering of explanation. "I could not think what to do, my lord. It arrived after midday, and I thought to send to Ciaran by morning for its disposition."

Donnchadh felt a keen dismay upon recognizing the royal seal, and, though it was addressed to Iaian, he opened it without hesitation. It proved to be a missive from Arran himself, calling Iaian to journey to France with Amalric Lotharing. Donnchadh studied it at length, trying to read something into or between the actual lines, for he could not believe it was an innocent afterthought on the part of Arran. Nay, someone had concocted the thought and planted it, but who? And why?

But after the better part of an hour, he still had no answer, so he dispatched a messenger to Waytefeld, charging the man with the urgency of his mission. Then he dressed meticulously and rode the short distance to Ciaran, not heeding the lateness of the hour. This summons needed to be discussed with Saelec Lotharing. Perhaps Amalric's father knew something that could put Donnchadh's mind to rest.

As it proved, he did not, looking as surprised as Donnchadh at Arran's words. They were polite enough, and though they held no warmth, neither did they hold a chill, as if written to a man in disfavor.

Saelec rubbed his ear. "I've no more understanding of this than you. Have you sent word to Iaian?"

"Aye, and suggested he await Amalric in Edinburgh. The messenger left this very night, for that was as soon as I knew of it." Donnchadh shook his head. "I like this not."

"You think it bodes ill for the lad?" Saelec asked worriedly, concerned more for Ceci, though he liked Iaian well enough for himself.

"I think 'tis possible, for the decision was too hastily made, and with no reason given. Aye, 'tis possible, but I see nothing to be done about it as yet." Donnchadh smiled reassuringly. "As many other of Scotland's nobles, I've eyes and ears at court. If there's aught to hear, trust I shall hear it."

"Aye, but I hope 'tis soon enough that you do so. News too late is of little use."

Donnchadh could not quarrel with that. "Aye, 'tis why I've thought to travel to Edinburgh myself, before the court moves to Stirling for the next season." He paused. What he would ask now was difficult to broach, for he knew he moved faster than amenities suggested. He cleared his throat. "Because the task before me will take me from here for some time and because I must return to see to my own properties as soon as may be, I'd ask your leave to speak to Rilla of my feelings. I'd ask her to be my wife."

Saelec smiled, though his worried look did not entirely ease. "'Tis not merely my leave you have, but my blessings. I do not think she is expecting you this evening. She is in the nursery with my grandsons." His pride in the boys was evident in his tone and in the way his eyes lit at the thought of them.

Donnchadh's smile held relief, though he'd not really expected to be refused. Still, there had been that small, niggling doubt. He knew how well Lotharing loved his family, especially his grandsons by Odwulf. "They'll not lose their heritage for being in my care. I promise you that." He clasped Saelec's shoulder, hoping the man would know his words were sincere.

Assailed by thoughts of the son lost, Saelec blinked quickly, then forced a jovial smile. "Shall I send word to the nursery?"

"Nay. If you permit, I'll seek her there unannounced."

"'Tis your neck," Saelec warned, thinking how ill-tempered his womenfolk could be when they considered themselves not attired correctly for guests.

Donnchadh was not thinking of his neck, however, as he took the stairs to the nursery. He was quite familiar with the way, for upon every visit, he made it a point to see the boys. He thought it far better for them to come to know him in the comfortable surroundings of their own home rather than the strange ones of his . . . should he be so lucky, of course, as to receive the desired answer to his proposal.

The door to the nursery stood open, and he paused there, taking in the sight of his Rilla. She was on the heavy Turkish rug with her sons, her skirts swirled carelessly about her. Her beautiful hair was loose, gleaming like melted ripples of red-gold in the lamp light. The lonely years since he'd lost his Catriona fell away from him, and he did not think his lovely wife would mind that he sought happiness once again.

"My lady," he said softly, drawing her attention from the toys scattered among the folds of her skirts and the tiny hands seeking to find them.

At the sound of his voice, Rilla looked up with laughter in her eyes. "Ros," she said softly, rather than the more formal *my lord.* She addressed him thusly because that was how she thought of him, and also to show him that she was not angered that he had ignored once again her pleas for advance warning of his visits.

She stirred as if to rise, and he lifted his hand in protest. "Nay. I'll join you."

Rilla's throaty laugh as she took in his fine clothes drew a rueful smile in response. "'Tis no matter if velvet does not fare well with these two," he said softly, dropping to his knees even as Theu took a toddling step toward him, arms outstretched.

"'Twill serve you right if they are ruined," Rilla agreed as she stopped Valdemar from snatching the gold chain that dangled appealingly from Donnchadh's broad chest. "You have caught me in my poorest gown, my lord."

"You are lovely however you are gowned," Donnchadh answered.

And his heart and soul were in his eyes, so that a rush of blood sent soft, warm color flooding Rilla's cheeks.

As she averted her eyes, Donnchadh protested hoarsely, "Do not turn from me, my love."

And her gaze flew back to his, for never had he addressed her so intimately. "Ros?" she asked questioningly, her voice hushed, her pulse racing.

He reached for Valdemar, pulling him close with Theudoric, and met Rilla's green gaze over their fair heads. "I'd be their father," he said gruffly. There was a long pause. "I'd be your husband."

His heart failed him when she did not answer, but studied his face gravely. Then her smile came even as tears filled her eyes. "And I'd be your wife."

Without dropping either child, he managed to draw their mother into his embrace as well. She nestled there on the floor against his broad shoulder, feeling loved as she had thought never again to be after word was brought to her of Odwulf's death.

Thus it was that Saelec and Giorsal found them, and with the approval in their eyes, Rilla's last doubt was vanquished.

Miles below the border between Scotland and England, Scots coin crossed English palms arranging the arrest of Geoffrey Lindael.

"And what would your master have the charge be?" The man who spoke kept his voice low, though the tavern was crowded and noisy enough that their conversation could not be remarked. He was a lord in his own right, but an impoverished one. Young and reckless, he was not so pure of reputation that he could not be approached, yet not so tainted that he was without connection.

A rough-looking man faced him across the table, holding a tankard of ale in a scarred hand. 'Twas obvious he was capable of taking care of any business charged to him. "Treason."

The young lord lifted a brow. "But what would the basis of the charge be? I've never heard the slightest hint that would involve Lindael in such."

"A Scots leman. A beloved stepson now loyal to Scotland. Nothing that would stick for long," the other admitted crudely, "but then it don't need to. Just long enough to draw his stepson back to England when he gets the word."

The noble frowned. He would rather his involvement were limited to England's boundaries. Not even for gold would he wish to expose himself to the crudities of Scotland. "Who will send this word?"

"Never you worry about that end of it," was his answer. "I'll see to that. You just be sure Lindael lands in the Tower."

"Who wishes the stepson back?" When there was no answer beyond a placid stare he sighed in exasperation. "Well then, what of the remainder of the gold?"

"Payment is yours when the deed is done."

The young nobleman smiled grimly. "Oh, it will be accomplished, I assure you." He could never arrange to make the charges permanent, but as long as they did not expect *that* of him, then, aye, it would be accomplished.

His rough companion cleared his throat. "You will have one final task."

"Which is?"

"When 'tis done you must ensure the Scots leman believes the charges serious. And convince her that only her son's return to England will allay suspicion."

"That will be difficult," the younger man protested. "The lady does not know me, nor has she any reason to believe my words."

"That, my fine lord, is your worry—if you would have the balance of your gold."

An hour later, the scarred and bearded one was riding back toward the border of Scotland. This was not the first time he'd played at being English, nor did he think it would be the last. He had little stomach for it, but gold was gold, and he'd been assured it was for Scotland's own good.

Chapter Eighteen

Sparkles of morning dew on the meadow grasses dampened Cecile's skirts as she walked away from the castle walls. There remained a trace of vexation on her face for the argument she'd had with the guard. He'd not been pleased to open the gate for her. Not that he would have dared to be rude. Indeed, he had been very polite—and, in her opinion, very insulting. "Do you have leave to go without escort?"

Straightening her shoulders, Cecile had imitated her mother's most commanding tones. "I am Lady Waytefeld. Of whom should I ask leave to do my own bidding?" Strange to think this old fortress came with its own title, but so it was. She was now Lady Waytefeld as well as Lady Gillecrist, when but a short while ago, she had been only Cecile Lotharing, untitled and unwed.

The guard looked at her in chagrin. What kind of a mistress had he now? But when her expression did not relent, he nodded reluctantly and gestured for the gate to be opened. His own expression told quite clearly that he expected this to be the end of his career, and he was not going to thank her for it! "May I send a lad with you?"

"Nay." Cecile relented at his look of misery. "I promise not to go beyond the clearing, and you may post a rider at the gate, waiting to come after me should I come to harm." Before he could protest further, she slipped through the gate, which had been opened at his gesture.

Escape! 'Twas what it seemed, if only for a brief time. The walls of Waytefeld were oppressive to her, more so than any place she had been. She lifted her chin to the rising sun, reveling in its warmth. Even in midsummer, Waytefeld keep was a cold, damp place. She did not care for it, but Iaian appeared to be in no hurry to leave here, so she held her tongue.

Iaian. Her steps slowed at the thought of him. They were so much closer, yet he remained apart from her in many ways. There was a wall she had not breached and did not know that she ever would—or even could. Yet, when she entered a room, his eyes sought her immediately, as if he had been waiting for her to appear. And if she left the hall before him of an evening, he hurried soon after.

And the nights were unlike anything she could

have imagined. She had begun to crave his touch as she knew some men craved their ale. Night after night, he set her on fire, matching her heat with his, and never again had she had to beg to share in the exquisite pleasure-pain of passion. But afterwards, though he held her and did not turn his back on her, his thoughts and feelings fled to places she could not follow. And that left her with a wound she did not know how to heal.

Her steps had taken her to the first edge of the trees, and she smiled faintly to hear the birds that chirped and warbled to her from the leafy branches. Remembering her promise, she obediently turned back, then stopped in surprise at the rider leaving the castle. Had the foolish man thought she would stray into the woods and sent someone after her?

But she frowned when she realized the sun was lifted fully above the horizon. She had not intended to walk so far nor so long. She could not fault the guard for his concern. Then, her heart gave a funny little leap as the rider neared at a steady pace. 'Twas Iaian.

Within moments, he scowled down at her from a snorting, blowing animal. Cecile smiled sunnily. That look was just like all the looks her father had ever bestowed on her when he considered she had given him cause to worry. A man did not worry who did not care.

Iaian snorted as loudly as his horse. "You look pleased enough, my lady, to have set my household in an uproar."

Cecile shook her head. “Pleased only to see you, my lord. I’d no wish to distress anyone by my wanderings.” She saw no need to pretend she did not know the cause for the uproar. “5’Tis something I do often enough that I hope the guards will become accustomed to my comings and goings.”

“They’ll not have the opportunity,” Iaian said flatly. “You’ll not leave Waytefeld nor any other keep unattended.”

Cecile opened her mouth to protest, but Iaian cut through before the words could come.

“I’ll not have argument to that, Ceci. I’m not your father, to twist about your every wish. I’ll walk or ride with you when I can, but you’ll not go alone. Or if I cannot—” he frowned as a thought occurred to him, “or if you’ve no wish for my company—you will take a groom with you.”

His scowl told Cecile better than words that he did not care to think she might prefer having a guard attend her. That pleased her. “I would always enjoy your company, Iaian, but I’ve no wish to disturb you so early as I like to wander.”

Before Iaian could answer to that, Cecile’s eye was caught by a movement along the crude road from Dunblane. “Iaian—someone approaches the keep.”

Iaian turned sharply, then relaxed. ’Twas a man alone, and no threat to Waytefeld. “Aye. A messenger, I’d say by his haste.”

Cecile’s heart tightened. Most messengers traveled in haste, but one carrying dire news traveled swiftest. As always, her thoughts went to her mother's poor health. "Iaian, we must hurry back to the keep, if you please."

The urgency in her tone drew a frown. She still made him wary with her uncanny way of discerning moods and feelings. And though she had assured him there was no knowledge in her of future events, he could not help but wonder at times.

With a nod, he took her up before him and turned his massive gelding toward the fortress. He moved the animal to a steady canter, but did not urge him to a greater speed. Cecile felt far too fragile in his arms. Though he knew her for a good rider, somehow the animal beneath them seemed too powerful for her slight form.

By the time they reached the hall the messenger had been made comfortable with meat and ale at one end of the long table. He rose hastily at their approach, his eyes moving quickly from the impressive viscount to the tiny figure at his side, who looked more sprite than noble lady. "Lord Gillecrist," he stammered, meeting a scowl as he turned his gaze once more to the viscount. Reaching into his short coat, he withdrew a small scroll and handed it to Iaian.

Iaian broke the seal, his scowl deepening as he read the short missive.

"My lord?" Cecile questioned softly, her fears still for her mother.

"'Tis from Donnchadh," Iaian said shortly.

Cecile's brows lifted questioningly. Ros Donnchadh had left them but four days earlier. He must have dispatched the messenger immediately upon his return to Daileass. "Is aught amiss?"

Iaian glanced at the messenger. "Rest a few hours, then I'll have an answer for you to carry upon your return."

The messenger stifled a groan. A few hours? He'd ridden from morning sun to morning sun. But the needs of nobility did not take into consideration a mere messenger's exhaustion. "Aye, my lord," he said, half to Lord Gillecrist's back as he turned away.

"Is my mother well?" Cecile asked at last in exasperation.

"Aye." Iaian lifted one brow in surprise at her sharpness. "At least, there's nothing here to say she is not. Should she not be?"

"Sometimes she is not," Cecile admitted in a low voice.

Iaian's look softened. "There is no mention of her. And I'm sure my uncle is enough at Ciaran's doors that he would know if there was aught amiss." He stared down into Cecile's huge eyes and sighed. She was still so much a child. He could not leave her on her own whilst he did Arran's bidding. "You know Amalric travels with your child queen to France?"

Cecile nodded, frowning because she sensed something to come that she would not like. Or Iaian's voice told her that he, at least, did not think she would like it.

"I am to join him."

She looked up at him puzzled. "We travel to France?"

Iaian sighed. This, then, was the point she would argue. "Nay. Donnchadh makes it clear I am to go alone. He suggests I return you to your parents' keeping for the nonce."

"I may not be called to go with you, but I'd not return to Ciaran. I'll stay at Daileass, by your leave."

The last three words of her speech surprised Iaian. He'd not have expected her to be the least submissive to his wishes after she'd followed him uninvited to Daileass. Perhaps she hadn't every intention of being a difficult, rebellious wife after all. Still, he did not understand why she would rather stay alone at Daileass than return to Ciaran. "Will you not be lonely there?"

"Ciaran is not too far for visits, and I'll surround myself with guards when I set forth," she added hastily, forestalling any protest or lecture. "I am mistress of your holdings, Iaian. I'd take my rightful place, for there is much I must learn if I am to make us comfortable."

But she knew that was not all of it. Something deep inside told her that this marriage had begun on too tenuous terms. If it was to strengthen, she could allow nothing to diminish her place in Iaian's life. Though she could not travel with him and remain at his side, she could give him thoughts of her in his home, directing his household affairs—sleeping alone in their marriage bed.

Perhaps a part of her feelings were simply insecurities, because she knew he did not love her. Nor was he like to. But she had not a doubt they could deal comfortably together as long as she let nothing diminish the one bond that was between them. Their vows to stand as one before the rest of the world would, in time, prove stronger than any steadfast declarations of love.

For long moments, Iaian said nothing in response to her request, and when he did speak it was not to answer her directly. "Donnchadh bids me await Amalric in Edinburgh. We'll travel there together, and I'll ask Donnchadh to meet us there as well. He can escort you home upon my departure from Scotland." He met her anxious eyes, and a slight smile warmed his face. "Home to Daileass."

Theirs was an easy journey from Dunblane to Edinburgh. Cecile had no doubt that had Iaian traveled alone, he would have completed it in one day. As it was, they stopped in Linlithgow, well before nightfall. The inn was comfortable, but entirely unremarkable. But, for Cecile, the journey itself was anything but unremarkable. She had never before been so near the sea, and the smell of salt and the rush of waves against the shoreline fascinated her. Their small entourage followed the strand from Linlithgow to Edinburgh.

"I'd go with you to France," she said once, on a sigh. But her voice was only plaintive and not pleading. "It must be wonderful to feel the water beneath the very deck on which you stand."

As Iaian watched, she lifted her face skyward at the sound of a seabird's mewing cry. The mist from the sea beading against the white gilt of her hair seemed to form a shimmering halo about her head. But he knew her for no angel and smiled at the realization that he'd not have her any more angelic than she was. He suspected no heavenly being would seduce a husband as Cecile was wont to do each night. Feeling his body respond to his thoughts, he turned his attention to her longing words. "I'd not know if 'tis pleasant or unpleasant. I've never been to sea, either."

She looked at him in surprise, her blue eyes wide. "I thought every young English lord was educated abroad."

Iaian's smile faded in memory. "My mother kept me close to her."

"She must have loved you a great deal." Cecile tread cautiously, knowing she must but feeling a pang of sympathy for the other woman in Iaian's life. "As she surely does, even now."

"Aye," Iaian's voice was harsh, "she loved me quite painfully."

And Cecile knew he was not speaking of his mother's pain. She ached to stretch out her hand and touch him. They were close enough, riding side by side, their horses so near to one another that their legs brushed on occasion. But there was something in Iaian's shuttered expression that warned her it would do no good, would surely be resented, spoiling the brief harmony between them.

But she wanted him to continue telling her whatever of his past he would. "Did you ever wish to run away to sea as a lad? I did."

"And when were you ever a lad?" Iaian returned easily, allowing her to draw him away from his dark mood. That other life was lost to him, after all; no need to pine for it, or hold tight to his regrets.

Cecile flashed him a smile, relieved that he did not withdraw from her this time as he had so many others when she walked on forbidden ground. "I *wished* to be a lad," she said stoutly. "And I wished to go to sea. And to other lands. I've three brothers who have seen Germany, one of whom is there even now. I've seen nothing but my little piece of Scotland."

Iaian smiled broadly at the chagrin in that last sentence. He'd certainly taken an uncommon wife. Most young girls dreamed of romance and luxury, not travel and adventure. "Perhaps one day we'll travel together." The idea of watching Cecile's rapt expression as she encountered new experiences was rather appealing. And the way her face lit at his suggestion was equally appealing. He wondered lately that he had not thought her particularly attractive at their first meeting. He still was not inclined to think her a classic beauty, but he had come to believe he would not change any of her piquant features even if he could.

But while he watched, Cecile's smile faded at the thought that occurred to her. "Iaian," she began hesitantly, "is there danger in this journey to France with our Mary?" A tiny frown marred her forehead.

For a jealous moment Iaian wondered if it were only trepidation for her brother's safety that made her ask. Then he smiled and answered easily, as he recalled anew that he did not wish for a wife who pined for his company and fretted for his safety. "I should think that the entourage of the Queen of Scotland is probably the safest place of any to be. And she travels to a country that greets her with open arms."

"But what of England? Will Somerset not try to prevent her from reaching France?" At some point, Cecile had accepted that Iaian, though he might never look wholly on Scotland as his country or Mary as his queen, had also severed loyalties to England and its monarch. That saddened her, for it seemed to leave Iaian lost somewhere in the middle.

"Perhaps he might," Iaian agreed, "if he could find a way to do so, but all of Scotland would rise against him were he to step foot toward Dumbarton."

"But at sea?" Cecile persisted softly.

"I think not even Somerset would dare to attack the French fleet. 'Twould mean war on a scale he is not prepared to match. In such case, all of Scotland, Catholic and reformer alike, would join with Henri of France to crush the English." Attacking an ally was one thing; attempting to wrest the dauphin's bride from the grip of the royal navy would be something else entirely in Henri's eyes. Iaian, however, did not doubt the English would be foolish enough to at least try. It was not quite honest to say there was anything Somerset did not dare. He saw no need, however, to alarm Cecile with the possibility of events she could do nothing to prevent.

And she had to be content with his assurances, though she did not like any part of the separation that lay ahead. She had just begun to know her husband and feared the tentative steps they had taken to find a meeting place in their marriage would be all to do over again upon his return to Scotland.

But a short time later her mind was completely taken over by her first sight of Edinburgh. As they passed through the gates of the city, she turned to Iaian in bitter disappointment. "'Tis dirty."

As the words left her mouth, slops were poured from an overhead window and splattered onto the cobblestones ahead of them. Iaian smiled sympathetically. "No more than London. Wherever people must live crowded together, filth abounds."

"But I had thought it to be grand." Her wail turned to indignation as she continued, "All my life I have dreamed of seeing our royal burgh."

"'Tis grand enough where royalty resides. Grand enough even for your greedy eyes to look their fill, I promise you."

Hearing the laughter in his voice, she caught her lip between her teeth. "I must sound like a child to you."

"I'd not have you jaded," he said softly, and knew it was true.

Cecile turned her attention back to the city, increasingly convinced that Iaian would be a tender husband if she could but peel away the layers of anger and resentment.

The Gillecrist home did not disappoint her. The servant who led their way stopped at the ornate front door. Massive walls of stone and mortar rose several stories, and tall windows were graced by stained glass. Iaian assisted her from her horse and led her up the broad steps just as the door opened and several servants stepped out to greet them.

Cecile looked sharply at an attractive young woman who claimed to be housekeeper. She seemed overyoung for her position but gave Iaian no more than his due as lord of the house, and then turned her attention fully to Cecile. And her manner was all that it should be.

As they moved inside, an older manservant shook his head in answer to Iaian's question. "Master Tavis is not at home. Was he expecting your arrival this afternoon?"

"No," Iaian answered evenly. "He was not expecting us at all." He glanced at Cecile. "Would you rest for a while?"

Cecile smiled and shook her head. "I would eat, if you please."

Iaian laughed at her words. "I fear you will never make a stylish wife. You should be swooning from exhaustion."

" 'Tis hard when I am fainting with hunger," she retorted, not the least dismayed by his portrayal of her. Nó man could truly wish for such a dismal wife.

As they followed the housekeeper, Elspeth as she was called, into a drawing room, Iaian considered that most well-bred young ladies, such as Lady Edra, would more likely be complaining than swooning. And he silently acknowledged that he did not wish for Cecile to swoon or complain. He could not, however, go so far as to admit he did not wish she were Lady Edra, either. Not yet.

They were dining quite comfortably by the time Tavis returned to the townhouse. When he entered the room, smiling but looking a bit disconcerted, Cecile was struck anew by his resemblance to Iaian. None could doubt they were brothers, and it seemed remarkably unfair that only Alasdair Gillecrist's lack of restraint had made the one an heir and the other a bastard.

Iaian waved toward a seat at his left. "Join us?"

Tavis's smile faded a bit. He had foolishly grown used to thinking of himself as master here, sitting where Iaian now sat, inviting guests to dine. With a mental curse at his own stupidity, he took the chair Iaian offered. Was he being more noble than he could afford by turning his back on Dunmar's offer of a chance to have it all?

Elspeth chose that inopportune moment to enter the room. A flash of her eyes told him that she, too, felt chagrined that another sat in the place they thought of as his. But her face was a quick mask as she oversaw the serving of the second course. Tavis felt a surge of resentment for his father, for Iaian, and even for Elspeth. Aye, 'twas no more than a servant that carried his seed, after all. A servant, like his own mother, taking what she desired heedlessly, never giving thought to the consequences, never giving thought to the life she marred by the very act of conceiving it. Self-knowledge twisted his lips. And if she were no better than his mother, was he any better than his father?

Cecile followed Elspeth's movements with thoughtful eyes. She had not missed the flash of fire in those brown eyes, nor the telltale flush of color as they met Tavis's glance. She was not so sheltered as to think noble men did not lie with serving wenches, though her father and brothers did not make that practice. Still, she thought there was something here besides a maid that had been tumbled.

Elspeth caught her gaze and flushed more deeply as she left the room. Then Cecile turned to study Tavis, who kept his eyes on his trencher until Iaian questioned him concerning how he had found this household on his return.

"As well as if my father still lived," Tavis answered readily. "I've no doubt you can safely turn your attention to your other properties."

"I can only hope there's no further need." Iaian's tone was rueful. "Arran claims my attention now."

Tavis almost choked on his basted pork. "Arran? What has he to do with you?" He felt the beginning of a cold dread, for he could see Dunmar's not so subtle hand in this. Did Arran call Iaian innocently forth to arrest him?

"It seems I am to travel to France with young Amalric Lotharing in escort of Arran's royal charge." Iaian spoke without inflection, as if he had no questions concerning this unexpected—and unwanted—appointment.

"But . . . why?" Tavis protested in spite of himself. Though he still did not doubt Dunmar was behind this, he could not follow the logic. How could such a signal honor bring Iaian low? He frowned, considering. Would even Dunmar be so brash as to place a five-year-old queen in danger in order to make her mother regent? Nay. That could not be. If aught happened to Mary, there would be no need of a regency. The crown would pass to the next in line, which could in no way benefit Dunmar, for de Guise would lose what little power she had.

"I've asked that of myself, and have come to no answers. Have you any?"

Tavis felt a sting of guilt, quickly suppressed. He had done nothing, after all. And Iaian could *know* nothing. "I've long given up trying to discern the whims of royalty," he answered. "Nay, do not look to me for answers." But he would look to Dunmar. The question yet unanswered, however, was whether he would do more than look.

Chapter Nineteen

Cecile was waiting when Iaian entered their bedchamber. He looked faintly surprised to see her sitting upright in the wide bed.

"I would have thought you well into sleep by now, Ceci." He felt a small, pleased warmth at the thought that she remained awake, waiting for his return. Almost at once, the realization made him scowl. He reached to unfasten his doublet, turning his face from her.

Cecile winced at his look, sure she knew what battles he fought within. "I was curious to know what you and Tavis discussed at such length," she said, careful not to let him think she had waited for the pleasure of his company.

"Nothing that need concern you, else I'd have had you join us." Iaian felt immediately shamed by the quick hurt that showed in her eyes. There was no need to punish her for his own feelings. He tossed the doublet to a chair and pulled his shirt over his shoulders before adding, "'Twas of little interest, after all. Details of how I found Waytefeld and of how he found affairs here."

Taking the olive branch he offered, Cecile dared a little more. "Do you really intend to give Waytefeld to his keeping?"

"Aye, though I've not yet spoken to him of it. I think he'd do well there—and he needs something to occupy him. I fear he'll fall into some foolish intrigue if left to his own imaginings too long."

"Intrigue?" Cecile could not imagine open, blunt Tavis involved in anything of secrecy.

"There's enough of it going on, I fear," Iaian said slowly. "And a royal burgh is a likely place to get involved. Tavis is my responsibility as surely as any of the properties my father left. I'd see to him, if I can."

"I cannot think he'd be pleased to know how you view him," Cecile retorted. "Much like a holding to be suitably disposed of." But her mind was no longer on their conversation as Iaian began to unfasten his hose. And then she blushed faintly, for the light still burned in the room, and Iaian looked up to find her staring. Even though she glanced away, her mind remained filled with the sight of hard, flat chest muscles and the dark hair she knew was crisp to her touch.

"What think you of the woman Elspeth?"

The question was unexpected, and Cecile turned back to face him, eyes wide. "I think," she said slowly, "theirs was a tumble turned serious."

"Aye." Iaian nodded grimly. "And I suspect another Gillecrist bastard is on its way into the world."

Cecile recalled the flash of pride in the woman's eyes, and the flare of resentment unwittingly revealed when Elspeth looked at Iaian. The woman's care for a babe she carried would make that understandable, at least to Cecile.

"Will he marry her, do you think?"

Iaian looked at her hard, trying to discern why she would ask. Why she would care. "And if he did? Would that distress you?"

"Distress me?" Cecile repeated in surprise. "Nay. Of course it would not."

She spoke hastily. Too hastily, Iaian thought, so that when he extinguished the candle and slid into bed beside her, he reached for her with more force than was his custom, pulling her hard against his body, as if she would resist.

For a moment Cecile almost protested, but then his insecurity wrapped itself around her heart, and she smiled into the darkness as she turned into his embrace. Her lips touched his throat to find a pulse strong and warm beneath his skin. She felt a shiver of anticipation when his hands tugged at the hem of her nightshift.

Determined to drive Tavis from her thoughts if he were, indeed, within them, Iaian wooed every inch of her flesh, caressing roughly then gently by turn, so that she did not know what to expect from one moment to the next. And he did it slowly. Inch by precious inch, he lifted the soft linen shift to expose, then touch, then kiss each curve, angle, and plane of her body.

Cecile had believed Iaian had long since forced her to leave all modesty outside of their marriage bed until his search bared her upper thighs and the dark curls between. But though she blushed, her heat was not from embarrassment as his mouth followed his hands upward. And though she moaned, her murmur was not a protest.

Cecile felt tears sting her eyes at the beauty of the gift he was giving, for mingled with the raw need he built in her was his desire to please. The fierce tenderness that washed over her with the breathtaking physical release came as much from him as from within her. When Iaian slid upward to catch the last of her quiverings with his body she had to bite her tongue to keep from giving him her love. And the tears overflowed and slipped down her cheeks.

Amalric and Donnchadh arrived together on a warm, misty evening, both in good humor. Amalric, because of the adventure ahead of him; Donnchadh, because he had come from Ciaran, and Rilla.

When Iaian and Cecile and Tavis stepped out into the bailey to greet them Amalric's first piercing look was for his sister. Satisfied with what he saw in her face and eyes, he turned to his brother-in-law with a smile. "Marriage sits well with Ceci, I can see. I hope you find it the same?"

"Well enough." Iaian's smile held a touch of wryness. "Although I find I must quarrel with your father's assurance that she is a biddable girl. That, or she's changed greatly in but a few scant weeks."

Amalric's grin broadened. "Nay, I'll warrant she's changed not at all, then." He ignored Cecile's exasperated glare as he put his arm around her and pulled her close.

Iaian asked Donnchadh if all were well at Daileass, and Amalric took that moment to whisper, for Cecile's ears only, "Are you content, lass?"

"Aye," she said simply, her eyes on her husband's darkly handsome face. "I am content."

Tavis, overhearing her soft reply and following her gaze to Iaian, stared at his half-brother with more bitterness than usual. Aye, Iaian had all Tavis had ever desired for himself. And he had Elspeth and her ill-conceived babe.

Only Donnchadh noticed anything amiss in Tavis's expression as the group turned to enter the house. He stared hard, but after a moment there seemed nothing wrong, after all. Tavis returned his look with a questioning smile, and Donnchadh greeted him affectionately. He'd known Tavis since he was a wee lad, and liked him well enough and knew him far better than he knew Iaian. But 'twas time Tavis accepted for once and all that Iaian was his father's heir. Donnchadh had believed he'd done so already, but something in Tavis's eyes made him wonder anew.

Dinner that evening proved pleasant enough. Iaian found himself quite comfortable with Cecile's brother. Amalric, though a sensible lad, had high spirits that found everything to be an adventure. The approaching journey to France gave him no qualms.

"Do you not regret a lengthy parting from your betrothed? I hear she's a lovely lass."

"Aye," Amalric answered Tavis's question with a smile. "Edina is a lovely girl—she is also but twelve years old. We do not visit much."

"Then 'tis a match arranged by your family?" Iaian asked curiously. "Are you content with it?"

"'Twas arranged with my blessing, though I was but ten when questioned concerning it. 'Twas a contract with an infant heiress or training for the priesthood." He grinned. "I'd no great ambition to garb myself like a crow."

"Amalric," Cecile scolded, looking up from her trencher of fowl, crisply roasted and dripping with juices, "'tis no way to speak of our holy fathers."

Amalric gave a shout of laughter. "A fine one you are to speak, who drove a priest from our very door."

Cecile blushed, sorry she'd spoken. "Nay, 'twas not I who bade him leave lest he not live the day."

"And what was I to do after he struck you?"

His attention arrested, Iaian paused with his wine goblet lifted to look at Amalric with narrowed eyes. "Struck Cecile? What priest is this?"

"He goes by the name of Father Aindreas," Amalric answered.

At almost the same moment that Amalric spoke, Cecile laid her hand upon Iaian's arm. "'Twas months ago and of no great moment." The heat of his quick rage flowed over her skin at her touch, and she almost gasped at its strength.

Amalric, seeing her start, looked more closely at Iaian and was pleased. This was clearly a man who felt protective of his wife and would let no other harm her.

But Donnchadh was watching Tavis, who had actually winced upon hearing the name of the priest. There was something afoot, Donnchadh decided, and it behooved him to discover what that was.

By the time Amalric completed relaying the tale of the fateful day that drove Father Aindreas from Ciaran, Tavis had himself in control. Perhaps he had not the stomach for intrigue that he had thought. He was sure his fingers would itch to squeeze the breath of life from the self-styled man of God should he approach Tavis with Dunmar's plans *now*. He'd not even care that it put the plot to place de Guise behind the throne at risk. Though Cecile would never be his, Tavis could not help the fierce instincts that rose in him at the thought of someone seeking to wound her, however slightly.

"Tell me of my family," Cecile begged in the first silence that fell into the conversation.

"You've not been gone that long," Amalric said in surprise. "And I've told you that all are hale, though Mother misses you greatly."

"But she is well?" Cecile persisted.

"She is better of late, I think. Stronger. Oh," Amalric added, almost as an afterthought, "we have had word of Raimund. He is safely wed, and their wedding journey will bring them to Ciaran for a brief stay." He grinned at his sister. "Perhaps Reynard will journey with them and pine to find you wed."

"And who is Reynard that he should care if you are wed?" The table grew quiet with the very weight of Iaian's cool displeasure.

"Reynard is Rilla's brother," Cecile answered evenly, "and a childhood friend, but otherwise of no consequence."

"But he would have had it otherwise?" Iaian asked, looking only at Cecile but very aware of Tavis. He wondered how many others had wished to marry this tiny slip of a girl.

Cecile smiled gently. "Though Reynard is of noble birth, he would aspire to be no more than a minstrel, and it behooves all minstrels to fall in love at every opportunity. 'Tis part of their calling to remain lovesick, I think."

Not wishing to look a jealous fool, Iaian nodded and turned the subject, but it did not leave his mind quite as easily as he dismissed it from his conversation. Would this Reynard return to Ciaran while Cecile waited close by at Daileass for her husband's return from France?

He found his mood did not lighten as the evening passed, and he was glad enough when it was time to seek his bed with Cecile. At least there he had no doubts of her. She had come to him an innocent, and he was sure she had no thoughts of another in her mind when she was in his arms. He did not believe her skilled enough in dissembling for that.

And though it bothered him faintly when Donnchadh drew Tavis aside as they left the dining room, he resolved to put it from his mind. If he did not trust Tavis he did trust his uncle. And though he harbored doubts of Tavis's loyalty, he was not unduly concerned. Tavis could do him little harm, after all, now that the crown had acknowledged his rights and the holdings had yielded to his authority.

With the others of the household finally abed, Donnchadh faced Tavis sternly. "I'd thought you long since accepting of Iaian's claiming of your father's properties. I fear, now, I was wrong."

They were in a small office with little more than a desk and two chairs of dubious comfort, but Donnchadh had brought a bottle of whiskey and two chased goblets. Watching the effect of his words on the younger man, he poured a goblet full and handed it to Tavis.

"I do not quarrel with his right to it." Tavis scowled at being taken to task as if he were a child. "And I do nothing to interfere." He took a long drink of the smooth liquid, more to hide his feelings than from thirst. Deep within him lay a nagging sense of guilt for what he knew of Dunmar's plans—and did not intend to reveal.

"Mayhap you do not, but I warrant you'd be filled with glee were aught to go amiss with Iaian." Still, Donnchadh could not be overly angry with Tavis. Indeed, he suspected he would feel much the same were he in Tavis's shoes.

"What would you have me do, then?" Tavis asked angrily. "Stand on a public corner and proclaim his right to all that I held dear for most of my life? Nay, you ask too much, that I should fawn over him and boast of his position."

"I do not ask that of you," Donnchadh said sharply, more than a little irritated. "I've not even hinted of that."

"Then what would you have of me?" Tavis's tone held a great weariness, even resignation.

"Perhaps gratitude for what he would do for you."

"Gratitude? Aye," Tavis said bitterly, "I suppose I should be grateful that I am given food for my belly and a roof over my head. He owes me nothing, after all, and 'tis better than a bastard should expect." He fair spat the word at Iaian's uncle.

Donnchadh fell silent. So, Iaian had not yet mentioned the seisin of Waytefeld to Tavis. Well, then, nor would he, for he did not know the reasons for Iaian's hesitation in broaching the subject.

Donnchadh emptied his goblet before he broke the silence that stood between them. "I think you wrong Iaian. He does not hold your lack of birthright against you. Indeed, I suspect that he would welcome the opportunity to look upon you as a brother in truth as well as in blood." He lifted a silencing hand at Tavis's snort of disbelief. "Remember you this, he has no family here beyond what we give him. Just as you have no family other than Iaian."

"I've Elspeth," Tavis said defiantly, though he'd not meant to speak of her to anyone—not just yet.

Donnchadh did not betray his surprise. "The housekeeper?" His tone was without inflection beyond a faintly questioning one.

"More than that to me. And it is for that reason, if nothing else, that I've cause to resent Iaian. What have I to leave my son?" The words came from the bitter depths of him.

"Ah-h-h," Donnchadh said softly on a breath, understanding at last why this renewed hostility. And then he sighed. "Have the Gillecrists not enough bastards to their credit, Tavis?"

"He'll not be a bastard." Tavis put into words what he had only hinted at with Elspeth. But saying them could not make their truth more palatable.

"You'd wed a servant?" Donnchadh was clearly disbelieving. Tavis had always held himself in higher regard than many a true-born noble.

Tavis shrugged. "Her blood's true enough, though her circumstances are lowered past anything her forebears might ever have imagined. She's a Leathann."

Donnchadh lifted one brow. "Aye, she's indeed reduced from what that proud name could once command." Though never a large clan, the name had once held as much power as that of Donnchadh or Gillecrist. And far more wealth. Greed had been their downfall. Greed, and poor judgment. From one feud to the next, they'd shed their blood and their gold on wasted effort.

"So you will wed the girl. And what then?"

Tavis stared at him, not seeing the direction of his questions. "What then?" he repeated.

"Aye." Donnchadh almost smiled. "Will you continue to spit in Iaian's face and make your own way in the world? Or will you take the hand he offers in friendship and turn it into a kinship between brothers? As you said, he owes you nothing."

"I will think on your words" was all that Tavis would promise.

With that, Donnchadh had to be content. "Well, if you will wed the girl, I will dower her. Two generations back, a Donnchadh married a Leathann, so I suppose I could claim some kinship on that." And with a dowry, Donnchadh reassured himself, and the seisin of Waytefeld, Tavis should do well enough to put aside his bitterness toward Iaian.

"Elspeth will be honored," Tavis said slowly, feeling some of the weight leave his shoulders for the first time since learning of the babe. If

Donnchadh would make some claim to her, then Tavis would not be marrying too far beneath what he might have expected had Alasdair Gillecrist himself had the arrangement of it.

"I'd ask one more thing of you," Donnchadh said. "An honest answer to a question."

Tavis waited in silence.

"What is there in mention of a priest to dismay you so?"

Tavis cursed silently that he had given anything away upon hearing Father Aindreas's name. "Nothing in itself," he lied, unable to give Donnchadh the honesty he wished. "Everything in learning that any man should strike someone I have ever cared for. You have long known my feelings for Cecile Lotharing. I would have wed her had her father not been averse to a bastard."

Donnchadh did not bother to correct his supposition. Tavis would never believe it was not his lack of legitimacy that had caused Saelec Lotharing to deny his suit. And though he was not sure he believed Tavis's explanation, he had nothing with which to refute it. Best to leave it alone, though he determined to be as watchful as events allowed. He was still uneasy over Iaian's call to journey to France and could only pray it had nothing to do with Tavis.

When the two parted company Tavis felt the weight of Donnchadh's gaze follow him into his chamber. And he knew that Donnchadh still felt some concern for his loyalties. He did not worry that Donnchadh would set someone to guard him, but he suspected if he were going to speak privately with Dunmar, the time should be now.

So it was that within half an hour, Elspeth closed the front door behind him, her pale face wearing a faint, worried frown. He knew she would wait there, downstairs, for his safe return. The thought warmed him. He'd been but a lad the last time anyone had a care for his well-being.

He found Dunmar still awake and not overly surprised to see him. As he was ushered into a drawing room, he was struck anew that everywhere he was accorded more respect than what Iaian seemed to grant him. The servant saw to his comfort, assuring him that Lord Dunmar would be with him shortly.

True enough, Dunmar entered the room but moments later. He glanced at Tavis before flicking his fingers at the servant bearing a tray of wine and sweets, indicating that he should place it on a side table and depart.

Then Dunmar turned his attention more fully to Tavis. "I had not looked to see you again so soon, sir. Have you rethought your decision to assist?"

"As I told Father Aindreas"—the name was sour in his mouth when he thought of the cold bastard striking Cecile—"I would do your bidding against any except those named."

"But you stand loyal to your father's son?" Dunmar chose his words carefully, seeking to do the most damage—and, thus, the most good.

"I will do nothing against Iaian Gillecrist nor

Saelec Lotharing," Tavis returned grimly.

"Then why are you here?" The question was almost idly asked, though Dunmar's fingers tightened around the wine carafe at Tavis's continued stubbornness.

Tavis accepted the glass of wine, though he did not intend to do more than play at drinking it. He'd had too much whiskey earlier with Donnchadh and he needed to keep his wits about him now. "I would know if you are behind Iaian's dispatch to travel with the queen to France."

"And if I am?"

"Are you?" Tavis asked again between gritted teeth.

So fierce was his expression, Dunmar felt a tiny shiver of something very akin to fear. "Aye. So then, what will you now?"

"Perhaps nothing," Tavis admitted. "But what will it gain you?" He'd not let Dunmar kill Iaian. There was much he'd look the other way and let happen, but not that.

His lack of reaction bolstered Dunmar's confidence. Perhaps Tavis was merely curious, and perhaps that could be turned to advantage.

"And if I tell you?" Dunmar lifted his brows, querying. "Ah, you'd have me trust you, yet you give me no trust in return."

"I've given you no cause to distrust me," Tavis said brusquely. "We still seek the same goal, though perhaps choose different methods to accomplish it. I'd have Marie de Guise rule Scotland as surely as you."

"Very well, then." Dunmar appeared to take his words as offered. "Gillecrist will never actually embark for France. Once he's seen more than any Englishman should of our defenses and the proposed sailing route, he'll return to England."

"He'll never do so," Tavis said flatly.

"Ah, but I assure you, he will." Dunmar met his gaze with a satisfied smile.

Tavis felt a chill run down his spine. This would not be a man to cross. "How will you accomplish it?"

"No matter. It is enough that I can. Now tell me, Tavis Gillecrist, will you betray my plans?"

Almost against his will, Tavis shook his head. God help him, he could not help but pray that Dunmar could, indeed, induce Iaian to return to England. 'Twas where Iaian's loyalties must still lie, after all. And as long as Dunmar did not plan murder, Tavis would not intervene. What would it truly matter to Iaian that he would never be welcome in Scotland again? Indeed, he would not even be safe if it were thought he carried Scotland's secrets back to England's lord protector.

Dunmar smiled at his silent answer, noting with satisfaction the look of guilt on Tavis's face. Aye, by holding his tongue, Tavis would be as implicated as if he'd had part in the deed. He would let the plans go forward, and once the deed was done he would be far too involved to betray what had been done.

Chapter Twenty

Anne's dark eyes flashed angrily. "The man is a fool!" Yet beneath her fury lay fear. Many a sensible man had died at the hands of a foolish one. She could not believe the vile tidings this young man had brought to her. Moments before she had lightheartedly prepared for her husband's return. Now, she must wonder if he would ever return to her safely. And if he did not?

"My lady, I pray you do not be overset." The young noble found himself caught between his admiration for her mature beauty and the need to speak carefully those things he had rehearsed so well. He had arrived midmorning at the Lindael manor house, stating the urgency of his mission so that he was shown immediately into Lady Lindael's presence. It had not taken her long to read the missive and erupt into fury.

"I am not," Anne answered his pleading more calmly, knowing she lied. She *was* overset. More, she was outraged—and terrified. "I must think," she said a bit desperately, as much to herself as to her visitor. "I must think."

This was the opening he needed. "My lady, all know these charges are lies. But for the King's own good, my lord Somerset must set forth an investigation."

Anne grasped at his opening words. "You believe my husband innocent?"

He affected a look of shock. "Indeed, my lady. And so does any man who loves justice. But I understand, too, Somerset's position. Until that innocence is proved, he cannot release your husband."

Perhaps this bearer of bad tidings could be of some assistance to her. "What is your name, sir? I confess I cannot recall anything beyond the vicious lies written upon this parchment." She held it from her as if it were a venomous reptile.

"Creighton, my lady. Rufus Creighton."

"Sir Rufus," she began.

He lifted a hand deprecatingly. "Nay, my lady. A mere squire, but a true friend, if you will but allow it."

"Then, friend Rufus, perhaps between us we can find a way to provide that proof of my Geoffrey's innocence."

Almost, the coin that awaited him at task's end was not worth the pain in the lady's luminous eyes. Almost. He heard the clink of gold as he answered, "Indeed, my lady. I dare say we can."

And he allowed the finding of it to take an entire evening, as he supped with the lady and drank of her wine, all the while tossing suggestions and countering hers. Still, by evening's end, he had not brought her to the line of reasoning he wished. So if it would not be her own thought, it must be his.

"Who could have planted these lies?" Anne beseeched for the dozenth time.

And for the dozenth time, Rufus answered quite calmly. "Lady, I know not. I but serve his grace Somerset and begged leave to bring this written levy of charges to your attention. I would not have Sir Geoffrey's lady hear such grievous tidings from other than a sympathetic tongue."

"And I thank you for it, Rufus. Indeed, I do, but my mind wearies of trying to find a way around these vile accusations. If I but knew what had occasioned such lies, perhaps the answer could be found therein."

"As to that, my lady, evil needs no occasion. But, at risk of wounding you further, 'tis Sir Geoffrey's very love for you that has given his enemies this opportunity."

Anne paled. "His love for me? Nay."

Rufus looked at her gravely. "Look once more at the charges brought forward to Somerset's attentions." He watched her bowed head as she poured over the elaborately scripted words on the parchment. The eyes she lifted to his were still perplexed.

"*Loyalty to adverse blood,*" he paraphrased softly. "All know Sir Geoffrey is loyal first to his love for you. Many a court lady can attest to that. And you are Scots. *Ties to a land hostile to Edward's rule.* Edward would rule Scotland. Your son—Sir Geoffrey's acclaimed son—is of the nobility there. What secrets might he carry to Arran for Sir Geoffrey?"

Anne was more than pale now—she was bloodless. "None. Before God, I swear to it."

"Swear not to me, my lady. There is no need. And 'twould be of little use to make such a vow to Somerset. 'Tis proof he needs."

"But what proof can I give to refute mere vapor? There is no substance to these charges. No one can prove them," she ended desperately, "for they are all lies!"

"And so it will be shown . . . but when?" Rufus shook his head sadly. "Sir Geoffrey could languish in the Tower for months before Somerset is satisfied."

"But he is well treated. Did you not say so?"

"Aye. For now. But even if he remains comfortably housed, his fear for you tears at his heart. Sir Geoffrey visits Edward's court when he must, but never because he wishes. Aye, he suffers merely being withheld from your love."

"My love is with him always," Anne responded disconsolately.

"And he knows this," Rufus reassured her. "But he cannot help but know, as well, that it is his very love for you that has placed him in such a tangled position."

"But what can I do?"

She lifted tear-filled eyes to Rufus, who smiled kindly. "Why, my lady, I should think but one thing could accomplish Somerset's ease of mind." He paused. "Have your son return to England to plead your husband's case. Only he can avow your husband's lack of duplicity, only he can explain turning his back on England to take his place among Scotland's nobles."

Staring at the young man seeking so earnestly to help her, Anne's heart sank. Iaian had forgiven neither her nor Geoffrey. She feared he would not return to help them now.

Chapter Twenty-one

The night before Iaian and Amalric departed for Dumbarton, Cecile's dreams once more were laced with urgency. Yet, as before, the details eluded her upon awakening. She knew only that she had again dreamed of Iaian. She lay in the faint gray of dawn, staring wide-eyed at nothing, trying to recall even bits of insubstantial images. She could not. Only the aura of the dream remained within her mind's grasp.

Beside her, Iaian stirred and pulled her close, seemingly aware through the depths of sleep that her thoughts were of him. Cecile smiled at the strong, hard feel of his arms cradling her gently. She would not weep if he never spoke love sonnets to her, for she did not believe any courtly passion could be better than what they had come to share. He was as protective of her well-being and comfort as he was his own. And that his thoughts were often on her she knew by the way his gaze was so often upon her, whether they were alone in their chamber or belowstairs with the others.

And a part of all that, neither more nor less important, was the fire that blazed between them. Even as the thought formed in her mind, Iaian's hand stroked lazily up her ribs to cup the heaviness of her breast. Unsure if he were awake or seeking her in his sleep, she caught her breath against the gasp that rose to her throat at his touch. The nipple, yet untouched above his palm, hardened in response to the shiver that coursed through her. But it was a shiver of need, not of chill, and it was all she could do not to turn demandingly toward the source of that need.

"You do not sleep." His voice came quietly into her thoughts.

"Nay. I think of your leaving," she said not dishonestly. The thought of it had not been far from her mind since the messenger had brought the news.

"My uncle will see you safely to Daileass." By his tone, it was meant to be a reassurance.

"I am not afraid."

"Perhaps you are relieved and look forward to being apart from me?" His hand moved slightly against her breast.

Cecile chuckled. "You are a demon, Iaian. Do not dare to tease me." As his hand moved again, she twisted so that her breast was full in his palm.

Their few weeks of marriage had taught her well. She slipped one slender knee between his own and smiled when he groaned and pulled her hard against him.

While her hands explored the corded muscles of his arms and shoulders, she gave herself up to the deliberate pleasure of his touch and the not-so-deliberate pleasure of his feelings. Cecile knew she was winning. She did not know what ghosts she fought, but she was winning, because he no longer thought of those ghosts when he touched her. And he no longer held his emotions in cold check when his body lost control. Cecile had come to dread that moment when his thoughts pulled away from her, for she believed he feared to call another's name in the heights of his passion. But the moment had come less and less, until it came not at all.

And though she could not help but wonder, still, who that other was, she knew contentment that she alone held his thoughts now. Just as she alone held his body. It was her lips gasping of need and delight against his. Her lips he claimed when his seed spilled deep into her. And when his son was conceived, it would be her womb that bore his heir. Aye, she would win—for once and for all.

Less than a half hour before he and Amalric planned to leave, Iaian faced his half-brother across the narrow table and frowned slightly. "I do not know how long I'll be gone from Scotland. It may be weeks or even months, and I'd not have all I've accomplished go undone in that space of time. I look to you to hold my properties secure."

Tavis lifted one brow and smiled grimly. "Art a fool, brother? Better you should turn to Donnchadh. Who but I would seek to take them from you?"

"You would not. You've too much honor. Aye, my uncle would do as well by me, but you're a Gillecrist. Besides," Iaian smiled faintly, "I do not think you are greedy. Waytefeld should be enough for you."

"You throw me a stewardship as a sop. I've not said I'll take it."

Iaian stared at him bewildered. "Steward? Nay, Tavis, that was not my intent."

Tavis was silent for long moments, searching Iaian's eyes for a jest as he tried to recall Iaian's exact words when he'd casually told Tavis that Waytefeld was to be his. "You'd give Waytefeld to me? Unencumbered?" He did not believe it.

"Unencumbered," Iaian agreed, "save for one legal binding. It is not to leave this family. Should you die without issue, it reverts to me and mine. Otherwise, it passes to your heirs with whatever binders you place upon it for them."

Cold guilt, like a stone, settled in Tavis's stomach. "When did you think to do this?"

"What does that matter?" And then, because Tavis did not answer, he shrugged. "I do not know when the thought first came to me. I decided upon Waytefeld when I saw how rich a property it was. But it comes with a burden—you must keep Hagaleah safe for me. You'll be the closer."

"You could have given me Hagaleah," Tavis said slowly.

Iaian looked at him in amazement, then laughed. "You may have the lesser of the two, if you wish. I'll not quarrel with that."

In spite of himself, Tavis smiled. "Nay. I do not refuse Waytefeld. 'Tis just that I did not expect this."

"Well, as to that, I did not expect anything that has happened to me these past months. And chose none of it. Not my name nor this land nor even my inheritance." *Nor you for brother.* The thought hung unspoken between them.

"Your wife, at least, you chose." Tavis still could not quell a faint regret for the loss of Cecile.

"Aye," Iaian said slowly, "my wife I chose."

And he no longer regretted the choice, Iaian decided, taking his leave of her moments later in the courtyard. Tavis, Amalric, and Donnchadh discreetly engaged in their own conversation as Iaian took Cecile's hand in his in a rare open gesture of affection. "My uncle will see to your welfare. And my brother."

Cecile smiled. "'Tis good to hear you call Tavis brother."

Iaian sighed. "Did you not hear anything beyond that, Ceci?"

"Aye, you seek to reassure me, but, Iaian, I need none. I am not afraid," she echoed her earlier assurance. Her smile turned impish. "And I like for you to call me Ceci."

"Minx might be more appropriate," he murmured, "or temptress." The sunlight sparkled against the blue of her eyes until he thought he had never seen anything so brilliant as their color. Even her gown of shimmering satin could not compete. His gaze was drawn to the square neckline, and he ached to touch the tempting swell of flesh above it. He touched her cheek instead, then sighed. "I'd bid you be obedient to those who would have a care for you, but I hesitate to give you more requests to ignore."

She laughed, half-dismayed that he read her so well. "Iaian, I would not! At least," she amended, "I will try not."

"I do not know if I'll be gone weeks or months," he told her, much as he'd told Tavis earlier. "But I'll be less fearful for your safety if you would promise to heed Donnchadh's wishes in all things."

"I will heed him," Cecile answered gravely, lifting her lips for his parting kiss and thinking that heed didn't mean *quite* the same thing as obey, after all.

And then she watched Iaian ride away from her at Amalric's side, and the sight caused her to feel more forlorn than she had thought she would.

Donnchadh moved to her side, noting the slight droop of her lips. He'd gotten used to their sunny tilt and found he did not like this look of sadness upon her. "'Tis an honor for Iaian, this call to travel with the queen."

"You do not think so," she challenged. "Nor does Iaian."

He looked at her in surprise. "Iaian told you this?"

"Nay. He would not worry me. But he cannot keep his feelings from me, though he tries."

"Nor can I, it appears," Donnchadh murmured, placing his hand beneath her elbow to escort her back inside.

"Not when those worries are of Iaian," she said quietly. "What is it you fear?"

Donnchadh sighed. "As to that, I do not even know, save I think 'twas too hastily decided and with too little reason given. Indeed, for most 'tis a signal honor to be selected, one vied for amongst courtiers." He shook his head. "But I take Iaian's selection amiss. Something of it does not sit well with me."

And, Tavis, falling into step beside them, felt the guilt grow larger in his belly until he thought it would rise up and choke him.

"Nay," Elspeth said fiercely. "You can do nothing. If you intercede for Iaian Gillecrist 'twill be your downfall." She paced to the far end of Tavis's chamber before turning to look at him.

Tavis rubbed his forehead wearily, not meeting her eyes. It had proved a long evening. He'd argued more with himself than with Elspeth, using her to test his thoughts aloud. But what she said was truth. Dunmar was too ruthless, too determined on Iaian's downfall to be swayed. Tavis could not go to Donnchadh without revealing his part in Dunmar's plot, and he could not go to Arran without hurting Marie de Guise's efforts to take the regency. "I *cannot* do nothing," he spat at her, equally fierce. "He is my brother."

"Half-brother," Elspeth reminded, feeling as if she fought for her very soul. She did, indeed, fight for her child and her own future. If Tavis placed himself in danger, he destroyed all her hopes. "Far less to you than the child I carry, Tavis. Do not lose all, I beg you."

"You'd have me stand and watch him destroyed." Tavis eyed her almost distastefully.

The look hurt. "I'd not have you seek to harm him, Tavis. I know he has tried to do well by you, after all. But can any effort of yours truly aid him? If Dunmar succeeds, you will have gained only that which should never have been taken from you. And if he fails, no fault can be held against you. You are no part of any of this—you've told Dunmar so. Your name is not linked to anything that happens."

"Dunmar is the master of lies. If he fails, he will still do whatever damage he can. How best could he deal one final blow to Iaian than to tell him that his own brother knew of the plot and did nothing to stop it?" Tavis did not think he could bear to see the disappointment in Iaian's eyes. When had Iaian's opinion of him come to mean so much?

He did not even notice when Elspeth left the room, and the realization made her even more bitter. Now, when she knew he would wed her, she should have been happiest. But he would throw it all away. She knew he would. Lost in her own thoughts, she did not see the Lady Gillecrist until they brushed together.

Elspeth heard Cecile's gasp at the contact before she drew away, saw the dismay in the girl's eyes. And Elspeth felt a chill. It was almost as if the other knew her thoughts, but that, of course, was not possible.

"Is aught amiss?" Cecile asked, hesitant against the flare of animosity and jealousy emanating from the housekeeper. Did the woman know Tavis had once sought to wed her? Did she think he still cared for her? Cecile did not know how to reassure her if it were so.

"Nay, my lady," Elspeth said flatly, "nothing is amiss." She turned back the way she had come, not even asking if she could fetch what the lady sought. Even in a plain nightshift, Cecile Gillecrist looked her part, noble and assured. Elspeth knew she could never match that regal bearing, not even if Tavis wed her and ended with all the Gillecrist properties. Nay, she would never be such a lady.

The feelings of envy and despair drifted away with the housekeeper's departure, and Cecile sighed. She had wed into a very troubled household, indeed, if Tavis thought to take this woman to wife. But 'twas his affair, and not hers. Her concern was for Iaian, and the empty bed that would not give her sleep.

Seeking exhaustion, she walked every corridor of the large house, wishing for the cold winds to be found along the battlements of Ciaran or Daileass. Elegant though the townhouse was, she found she did not care for living in Edinburgh. 'Twas too close and too dirt-ridden within the city walls. There grew a longing within her for the clean, open air of the country, and she made up her mind to have Donnchadh take her away from the city at once. They would travel as hard as he would allow her to push herself, and perhaps she would be tired enough each night to find her sleep alone. Strange that she should have slept without Iaian's arms around her for sixteen years and now, after only weeks, she could not.

Preferring to rely on speed rather than numbers for their safety, Iaian and Amalric traveled with no more than the dozen armed men who had escorted Amalric to Edinburgh. The countryside they traveled, though with its share of brigands, was fairly civilized. And the brigands had pickings enough amongst unwary travelers that these, who were so obviously warriors, were given wide birth.

Iaian found Amalric a good traveling companion, neither overly talkative nor morose, but his snoring presence in the night did nothing to ease Iaian's longing for Cecile's small body pressed to his. He found it irksome to miss her. He'd not intended her to become in any wise important to his peace of mind. Yet she had. Thus Iaian found he slept poorly, listening to the soft night sounds long after the others were lost to their dreams.

He found himself glad enough to reach the seafaring town of Dumbarton Rock at the mouth of the River Clyde. The port bustled with the importance of its mission, to keep the small girl upon which all of Scotland's future rested safe until her departure for France. And the French, themselves, overran the place. Everywhere Iaian and Amalric turned there were Frenchmen and other foreigners.

The inns were full of them, so that it was not easy to find a room, and impossible to find a private one. As they placed their belongings in the mean room they would share, Amalric glanced at Iaian ruefully. "'Tis not Ciaran nor Daileass."

"Nay," Iaian agreed, "but it will provide a roof over our heads and a floor beneath our feet"—he grinned and looked around him—"though not much more, I confess."

Amalric snorted. "And for a very dear price."

Iaian could not argue and almost suggested they sleep in the stables with their men. 'Twas only because he had little liking for vermin and had found none in the sheets upon the bed that he did not.

"'Tis early yet to dine," Amalric said, "and there's nothing here to delay us. I'd suggest we look for this Captain Archard on whose ship we are to sail."

Iaian agreed, and they left the inn after asking directions of its keeper. It seemed d'Esse, who headed the French fleet, had established a central quarters in a building near the water. From there his captains commanded the 6000 men who had descended upon the small port. Those men included German and Italian mercenaries as well as the French seamen. No chance would be taken with the security of the queen, who waited in well-guarded comfort on dry land for the weather to settle enough for a safe journey to France. At these central quarters, they discovered that Captain Archard had been rowed out to his ship but a hour earlier. It was a daily practice with him, and he would return before nightfall.

Iaian frowned at the young officer who had answered their question. "Has any date been set for the fleet to depart?"

"Who can foretell this miserable Scots weather?" The young Frenchman immediately blushed. D'Esse would have his tongue if he did not cease to insult these hot-headed Scots nobles. "My pardon, my lord, 'tis that I am unused to such storms as we have seen these past weeks."

To his relief, the grim young lord smiled as he answered, "I, too, find the weather here frequently extreme. What would you suggest we do until the seas calm?"

"What every other man here has done these past few weeks—eat, drink, and whore," the officer answered with a half-disgusted, slightly rueful grin. "God knows there is little else *to* do."

Iaian laughed out loud at Amalric's expression of delight. At least one of them would not be miserable during the enforced idleness.

They stepped back out into the salty air, and Iaian heard the dash of waves against the rock on which the town stood. If current conditions were any indication, their wait could be long indeed. It was July now, and the French fleet had been landed since June. The thought of the wasted time chafed.

Neither Iaian nor Amalric noticed the man who fell into step some distance behind them, neither falling behind nor closing the gap between himself and the two he followed. At Amalric's suggestion they turned into a small public house from which wafted some fairly palatable aromas.

The Englishman growled at the delay as he posted himself some slight distance away. He, too, would prefer to eat and drink, but he was wise enough to keep his distance from any establishment. He'd passed for Scots on more than one occasion, but never by pressing his luck. Nay, he would seek Iaian Gillecrist when he was alone, give his message, and depart. His hunger and thirst would wait until he could be safely away from this swarming den of foreigners.

The food was better than decent, and Iaian felt slightly less unhappy about their situation when they returned to meet Captain Archard. To his relief, the captain turned out to be no pretty officer but a true seafarer. The good captain could not, however, give any better news than that all waited, now, upon the weather. He met Iaian's scowl with a calm, gray gaze. "It pleases no one, but what choice have we?" he asked with a shrug.

"None," Iaian admitted, forcing himself to smile. It was not this man's fault, after all, that the pattern of his life had been totally disrupted after he had just begun to piece it back together.

"Would you care to quarter aboard ship? 'Twill be as comfortable there as here, and perhaps less crowded." To the captain's disgust, he had more than a little difficulty in keeping sufficient men on board for the safety of the ship.

Amalric shook his head emphatically. "We are not sailors by choice, Captain, and may not prove good ones. I think it best we keep our feet planted on solid ground as long as possible."

The Frenchman shrugged. "If you change your mind, you've only to say. Arrangements will be made. Until such time as we are called upon to sail, my lords, your time is your own. If you have need of me, however, I will be at your immediate disposal."

At Amalric's request, Captain Archard explained the defenses of the fleet, which impressed Iaian, and the route they expected to take to France, which did not. "'Twould have been a far easier voyage for the child had you landed at Edinburgh, or mayhap St. Andrews."

"True," Captain Archard agreed, "but English eyes will be upon the east coast. 'Twas agreed the longer voyage would be the safer for your queen, if not the easier."

Iaian suspected Somerset was wise enough to have spies at every likely port, east as well as west, but he did not say so. He simply nodded as the captain rolled up the maps upon which he had been outlining their route. The sea path chosen would take them past the Isle of Man, Wales, and the point of Cornwall, and thus to the English Channel and on to the coast of France.

Dark had fallen when they left the captain's cramped quarters to return to their own. Iaian would not have been surprised if Amalric had expressed a desire to change clothing and return to the streets of the harbor town, but he did not. He simply purchased a bottle of wine, laughingly lifting it for Iaian's inspection as they climbed the stairs to their room. "French wine. I doubt if you could purchase anything else in Dumbarton, now."

"At least it's good wine," Iaian remarked upon reaching their room. "Do we now drink ourselves to sleep?" It did not seem such a bad idea in view of the previous sleepless one.

"Aye, and perhaps you will cease your tossing," Amalric retorted, proving Iaian's restlessness had not gone unnoticed.

Before Iaian could answer a sharp rap sounded upon the rough oak door. Suddenly cautious, Iaian gestured for Amalric to stand away, ready, while he opened the door. "Aye?"

"I've a message for Iaian Lindael." The man spoke softly, obviously not desirous of drawing the attention of other than the room's occupants.

Iaian stiffened at hearing the name Lindael. "What mischief is this?"

"None, my lord. I've a message for the man who was known as Iaian Lindael."

"I am Iaian Gillecrist." He opened the door more fully, permitting the messenger entrance. Amalric's curious gaze bored into his back as he closed the door behind the man. "Where is the message?"

"I am not so foolish as to carry anything in writing, my lord." There burned a faint tone of contempt in the words.

"Who sends you?"

"Lady Anne."

Shock reverberated through Iaian's bones. "And the message?" He kept his tone carefully neutral.

The messenger glanced suspiciously at Amalric. "I'd speak to you alone."

Though Amalric stepped forward, Iaian stopped him with a lifted hand. "He stays. The message can be delivered in front of him."

The messenger scowled, but did not argue the point. "Lady Anne has need of you, my lord. Sir Geoffrey has been placed in the Tower of London on charges of treason."

"Impossible!" Iaian said sharply.

"Nay, my lord, 'tis not impossible. 'Tis true."

"Who brings these charges?"

The Englishman shrugged. "I know no more than I've been bid to tell you. Sir Geoffrey has been arrested, and Lady Anne asks for your aid." His face remained expressionless. "If you would know more, return to England."

"Iaian?" Amalric stepped forward, concerned at the consequences, both of the message and of Arran's reaction were Iaian to simply ride away from his appointment.

Iaian shook his head, still trying to absorb the possibility that the man who had kept Iaian secure through childhood should now be in danger of losing his very life. Treason carried but one penalty, though in several cruel guises. There were many ways to take a man's life. Iaian's mind held an image of Sir Geoffrey as he had seen him last, his eyes almost pleading, his expression burdened with sadness. And Iaian had hardened his heart and turned away from the two people who had loved him unconditionally through all the years of his life.

The messenger broke into his reflections. "I'll be gone within the hour, my lord. Have you a message for me to carry to Lady Anne?"

Iaian looked at him almost unseeingly. "Nay," he said hoarsely. "Nay. I'll carry it myself."

And the messenger turned to go lest the two men see the satisfaction in his eyes.

"'Tis folly," Amalric warned, even as his sister's husband began to gather his belongings.

Iaian looked at him bleakly. "Aye. But I've no choice. He was as a father to me."

And Amalric, who would have shed every drop of his life's blood for his own father, said no more.

Chapter Twenty-two

Iaian returned to Edinburgh far more hastily than he had departed from there. Though a part of him chafed at the delay in reaching England, he could not go without a word to Cecile. He did not examine with any great care the feelings that drove him, neither those for his wife nor those he felt for the man who had reared him. His speed did not allow much time for retrospection, which he thought was perhaps just as well.

But he could not deny a piercing disappointment when Tavis greeted him with the news that Donnchadh had taken Cecile south to Daileass. Still covered with the dust of his travels, he had been shown into the library just after midday. From the ledgers spread about, and the crudely drawn map of Waytefeld, it appeared obvious that

Tavis had begun to plan his finances for a future there.

"Iaian!" Tavis regarded him in thunderstruck amazement as he was announced. Half-rising, he pushed aside the clutter of papers and gestured for Iaian to sit.

"Where is Cecile?" Iaian cared nothing for making explanations at this point. He wished only to see his wife.

"Halfway to Daileass, I should think."

"Damnation." It was a halfhearted curse, more weary than anything else. Iaian sank into the chair across from Tavis.

Tavis eyed Iaian's slumped shoulders with interest. He'd not thought the match between his half-brother and Cecile Lotharing one of affection. Yet, he could not deny that she'd moped after Iaian's departure, and now he had Iaian's reaction to finding her gone on his precipitous return. And why *had* he returned?

When he voiced the question, Iaian closed the door of the library before sinking to a chair opposite Tavis. "I must return to England. At once." And a sense of urgency warned him he could not delay further, not even to follow Cecile to Daileass.

"England? But why?" Tavis regarded him with dread. How had Dunmar accomplished the task, and so soon?

"My father—" Iaian broke off at Tavis's expression and started again—"the man who raised me as such is in peril. My mother begs aid of me."

Seeing the tired lines in his half-brother's face, the gray look of anxiety, Tavis knew he could not hold his peace even if he damned himself with his own words. As doubtless he would. "'Tis a trick," he said slowly. "'Tis Dunmar's treachery."

Iaian's brows drew together. "Continue." He spoke evenly, and not yet with the anger he suspected would come. He did not question that Tavis knew something of this. His uncle had tried to warn him of Tavis's bent for intrigue even as he urged him to treat Tavis as the brother he might have been.

"There is a plot afoot to place Marie de Guise at the head of Scotland until Mary is of an age to rule with her consort. Dunmar is heavily involved."

"And you?" Iaian probed.

"I . . . have knowledge of it. I have not acted upon any of it, though I was approached."

"And what has this to do with me? And England?"

"'Twas felt—Dunmar felt Arran could be defeated by reducing the circumstances of those loyal to him."

"Of which I am perceived to be one."

Tavis flinched at the ominous tone of Iaian's voice. "I think it suited Dunmar for you to be considered so. I suspect he has other purposes than the prospering of de Guise."

"I suspect so," Iaian agreed. "And you were approached with this plan?"

"Aye," Tavis admitted in a low voice, adding, "I refused."

"Thank you for that—if not for the lack of warning." Iaian made no effort to keep the bitterness from his words.

Nor did Tavis try to excuse himself. There was, after all, no excuse to be made. "What will you do now?"

"Whatever Dunmar has set in motion I cannot let him bring harm to Sir Geoffrey."

"You cannot go to England!" Tavis struck his fist against the table in frustration. "Dunmar will somehow use that against you." God help him, he wished he knew more of what Dunmar had wrought. There had to be a way to thwart Dunmar without hurting de Guise.

"I have no choice." Iaian smiled at Tavis's frustrated expression almost ruefully. "Console yourself, brother. Waytefeld is yours, and if I do not return, the rest will be also."

"Damn you," Tavis said angrily. "I do not want it."

Iaian gave a shout of laughter despite the gravity of the situation. "Then more fool you, but," his voice softened, "thank you for that also." He got to his feet and circled the table to place a hand on Tavis's shoulder. "I'd have one thing of you."

"Anything." Tavis could not meet his eyes until Iaian's silence forced him to look up.

"Send word to Cecile. I'd have her know that I will return as soon as is possible."

Tavis nodded. "What shall I tell her draws you back to England?"

"Tell her . . . tell her simply that my mother has need of me." He smiled. Never was a girl more tender-hearted than his Ceci. "'Twill be reason enough for her, I think."

Tavis gained his feet and stood facing Iaian awkwardly. "Should you have need of me . . ."

"I'll send word at once." Iaian found it comforting that with all the family he had lost, he had gained some, as well.

With a deep sense of relief, Tavis accepted the hand Iaian offered to him. And he vowed to do more than the one thing Iaian had asked of him. Aye, he'd send word to Cecile, but he would find a way to declaw Dunmar as well. Even if it cost Marie de Guise all hope of the regency. Nothing would come before family.

As Iaian's boots echoed against the polished floor, Elspeth pulled away from her tautly held position at the door to the library. She had not heard all, but she had heard enough. Her skirts were only a whisper of sound in the corridor as she whisked out of sight. Behind her, she could hear Tavis's voice as he bade Iaian Godspeed. She could not hear Iaian's reply, but it was more because of her turmoil of thoughts than the distance she had placed between herself and the two men.

She was not sure of any course of action, but she knew instinctively there must be nothing in writing to indicate that Iaian had plans of returning to Scotland. Somehow, she would convince

Tavis of what must be. Somehow. But she knew it would not be easily or quickly done. For now she must act alone.

Because of her acknowledged place at Tavis's side, his secretary merely felt grateful when she offered to arrange for the delivery of Tavis's message to his brother's wife. The young man handed her the sealed scroll without demur, never doubting that it would be as carefully tended to by her as it would have been by him. And when Tavis questioned him later, he assured his employer in good faith that the missive was well on its way south.

Elspeth's heart raced guiltily as she held the parchment to a candle flame. But she was only doing what she must for her child's sake. And for Tavis's too, did he but realize it.

Amalric remained in Dumbarton but one day longer than Iaian. He spent that day in wrestling with his conscience on conflicts of duty and family loyalty. In the end, family loyalty won. Saelec had taught his sons one precept from birth: the ties of blood came first, followed by bonds of friendship. Only then did a man consider the needs of whatever powers were currently governing their adopted country.

In walking the narrow lanes of Dumbarton, Amalric could not help but realize that his presence would do little more to safeguard the queen than could be accomplished by 6000 French-paid guardians. There might be much, however, he could do in aid of his sister's husband.

Thus it was that one day later Tavis faced Amalric with much the same surprise he'd felt upon seeing Iaian.

"I feared he would have need of me," Amalric said simply, by way of explanation.

"And I fear he has need of more than either you or I can accomplish." And, because he had been unsuccessful in concocting a plan to defeat Dunmar, Tavis told him everything.

Amalric was livid. "The puling bastard! Where is he now?"

"Dunmar?" Tavis shrugged. "I only know he is not in Edinburgh. Or if he is, he is in hiding from me." But Tavis did not believe Dunmar had any fear of him. He did not think the man would hide from anyone.

Nor did Amalric. "In Stirling, then, with Arran?"

"Perhaps. I've not been able to learn even that much."

Amalric gave him an almost wolfish smile. "Then I suggest we travel to Stirling. If we cannot rout Dunmar, we will see what damage we can do to his standing with Arran. Perhaps 'twill be Dunmar who is brought low, rather than Iaian."

Tavis felt a surge of relief. Here was activity at last, and if not well thought, at least sincere. "Aye. We'll go to Stirling within the hour."

And he held fast to his determination through Elspeth's pleading, which turned to cursing when he would not be swayed.

"What of our babe?"

"He will have a father of whom he need not be ashamed." Tavis turned from his hasty preparations to place both hands on her shoulders. "I cannot live with myself if I let Dunmar succeed in this."

"You are no match for him," Elspeth said bitterly, seeing all her dreams fade.

"I would have you place more faith in my ability to contrive," Tavis told her lightly, hiding his disappointment that she thought so little of him.

"And I would have you listen!" she spat at him. "That English usurper is nothing to you! Nothing!"

Suddenly angry, he thrust her from him. "You've lived too long outside your clan, Elspeth Leathann. You've no feeling for family left within you. 'Tis a sad thing for a man or woman to lose, and I'll not let you destroy it in me."

"Bastards have no family!" But she spoke to his back as he left her, and he did not turn to look at her again. "Damn you." She sobbed the words as his measured stride carried him down the hall away from her. "Damn you."

But there was no one to hear.

The coastline between Edinburgh and Stirling was as quietly beautiful as always. Tavis found the ride a time of healing, a time in which he forgave himself for past mistakes, aided by the fact that Amalric did not seem to think him past redemption for the part he had almost played.

Indeed, Amalric Lotharing seemed to hold him in respect for the risk he was now willing to take to aid Iaian. And risk it was. Tavis had little to lose besides his life, and that would be quickly forfeit if Arran discerned the underlying intent of the plot had been to depose him as regent—and that Tavis had been a willing part of that plot until the point of involving Iaian.

They had not yet contrived a clear plan of action when they led their small troop of men up the headlands toward the walls of Stirling Castle. The fortress sat high over the town, surveying the sweep of plain on one side and the grand rise of mountains on the other. The River Forth, given birth in the wild hills to the west, wandered through those plains before widening to a firth at the face of the sea. From the castle gates Tavis gazed at the river one last time, wondering if it would be his last view of Scotland. Then he turned a smile upon Amalric and said, "Let us be to it."

But it proved not so simple. Whether because of truly pressing matters of state or simply because Arran was displeased that Amalric was at Stirling rather than Dumbarton, they were not given an immediate audience. After two days of enforced idleness, in which all that was accomplished was to ascertain that Dunmar was not at Stirling, Amalric could stand no more.

He glared about the hall, crowded with courtiers. "I ride south on the morrow," he told Tavis, while still pretending to watch a band of singularly unskilled jugglers.

"Aye," Tavis returned with equal frustration, "and I'd ride with you save I dare not."

"One of us must gain Arran's ear," Amalric agreed, "and he has too much cause to be angered with me. You'll have the better luck in getting a sympathetic audience of him, I fear." Unless, of course, Tavis was so witless as to confess his willingness to replace Arran with Marie de Guise.

"If I get an audience at all. Do you ride for England?"

"Eventually. First, I think, I need to apprise both my father and Donnchadh of Dunmar's game. We'll need them if we're to free Iaian from this tangle." He glanced about to make sure their conversation was still unattended by any other. "Have a care in what you tell Arran. There's no great need to place your neck on the chopping block." It was a warning he'd given several times.

Tavis sighed. "I could have stopped this 'ere it got started by going to Iaian. I was a fool. Now I'll tell Arran whatever I must to turn his belief from Dunmar."

And no further urging by Amalric, either then or at their parting the next morning, could gain a promise that Tavis would have at least as much care for his future as he did for Iaian's.

"Would you have me carry any word to Iaian?"

Tavis smiled grimly. "Only if I do not survive Arran's wrath. I'd have you remind him of his pledge that Waytefeld should go to my heir after me."

Amalric sent him a curious look, but merely nodded. "I hope 'tis one message I do not have to deliver."

"No more than I," Tavis responded, taking the hand Amalric offered. "Godspeed, Lotharing."

"And God's good luck to you, Gillecrist."

Chapter Twenty-three

Cecile slipped from her mount before even the groom could reach her. While Donnchadh watched with a smile, she turned slowly in a circle, savoring the sights of the familiar courtyard of Ciaran Castle, bathed in a midmorning glow of sunlight.

Dismounting, Donnchadh tossed his own reins to a groom. Before he could speak, Saelec burst through the wide-flung doors of the hall, the wrinkles in his face arranged to a smile.

"Father!" Cecile ran to him, feeling the weeks fall away from her, though she knew herself forever changed from the child he'd last known.

"So, lass, you've returned home at last," Saelec said gruffly, enfolding his daughter in a crushing embrace. But even as he spoke, he looked over her head to Donnchadh, who shook his own head.

Donnchadh had much—and nothing—to tell the man. Time enough later to explain that Arran had left Edinburgh for Stirling before his own arrival there. And that, once Iaian was gone, he had deemed it best to remove Cecile from Edinburgh before he pursued the question of Iaian's appointment. He'd been glad it was the lass's idea to leave, else he would have had to persuade her, and if he knew one thing of Cecile Gillecrist, it was that she was not easily persuaded of anything not her own notion. He did not envy Iaian his wife.

Cecile savored the scent of sandalwood and leather that clung to her father, just as it had since her childhood. Some things appeared unchanging. Even her mother, brought running by the servant sent to fetch her, looked no different than she had on Cecile's leaving.

With a glad cry, Cecile traded one parent's embrace for another, leaving Saelec free to draw aside with Donnchadh, who spoke hastily. Iaian's uncle ended by shaking his head. "So now I'm for Stirling as soon as I see the lass safely settled."

"She's home now," Saelec protested. "Safe enough."

Donnchadh smiled wearily. "She says not. She would have it that she must wait at Daileass for my nephew's return."

"I'll not have it," Saelec said flatly, and he was still saying the same at the evening table. He stared in exasperation at his only daughter. How could such a fragile-appearing girl bear such a determined nature?

"I love you, Father, but I will wait for my husband in his home. 'Tis an argument you lost some weeks ago," Cecile reminded gently. "Must we have it again?"

"Mind your tongue with me, minx! I've not forgotten. But it could be months before Iaian and your brother return from France. I'd have you safe under my roof."

"And I prefer to be safe under my husband's roof," Cecile returned calmly. "Daileass is well defended, is it not, my lord?" She looked to Donnchadh to bolster her argument.

"Aye," he admitted uncomfortably, "but I do not think it would come amiss that you remain at Ciaran."

"I will abide at Daileass until Iaian's return." Cecile was sure of her ability to win this argument, for she did not intend to lose.

As always, she looked to her mother for support, and was not disappointed. When all Saelec's arguments had failed to dislodge Cecile's resolve, Giorsal spoke gently to her husband. "I see no harm in it, Saelec. She will be close at hand—within but a few hours' ride. You can see her often, and she will journey to see me often, will you not, my love?"

Giorsal's gaze caressed her daughter from the shining pale gold waves at her temple to the healthy color on her cheeks. In truth, Giorsal was relieved to see her daughter's fierce determination to remain in her husband's home though she could not be at his side. Clearly, the marriage was proving a solid one.

"Aye, Mother. 'Twill occupy me to travel often betwixt here and Daileass." Just as the journey from Edinburgh had occupied her hours and kept her loneliness for Iaian at bay, if only for a little while.

Saelec sputtered a few moments more, but he could never win an argument against Giorsal. And rarely tried, of late. He did not like to see the way it tired her.

With a feeling of relief, Cecile focused attention away from herself by asking Rilla how Theudoric and Valdemar fared. Rilla blushed as all eyes turned to her, for it was immediately obvious that she and Donnchadh had been engrossed in a private conversation of their own. "Mischievous as always," Rilla answered softly, "and they will be delighted to see their Aunt Ceci."

Cecile smiled warmly, thinking how lovely Rilla looked in her newly found joy. Her soft green eyes were lit from within by that joy. Cecile could not believe Odwulf would have begrudged Rilla that happiness. His parents certainly did not, if their peaceful smiles were any indication. "I will visit with them this very evening, for I return to Daileass in the morning. Donnchadh would see to its defenses before he leaves to attend urgent business in Stirling." Then Cecile laughed at herself as she realized Rilla was more than likely privy to the nature of the business, while she only knew that it existed.

True to her word, Cecile retired to the nursery immediately following dinner. Rilla, and to her pleasure, Nearra and Giorsal as well, joined her in leaving the men to their whiskey and talk.

Well used to the strange hours kept by the boys' mother, their nurse did not demur at the late-evening company. There had been many a night after the young master's death that his lady had sat holding her bairns through the long hours until dawn. Poor wee ones with no father. But then, the nurse sighed as she remembered, that was soon to be remedied. She took to her chair in the corner, shaking her head to see the ladies of the household join the little lads on the rug, heedless of their fine skirts crumpled beneath them.

Cecile laughed as Valdemar launched himself at her. "I'd have boys," she said stoutly. "A great many of them, all as strong and dark as their father."

"You're happy then?" Giorsal could not help asking as she brushed an errant curl from Theu's round cheek.

"I've not had a moment's regret," Cecile replied gently, not quite answering her mother's question, but hoping the lack was not noticed. She was not unhappy, though there was always that part of Iaian that he withheld from her. But, aye, she was happy enough, she supposed. "And I will bear my husband fine sons." And bind him solidly to her.

"Boys can be as demanding as grown men," Rilla warned.

"I'd have girls," Nearra said softly, "at least a girl first."

She was close enough to Cecile that their shoulders brushed, and Cecile turned to look at her in amazement, drawing back so that she could study her face. For the first time in Cecile's remembrance, there was no wistfulness in Nearra's face, no longing wrapped around her heart.

"Nearra, you're breeding," she crowed indelicately.

Nearra blushed and slipped her hand into Giorsal's waiting one. "'Tis true," she said softly, looking into her mother-in-law's loving eyes. "Berin and I waited to tell you until we were sure."

"Sweetheart," Giorsal said with a small chuckle, "*I* have been sure for weeks."

"Father Saelec?" Above all things, Nearra wanted to give Berinhard's father, who had wholeheartedly accepted her as his own, another grandchild to adore.

"Aye. I told him," Giorsal admitted with a twinkle in her bright blue eyes, "but I threatened him direly if he mentioned it before you were ready to tell us."

And Cecile, whose time had come upon her most inconveniently while she had traveled homeward with Donnchadh, wondered when such sweet news would be hers to share with her family. A wife could not get with child when her husband was leagues distant.

That night she dreamed of laughing babies with dark eyes and dark hair. And woke longing for Iaian to hold her and give her a child.

The next morning as she bade her family another farewell, she embraced her eldest brother and went up on tiptoe to whisper in his ear. "Nearra tells me she wishes for a girl child first."

"I'll beat her if 'tis so," he whispered back gruffly, "for I fear she would be as willful as her aunt." But he embraced her fiercely nonetheless. "I'll visit often, Ceci, just to be sure you have need of nothing until Amalric and Gillecrist return."

"And I'll be glad to see you, Berin. Take care of Nearra and Mother."

And then she embraced them all in turn, this time truly understanding what her marriage had meant. Ciaran was home to her no more. Just where home *was,* she could not say, save that it was with her husband, wherever he might lead her.

At last she allowed a groom to assist her into the saddle and turned her rueful smile upon the patient Donnchadh. "I am ready at long last, my lord."

Donnchadh, who had taken his leave of Rilla in private earlier that morning, smiled in sympathy at the hint of sadness in her eyes. But he did not remind her that she had no need to leave. It was her wish and, in truth, the parting would come sooner or later whether she wished it or not. Nor was he surprised when her natural good spirits overcame her small sorrow at being parted again from her family. It was not in Cecile's nature to be morose.

"Will you return to Daileass when your business is concluded in Stirling?" Cecile asked when the castle loomed into sight before them.

"Aye. For a brief time." He chuckled self-consciously as he admitted, "Long enough to plan my wedding with Rilla."

"She will make a good wife to you." Cecile knew she spoke needlessly. If Rilla made the worst wife in the world, she suspected Donnchadh would care not a whit. Not so long as he had her love.

She gave a tiny sigh. It seemed to matter far more to Iaian that *she* be an obedient wife than a loving one.

Donnchadh remained at Daileass for three days, busy every moment of every hour inspecting each aspect of its defense. When he was satisfied he took his leave of Cecile, charging the captain of the guard with her safekeeping, failure to do so being the cost of his life. Cecile smiled sympathetically at the look of outrage on the man's face that Donnchadh should doubt he'd guard her with that life. Freyne, who had come with Iaian from England, knew better than any man here how to guard that which belonged to his lord and master.

Alone, Cecile settled happily into her role of Daileass's chatelaine. The steward, Ewen, and her maid, Iseabal, provided the only relief to the peaceful stretch of hours the first few days.

"Iseabal, are you jealous of me?" Cecile asked on a laughing note as the older woman completed her recount of a list of grievances against the steward.

Iseabal glared at her indignantly. "Indeed, I am not, little miss," she retorted, deliberately not giving Cecile the title that was her due. "And if you wish to be bothered with the man every hour of the day, I'll gladly stand aside."

"'Tis his job to bring me anything he considers of concern," Cecile said softly, "and mine to listen."

"His concerns are trivial matters."

"Perhaps," Cecile agreed, for she had found some of them to be so, "but I would prefer to listen to the inconsequential than to have the important withheld from me as well. Ewen is overzealous, I think, because of the many changes that have come to the Gillecrist properties. He is finding his way in Iaian's life, much as I must do."

"You are Lord Gillecrist's wife," Iseabal protested sharply. "There is no doubt of your place in his life."

"Mayhap," Cecile returned noncommittally, "but I can still have an understanding of Ewen's uncertainties."

And though Iseabal did not, she ceased to place barriers in the steward's way when he wished to speak with his mistress, no matter how small the issue appeared to her.

And on the day Dunmar arrived at Daileass, Iseabal was glad enough to have him hovering in the background as her lady received the elegant gentleman and the black crow that traveled with him.

Summoned by the watch, who recognized his standard, Cecile waited upon the steps of the hall while the fairly large band was permitted entrance at her reluctant orders. Though she had no fear of treachery, she was aware that Captain Freyne quietly positioned his men in the background for her protection.

Cecile watched Dunmar dismount and walk toward her. She knew he desired her, just as she knew he despised Iaian. This visit could neither be one of pleasantry nor a paying of respects. Nor, in the normal course of things, could it be that Dunmar sought the hospitality of the keep as a mere wayfarer. Daileass was not on a well-traveled route, and this particular traveler would be much more likely to seek hospitality of the Lotharings than of Iaian Gillecrist.

But all these thoughts Cecile kept from her face as he approached. Her expression was schooled to polite, if not warm, welcome.

"My Lady Gillecrist," Dunmar greeted her softly, bowing low over the hand she extended to him. He was pleased to feel a slight trembling, but was doomed to disappointment when he rose and found that her shiver was not a reaction to his attention. She looked over his shoulder at the priest, still mounted and staring at her with glacial dislike.

Dunmar took that instant of discomposure to study Cecile Lotharing Gillecrist. He could see little difference in this titled lady and the lass he had thought to tumble. Gilt waves escaped the confines of her pins, slipping in tumbled strands from beneath her satin cap. Blue eyes caught and held what little sunlight filtered through a heavy layer of mist and clouds overhead. Rose and cream skin glowed until a man ached to touch that perfection.

Then her attention returned to him and he saw, too, that she would not shrink from his open lust now any more than she had as a maid in her father's home. The light in her eyes held no fear, only aversion. Instead of recoiling from what he deliberately allowed her to see, she smiled faintly.

"You waste your time, my lord," she said simply.

The calm certainty in her words stung him more surely than any arrogance. He clenched his teeth until his jaw twitched. Then, forcing himself to relax, he shook his head. "I think not."

Cecile tilted her head consideringly, then shrugged. "You will be welcomed here as long as you take only that which is offered to you. But," she warned, "do not think to repay hospitality with treachery. My lord would see it cost you dearly when he returns from France." She knew she told him nothing he did not already know of Iaian's whereabouts. Indeed, she suspected he would not have traveled here had he not been certain she was alone.

Dunmar had begun to enjoy the exchange. This lady seemed unlike any other he had ever known. Recognizing his desire to possess her, she showed neither fear nor anger, displaying, instead, a spirit he would enjoy crushing. She would pay for her disdain before this evening had drawn to a close. Too, her confidence in her husband irked him. Clearly, she feared no man while she considered herself safe within his care.

But there had been at least a moment of something akin to fear in her eyes when she regarded Father Aindreas. Dunmar turned to cast a considering look at the priest, storing her reaction as something to be used against her.

He would enjoy toying with her, allowing her to speak glibly of her husband's protection. Then would he tell her that she had been abandoned to any man who cared to claim her. And he would watch the fear come to her eyes when she learned Iaian Gillecrist had returned to England—without a word of farewell to her.

Cecile steeled herself to greet Father Aindreas when he tired of watching the parry of looks between them and beckoned a groom to aid him in dismounting. He approached her with no pretense of civility between them, his eyes flashing his enmity for her.

"Father." Cecile inclined her head, taking her

cue from him and neither smiling nor offering her hand in greeting.

"Madam." It was a mere acknowledgment that she had spoken.

Cecile felt the flesh quiver between her shoulder blades when she turned to lead them into the keep. Freyne's grave nod as she glanced his way was reassuring. He would not relax his vigilance toward the troop of men Dunmar had brought with him.

Ewen waited correctly just inside the doors of the hall, and Cecile smiled at him warmly and requested food and drink for their guests. Ewen's look, too, was deliberately reassuring, and Cecile regained some of the composure she had lost to Father Aindreas's undisguised condemnation of her.

When Cecile had seen them comfortably seated before a light meal, quite elegant considering the speed with which it had been gathered, she took her leave, saying graciously, "Ewen will have you shown to comfortable chambers. Anything you need, you've only to ask of him. I've household matters requiring my attention in my husband's absence, but I shall join you for dinner this evening."

Dunmar responded with equal grace while the priest deigned not to notice her speech, fixing his eyes instead on the expensive tapestries, none of which depicted any religious scenes.

Pagans, he thought. Pagans all, as the girl still was. His very blood cried out to him that he took his rest in a Godless hall. "She should burn as the veriest heretic."

Dunmar dragged his gaze from the gently swaying skirts of the departing girl to the priest. He scowled at the priest's muttered words. Char that exquisite flesh? He, who had smiled to watch the most horrible sufferings a man could endure, shuddered at the thought. "Nay," he said harshly. "She will not be harmed."

"She will bring you to damnation," Father Aindreas warned. "Have a care for your soul."

"My soul is safe enough." Dunmar spoke almost carelessly. "'Tis only my body that burns for her."

Father Aindreas frowned, but said no more. He had long suspected that Lord Dunmar held none of the religious fervency to be found in most of Marie de Guise's minions. But he alone seemed willing to act on her behalf. Which, though he might not intend it, was also to act on behalf of the one true church.

Cecile dressed with as much care as if for a coronation—or an execution, which was more accurately how she felt about the coming evening. At least she need only endure this one evening alone with her guests. Even now, a messenger carried word to Ciaran for her father or brother to come to her.

Her gown was of gold damask, stiffened with buckram, and as she donned it she smiled wryly at Iseabal. "'Tis to be wished that I could add stiffening to my spine. I confess I do not look forward to this evening."

"'Tis the priest," Iseabal sniffed darkly. "I'd warrant God, himself, frowns with disfavor upon that one."

Cecile did not scold her for the irreverence. She could not help but feel the same. "'Tis Dunmar, as well. The man chills me, though I'll bite through my own tongue before I let him know."

Obediently, she sat in front of a mirror of polished silver while Iseabal dressed her hair. Without being asked, the maid piled it high, threading it with ribbons to hold it secure. Although it would not add much to her stature, it would give some height. The cap placed atop the gleaming mass was almost a nonsense, it was so tiny. But it, too, added a bit to her inches.

Uncomfortable in her vasquine, which held her skirts in a full circle around her, Cecile smiled. "A man would have to fight dearly to get past this." Not to mention the scratchy taffeta of several petticoats.

Of course, any man bent on rape would not be more than mildly hindered. But that would not be Dunmar's way, Cecile knew beyond a doubt. Nay, his would be to press nearer than propriety allowed, giving discomfort and building upon unease, but never blatantly enough to force a confrontation. Instinctively, she knew he thought to intimidate her, though she could not fathom what he thought it would gain him. Whatever his reason, she had determined he would not find it an easy task. She was her father's daughter and

Iaian Gillecrist's wife. She would do both positions honor.

Dunmar and Father Aindreas were taking their ease in deep leather chairs situated on Turkish rugs near the hearth that was not in use in this warm weather. The arrangement was Cecile's in her attempts to soften the fortress aspect of Daileass. She feared she had not been much successful in the hall at least. New tapestries would be needed for that. These fairly dripped blood, so real were their battle scenes.

The men rose at her approach, though she suspected Father Aindreas made the respectful gesture on Dunmar's command alone.

When they were seated at a table laden with expensive plate and jeweled goblets, the master of the kitchen had the first course placed before them. Cecile smiled her approval of the pork with its carefully browned skin and bed of new peas cooked in a rich sauce. She knew her pleasure would be relayed to the cook.

After several pleasantries Dunmar began leading her to the kill. "And how do you find wedded life, my lady?"

"As pleasant as I had expected." Cecile kept her tone neutral, knowing anything could be made of that statement. She might have expected much or little.

Dunmar eyed her with respect. She would give nothing away, then. He made a show of looking around him at the comfort of Daileass. "Gillecrist has provided well for you."

"I have found no lack." Cecile knew very well Dunmar's conversation bordered on the improper, and that most ladies would take offense, bringing it to a halt with a cold word. But she suspected Dunmar had a game to play, and she wanted to know what that game was. Iaian might have need of what she could learn.

Abruptly Dunmar appeared to change the subject. "Did you find Edinburgh to your liking?"

"'Twas confining," she admitted, seeing no harm in that much.

"As is any city," Dunmar agreed. "Yet, Edinburgh can also be very exciting when the court is in residence."

"I am not one to crave a great deal of excitement, my lord." Her eyes gleamed at her own falsehood. It amused her to lie to this man. "I much prefer quiet."

"Your husband's bas . . . half-brother abides in Edinburgh, does he not?"

Cecile grew still, then nodded slowly, reaching for her goblet. Dunmar asked her something he clearly knew to be a certainty. Why?

"Tavis lost much when Iaian Gillecrist stepped forward as his father's heir." The words were almost casually spoken, while Dunmar watched her reaction with hooded eyes.

Again Cecile nodded without answering.

"And he would gain much if Iaian Gillecrist were to leave as suddenly," Dunmar added softly.

Cecile lifted her chin, recognizing the challenge. "Iaian will not leave."

"Ah, but my lady, he has done so already."

"By Arran's command," she pointed out, "but he will return as surely as I shall await his return."

"I think not." Dunmar watched her much the way a hawk would watch its prey just before the swoop. "He does not travel to Arran's bidding. His path has taken him south—to England."

"You lie." But catching Father Aindreas's grim look of satisfaction, she knew Dunmar did not lie. She fought the confusion that would entangle her thoughts, careful to meet Dunmar's gaze boldly. "But if his journeys *should* take him to England," she said, with far more confidence than she felt, "I trust him yet to return."

"And when you tire of waiting?" Dunmar smiled hatefully.

"Whatever it is you think you know," she said evenly, gaining her feet as she spoke, "know this also. Iaian Gillecrist is my husband. A lifetime would not tire me of waiting for his return."

Dunmar knew he had drawn blood for all her proud speech. Before he could close for the kill, however, the doors of the hall were flung wide. Dunmar cursed under his breath while Father Aindreas paled at the sight of Saelec Lotharing and his eldest son entering the room.

Cecile drew a breath of relief, drawing on her resources to greet them calmly. "Father, Berinhard. You are well come to Daileass." Her father's hawklike gaze perused her carefully, and whatever he saw deepened the lines in his face. Never had two men, roughly dressed and dusty with travel, looked so wonderful to her eyes.

Taking his cue from Cecile, who did not acknowledge that she had sent for them, Saelec shrugged in seeming amusement. "Donnchadh sent word of his departure. And your sainted mother would have it that we should ensure your safety." He gave Dunmar a wintry smile, placing a heavy hand on Berinhard's shoulder when he surged forward at sight of Father Aindreas. "Of course, had I known you to be so well attended already, I could have reassured her."

Dunmar smiled between gritted teeth. "Lothаring, 'tis indeed good to see you." He nodded civilly at both men, though he did not bother to acknowledge the younger with speech.

Saelec turned his full attention to his daughter, noting the lines of strain about her mouth and eyes. It appeared he had not arrived any too soon. "What is amiss, Ceci?"

"My lord Dunmar has brought unhappy tidings . . . if they be true." She threw Dunmar a bitter glance. "He claims Iaian travels not to France, as bid by our regent, but to England instead."

"'Tis true enough," Dunmar told Saelec casually. "Though I doubt not that the Lady Gillecrist would prefer not to believe it."

"What proof have you?" Berinhard growled.

Dunmar shrugged, careful not to insult this bear of a man. "Proof? I have need of none, after all. Time will prove my tale."

"Why should he go to England?" Cecile flung the question at him as if it were a challenge, which indeed she intended it to be.

"Perchance for the reasons that drew him to Scotland in the first place."

"His inheritance?" Saelec scowled at Dunmar. "Make sense, man."

Dunmar ignored the open affront. "But if it were not his inheritance that brought him here? If that were merely a cover for other, darker reasons? Somerset would pay a man well for Scotland's secrets. And Gillecrist has no loyalties to Scotland, after all."

"You lie," Cecile spat at him. "Iaian is too honorable for what you suggest."

But Saelec, despite his inherent dislike of Dunmar, knew there was an element of truth possible in the words. He gave Cecile a worried frown. Had he bound his only daughter to a traitor?

"Nay." Cecile answered that doubt proudly. "Nay, Father, Iaian practices no deceit." She turned a hard expression toward Dunmar. "You accuse my husband with lies and treachery. Go. You are not welcome here longer."

Dunmar's face darkened. "You are proud now, my lady, but you will not remain so."

But he hastily gained his feet, the priest with him, at the savage look Lotharing gave him at his threat. He would leave, aye. But he would not forget—and he would return to claim this arrogant bitch. And to tame her.

Chapter Twenty-four

Cecile paced the length of the hall, oblivious to the wary eyes of her father and brother, following her restless movements. Aye, they knew what thoughts raced through her mind, knew what she intended. They knew, too, she would fall headlong into danger if they did not stop her. But—and this was the rub their silent exchange of glances admitted—they did not know how to keep their Ceci from that which she made up her mind to do.

She paused to look at them. "I *wish* Donnchadh were here. He knows Iaian best of us, I think."

"I'll send for him," Berinhard suggested hopefully, seeing, if not a way out, at least a delay. His blue-green eyes held almost a hint of pleading.

Cecile's face brightened, then fell. "'Twill take too long. I do not know how much time there is to us."

"Time until what?" Saelec asked, though he knew full well what she thought and suspected she had the right of it. "Dunmar made no threats."

"Aye," Cecile said slowly, "but the threat was there. I *must* get to Iaian. He must be warned."

"Warned of what? And where? Lass, we do not even ken where he is now—Dumbarton, France, or England."

"Has the fleet sailed, then?" She had not expected that.

Her father shrugged, looking more weary by the moment. "Perhaps yesterday, today, tomorrow. Or perhaps in a month. 'Tis in the hands of God." And d'Esse.

Cecile began to pace again. "It must be," she said at last, "that Dunmar has told half-truths. He gains nothing by telling us Iaian has gone to England if, in fact, he has not. 'Tis the reason he twists to his own meaning."

"And if he has the right of it?" Saelec hated saying the words, but the niggling doubt remained.

As he had feared, his daughter whirled on him with angry eyes that flashed a blue fire. "He does not! There is much I do not know of Iaian," she admitted in fiercely steadfast tones, "but that he is honest, I am as sure as I am of your love for me."

"And I," Berinhard said, surprising them both. Saelec had not thought his eldest cared much for the man.

Saelec shrugged. "Well, then, what has taken him to England, and how does Dunmar hope to profit by it?"

Cecile stopped in midstride, turning to face him so abruptly her skirts settled about her like some golden flower suddenly wilted. Saelec groaned silently, for her expression said clearly that she had come to the conclusion he had known she would.

"I think," she said slowly, thoughtfully, "I think the answers lie in England."

"I'll not have it, lass."

Her gamine's grin peaked through her worry. Did he have any idea how often he repeated those same words to her—and with as little result? "Father," she appealed to him, "would my mother do less for you?"

"'Tis dangerous."

"I'll go." Berinhard saw no other way to stop her. Sweet mother of Jesus, but he hoped his Nearra had only boy children.

"'Twill not serve," Cecile said with a shake of her head. "As his wife, I can gain admittance where you could not. England would be dangerous for a Lotharing of Scotland, but not for the daughter-in-law of Sir Geoffrey Lindael."

And that was something neither man could dispute.

"You could waste weeks trying to find your way about England." Saelec pictured her blundering through all manner of English defenses with a full troop of men. He cringed at the thought of the danger that would bring to her.

Her sunny smile did *not* reassure him. "Nay, for I shall have a guide who will know how to lead me directly to Iaian's mother." She knew that was where the beginning, if not the ending, of the answer would be found. With Iaian's mother.

Ewen, who had been hovering within call, answered her summons with alacrity. "Please fetch Captain Freyne to me, Ewen."

Captain Freyne, having surmised from Lord Dunmar's furious departure that something was afoot, had been waiting for just such a summons. Within moments he was bowing low before her. "My lady, you have need of me?"

Cecile nodded slowly. "More importantly, Captain, I think Lord Iaian has need of you."

Freyne straightened abruptly. He *knew* Lord Gillecrist should not have left him behind to care for this pile of mouldering rock. "I am yours to command in his behalf, my lady."

"As I am yours to lead. We go to England, Freyne."

"We, my lady?" Freyne swallowed hard and glanced at her father. No help there. The man's expression held only defeat.

"Aye. You must lead me to Iaian's mother, to the home of Geoffrey Lindael." She smiled at him encouragingly. "We must find Iaian, and I think Lady Lindael can help in that."

"But . . . but I thought Lord Gillecrist journeyed to France." Freyne made no secret of his confusion.

"He was to do so, but I fear some deceit has taken him to England. I would go to him, and you must guide me."

Freyne bowed again. "I'll ready a full troop to escort us. When would you leave?"

"Within the hour, Captain, but," she added gently, "we take no more than a handful of men. I'd not have us stopped as hostile forces. Nothing must keep me from getting to Iaian."

"Now, Ceci, I'll not let you go without enough men to safeguard you." Saelec had yielded too much as it was. He would not yield on this.

One look at his face told Cecile she had reached her limit. "Very well." She turned to the captain, who looked relieved. "A full troop, Freyne." Her father need never know how many she intended to turn back at the border.

"And I'll go with you," Saelec determined, rising to his feet.

Cecile had prepared herself for that pronouncement. "Mother has more need of you," she reminded, certain her father's care for her safety would conflict with her own desire for speed. "You must not add to her worries. Indeed, 'twould be better for her health were she to think me safely here at Daileass awaiting Iaian's return."

Saelec scowled. 'Twas true, Giorsal took excitement less and less well of late. "Berinhard, then, shall go with you."

"And how will you explain his absence? Mother will fret that there is aught amiss if you return without good reason for Berin having remained here with me." Again, seeing Saelec hesitate at the thought of Giorsal's flagging health, Cecile pressed her advantage. "Captain Freyne will protect me, Father, and I'll take no undue chances."

Saelec stared at the captain, who drew himself up proudly. "She'll come to no harm with me, my lord."

Though not content, Saelec once again acknowledged defeat at the hands of his daughter. And as he conceded the point, he wondered again how she came by her nature.

Dismissing Captain Freyne to his preparations, Cecile embraced her father. "I must prepare myself to travel, Father. You are welcome to Daileass's hospitality if you've no wish to return to Ciaran tonight."

"Nay, Berin and I will go now." He had a strong need to be with Giorsal. Every moment was precious to him, for he knew not how many more they would have together. Even his worries for his daughter were secondary to that. Cecile was young and strong and had ever contrived success in all she turned her hand to.

Berinhard was equally ready to leave. Cecile made him nervous. Too, Nearra did not like having him sleep away from Ciaran, and the babe, so many years prayed for, was more than sufficient reason for him to wish not to distress her.

As they embraced, Saelec cautioned her, "Take every care, and when you reach Lady Anne, send word to me of your safe arrival." He remembered Anne Donnchadh of old. She would not let harm come to his Ceci, but he would worry every moment until Cecile was in her safekeeping.

Cecile did not escort them to the bailey. Time was too precious. The doors of the hall had barely closed behind them before she whirled to mount the stairs leading to her chamber. Iseabal, dozing by the bed, jumped up, startled at her precipitous entrance.

"I ride for England within the hour, Iseabal. I'll need a sturdy riding habit and a small bag with but one gown and slippers."

Iseabal stiffened in immediate disapproval. "England! But, my lady—"

Tired of arguments, Cecile stamped her foot in frustration as she cut her off midsentence. "Nay, Iseabal, no protests. What my father allows is not for you to forbid."

To her surprised relief, Iseabal said no more, but her every movement as she assisted Cecile to change spoke of censorious reproach. She relented only when Cecile paused to give her a quick hug. And then she sniffed and begged Cecile to have a care for her safety until Cecile decided she preferred her in a huff.

But soon enough, she stood in the courtyard, looking over the preparations Freyne had made for their journey. She smiled at the horse led forward for her. There was nothing feminine about either the mount or the trappings. Freyne intended to travel as she wished, hard and fast, with no concessions to the fact that she was Lady Gillecrist.

For a moment, surveying the full score of men who gathered about them, she considered cutting their number before even leaving the keep. But she feared Captain Freyne would argue the issue whilst they were still safely within Daileass walls, and she did not wish to waste the time. Instead, she merely asked him to let her know when they approached the border.

Cecile felt a surge of excitement as they clattered through the gates of Daileass. The night was soft and warm and almost clear, with only a cloud or two lying low against a velvet sky. She knew she would be inexpressibly weary by the next evening, but for now she was enlivened with purpose. And she was certainly strong enough to withstand going this one night without sleep. It would not have been possible for her to sleep now even had she delayed their departure until morning. Her very veins pulsed with her drive to reach Iaian.

Just after first light Captain Freyne turned to her and said simply, "My lady, behold England."

They traveled now at a slow pace, resting their horses before resuming a full gallop. Despite her courage, Cecile shivered slightly. Living so near the border, she had been reared with tales of the bloodthirsty English marauders. But, she reminded herself, Iaian was English and no more cruel nor fearsome than any of her brothers.

When she drew rein Captain Freyne followed suit with a frown of surprise. "My lady?"

"Return all but a half dozen men to Daileass."

"I dare not, my lady," he said flatly, wondering how many ways his lordship could find to kill him if he let anything happen to his lordship's lady.

"If you will not give the command, I will do so." She took pity on his terror. "Captain Freyne, we are far safer in flight than in battle, and in flight numbers are insignificant."

Everything about her bespoke her determination, and Freyne knew she would not back down. He could continue the quarrel fruitlessly, he could refuse her request—or he could do her bidding.

"If you will heed me in this, I will follow you in all else. I swear it." Her eyes pled as eloquently as her words.

Freyne's doubts were not proof against her conviction. With a few quick commands, he selected those men he wished to continue on, sending the others back in the direction they had come. God held him, if he had made the wrong decision. Yet he could not help but be reassured by his lady's confident smile as they began their plunge into England.

Wearily, Iaian surveyed the home of his childhood. He had traveled swift and hard to reach the Lindael estates, but he found now that he dreaded to enter. His eyes blurred against the pain that struck him when he surveyed the sprawling manor home he had once thought to inherit. Every stone of it was beloved and as familiar to him as his own skin. His sons would have scrambled through the same hills he had wandered as a youth. His daughters would have played in the gardens his mother tended with such love. His children—and Edra's.

He had departed from here with five score of warriors at his back, angry and hell-bent on the destruction of anything that stood against him because he could not destroy the one thing that had ruined his life: his own history. He returned alone and still wounded, but no longer angry. For some time, he had suspected that Cecile drew that poison from him, though he could not fathom how she did so. The thought of Cecile made him smile. He would be glad to return to her, even to Scotland. The realization surprised him but did not fill him with the dismay it once would have.

Nudging his horse forward, he slipped his helmet from his head, cradling it in his arms so that the sentry could have no doubt of who approached. And so it was that he was not even challenged, but allowed to ride slowly through gates flung open in welcome.

There was the glisten of tears in the old captain's eyes as the man rushed forward to greet Iaian as he dismounted. "Sir Iaian!" And then he could say no more as he embraced the young man who had been both the joy and the bane of younger years. Sir Geoffrey had looked to him to keep the lad in line, and that had not always been an easy task. But all that was forgotten upon feeling the hard lines of the young man's shoulders against his hands. He stepped back to peer into Iaian's face. "Your sainted mother will be so heartened to see you. 'Tis been a damnable time for her since Sir Geoffrey's arrest."

"Do you know aught of that? 'Tis why I am here."

The older man shook his head. "There's been little word, save that he is well treated."

Iaian's lips thinned. "I do not think that imprisonment for a lifetime of loyalty can be considered good treatment." But at the captain's look of distress, he clapped him reassuringly on the shoulder, thinking on the incongruity of the reversal in the roles they had played with each other for so many years. "But I shall soon see him freed." And be perhaps imprisoned in his place. "Now, where might I find my lady mother?" he asked, his voice gentling at the mere thought of her.

"Midmorning, it be," the captain reminded him. "She'll be amongst her roses."

Iaian left him then, his feet finding the way on their own, leaving his mind free to wander. Though he remembered the anger he had felt toward her with his mind, he could not now recall it with his heart. All he recalled was the anguish in her eyes when he left her without so much as a farewell. She, who would have given her life for him, had received nothing of the loyalty and understanding that was due her. And Sir Geoffrey—would Iaian have an opportunity to beg his forgiveness for the ingratitude? Or was it now too late?

Anne Donnchadh was not difficult to find. Iaian stopped at the edge of the garden to watch her for some few moments. She was as lovely and graceful as he recalled, but there were lines of pain in her face that tore at his heart. Sir Geoffrey's imprisonment might be the cause of most of them, but Iaian knew his own cruelty had drawn too many. He would give much to unspeak the words he had flung at her on learning the truth of his parentage. Because that was not possible he could only hope that by somehow freeing Sir Geoffrey, he could make up for the damage he had done.

As he stepped forward, Anne froze, arrested at the sight of the son she had once given up hope of ever seeing again. Her lips formed his name, but no sound came forth. She felt again the sharp pain of her betrayal of this young man, this stranger who was her beloved child. She did not blame him for his fury and his condemnation of her that day. They were but her payment for her years of selfish happiness with Sir Geoffrey. But, God help her, she could not regret those years.

Iaian nearly wept at the gathering of tears in his mother's eyes, at the fear and pain that caused them. He walked to her, unable to force his feet to move swiftly, stumbling once because he could no longer see the path beneath him through his own tears. And when he reached her he fell at her feet.

Freyne had no further cause for complaint. True to her word, Cecile obeyed him in all things. Freyne set the pace, as well as the hour for sleeping and rising. He suspected he was merely fortunate that his desire for haste matched hers. He did not doubt she would do more than protest if she thought they were traveling less swiftly than possible.

Only once did she complain of their crooked path, but when he named nearby English strongholds that were best avoided, she nodded with understanding. Though she grew dismayed at the length of time their journey was taking, she could not quarrel with his reasoning. She could do Iaian no service imprisoned in an English keep.

And because they had avoided all other habitations, she knew at once that the keep that loomed before them on the fourth afternoon was the home of Geoffrey Lindael. Her heart rose. Even now, Iaian might be within those walls.

Chapter Twenty-five

"My brother is no traitor." Tavis wondered if it were the fourth or fifth time he had said those words, and with seemingly the same lack of impact. He glared at the elaborate frieze adorning the walls of the privy chamber, afraid that if he did not, he would glare instead at Scotland's regent.

Arran eyed him consideringly, until Tavis was forced to meet his gaze once more. "Mayhap he is not. But," Arran's voice threatened softly as he asked, "is your brother Scots . . . or is he English?"

"His home, all of his wealth, is here," Tavis reminded him. "And he wed the daughter of Ciaran, a Scots lass." These things, too, Tavis had said more than once.

This audience had proved even more nerve-racking than Tavis had anticipated. He wished heartily that Amalric had waited the one more day it had taken Arran to decide to grant an hour of his time. Arran had made his disapproval of Amalric's actions clear. When a duty was given it was to be carried out, not abandoned. Clear, too, was the fact that Dunmar had already planted his seeds of doubt in the regent's mind. And likely it had been done in the past few days, whilst Arran had kept Tavis and Amalric, and then Tavis alone, waiting. That probability in itself had increased Tavis's frustration with the regent immeasurably.

Arran leaned back in his chair, Dunmar's insidious whispers still lingering in his ears. But—and this alone made him listen to the man—Tavis Gillecrist stood only to benefit if Iaian Gillecrist were to be named traitor and his estates confiscated. Arran had within his possession a writ signed by Alasdair Gillecrist's own hand, naming Tavis as his heir. Of course the young man could not inherit any title, but Alasdair had requested that the title be granted to him by royal boon.

"If as you say," Arran began slowly, "his loyalties are here, why does he risk all for this Englishman?"

"I think, your Grace, he saw not the risk, but the need. Geoffrey Lindael cared for Iaian as for his own son. Indeed, until just months ago, Iaian thought he *was* the man's son. Which of us could turn our back on one we consider our father?" Tavis was growing weary and less and less hopeful. The audience, already an hour old, had brought him no closer to persuading Arran of Iaian's loyalty to his new country than when he had begun. The most he could hope for, now, would be to persuade the regent to take no action, at least not until Iaian had returned. Only failing that would he denounce Dunmar openly, betraying Marie de Guise and sealing his own doom.

"And you would have me yet trust the man. Gillecrist has seen the French fleet at Dumbarton, can attest to both the defenses of our queen and the route she would take to France. And on the heels of gaining this knowledge, he returned to England. Yet, you would have me believe this knowledge will not find its way to English ears."

"Your Grace, I would stake my life on it."

Arran smiled faintly. "Sir, you may be doing just that."

"You will wait, then, for his return?" Tavis pressed his advantage, knowing he risked Arran's temper for his persistence.

Drumming his fingers on the polished table of inlaid stone between them, Arran studied Tavis for several tense moments before he nodded. "Aye. I'll wait. Two sennights. Then God help you both if you do not stand before me at that time."

Tavis found he was sweating when he left the privy chamber of Scotland's regent, and he did not think it was because of his formal dress of satin doublet and full ruff. He had two weeks to find Iaian and ensure his return to Scotland. And during those two weeks, Dunmar would be free to pour further lies into Arran's waiting ears. It did not bode well for any who bore the Gillecrist name.

Heart pounding and blood racing, Iaian stood in the long, shadowy corridor and waited for the drugged wine to take its toll on the guards positioned near the chambers of Edward Seymour, Duke of Somerset and Protector of all the Realms and Dominions of the King's Majesty. Until now, all had been easy, or at least not overly difficult. His entrance to the city, even at so late an hour, had not been questioned. With his rich garb and careless attitude, he appeared simply one more wealthy noble among the many that thronged the streets of London.

Nor had he been challenged at any of the well-guarded entrances. He had housed all but one of his men outside the palace walls, and with but one retainer at his side, he appeared no apparent threat to anyone. His charm, more than his gold, convinced the pretty little serving wench to take a flask of wine to the guards. A payment he owed, he told her by way of explanation. And he knew it was a common enough occurrence, after all. The guards themselves usually parted with the coin it took to have wine or ale brought to quench the thirst of a long night.

Galen, who posed as his retainer, had seen to the drugging of the wine while Iaian dallied with the wench. Now the serving maid was long gone to her sleep, Galen stood as sentry close to the stairway that led to this darkened hallway, and Iaian waited.

At long last the second guard followed the first into slumber, and Iaian stepped quietly over their sprawled legs. Inside the antechamber, Iaian froze. All was not in darkness as he had anticipated. A late-working clerk had given way to weariness, his head laid upon crossed arms. He snored softly, heedless of the papers he crumpled beneath him. Beside his head, a candle flickered softly.

Regretfully, Iaian unsheathed the jeweled knife at his waist and brought it hilt down upon the skull of the unsuspecting young man. It went against the grain to strike such a blow, but Sir Geoffrey's life was at stake. Iaian would have killed the young man to save Sir Geoffrey if that had proved necessary.

Nevertheless, he was relieved to see the blow had not drawn more than a trickle of blood from a swift-rising lump. He lifted the candle and turned toward the chamber where Somerset lay sleeping. The shadows fell away from the light of the candle as Iaian approached the bed. He lit the stand of candles on the nearby table, then held his breath and slid the bedhangings quietly open. Still silent, he stepped away from the bed. Oddly enough, he was not yet angry with the Lord Protector of England. If what Tavis believed was true, Somerset was but a pawn in plans that had begun leagues away in Scotland.

"Your Grace." Iaian spoke the words quietly into the silence.

In the candle glow, Iaian watched Somerset's eyes flicker open. To the man's credit, Somerset was instantly alert and undismayed at his unexpected guest. He sat, managing to look regal even in his nightrail. For long moments he studied Iaian's features in silence, then sighed and swung his legs out of the bed. Iaian wondered if he recognized him.

Somerset's first words answered the question. "You risk much to aid your foster father." Somerset spoke bluntly, for he was not one to play games. And for that, Iaian was thankful.

Iaian nodded, knowing how much truth lay in those words. He *did* risk much. "I felt it was necessary, your Grace."

"And if it cost your life?" Calmly, Somerset reached for a robe.

"I would choose to do no different, no matter the outcome. Sir Geoffrey is more true father than foster, your Grace. I've never known any other."

"And he would do anything for you?" Somerset probed.

Iaian saw the not-so-subtle trap and smiled faintly. "Not *anything*."

Somerset smiled in return. His was a thankless task, this minding of England's business until its prince was of an age to take the reins of government. And he knew he was not popular. Not with the nobles of England, who could not take advantage of him for the purpose of gaining riches, nor with the populace, who considered him dry and lacking in kingly graces. But then, he was no king, nor had he any desire to be. He believed he did possess, however, more of a sense of humor than most credited to him. And he had, as well, an earnest sense of duty to the realm of England. He did not believe Sir Geoffrey Lindael stood as a traitor to England, but there had been seeds of doubt planted liberally amongst the court nobles and finally brought to his ears. And though he could not simply ignore the warnings as he felt inclined to do, he had refused to either dishonor or discomfort Sir Geoffrey with more than a token imprisonment in rather lavish Tower apartments.

Now, Sir Geoffrey's foster son, the young man accused as the other half of the traitors' web, waited before him no doubt ready to plead the knight's innocence. Somerset held that foster son's gaze, measuring and judging him. "He stands accused of giving you England's secrets for Scotland's use. What have you to say in his behalf?"

Iaian smiled somewhat ruefully. "Just what you would expect of me. Sir Geoffrey—if he even has secrets to tell—has given none to me. Nor would I have any use for them. I do not intrigue for the downfall of either England or Scotland." His expression softened from the half-angry cast he could not help wearing over this tangle of lies involving himself and Sir Geoffrey. "Though no longer the land I can claim as my birthright, England will always be beloved of me. But

Scotland, because of my blood, has equal right to my loyalty. I will defend what is mine," he said strongly, "let no man mistake the matter, but I will never bring deliberate harm to this realm."

Somerset was more convinced than ever that he had been wise to bring no harm to Sir Geoffrey. This young man's words had the ring of truth to them. Still hiding his thoughts, he looked beyond Iaian to his unfortunate clerk. "Have you killed him?"

Iaian followed his gaze. "No, your Grace. He will merely suffer with an aching head upon the morrow."

"And my guards." Somerset's lips twitched in a smile. The young man had been determined, indeed. Or desperate.

"Ill stomachs to go with their aching heads." Iaian smiled. "They should have refused the wine whilst guarding your Grace." Iaian had finally begun to relax. If Somerset truly believed Sir Geoffrey guilty of treason, he would at least be showing some alarm by now.

"You will be fined for this intrusion, my lord. Stiffly fined." He could not, after all, have his nobles thinking they could force an audience upon him at their whim. As for the guards, they would soon realize their lack of prudence. They would have to deal with more than the effects of the drugged wine on the morrow.

"I can only consider it coin well spent," Iaian said, grateful to learn gold would be all he lost in this endeavor.

Somerset rubbed his brow. This was, in truth, an ungodly hour to be disturbed. "I will see to Sir Geoffrey's release."

Iaian stared at him. As simply done as that.

Somerset laughed shortly at his expression. "I've two choices, my lord: free Lindael or imprison you with him. It needed only your presence to disprove the accusations. You may leave or join the hospitality of the court." He reached for a bellpull, sighing at the explanations and reassurances that would now have to be made.

To his amazement, Iaian found himself in a comfortable chamber just moments later, waiting for Sir Geoffrey to join him. He found, too, he was more in dread of this meeting than he had been of the one with his mother. Anne Donnchadh could not deny their kinship no matter how great the wounds he had inflicted. Sir Geoffrey, however, was not bound by the same ties. He could simply turn his back and walk away from Iaian as if the bonds of a father and son's love had never existed between them.

When the door to the chamber slowly opened Iaian stood his ground with pounding pulse. He had cursed this man when last they'd been face to face. Too late, now, to wish his tongue had been struck mute at birth.

Sir Geoffrey, none the worse for his confinement, dismissed the page who had accompanied him. His gray eyes assessed Iaian swiftly, then he smiled. "Your mother sought your aid on my behalf?"

"Aye," Iaian said hoarsely, unsure how to breach the barrier of his remembered angry words.

"Then I must be grateful to you both for my freedom." Sir Geoffrey studied Iaian almost hungrily and, with many years of living to his credit, saw the need in Iaian's dark eyes. Saw, too, the pride and the young man's fear of his own reaction. Shaking his head, Sir Geoffrey opened his arms. "I thank God for the chance to see you again. My son."

And Iaian, holding tears at bay, embraced him fiercely. "Father."

Chapter Twenty-six

Cecile remained mounted, looking about the well-kept bailey while she waited for Anne Donnchadh to receive her or turn her away. Curiosity, strong within her, was tempered by the knowledge that Anne might find her presence a too-painful reminder of the son she had lost to another land, another life. She had bade the servant tell Lady Lindael, as she was known here, that her son's wife awaited her pleasure.

When the woman swept gracefully into the bailey Cecile knew her at once by her resemblance both to Iaian and to Donnchadh. Iaian bore her stamp in his deep, dark eyes and crisply curling hair. Her resemblance to Donnchadh, even more than of coloring, was in the serenity of expression and the wisdom to be found behind wide-set eyes.

Anne drew near, gazing up at the young woman who had married her son. For long moments she stood, enjoying her beauty as naturally as she enjoyed that of the flowers in her garden. Not even Iaian's stumbling descriptions had prepared her for the lovely piquancy of the girl's features, the blue brilliance of her eyes, or the pure silk of hair that gleamed white-gold in the sunlight. And she was, indeed, as tiny as Iaian had claimed, a perfect miniature.

"You are my son's wife," Anne said at last, unable to stifle the hint of pain that came with the knowledge of the beautiful babies this woman would give her Iaian. Babies who would be nurtured to adulthood far from her loving arms.

Seeing the welcome in her sad smile, Cecile allowed a groom to assist her in dismounting. And then it seemed natural to slip into Anne's embrace. This was the mother of her husband, and Anne's love for her son was obvious, no matter how Iaian felt about the turmoil her actions had wrought in his life.

Cecile drew back to smile at her, answering unnecessarily, "Aye. I am Iaian's wife."

Pride warmed her voice, and Anne smiled back, relieved of one last fear that her talks with Iaian had given her. "And you love my son."

"Aye . . . but do not tell him." Cecile grinned at her a bit ruefully. "The knowledge would make him most uncomfortable."

Stifling her surprise, Anne bade her enter the manor. It would appear that her son and his wife lived in mutual confusion, as most young couples seemed to do.

Cecile followed Anne to a graciously furnished drawing room that opened onto an inner courtyard blooming with flowers. Youthful voices drifted through the open doors, and Anne smiled at her as they sat together on a low sofa. "The younger of my children."

"They sound happy."

Anne's smile faded. "Indeed. 'Tis only Iaian that I have caused to suffer."

"Iaian will come to accept what must be."

"I believe he is close to that now," Anne said in a low voice. "At least he cares enough for us yet that he did not refuse to come to my aid."

"Then *you* sent for him! You have seen him?"

Anne stared at her, bewildered. "Did you not know? He sent a message to you."

"I received no message," Cecile said with a shake of her head. "My only knowledge is that he was charged with accompanying Queen Mary to France. Then I was told he had left Scotland to return to England." Her lips thinned at the memory of Dunmar's accusations.

A servant bearing food and drink interrupted Anne's answer. And Anne, knowing what healthy appetites the young have, would speak no more until Cecile had eaten. When she did resume she told Cecile of her Geoffrey's arrest, and that it had seemed best to a friend of Sir Geoffrey's that Iaian be called home to plead his foster father's innocence.

"I fear Sir Geoffrey's 'friend' is no friend to Iaian," Cecile said darkly.

Anne's brows knit with her confusion. "Why do you say so?"

"'Tis too opportune, this arrest and the need for Iaian to return to England. The timing of it looks fair to damn Iaian with Scotland's regent. Perhaps at the cost of his inheritance."

Anne paled. "You must tell me everything."

And Cecile did so, concluding, "Iaian must return to Scotland to clear himself of charges as false as those brought against Sir Geoffrey."

"Have these charges been made?"

"I've no doubt they will be," Cecile answered, picturing Dunmar's expression as she had seen him last. "I must reach Iaian."

Anne grasped her hand. "I've heard nothing from Iaian or Sir Geoffrey," she said anxiously. "It could be very dangerous for you at court."

Her meaning was clear, and Cecile felt as if the ground had fallen away from beneath her. She had not considered this, believing all danger to Iaian lay in Scots hands. "How long since Iaian left you?"

"Several days ago."

"Will you take me to him?" Cecile asked in a low voice.

Anne thought of all the years she had avoided the knowing eyes of the court, the titters and the gossip. Even in her youngest years, she suspected she would not have been as brave as her son's wife, traveling to a country hostile to her own, willing to risk imprisonment and even death to aid the man she loved. She no longer feared the court gossips nor danger to herself. Her only fears, now, were for her children. What would become of the younger ones if they had neither mother nor father to see to their protection? At last she sighed. "I will take you."

To her touched surprise, Cecile placed her small hand on Anne's. "Do not be fearful. I will not let harm come to you." And though Anne knew Cecile could not withstand England's Lord Protector if he chose to hold them as tightly within his grasp as he held Geoffrey, she was somehow reassured.

"We leave on the morrow. I can discover nothing."

Iaian heaved a sigh of relief at Sir Geoffrey's words, though he sympathized with the frustration behind them. Sir Geoffrey had been determined to remain at court until he discovered who was behind his imprisonment. It had been six days since his release, and he had uncovered nothing. No one seemed to recall just who had begun the whispers. And, of course, he was constantly assured, no one had truly believed the campaign of lies.

Sir Geoffrey was flooded with murmurs of audiences sought with Somerset in which his innocence was proclaimed. By neither word nor expression did he reveal his disbelief that any had sought to aid him. Iaian could not stifle a bitterness on his father's behalf, but Sir Geoffrey merely shrugged. Theirs was a political world. Friends would always be scarce when trouble threatened. And, indeed, he needed no one save Anne. And he longed to return to her.

Iaian felt a growing need of his own to return to Scotland and his neglected keeps—as well as his neglected wife. Too, he knew he would have some explanations of his own to make. Arran would not be pleased that he had gone haring off to England when he'd been charged with an entirely different task.

One more evening to endure of artificial smiles and suspicious eyes, then he could leave Sir Geoffrey and his mother with a far lighter heart than their last parting, knowing it would not be forever. Perhaps he and Cecile could visit in the not too distant future. He longed to show her off to them, and them to her.

One thing had these past several days of idleness ensured—he understood far better the strength of feelings that had caused Sir Geoffrey to keep Alasdair Gillecrist's young wife from him all those years ago. When Sir Geoffrey spoke of the faded bruises on Anne's fair skin, witness to past beatings, Iaian pictured Cecile marred by such harsh treatment and shuddered. "It was impossible not to love Anne," Sir Geoffrey had said at one point, and Iaian had sat frozen at the word. Love? Aye. And his desire to return to Cecile had burned the hotter for the discovery.

On the heels of knowledge came proof. The evening before they planned to leave, Lady Edra Byreham came to court.

Iaian had already taken his seat at the well-lardered table when he heard her family name announced. A flash of remembered pain made him stiffen, and Sir Geoffrey placed a hand upon his forearm in silent sympathy. Despite himself, Iaian's eyes were drawn to the statuesque beauty entering the room upon her father's arm.

Lady Edra shone as lovely as his memories of her. Her honey-colored hair gleamed in the candlelight, and her eyes glowed a tawny shade of brown. Full breasts teased the eye as they swelled enticingly above her costly gown of dark green velvet. Jewels sparkled against that tempting flesh, as well as against the rich sheen of her hair. Aye, Lady Edra remained everything she had been, a promise of passion as well as a pledge of her father's wealth.

But Iaian tasted only bitterness for what he knew lay within her. His Ceci, for all her willfulness and disobedience, was inherently good and sweet. "I thank God the lady refused me," he spoke his thoughts aloud.

Sir Geoffrey gave a start of surprise, though he had suspected as much by Iaian's voice when he spoke of his wife. Beneath the faint frustration the girl seemed to engender in Iaian lay a very real pride and affection. And though Iaian had very naturally not spoken of passion between them, Sir Geoffrey had heard that, too, in his voice.

After the last course of sweets, when the court nobles and ladies mingled for gossip and the arranging of trysts, Iaian stood waiting. He knew Lady Edra would be told of his presence, knew she would not be able to keep herself from seeking him out, if only to taunt him with what he had lost.

And he was right. He saw it when he watched her flirt with some young knight, saw the way her chin lifted when she turned from her flirtation, her eyes searching the room until she found him. She smiled slowly and began making her way across the crowded room, her attention focused on him as if there were only the two of them in the vast hall.

"Iaian." Her voice purred low and husky, without a trace of the insults she had heaped upon him in renouncing their troth long months ago. She had scarcely believed her ears when the young knight had revealed that Iaian Lindael was once again upon English soil.

"My lady." Iaian bowed over her hand, feeling her pulse leap to life when he turned it palm up to place his kiss against her wrist. He gave her a deliberate reminder of the passion that had been between them, unconsummated but never ignored.

Edra's heart almost wept at what would never be, but she forced a return of the hardness that protected her at all times. She was Lady Edra Byreham. Her duty would ever be to uphold and enhance that name at all times. In only one thing had she determined to think of herself first. Though her hand had been pledged to one of the wealthiest men of the realm, his blood was as cold as it was pure. Edra had determined that her body would be given, first, to one who could warm it. She would ensure no issue came of the giving, and she would ensure, too, that her husband never knew she did not come to him chaste. There were women of her acquaintance well versed in those arts who had vowed to assist her. It amused and titillated them to do so.

Forever after that one time, Edra knew she would honor her wedding vows, not for the sake of those vows or the man she would wed, but for the sake of her family pride. But she would have one memory. One night. The man who would give her that memory would have to be carefully chosen. One who fired her blood, but would also hold his tongue for an eternity. Two completely different but exciting men had been vying for her attention. But now there was Iaian, as wildly handsome and devastatingly seductive as she remembered him to be.

She placed one perfect hand against the broad expanse of his chest, feeling the rich texture of satin covering hard muscle. "I have thought of you," she admitted in a low voice.

Iaian looked up from her deceptively sad eyes and sweetly curved lips into the composed fury of his wife's face. And behind her stood his very disapproving mother.

* * *

"Who is she?" Cecile asked in a low, contained voice.

"Lady Edra Byreham," Anne answered on a sigh. "Iaian was pledged to her until he learned of his true parentage."

"Who broke faith?"

Anne hesitated, knowing the truth would tell Cecile much. Finally she admitted, "Lady Edra."

Cecile lifted her chin, meeting the stunned gaze of her husband. The knowledge steadied her. He *was* her husband. In a gown borrowed from Anne, skillfully altered to fit her shorter stature and every bit as elegant as those around her, Cecile walked gracefully to her husband's side.

Anne, who knew her children must find their own way, turned her thoughts and attention to the man rushing through the crowded room to take her in his arms.

Beside Iaian, Lady Edra felt his withdrawal, followed the line of his gaze, and stiffened. The look in the approaching blonde's eyes spoke of ownership. She was clearly come to claim her own.

"My lord." Cecile spoke first to Iaian, ignoring the beauty at his side. She struggled to quiet the turmoil deep within her, the fear that she had lost him long before he'd ever truly been hers.

"Cecile." He half-turned to the woman at his side, though his eyes never left the blue ones daring him. "Lady Edra, my wife, Lady Gillecrist." Iaian's lips twitched in amusement at the situation. He knew he should be furious, but he was too glad to see her. He barely heard Edra's acknowledgment before he spoke again to Cecile. "I don't know why I thought you safely at Daileass." His gaze caressed her, an echo of his body's craving to drag her against him.

Cecile felt his welcome wash over her, and the shock of it widened her eyes enormously. To her relief, there was no anger in him for her intrusion upon what had looked to be an intimate moment. He almost looked pleased. She smiled somewhat mischievously, for the Lady Edra's benefit. "Nor do I ken why you would think that, my lord. You know I do not care to be left behind."

Hearing the exchange, or rather the tones behind it, Edra knew she had lost all chance of Iaian being the man who took her maidenhood—if, indeed, there had ever been any hope of it at all. Judging by his wife's confidence and the hungry way he was looking at her, she more than suspected there had not been. With murmured words, she took her leave, wondering if they even heard her, knowing they did not care.

Cecile knew the moment she left them, though she gave her not a glance to recognize it. Instead she glared at Iaian furiously. "If you have dallied with her, my lord, I will cut your manhood from you."

And Iaian, at peace with his parents and thus finally himself, simply smiled at her. "Before or after I beat you for journeying half the length of this country without my protection?" He gave into his longing to touch her, drawing one finger lightly along the fragile line of her jaw.

"You will not beat me," Cecile said with only a trace of uncertainty in her voice. She resisted the urge to turn her cheek into the warmth of his palm.

"Nay, I'd rather love you into obedience." It was an admission of more than his physical need for her. His hand moved up to caress the silken ripple of her hair, heedless of a hundred watching eyes.

"I think," Cecile said unsteadily, "we should find a more private place for these . . . disclosures." Her legs were trembling with her need for his touch.

Iaian caught his breath at the frank look of desire in her eyes. "Which chamber have you been given?" he asked in a low voice, the huskiness of which betrayed his own hunger.

"I think I could find my way there again," she admitted, "but 'tis one I share with your mother."

"I trust my father will not mince words at an exchange of bedpartners," Iaian said with a smile. His eyes found the pair, their arms entwined, surrounded by the curious. Preferring to avoid that fate, he grasped Cecile's hand and pulled her toward the stairway leading to the long corridor of chambers above.

Cecile refused to blush as Iaian led her from the hall, though she was certain every person there watched and knew why they departed with the evening still young. Iaian's love surrounded her like the warmest cloak, and nothing else mattered.

Iaian routed the maidservant from the room without a trace of pity, then barred the door before turning to face Cecile. His wife. Never before had the words thrilled him quite so thoroughly. He'd been a fool not to realize what a prize he had gained in her.

"Come here."

Cecile did so without hesitation, standing before him as he drew the pins from her hair. When it spilled into his hands, cool and silky, he drew a shaky breath of desire.

"Turn around."

Again Cecile obeyed wordlessly, presenting her back to him with the tiny row of hooks fastening her gown. His hands were clumsy with his reaction to her, and she was glad to realize it. She was near to breaking with her own desire.

Cool air caressed her as he pushed the loosened gown from her shoulders. Then she felt him lift her hair and press his lips to the nape of her neck. She shivered, moaning slightly. His hands peeled her shift from her, his lips following its descent, so that his kisses touched her from shoulder to hip to calf in slow procession.

She turned as she stepped from the discarded clothing, only to gasp as his hand slid up the inside of her leg as he rose. His caress skimmed her flesh, taunting her, before he turned his attention to his own clothing. He left her standing there, watching him, quivering, while he disrobed.

And then he lifted her in his arms, carrying her to the cool linen of the bed, where he placed her. The contrast from the warmth of his flesh brought her eyes open wide. He was smiling down at her, enjoying the effect he had on her. "I love you, Iaian," she said clearly, opening her arms to him.

For answer, he pressed his mouth to hers, parting her lips with his tongue, driving deep until she arched in helpless yearning against him. The tips of her breasts ached for his touch, as did the tormented flesh that pressed upward against him. "Please," she gasped. "Iaian."

But he seemed not to heed her as he touched his fingers lightly to her taut nipple. She wondered if he truly did intend punishment. If so, he would have to wonder which of them suffered the most. With the thought, she slid her own hand down the ripple of his ribs to glide her fingernails gently against the hard muscle of his hip. She heard him gasp with pleased satisfaction, and then knew nothing else as his body responded to her teasing and he shifted her abruptly, entering her with gently driving force.

She said his name on a soft scream of uncontrolled pleasure, and he smothered the sound of it with his kiss. And with his words. "I love you, Ceci."

Chapter Twenty-seven

"I saw the men preparing to leave with Ceci," Saelec argued. "A full two dozen of them, there were." His voice rose to a roar that seemed to echo against the stone walls of Ciaran's bailey.

"Aye, but she turned more than half of them back at the border." Amalric brought to Ciaran the unwelcome news that his sister had departed for England with only a fraction of the men her father thought to be traveling with her. Traveling first to Daileass, Amalric sought knowledge of Iaian, only to be regaled with tales of Cecile's courage by the master of arms. Ceci, it seemed, had captured the imagination of every warrior at Daileass, but to a man they were relieved to give the truth of her circumstances to one of her menfolk.

Saelec had barely absorbed Amalric's tidings when Donnchadh and Tavis arrived close on his heels the same day. They brought with them more news to turn a father's heart to ice, dire warnings of Dunmar's perfidy and the need for Iaian's hasty return. Whatever dangers Cecile and Iaian faced in England, they faced their equal in Scotland.

Saelec, with his two sons, Donnchadh, and Tavis, determined to journey as far into England as need be to see to the safe return of the young couple.

"I'll kill the girl," Saelec thundered as he chose his weapons, picturing every ill imaginable befalling the child of his heart.

Berinhard buckled on his breastplate and told his wife grimly, "If you have a girlchild, I'll disown the both of you."

Nearra and Giorsal exchanged looks of silent resignation. Men would always be angry when they were affrighted.

Within an hour of Donnchadh's and Tavis's arrival, the courtyard of Ciaran boiled with men preparing for travel and battle, both. And it was into this turmoil that Iaian rode with Cecile at his side.

All activity stopped with almost ludicrous speed as they were heralded into the bailey.

Saelec glowered at Cecile, who smiled down at him sunnily. "Are you harmed?" He fairly barked the question at her.

"Nay, Father."

Berinhard glared at Iaian. "Did you beat her?"

Iaian looked at him in surprise. "Nay."

"Fool." Berinhard turned away toward the keep, leaving Iaian staring at his back while Cecile burst into peels of laughter.

Amalric looked disappointed that they would not be charging into the midst of England, while Donnchadh merely looked relieved. The warriors around them began to melt away, some sharing Amalric's disappointment, some Donnchadh's relief that there would be no fighting their way through England.

Tavis frowned impatiently while he waited for Iaian to dismount and to aid Cecile in dismounting. "You've time for a rest," he warned as he escorted them into the hall, "but not much more. I've no doubt Dunmar has been very busy these past few days."

"It appears he's been busy for some time before that," Iaian retorted, his arm possessively around Cecile's shoulders. He concurred with her belief that Dunmar had been behind Sir Geoffrey's arrest, rather than some Englishman jealous of his father's wealth or influence.

The men gathered at the long table and were soon served with mugs of ale by scurrying servants. Cecile pulled a low stool close to Iaian's thigh, wanting to be near without intruding, and her father looked at her in disbelieving approval. Perhaps this husband of hers could teach her some discretion, after all.

They all listened to Tavis relay what had passed between him and Arran. It was not encouraging.

"And I could find nothing more to pin on Dunmar than that it was he who persuaded Arran to appoint you to the queen's protection whilst she traveled to France," Donnchadh admitted.

"Little enough," Iaian said finally. "I fear Dunmar is so well versed in intrigue that we will find nothing further. There will be no proof he was involved in Sir Geoffrey's arrest, thereby ensuring my return to England."

"What will you do?" Tavis asked, feeling the heavy guilt of his own part for having allowed any of it to occur.

"Face Arran openly. I've done nothing wrong, after all."

"I do not think that overly risky," his uncle agreed, "though it is always possible Arran could be persuaded to arrest you on the same sort of whim that saw your foster father imprisoned."

"Risk or no," Iaian said slowly, "there's nothing else that can be done. Arran has the power to seize all I have fought to gain." He felt Cecile's gaze burning into the back of his skull and turned to answer her silent question with a wry grin. "Nay, I'll not leave you behind, minx." For what good would it do, his eyes asked her silently, unless I were willing to bind you with irons?

And she smiled in relief, though she said nothing at all.

But hours later, in the comfort of her childhood chamber, while she was yet within the safe circle of her family, Iaian offered to free her of her marriage vows.

He sat propped against enormous bedpillows, Cecile cuddling contentedly against him.

"I would understand if you did not go with me, Ceci."

"Truly?" she asked in curious tones. "I would not." She stifled a hint of indignation in the last, knowing what demons drove him.

"You do not know what it is to be exiled," he warned. "Dunmar could yet prevail, and if I do not lose my freedom, I may yet be banned from Scotland—forced to return to England." The land of Cecile's enemies, as Scotland had been to Edra, the thought came unbidden to him. "No one would blame you for not choosing that risk."

"Not even God," she persisted, "for turning my back on the vows I made in his presence?"

The question sent a dart of bitter poison through the heart of him. Was she considering the possibility, then? Yet, the choice must be hers, and freely made. "Not even God," he answered softly. He thought of all he had lost and all he had gained in the months past. And how much more he stood to lose now than then. A coldness seeped into his veins as he waited for her answer.

His doubt of the strength of her love was a palpable thing, and insulting. Yet his fear for her loss touched her to the soul. "I married a fool," she said with equal softness, burrowing against the warm fur upon his chest.

And Iaian, who had not really wished to wed this girl, who had been too tiny, too blonde, and much too wayward for his preference, locked her in an almost painful embrace. If he lost everything material and retained only her, he would be a man truly blest. And healed at last.

It took all of Donnchadh's persuasion to convince Saelec Lotharing and his sons to remain at Ciaran. Only the knowledge that Iaian and Cecile might need a place to run, and people prepared to help them, gained their agreement not to travel with Iaian to Edinburgh and from there to Stirling. And, truly, Saelec knew he fared better on a battlefield than in a grand hall filled with courtiers.

But he remained unhappy with the arrangement, even in the moment he bade his daughter and son-in-law farewell. Pounding Iaian rather stoutly on the back, he said, "Do not let that volemouse wrest from you what is yours. I'd mislike having to slay him." Then he pulled Cecile from her mother's lingering embrace and whispered in her ear, "No son could make me any prouder than I am of you, lass. Go with God."

Donnchadh, who had moved a little apart with Rilla, stepped away from her with a light touch of her cheek, and within moments, his brisk manner had them mounted and prepared to depart. They did not travel with a large group. A dozen armed men rode with them, more for Cecile's protection, and her possible hasty return to Ciaran if all did not go well. This was a battle that could not be won by force of arms.

At his own request, Freyne captained the small force. Though a signal honor, captaining the guard at Daileass had proven too tame. The foray into England had brought that truth forcibly home to him. And if Iaian had to fight his way to freedom, Freyne wanted to be at his side.

Once away from Ciaran, they traveled amidst bantering and laughter. Among them, Donnchadh felt only he truly accepted the possibilities of defeat. Perhaps because he had lived longest and thus seen more of the evil that others could do. But he admired Iaian's quiet confidence and Cecile's cheerful determination, even while he was proudest of Tavis. The lad had clearly aged in the past weeks, but he was facing up to his mistakes and shouldering his responsibilities. Aye, he was proud of Tavis Gillecrist.

Edinburgh received them as unobtrusively as they wished, the sentry opening the gates of the city quickly once the Donnchadh standard was recognized. The fog, which had enveloped them several miles back, turned more into a mist within the city walls. Cecile found it softened the ugliness of the crowded buildings, hiding the filth that fouled even High Street and hiding their small group, as well, from curious eyes.

Because it was early evening, the household servants were still awake and about their final duties for the day. Elspeth stifled her soft, glad cry at the sight of Tavis when she looked beyond him to his traveling companions. As they entered the front room, Tavis smiled warmly at her so that she stepped nearer, but his smile faded with her words. "You should not be in his company, Tavis. 'Tis common knowledge he is soon to be arrested as a traitor."

"Bridle your tongue, woman. My brother is no traitor."

Elspeth's eyes narrowed as he confirmed her worst fears. "Brother, is it? And will you go to the gallows with your arm about his shoulders?"

"If need be," Tavis said quietly, seeing the gulf between them widen. As he had feared, Elspeth Leathann had lived as servant too long. She was no longer bound by any code of family honor. When she would have opened her mouth he stopped her with a furious look and even harsher words. "Hold your tongue, I say. If we've aught to speak of, 'twill be later."

Elspeth stared at him aghast. If they'd aught to speak of? And why should they not? She bore his child and would be his wife. But then her eye caught the gaze of Cecile Gillecrist, and she recalled that Tavis had once thought to wed the girl. Had he hopes, now, that she would turn to him when her husband was safely behind some prison bars or upon the block?

Cecile felt the hatred of the woman, Elspeth, and wondered at it anew, even while she withdrew from the unpleasant force of it. Her eyes sought Donnchadh's, and she was reassured by his watchful expression. More than anyone else, it was Donnchadh she trusted to aid Iaian. His was an authority and quiet strength that few could ignore.

The following morning, however, she was far less pleased with him when he agreed with Iaian on a point they had quarreled most of the night. "Nay, lass, 'tis best you remain here."

"I would be at Iaian's side." Cecile had been unable to convince Iaian to allow it. Donnchadh had been her last hope, and he, too, was against it. "Arran should see that my family stands with him."

"'Twould be helpful," Donnchadh acceded the point, "but you'd be safest here. And," he continued, before she could pounce on that, "Iaian will think best and quickest if he knows you are safe. His wits are what will win or lose the day, Ceci. Do not cloud his thoughts with fears for you."

Distressed that she could only sit and wait, Cecile nevertheless sent Iaian on his way with a loving smile and soft words of encouragement. Her heart was heavy and was made no lighter when she turned from the last glimpse of Iaian's dark cloak to find Elspeth Leathann watching her with hostile eyes.

Elspeth, who had a future to ensure, had made it a point to learn all she could of the secrets in which Tavis was involved. Some of the precious gold Tavis had given her for her care and the babe's had been spent for information, the rest carefully hoarded. Her only opening had been the priest who had met privately with Tavis that morning weeks ago, but well-paid eyes had linked him to Lord Dunmar. And Dunmar had the ear of the regent, as well as the dowager queen. Elspeth had learned very little beyond the fact that the priest and Dunmar were as hostile toward Iaian Gillecrist as she herself. Their reasons mattered not at all to her, but their help might.

Watching as Cecile Gillecrist returned to the house and upstairs to her room, Elspeth made a quick decision. She did not know what use to make of the lady's undefended presence here, but others might.

Dunmar neared desperation. Even with Gillecrist in England, he had come no closer to convincing Arran to put the man to the horn as an outlaw and a traitor. If that were done, the young upstart's life would be forfeit to any man who chose to take it. But Arran would only bid him be patient. Queen Mary remained safe and protected. And there had been no movement by the English toward Dumbarton Rock. Nothing, in fact, to indicate that Iaian had been a part of any plan to seize her.

On this morning, well received in Arran's privy chamber, he did no more than boost Arran's ego as subtly as he had learned to do. He had said all he dared to say and could only hope that Iaian Gillecrist did not return to prove his loyalty within the space of time Arran had allotted.

He watched with interest the chamberlain who bent to whisper in Arran's ear.

Arran sent him out with a quick gesture, then turned to Dunmar. "My lord, we will have our answer at last."

Dunmar's heartbeat increased. Arran could mean only one thing. His mind raced over the lies he had built so carefully, tales of secret meetings observed while Iaian was in Dumbarton, a troop of Englishmen seen near Daileass. Nothing that could easily be proved or disproved, but that, hopefully, with Iaian's own flight to England, could continue to at least cast doubt on the direction of his loyalties.

But when Gillecrist strode boldly into the privy chamber, flanked by his half-brother and Donnchadh, Dunmar tasted defeat. He'd not expected either the bastard or Donnchadh to remain loyal in the face of adversity. Why should they, after all?

Iaian Gillecrist had obviously garbed himself for effect, the scarlet of his doublet and hose so dark as to be almost black, unrelieved save for one heavy chain of beaten gold—and the gleaming sword at his side. Donnchadh wore black and Tavis a deep midnight blue. Beside them Dunmar felt a court jester in his brilliant robe of green and gold. He sneered to hide his discomfort when Gillecrist's gaze raked him lightly.

The trio made an impressive entrance. But, even alone, Donnchadh was a force to be reckoned with and he greeted Arran first, with the ease born of familiarity.

Arran acknowledged him with an enigmatic smile, before his gaze touched on Tavis. "So, then, you managed to find your brother and return here within the allotted time."

"Your Grace left me no choice," Tavis returned smoothly, with a touch of cool disdain the regent remembered as being typical of Alasdair Gillecrist. Legitimate or not, Tavis was definitely his father's son.

"But actually," Tavis continued, "Iaian found me. He had returned *home* before I ever left Scotland to go in search of him."

Neither Arran nor Dunmar missed the slight emphasis he placed on the word.

For one brief moment Dunmar's gaze clashed with Tavis's as he considered speaking out once more against the upstart Englishman. But Tavis Gillecrist had matured in the space of a few weeks. He did not back down from that silent duel, his eyes hard and cold. He would, Dunmar realized, sacrifice himself—and Dunmar and the dowager queen with him. Dunmar cared nothing for Marie de Guise, but he did not believe he was one to live happily in either captivity or impoverished exile.

Not unaware of the flare of anger between the two, Arran waited only another moment for Dunmar to stand openly against the young viscount. When he did not Arran turned his attention to Iaian, himself. "What cause can you put forth for abandoning the task given to you, my lord?"

"Family duty, your Grace." Iaian spoke easily, even knowing his future hung in the balance mayhap on no more than this man's whim.

"Not duty to country?" Arran questioned softly.

"Your Grace, my mother had need of me. I could not refuse, though it placed my lands in jeopardy." Iaian did not honor Dunmar with so much as a glance.

"And you carried no secrets to England? No word of the queen's presence at Dumbarton? No mention of the French fleet landed at last?"

Iaian smiled with honest humor. "Secrets? Do you truly think Somerset did not know the moment the first ship cast anchor? And could six thousand men quartered on Scotland's coast be kept quiet? But, indeed, had I carried word of German and Italian mercenaries ready to fight on the queen's behalf, it would serve only to ensure no futile attempt was made to reach her."

Arran knew full well that Scotland crawled with Somerset's spies. And there was much truth in Gillecrist's words. Nor yet had Dunmar spoken, and Arran realized he would not. Arran's gaze flicked to Donnchadh, who was propped unconcernedly against a wall. "You vouch for the lad, Ros?"

"Aye, though I've not seen the need. His blood speaks for him. And I've yet to hear anyone speak against him."

Arran accepted the small jibe with only a faint smile for Dunmar's scowl. At least Arran had not acted against Gillecrist on accusations that were proving to be no more than vapor. He knew there were those who thought him a fool and played him for one, but he doubted many of those would fare much better at the hands of self-seeking nobles and the clever Marie de Guise.

"Your Grace?" Tired of the waiting and sick of the games, Iaian broke the silence that had fallen upon Arran's ruminations.

Arran, uncomfortable with his garb and with this interview, sighed. He misliked these new padded doublets with their pinched waists as much as he misliked the taller, stiffer ruffs that choked a man as surely as lies. He studied Iaian gravely. "There are no charges against you, my lord, but it would behoove you to give no further cause for doubt."

With a feeling of regret at the thought of Cecile, Iaian sighed. "I am prepared to return to Dumbarton at once, your Grace, yours and the queen's to command."

"Little use there," Arran returned unexpectedly, "as the fleet sailed on the morning tide." He noted with satisfaction that even Dunmar looked surprised at that news. It irked him that his nobles often knew the business of the realm before he did. "And you may tell young Amalric Lotharing that I am not best pleased. He'd be wise to present himself to me forthwith."

"I will do so, your Grace," Iaian said smoothly.

The audience concluded amicably, and Iaian had almost forgotten Dunmar's presence until he turned to go. The furious look of defeat on the other's face was revenge enough, he decided. And his thoughts were of Cecile and the future as he left the privy chamber, Donnchadh and Tavis at his shoulders.

Chapter Twenty-eight

"What are you doing here?" Cecile faced the pale green gaze of Father Aindreas and flinched from the waves of loathing he felt for her.

From the corner of her eye she saw the hem of Elspeth's skirts disappear around a corner. The servant, or Tavis's affianced, or whatever her position had summoned Cecile from her room with word that she had a visitor. Not even pausing to smooth the creases from the yellow silk of her gown, Cecile had rushed down the stairs only to be brought up short by the black-cassocked figure of the priest. She had expected a messenger from Iaian—or from Donnchadh, if Iaian were prevented from sending word to her.

His face passive, the priest surveyed her disdainfully. Her vibrant, colorful beauty offended him. She wore tumbling curls like a madonna's gilt halo, and her eyes rivaled the heavens in color and brilliance. Aye, with such did Satan tempt men.

"What are you doing here?" Cecile questioned again, her voice harshened by a sudden brush of fear. What did this evil man have to do with Iaian's plight? And did it bode ill for Iaian that he came here so openly?

The priest flicked a contemptuous gaze over her face. "You will come with me."

Cecile's chin lifted in response. Though his animosity rocked her, she met his look with more calm than she felt, determined that she would not let him see her instinctive recoil. "Where would you have me go?" She asked the question to delay and to give herself time to think, for she had no intention of leaving with him. And she did not really expect a truthful answer. "And why?"

"That is not for you to ask." The priest felt a rush of adrenaline. If the sinful wench refused, he would force her. For God's holy cause. "You will do as I bid."

There was no mistaking the pleasure he would take in bending her to his will, in breaking her own. "As to that, you may answer to my husband," Cecile spat at him, suddenly furious. "Or you may leave before you must face him."

"'Tis he who must face us, mistress." His hand itched to strike her for her defiance. Instead, fearing she would flee, he placed a heavy hand on her shoulder.

Cecile shivered at the hostility burning through the thin material of her gown as his fingers bit into her shoulder. "Iaian will kill you." The words were wrenched from the depths of her, but with them came almost immediate calm. Iaian would indeed kill him for her protection. But how long until Iaian returned? And who was the "us" he must face?

With the composure that strengthened her at the thought of Iaian, she straightened her spine. "Remove your hand from me."

Almost in spite of himself, Father Aindreas did so, but her imperious tone brought a darkened tone to his face. His eyes narrowed and his mouth became even more pinched.

"Whose orders do you follow?" Even as she asked, she knew the answer. 'Twas Dunmar.

"Jezebel!" he thundered. "I answer only to God."

"Did God bid you remove a wife from her husband's protection?" A movement behind her drew her attention momentarily. Elspeth hovered partway up the stairs leading from the entry. Deliberately, she did not turn to look at her, but kept her gaze warily on the priest. "And does the voice of God come in the form of a female servant?"

For the second time in her life, Cecile felt the sharp pain of the priest's hand against her face. Though her cheek burned from the feel of it, a warm caress brushed immediately behind it from an unseen palm.

Father Aindreas stared, amazed, at the smile that curved her lips. Was this insanity? Equally unexpected, her attention turned from him to the solid oak door. A chill rippled down his spine as she stood unmoving, expectantly waiting.

With every stride of the horse that carried him away from Stirling, Iaian felt an increasing urgency. When he nudged his horse into a trot Tavis followed suit without question, but Donnchadh frowned at him.

Iaian's expression was not that of a man just victorious over a foe who would have wrested his inheritance from him. "What's amiss?"

The lines furrowing Iaian's forehead deepened as he shook his head. "I do not know. 'Tis but a vague feeling of unease."

Yet it was more than that. Thoughts of Cecile enveloped him, neither fearful nor unhappy, but gently touching every part of his inner being. A sense of urgency drove him to reach her sooner rather than later.

When he urged his mount to a canter Donnchadh did also, sending a worried glance toward Tavis. He had no doubt this was to do with Cecile, whose magical quality could not be denied, though there was no true magic in her.

The townhouse came into sight, and he was surprised when Iaian did not ride to the small courtyard at the rear, but dismounted in the street at the front door, dropping his reins to the cobblestones heedlessly. Donnchadh dismounted with equal haste, seeing, too, that Tavis's face held a suddenly brooding look.

Tavis could not dwell on Iaian's sudden anxieties, for he had his own to conquer. What was he to do about Elspeth? Now that the differences between them could no longer be discounted? At least not by him. But, God help him, he wanted the babe.

The urgency that had penetrated to Iaian's soul dropped before the rage that suddenly consumed him when he flung open the door. His first glance gave him Cecile safe and lovely. The one that followed gave him the unmistakable imprint of a man's hand against her fair cheek. With a roar, he seized the fool who had dared, scarcely aware and completely uncaring that it was a man of God in his angry grasp. The savagery that rushed through his veins blinded him to all but the fact that Cecile had been hurt and frightened by this man.

Father Aindreas looked into the burning depths of hell when he met the dark gaze of Iaian Gillecrist's fury. Strong, broad fingers closed against his throat, and he fumbled desperately beneath the folds of his robe.

Donnchadh alone saw the glint of iron in the pale hand of the priest and did not mistake it for a crucifix, even though the hilt crossed the length of the blade in a travesty of the cross. Without conscious thought, he slipped his own dagger from its jeweled sheath and between the ribs of God's erring servant.

Cecile gasped at the speed of events. Her whispered "Nay" came even as the priest sagged in Iaian's grasp, blood soaking his garment. The priest might be truly evil, but she would not have had his death on their hands. Then the crude iron knife he carried slipped from lifeless fingers, falling to the polished floor at his side, and she realized it had been his life or Iaian's. Her thanks, trembling on her lips, were halted as Tavis brushed past her, his attention drawn from the grim scene in the entryway.

Above them, Elspeth backed up the steps, her eyes filled with dismay and regret at the realization in Tavis's. Despite the condemnation she saw in his face, her regret was not for what she had done. Only the outcome. Turning to flee from his growing rage, her slippered foot found no purchase on the rounded edge of the carpeted stair. From a great distance she heard his hoarse shout as the added weight of her pregnancy overbalanced her.

Chapter Twenty-nine

Laughter bubbled from the throat of Cecile Gillecrist as she lifted her face to the sun. A light morning wind tossed her carelessly tumbled hair, and meadow grasses tugged playfully at her skirts while the tiny girl at her side tugged at her hand.

Cecile swooped the child up into her arms, gazing lovingly into eyes as blue as her own beneath hair unexpectedly dark. The serenity of the morning seeped into her soul, carrying the peace she had found here on the border lands of Castle Coire. She kissed her daughter's silken curls, whispering, "The sun's getting high, sweet-heart, we'd best be getting back."

Her eyes lifted to the two men standing at a respectful distance, holding their horses and hers. Iaian did not tolerate her early-morning jaunts unless she and their daughter were accompanied by stout guards. He teased her frequently that she had taught their Lindael her wandering ways, but he did not prevent her wanderings so long as the two of them were safe.

The name she had chosen for the child born little more than a year after their marriage had touched and pleased him. That it was unusual did not deter them, though they couched it suitably between Anne and Cecile. And Anne Lindael Cecile Gillecrist cared not at all that her name was an oddity. A sunny two, she knew only that she was cherished.

Even as Cecile moved toward her escort, her eyes lifted to the rider emerging from the newly rebuilt walls of Coire. A smile touched her lips, for Iaian was an unmistakable figure. No man, she was sure, had shoulders as broad or strong, nor sat a horse with as much skill.

She stood waiting, her love in her eyes, while she gently rocked their daughter in the cradle of her arms. When Iaian reached her she lifted Lindael to him with a smile, then turned to the man leading her horse to her.

Once mounted, she leaned forward for Iaian's kiss, basking in the love he did not fear to show her. The pressure of his lips, both gentle and demanding, drew a tiny shiver from her. As they pulled apart, he grinned, aware of her reaction. She wrinkled her nose at him, then laughed. "Would you have me otherwise?"

Iaian gave a shout of laughter for her unabashed

admission of desire. "I count myself the luckiest of men that you are as you are. Sometimes," he amended, thinking on all the times she had defied him. The latest being her presence at Coire before its completion. Though he had left her in the comfortable security of Daileass, within a week of his departure she had gathered her belongings and bundled their Lindael, still a babe, into traveling blankets. Amidst his half-hearted protests, she had burrowed snugly into the few finished rooms of the castle just as she had burrowed her way snugly into his life—and his heart.

Her only response to that amendment was a gurgle of laughter. Because she was so free with her laughter, Iaian had learned to laugh again. Just as he had learned to forgive and to love. His joy in her reminded him of the reason he had ridden for her instead of waiting for her to return to the keep. At least it was one of the reasons. The other was that he was not comfortable when she was out of his presence for too long a time.

"I've had an answer from Lord Muirdach. He has accepted Tavis's suit for his daughter."

Cecile chuckled at the blatant satisfaction in his voice. "And just when will you tell Tavis that *he* has offered to wed this girl?"

"I shall dispatch a messenger this afternoon." His satisfaction did not diminish at her reminder of the difficulty ahead.

"Which should bring him posthaste," she murmured.

"Just so, and that, my sweet," he told her, "is

when you will convince him of the wisdom of this union."

"Wisdom? Nay, I shall tell him how lovely I found the girl, and how very like me I thought her in temperament."

Iaian looked at her aghast. "You would not!"

"Do you think that would not sway him in the desired direction?" she asked wickedly. At his dismayed expression, she relented. "Do not fear, Iaian, I shall do all I can to smooth the way." And she would, because she wanted to see Tavis as happily joined as she and Iaian. His wounds had been long in healing, for he had taken upon himself the guilt of Elspeth's death and that of their unborn child. He believed if he had not embroiled himself in Dunmar's evil, the events of that morning would never have occurred.

Iaian relaxed. If anyone could bring Tavis to willing acceptance of this marriage, it would be Cecile. And if it were true that Tavis, as most other men, would not want such a wayward wife as Cecile had proved to be, Iaian knew he would never want her to change. "I love you," he said softly, putting more into those three words than any other man, past or present, could have.

"And I love you," Cecile returned as softly, only dimly aware of their daughter in his arms and the men riding behind them. Nothing encompassed her as completely as what she felt for Iaian Gillecrist, an exile returned home at last.

Firestar

"Strip him! Strip him naked! Let's have a look at what we're bidding on!"

The strident female voice rose on the sweltering air, stirring a ripple of movement in the sullen, sweating crowd. All glanced in the woman's direction. Then, with a collective sigh, the people turned back to the huge, raised platform in the city square.

"She's right," another female cried. "These males come too highly priced as it is. He's pretty enough but we're not buying his looks. We're buying his breeding abilities. Strip him, I say!"

The auctioneer, a huge, hairy bear of a fellow, grumbled and mumbled to himself as he strode over to the bare-chested blond man pinned between two guards. "Damn them," he growled. "I'm a busy man and haven't the time to display each slave that passes through here."

He halted before the prisoner. Hard, dark brown eyes slammed into his. The auctioneer paused, startled by the savage look of warning. Then he grinned, his aterroot-stained teeth gleaming in the midday sun.

"You've only yourself to blame, you high-and-mighty off-worlder," he said to the man. "Strutting out here as cocky as you please, flaunting yourself before these women. You're lucky they don't swarm up here and tear you to pieces." His smile widened. "We had that happen once, you know."

The auctioneer's hands moved toward the prisoner's breeches. "Now, be sensible and don't give me any—"

A booted foot snapped out and upward, catching the auctioneer squarely in the groin. "Be damned!" Gage Bardwin snarled. "I'll not add to anyone's entertainment!"

With a whoosh of exhaled air, the big man clutched himself and sank to his knees. His face twisted in agony. For long seconds he knelt before Gage, breathing heavily. A stream of aterroot juice trickled down his chin to drip onto his shabby tunic.

Behind him, female voices rose to a wild shriek, a cacophony of primal excitement mixed with a growing bloodlust. "Strip him! Strip him! Teach the arrogant male a lesson!"

A small, scrawny man hurried over, nervous and perspiring profusely. He mopped his brow with the back of his sleeve, then grabbed at the auctioneer's arm, tugging him to his feet. "Get up, you fool! You should know better than to stand too close to a breeder."

He pulled the auctioneer out of harm's way, then motioned over four more guards. "Do whatever is necessary." He indicated the prisoner. "Just give the women what they ask. I want this one sold and out of here before he starts further trouble."

They advanced on Gage, all eyes riveted warily on his legs. He fought against the two men who held him, struggling to break free.

Helpless frustration welled in Gage. Gods, what else could go wrong? Beryllium shackles bound his wrists and arms, he faced four other men and he was trapped on an unfriendly planet with no weapons or money.

Curse the lapse of vigilance in that tavern on Locare, the final transport station before Tenua! If he hadn't been so exhausted from a particularly long and difficult transport process, if he hadn't imbibed one mug of Moracan ale too many or been so overly attentive to that seductive little barmaid, he'd have seen those off-world bounty hunters coming. But none of that mattered now. He'd been careless. He must extricate himself as best he could.

There was only one consolation. He *had* arrived at his destination, the capital of Eremita on the planet Tenua. He just wasn't in any position to do anything about it right—

With a shout, the extra guards rushed Gage en masse. Two leaped simultaneously for a leg. Another slipped behind to snake an arm about his neck and throttle him.

Gage fought wildly. He threw the full weight of his heavily muscled body first into one guard, then another. He managed to fling one man free of his right leg, then lashed out, kicking him full in the chest. The guard snapped backward, the wind knocked out of him.

Pivoting on his still encumbered leg, Gage kicked at the other man. Something flashed in his peripheral vision. A fist slammed into his jaw, then his gut.

The fourth guard.

Gage staggered backward, his knees buckling. Bright light exploded in his skull. Pain engulfed him. He battled past the agony, shaking his head to scatter the stars dancing before his eyes.

It was too late. The six men wrestled Gage to the platform, encasing him in a body lock he could only jerk against in impotent fury. His upper torso pinned, his legs held down in a spread-eagle position, Gage fought with all the strength left in him. Finally, as oxygen-starved limbs weakened, his powerful body could give no more. He lay there, panting in exhaustion, his face and chest sheened with sweat.

The sun beat down, its radiance blinding him. Gods, but it was hot on this hellish planet. So very hot. So draining...desolate.

A huge form moved to stand over him. "Proud, stupid off-worlder," the auctioneer snarled. "You'll pay dearly for your defiance before I'm done and satisfied, but first we'll give the women what they want."

He knelt between his prisoner's outspread legs. With a smirking grin, the man grasped the front of Gage's breeches and ripped them apart.

"No, damn you!" Gage roared. With a superhuman effort he reared up, sinews taut, muscles straining.

The guards' grips tightened, strangling the life from him. A swirling gray mist swallowed Gage. He fell back. At the sudden lack of resistance the guards' holds loosened.

Gage dragged in great gulps of air, fighting past the loss of consciousness, sick to the very marrow of his bones. Sick with his sense of helplessness, of defeat.

It didn't matter that they'd bared his body. What mattered was the implied submission of the act—the utter *subservience*. And he'd never, ever, allowed another to use him without his express consent. Never, since that sol he'd confronted his mother. . . .

Rage swelled, white hot and searing. In a sudden, unexpected movement, Gage twisted to the side, dragging all six guards with him.

"Let...me...go!"

The endeavor took all he had. They quickly wrestled him back to the floor, slamming him down, crushing his head into the rough, splintered wood. Gage tasted his own blood, then his despair, bitter as gall.

"Damn you all! Let me go!" he cried again, choking the words past his sudden surge of nausea.

"Do as he says," a new voice, rich with authority, commanded. "Free him. Now."

The guards paused, looking up in surprise. The auctioneer glanced over his shoulder. With a strangled sound he released Gage, then climbed to his feet.

"Domina Magna," the man murmured, bowing low to the

woman who was Queen and ruler of the planet. "I-I am honored that the royal family chose to attend my humble sale."

"And why not?" the Queen's voice came again. "Haven't you some of the finest breeders in the Imperium? Now, get out of my way. Let us have a closer look at the male."

"As you wish, Domina Magna." The auctioneer stepped aside.

For a moment all Gage saw was color, a bright, vibrant swirl of crimsons, blues and greens. Then the hues solidified into folds of shimmering, ultralight fabric, and the fabric into gowns. Gage levered himself to one elbow and glared up at the two women.

One was young with glossy black hair tucked under a sheer veil and striking, deep violet eyes. She was dressed in a loose, bulky gown that completely disguised whatever figure she might have. At his direct scrutiny her lashes lowered. A becoming flush darkened her cheeks.

A maiden, Gage thought wryly, and as shy as they came.

He shifted to the other woman. She was equally striking—her ripe femininity blatantly accentuated by the voluptuous bosom thrusting from her low-cut, snugly molded dress. There was no doubt as to the quality of her figure.

She met his hard-eyed gaze and held it for a long moment before turning to her younger companion.

"Well, daughter? Are you certain he's the one for you?" Her bold glance lowered to Gage's groin. "Your maiden's flesh will be sorely tried by a man such as he. And he strikes me as none too gentle, if his antics a few seconds ago are any indication."

"Mother, please." The girl bit her lip, turning nearly as crimson as her gown. Her hesitant gaze lifted, meeting Gage's for an instant before skittering away to slide down the tautly sculpted, hair-roughened planes of his body.

The girl's eyes halted at the gaping vee of his breeches. A river of dark hair arrowed straight down from his flat belly to a much denser nest and a hint of a large, thick organ before disappearing beneath the torn cloth. She swallowed hard, dragging her gaze back to her mother's.

"H-he couldn't help it. His pride was at stake. He had to fight them."

A slender brow arched in amusement. "Did he now? I think the sisters at our royal nunnery filled your head with too many tales of days long past. Days when men still possessed some shred of gentleness and integrity. And I think," the Queen said as she took her daughter's arm and began to lead her away, "that I called you back to your royal duties none too soon."

"Mother. Wait." The girl dug in her heels.

"Yes, child?"

"May I have him or not? You said it was my choice."

The Queen eyed her daughter, then sighed. "Yes, you may have him if your heart is set. The law dictates that you take a breeder before commencing a royal life mating. But heed my words. You'll regret it. He's not the male for you."

She glanced at the auctioneer. "We'll take him," she said, indicating Gage. "Have him sent to the palace immediately."

"Er, pardon, Domina Magna." The small, scrawny man stepped forward.

"Yes?"

"This is an especially high-quality breeder. He'll cost extra."

The Queen's lips tightened. "How much extra?"

"Five thousand imperials."

Her nostrils flared. "No breeder, not even one for a Royal Princess of Corba, is worth that much! I'll give you two thousand and not an imperial more!"

"But Domina Magna—"

"Enough!" The woman held up a silencing hand. "Another word and I'll forget I'm your queen and simply confiscate the male." She smiled thinly. "And everything else you possess as well."

"As you wish, Domina Magna," the little man croaked, bowing and backing away. "The breeder will be delivered immediately."

Triumph gleamed in the Queen's eyes. "Good. See that he is."

"You will mate with my daughter and impregnate her. An easy task, I'm sure, for a beeder of your 'quality'," Queen Kadra proclaimed, leaning back with an air of finality in her ornately gilded throne.

"Indeed?" Gage Bardwin drawled.

The woman glared down at the prisoner, her patience at an end. Though still bound and ensconced between two burly guards, the man was as defiant as he'd been on the auctioneer's platform. Obviously, more drastic measures were needed to ensure his cooperation.

She motioned to the guards. "Leave us."

At the order, Gage arched a dark brow. His lips twisted in cynical amusement.

Kadra waited until they were alone. "Have you had an opportunity to observe my palace?" She indicated the room with a regal sweep of her bejeweled hand.

Gage shrugged. "It appears adequate."

"Adequate?" Kadra nearly choked on the word. "It's *impregnable*, both from within and from without." Her smoldering gaze met his. "There is no hope of escape."

He eyed her, knowing there was more to come.

"You will service my daughter and impregnate her, or you will die. It's that simple."

"Is it now?"

Gage slowly surveyed the room. She was right. This chamber was just as heavily fortified as was the rest of the palace. The doors and windows were barricaded by a sturdy grillwork of what looked to be a beryllium-impregnated alloy. Not even a laser gun could cut through that metal. The exterior walls were of solid rock and several feet thick. Add to that the highly complex video monitoring system Gage had noticed in his journey through the palace, and escape seemed a near impossibility.

He clamped down on a surge of angry frustration and turned back to the queen. "And what's wrong with your own men that you must turn to an off-worlder for breeding purposes—especially for your own daughter?''

The Queen's grip on her chair tightened. ''Tenuan men are not the issue here. I have given you a command. The consequences are clear. What is your decision?''

Gage's eyes narrowed. Damn her. She held the advantage—at least for now—and she knew it.

`He was on a mission of vital importance. The issue of his pride, no matter how dearly cherished, paled in light of the threat of Volan infiltration. And there *were* potential benefits to stalling for time, for being in the Tenuan Royal Palace. Information could be gleaned, conversations overheard....

''She's a pretty one, your daughter,'' Gage said, conceding the Queen a temporary victory. ''What's her name?''

A smile glimmered on Kadra's lips. ''Meriel. Do I take this to mean you accept my terms?''

''A mating with your lovely daughter in exchange for my freedom?'' Gage nodded. ''In reality, I win all the way around. How soon do you require my services?''

''My daughter's fertile time spans this very day. You will be bathed, dressed more appropriately, then taken to her. I expect several matings to assure your seed is properly planted. Do you understand me?''

Gods, there went his opportunity for leisure to explore the palace. Well, the girl herself might be the best source of information anyway. He nodded. ''Yes. And on the morrow I am free to go?''

''But of course. There will be no further need for you.''

COMING IN OCTOBER 1993
FUTURISTIC ROMANCE
FIRESTAR
Kathleen Morgan
Bestselling Author of *The Knowing Crystal*

From the moment Meriel lays eyes on the virile slave chosen to breed with her, the heir to the Tenuan throne is loath to perform her imperial duty and produce a child. Yet despite her resolve, Meriel soon succumbs to Gage Bardwin—the one man who can save her planet.

_0-505-51908-9 $4.99 US/$5.99 CAN

TIMESWEPT ROMANCE
ALL THE TIME WE NEED
Megan Daniel

Nearly drowned after trying to save a client, musical agent Charli Stewart wakes up in New Orleans's finest brothel—run by the mother of the city's most virile man—on the eve of the Civil War. Unsure if she'll ever return to her own era, Charli gambles her heart on a love that might end as quickly as it began.

_0-505-51909-7 $4.99 US/$5.99 CAN

LEISURE BOOKS
ATTN: Order Department
276 5th Avenue, New York, NY 10001

Please add $1.50 for shipping and handling for the first book and $.35 for each book thereafter. PA., N.Y.S. and N.Y.C. residents, please add appropriate sales tax. No cash, stamps, or C.O.D.s. All orders shipped within 6 weeks via postal service book rate. Canadian orders require $2.00 extra postage and must be paid in U.S. dollars through a U.S. banking facility.

Name____
Address______________________________________
City __________________________ State______ Zip______
I have enclosed $______in payment for the checked book(s).
Payment must accompany all orders. ☐ Please send a free catalog.